GORDON R. DICKSON'S *CHILDE CYCLE*

"An inspiring and uplifting saga!"

—*Jackson Sun*

"Ambitious!"

—*Washington Post*

"In their day, Isaac Asimov's future of the Foundations and Robert Heinlein's of the 'Future History' seemed impressively complex and real. Gordon Dickson has been building a future of his own that is far more logical, more humanly real, and with a stronger philosophical foundation than either of those classics."

—*Analog*

Tactics of Mistake

"Dickson has no problem bringing new thought and freshness to the story line . . . reading provides new insights. *Tactics* is a thoroughly good adventure story with some depth."

—Lester Del Rey

"Imaginative . . . There is so much action that it kept me continuously interested."

—James Blish

Lost Dorsai

"A real treat for Dorsai fans and Dickson devotees . . . A worthy addition to one of the most popular series in sf."

—Amazing

"Strong . . . fascinating . . . good, entertaining reading from an award-winning author."

—Buffalo News

"A feast for Dickson's many readers!"

—Booklist

The Spirit of Dorsai

"Some of the best writing in the field . . . could well serve as a model for all sf writers."

—Science Fiction and Fantasy Book Review

"Dickson at his best! . . . The richness of description and multiple layers of meaning demonstrate that where Dickson was strong before, he is now all but unmatchable . . . Dickson has seldom written more powerfully."

—Galaxy

"Savor the beauty . . . experience the fierce, enduring courage that is the spirit of the Dorsai."

—Galileo

"*The Spirit of Dorsai* is a winner! . . . one of sf's old masters demonstrating why he deserves that status . . . contains some of the finest writing Dickson has ever done."

—Booklist

The Final Encyclopedia

"A richly textured, carefully constructed book that teems with extraordinary characters ... At a time full of preachments of nuclear winter, Dickson's faith that humankind can evolve into something almost godlike makes me want to stand up and cheer ... fascinating."

—*Analog*

"A great hero in a great story!"

—Frank Herbert, bestselling author of *Dune*

"In *The Final Encyclopedia*, Gordon Dickson has brilliantly continued the classic future legend begun in the award-winning *Soldier, Ask Not*."

—Anne McCaffrey

"A fitting climax to the grandest saga in the history of sf!"

—Ben Bova

"An important book ... but even better, it's an entertaining book."

—*Amazing Science Fiction Stories*

"Worthwhile ... intriguing!"

—*Fantasy Review*

THE DORSAI COMPANION

Gordon R. Dickson

ACE SCIENCE FICTION BOOKS
NEW YORK

"Amanda Morgan" and "Brothers" were previously published in *The Spirit of Dorsai,* an Ace Science Fiction Book. Copyright © 1979 by Gordon R. Dickson. Portions have also previously appeared as "Brothers" in *ASTOUNDING: John W. Campbell Memorial Anthology,* copyright © 1973 by Random House, Inc. "Warrior" and "Lost Dorsai" have appeared as part of *Lost Dorsai,* an Ace Science Fiction Book. Copyright © 1980 by Gordon R. Dickson. "Warrior" first appeared in *Analog,* copyright © 1965 by Condé Nast Publications, Inc. A shorter version of *Lost Dorsai* appeared in *Destinies,* Vol. II, no. 1; February–March 1980. Copyright © 1980 by Charter Communications, Inc.

THE DORSAI COMPANION

An Ace Science Fiction Book/published by arrangement with
the author

PRINTING HISTORY
Ace Science Fiction trade paperback edition/June 1986

ISBN: 0-441-16026-3

Ace Science Fiction Books are published by
The Berkley Publishing Group,
200 Madison Avenue, New York, New York 10016.
PRINTED IN THE UNITED STATES OF AMERICA

INTRODUCTION:
See a Thousand Years

I have a disability. It consists of remembering where, in those books I've written that are part of *The Childe Cycle*, such and such an event took place, or such and such a character appeared—or did some particular thing.

It is a disability that is most troublesome during the question-and-answer period that follows any speech of mine, but particularly one on the *Cycle* itself. Someone from the audience asks, perhaps, about the extent of central government's powers on the planet Dorsai—and I find myself prefacing my answer by saying something like:

"You might remember that Mahub Van Ghent's oldest son was the one member of the Van Ghent family who sided with the old man when he tried to set up what was to be, in effect, a strong central government—"

And at about this point (if I'm lucky) the blank looks on the faces before me stop me.

Mahub Van Ghent?

Eldest son?

??

It's true Van Ghent is referred to in *Dorsai!*, the first book of the *Cycle* to be written. But nowhere in any of the books so far written is there anything about his having sons, let alone an eldest son who is the only one who sides with his father in trying to create what is, in effect, a revolution.

This is part of the great volume of information about the story of the *Cycle* as a whole accumulated in my head over the last thirty-five years but not put to use in one of the books I have so far completed. The confusion that causes me to cite things like this that my audience could not possibly know arises, first, from the very mass of the *Cycle* itself, which when done will be in effect one very large novel in twelve or more sections; and, second, from the fact that I myself must work with the living mass of known history plus the logical fictional extensions of it that are found particularly in the books of the future section.

Accordingly, in this introduction, I am going to try to make some sense out of the *Cycle* for you and distinguish, generally at least, between what is in the books, will be in the books, and that which I must know but in all probability will not have time to put down in book form.

The rules I imposed upon the *Cycle* books when I first conceived them was that each book should be a complete story in itself—not merely a segment of something "to be continued with next publication." At the same time, for my own requirements, I needed each novel to fit thematically (and in some cases actively) with one or more other novels so that my final goal could be accomplished.

This goal was to use known history and logically generated future history to argue that the human race not only was presently in, but had been, at least since the first upwellings of the Renaissance in Europe, in a process of evolution—a form of evolution which I will here call *ethical*, for want of a better word, which has not been invented yet.

In short, the twelve or more books and any shorter works about the *Cycle* should fit together to make a single, very large novel of a new type, which I had named—with more truth than thought about how ponderous the name would be—the *Consciously Thematic Novel*.

To succeed in fulfilling this second requirement, I myself had to see the story of the *Cycle* as a whole. Perhaps the best illustration would be to suggest that you imagine the *Cycle* as a long tapestry on which are shown in detail certain critical events taking place over a thousand-year period—from the fourteenth century into the twenty-fourth century.

At first glance, such a tapestry would seem merely a linking together of unconnected events, like a string of dissimilar beads. Then, hopefully, if the reader had the whole *Cycle* before him or her, or even a significant chunk of it, the interior war of the human soul would be seen in conflict— in victory and defeat—as humankind built their history forward from the end of the middle ages to a time not yet come.

Given the tapestry, now let us assume that sections of it are cut out of the whole, copied, and published as separate entertainments, which are the novels plus the shorter works so far published and collected here. It was no wonder that, with the larger story presented as bits and pieces complete in themselves, the great majority of those who find them entertaining have not yet begun to put together the implications that, hopefully, will eventually echo from book to book of the complete work to tell that larger story.

The latest book in the *Cycle*, *The Final Encyclopedia*, gives the most so far of this background information. The story of Hal Mayne begun in it is to be continued in a more regular sequel fashion through *Chantry Guild*, which I am now writing, and *Childe*. With these last three novels, the future leg of the Cycle, once completed, should all together give at least a picture of what I as an author have been aiming at.

In short, the argument will have been laid out, demonstrated for those who want to reach below the surface of the books' entertainment for their deeper story.

That argument will still, however, be unproven. It will require the three historical novels dealing with known historical characters and the three novels laid in our own twentieth century, with fictional characters but based upon real and historically recent events, to build the base upon which the future leg, already by that time written, must stand.

When the *Cycle,* from the beginning of the real Sir John Hawkwood (who actually became Captain-General of Florence, Italy in the fourteenth century) to the fictional Hal Mayne (who breaks through at last to the Creative Universe in the twenty-fourth century) is at last finished, it will be seen that all the people in its books and all the things that happen there are linked by the chains of cause and effect that make up our historic process.

For example, the Final Encyclopedia itself is foreshadowed by the very real Theater of Memory, which Guilio Camillo Delminio spent his life trying to construct in the 16th century. The line of known philosophical thought runs squarely into the culture of the Exotics, and the political factors that produce the mercenary warrior culture of the Dorsai mirror those that produced the rise of the mercenary forces and their captains (the *condottieri* like Sir John Hawkwood) in the fourteenth to sixteenth centuries in Italy.

This then is the plan, which has so far produced five novels—*Dorsai!*, *Necromancer, Tactics of Mistake, Soldier, Ask Not,* and now *The Final Encyclopedia*—plus what I call the *Illuminations to the "Cycle,"* which are the short novels *Amanda Morgan* and *Lost Dorsai,* as well as the novelette *Brothers* and the short story "Warrior," all contained in this book. Still to come in the future leg of the *Cycle,* as I say, are *Chantry Guild* and *Childe*.

The last two will be large novels—with luck, though, not so large as *The Final Encyclopedia,* which is in excess of 300,000 words. Agents and editors, who read massive amounts of words weekly and mostly in their off hours, do not ordinarily turn pale at the sight of a manuscript. But any of them might be forgiven for turning pale at the sight of one that consisted of the equivalent of three reams of typing paper stacked vertically. I turned pale when the stack of printed galley sheets was returned to me to be read for errors.

And if that image strikes home to you at all—those of you who have ever been stuck with a great deal of reading to do in the line of duty—you might consider that, simultaneously with the reading of those galley sheets at my end of the operation, three members of the publisher's staff were reading other copies of the same galleys. There is a human failing that leads the best of us to mentally correct misspelled words or to supply one that has been mistakenly dropped from the text, and the only way to deal with this is to have a number of different sets of eyes examining the same text, in hopes that what one misses another will catch.

Nonetheless, mistakes get through into the finished book. There have been, in the case of the *Cycle* books, typographical errors, copyeditors' mistakes, and flat-out mistakes on my part, where I disagreed in one book with what I had written in another because my memory played tricks on me.

The classic of all these errors is perhaps the title of one of the sections in *Dorsai!*, where the book is divided into parts, each with its own subtitle. One of those subtitles—and you can check this for yourself if you have a copy of one of the earlier editions—is a title that I had plainly typed in manuscript as "Part-Maran" because it referred to the fact that Donal Graeme has an Exotic grandmother who had come originally from the planet Mara.

In the original magazine version of the book—the book was serialized in the magazine now called *Analog*—some copyeditor evidently assumed that I myself had been guilty of a typographical error. Possibly he or she checked with a dictionary and found that there is no such word as *maran*. In any case—and we authors, of course, never see galleys of magazine stories—I only discovered on reading the published story that that particular heading now read "Part-Moron."

I spoke to and wrote to editors on the immediately succeeding publications of the story in book form, and each one of them carefully noted that the spelling was to be put right "in the next printing." But somehow, through a number of printings and a number of publishers, "Part-Moron" kept its place. Eventually I became almost superstitious about it and very diffident about mentioning it to editors and publishers as something to be fixed.

The error was caught and corrected for the British editions, and, mercifully, the translator of the French edition, having translated all other headings verbatim, merely replaced that one with the number *3*.

On my part, I did some interesting things like mislaying Coby, which is one of the planets under the star Procyon, but which at the end of *Dorsai!* I put, along with the Dorsai world itself, under the sun of Vega, which is in fact beyond the sphere of inhabited worlds in the *Cycle*. The left knee of Cletus Grahame in *Tactics*, on which he limps at the beginning of the book, unaccountably became the right knee a couple of chapters later.

Then there is a slight mix-up between what is told in *Dorsai!* and what is told in *Soldier, Ask Not*. A battle in which Donal is engaged in the first book is mentioned as having taken place five years afterwards in the latter. In *Soldier, Ask Not*, Tam is injured in battle on New Earth, which is later incorrectly referred to as *Newton*. (This has been corrected.) Anea's hair is chestnut brown in *Dorsai!*, but by the time of *Soldier, Ask Not*, it has turned blond. (Corrected.) The two warring cities of Blauvain and Castelmaine, which everybody knows, of course, are on the world of Sainte Marie, somehow got put on New Earth in the early editions of *Soldier, Ask Not*.

Rudyard Kipling, that thoroughly real and thoroughly documented English poet of the late nineteenth and early twentieth centuries, is noted in an early edition of *Dorsai!* as having lived eight hundred years before the time in which *Dorsai!* is laid—instead of four hundred.

Hendrick Galt, a Dorsai general of merit mentioned in *Dorsai!*, suffered much from having his name misspelled in subsequent writings where he is mentioned. His first name is switched to Heinrich in one instance, and his last name to Gault in another.

Probably of most importance to the *Cycle*, for reasons which will become more apparent in the last two books, James Graeme, the youngest uncle of Donal Graeme and whose death has such a strong effect on Donal as a child, is mistakenly referred to as a brother, rather than an uncle, of Donal's in the manuscript of *The Final Encyclopedia* itself. This was corrected in time.

Finally, the correct total of human-inhabited worlds are sixteen, under nine stars, including our own Sun. Accept no substitute figures, no matter what the page before you may say.

There are undoubtedly other such errata, and I will appreciate any of you pointing them out to me as I go along, since we need to catch as many as possible if the whole *Cycle* is to work logically.

Luckily, a scapegoat for all this has been found.

It has become a practice these last few years for me and those who have worked with me on the *Cycle* to blame anything that hampers my building of it—from ill health to a long-overdue check lost in the mail—on Bleys Ahrens, that sad Satan of a man who is the opposite number of Hal Mayne in the last three books. Bleys represents the spearpoint of the forces opposed to evolution, as Hal represents the spearpoint of the forces striving to bring that evolution to its culmination in the emergence of *Homo sapiens crean*—"Creative Man."

It is human nature, after all, to blame someone. Our thoughtful race has always liked to pin a name on whoever is responsible for bad luck generally. It is a great relief to have someone or something specific to blame for everything adverse, whether gods or the weather—and the more specific the guilty party the better. Since Bleys is a master of machination and it is clearly to his advantage, up there in the twenty-fourth century, to see that the *Cycle* not get finished here in the twentieth, clearly no one but he can be responsible for the difficulties that I've been encountering in the process of getting the books done and published.

And his efforts to impede my work, I may tell you now, have not been small. What makes them endurable is something that, paradoxically, is required for the very writing of the *Cycle* itself—the ability to see the whole of the past and future tapestry I spoke of as a continuous whole.

I call it the "thousand-year view."

Imagine for yourself that you begin to step back from the current web of history to which you belong. Your first step, say, takes you the equivalent of only housetop level, so that you hang in midair with a view of your immediate neighborhood spread out before you. You take another step and you now can see not only the city in which that neighborhood belongs, but a fair amount of the open countryside surrounding.

Another step and you are above the atmosphere. You look down and see the continent you inhabit and a good share of the rest of the face of the earth currently turned toward you. The next step (you'll notice each one is increasing) and you see our world as a whole, from a distance, caught in its present moment of time, from which you now are detached.

Take one more giant step backward—step back seven hundred light years, while magically keeping the close-up view of the earth that you had a moment before. Now you see not only the present moment of Earth, but—borne to you on light that has taken six hundred and more years to reach you—each moment of Earth's history from the fourteenth century to the moment at which you left Earth's surface in the twentieth.

Now, squint your eyes a little and look forward. Squint tightly enough, try hard enough, and you can see the causes and the effects they produced becoming causes in their turn, projected forward another four hundred years.

Now, at last, you see six hundred years of the past and four hundred years of the resulting future as one long tapestry of cause and effect.

More than that, now that you are so far out from it all, so remote in space, you see how small are the concerns and troubles of any particular period in all that long time. One evil, whether it be the Black Plague or the imminent threat of nuclear war, each of which at its own moment seemed both inevitable and a certain end to the human race, passes away, to be replaced by another possibility for race-end, no less horrifying and apparently certain for the historical period in which it exists.

With that awareness, you begin for the first time to see other forces at work, more massive, more slowly developing forces gathering weight, mass, and momentum from generation to generation, from century to century, toward inevitable meetings, inevitable conflicts.

You see two parts in particular of the human soul—one which yearns to grow and reach out, one which is determined to conserve and stop all such adventuring into unknown futures. And you see these two originally as a battle within the individual human soul which expresses itself more and more through external means as the technology is created to manifest them, until eventually, the distinction becomes not only external, but irresistibly demanding of a resolution.

There, at the far end of the future four hundred years, comes that revolution—a point at which individuals in the race enlist themselves on one side or another, and the conflict over the direction in which the race will go from there is finally settled, not by material war, but by a war in a place that is already with us, but as yet unidentified, a place where victory can only be won by mind convincing mind.

The Creative Universe.

It is the shaping of this battle and its outcome which takes the bits and pieces that are the individual books and stories of the *Cycle* and ties them all together into one master story which covers a millennium. Now you see the tapestry as I have lived with it for thirty-five years, and it is this that, finally, makes even the machinations of such a one as Bleys Ahrens bearable—because I know, if no one else does yet, that all his roadblocks will be ineffective, all his oppositions will be futile.

We, we humans, I believe, shall emerge at last, as the butterfly comes from the cocoon, to ride the air currents that as caterpillars we had no way of imagining would ever bear us. We shall emerge into a larger universe, and there we will begin our true work, the work for which we have been unconsciously training ourselves since we first looked up from the soil below our earth-bound feet and saw the heavens.

Gordon R. Dickson

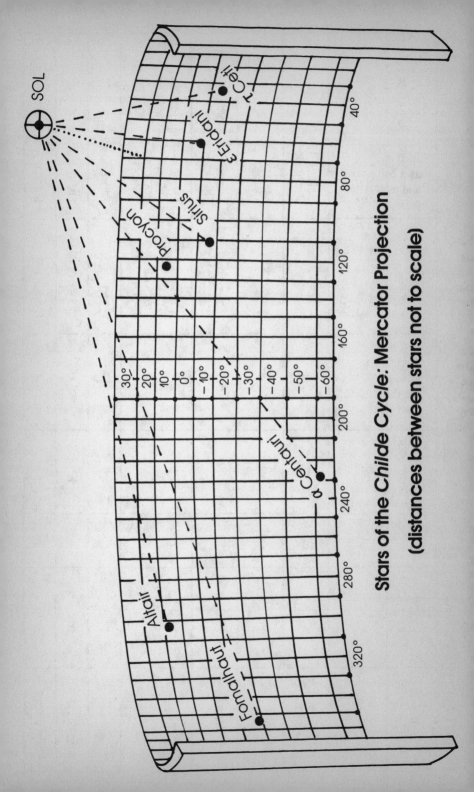

Stars of the Childe Cycle: Mercator Projection

(distances between stars not to scale)

SOL

τ Ceti
3 Eridani
Procyon
Sirius
α Centauri
Altair
Fomalhaut

40° 80° 120° 160° 200° 240° 280° 320°

30° 20° 10° 0° -10° -20° -30° -40° -50° -60°

Worlds of the Childe Cycle

Star	Distance (Light-Years)	Type	Diameter	Absolute Magnitude	Planet	Dominant Culture or Group
Sol	—	G_2	1.00	4.8	Venus Earth Mars	Scientists (research base) Full-Spectrum Scientists (research base)
α Centauri A α Centauri B	4.3 4.3	G_2 K_1	1.07 1.22	4.4 5.8	Newton Cassida	Scientists Technocrats
Sirius A	8.7	A_1	1.8	−1.42	New Earth Freiland	Mixed Mixed
ε Eridani	10.8	K_2	.9	6.1	Harmony Association	Friendlies—Faith-Holders Friendlies—Faith-Holders
Procyon A	11.3	F_5	2.6	2.7	Kultis Mara Ste. Marie Coby	Exotics—Philosophers Exotics—Philosophers Farmers Miners
τ Ceti	11.8	G_8	.9	5.7	Ceta	Merchants
Altair	16.5	A_7	1.5	2.0	Dunnin's World	Fishermen
Fomalhaut	22.6	A_3	2.0	1.7	Dorsai	Dorsai—Warriors

The Morgans

Amanda Morgan I & (1) Lloyd Jones   & (2) Cecil Kalsa Singh   & (3) Falco Lucano y Perez

James ap Morgan & Willa Saarinen   (other children)   (other children)

Llewellyn

David I & Lorna Tormai

David II & Caiya Charanis   Betta & Saburo Hasegawa

       Roger

Alban & (1) Fosima Kante   (2) Millicent Eastlake

     Amanda (Elaine) II   Charley & Elizabeth Aras

                     David III & Auste Romanowski

                     Thomas & Delia Whyte

    Amanda III   Elise & Hans Debigné   Megan

Note: Only principal lineages are shown, not collateral lines.

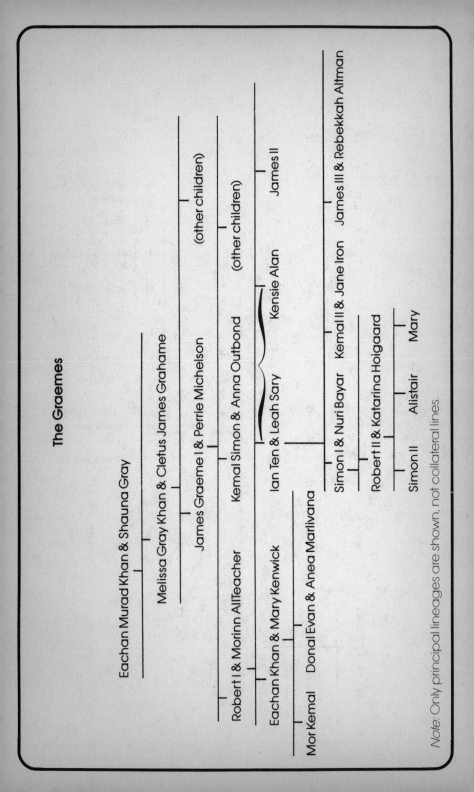

The Graemes

Note: Only principal lineages are shown, not collateral lines.

Chronology of the *Childe Cycle*

STORY	DATE	EVENTS
	2090	Phase shift transport and terraforming under development. First probes to other stars. The Chantry Guild fights dominance of technology on tense and crowded Earth
Necromancer	2093	Paul Formain awakens to destiny after losing an arm. Amanda Morgan I born on Earth
	2094	After joining the Chantry Guild, Paul divides the Racial Psyche, launches Splinter Cultures, and dies
		Terraforming and settlement of Younger Worlds continues throughout the early twenty-second century
	2128	Amanda I emigrates to Dorsai
	2130s	Outlaw Years on Dorsai
	2177	Destruction of Rochmont by outraged Dorsai troops
Tactics of Mistake / *Amanda Morgan*	2184	Cletus Grahame emigrates to Dorsai, founds Graeme dynasty
	2185	Amanda I leads defense of Foralie District. Cletus defeats Earth's leader, Dow deCastries. Younger Worlds gain independence
		Splinter Cultures come into full bloom for the next century
	2201	Amanda I dies
	2228	Building of Final Encyclopedia begins
	2238	Tam Olyn born on Earth
	2245	Ian and Kensie Graeme born on Dorsai
	2248	Amanda II born on Dorsai
	2258	Donal Graeme born on Dorsai
"Warrior"	2269	Ian wins justice for betrayed soldiers on Earth. Donal dedicates his life to fighting evil

STORY	DATE	EVENTS
	2270	Tam begins career as journalist
	2271	Van Ghent's Rebellion on Dorsai
Lost Dorsai	2273	Michael de Sandoval's victory on Ceta; Amanda II rejects Kensie
		Ian marries Leah on Earth
Brothers	2276	Donal graduates from Dorsai Academy
	2280	Kensie assassinated on Ste. Marie Tam amends his life and joins Final Encyclopedia
	2289	Donal defeats William of Ceta, brings peace and order to the inhabited worlds
		Splinter Cultures begin to fade
	2291	Donal disappears during solo spaceflight
	2321	Emergence of The Others, cross-cultural hybrids bent on ruling the human race
	2334	Amanda III born on Dorsai
	2338	Rukh Tamani born on Harmony
	2339	Ajela born on Mara
	2344	Baby Hal Mayne found in wrecked spacecraft
	2350	Ian dies Ajela comes to Final Encyclopedia
	2354	Amanda II dies
	2355	Ajela becomes Tam's assistant
	2359	Hal's three tutors killed on Earth
	2364	Bleys Ahrens assumes command of The Others
	2366	Backed by the talents of Amanda III, Rukh, and Ajela, Hal succeeds Tam as head of Final Encyclopedia. Bleys's minions lay siege to Earth

Soldier, Ask Not brackets *Lost Dorsai* and *Brothers*.

Dorsai! brackets 2276–2289.

The Final Encyclopedia brackets 2359–2366.

[To be continued in future stories]

THE
DORSAI
COMPANION

AMANDA MORGAN

DORSAI, 2185

Stone are my walls, and my roof is of timber;
But the hands of my builder are stronger by far.
The roof may be burned and my stones may
be scattered.
Never her light be defeated in war . . .
Song of the house named Fal Morgan

Amanda Morgan woke suddenly in darkness, her finger automatically on the firing button of the heavy energy handgun. She had heard—or dreamed she heard—the cry of a child. Rousing further, she remembered Betta in the next room and faced the impossibility of her great-granddaughter giving birth without calling her. It had been part of her dream, then.

Still, for a few seconds more, she lay, feeling the ghosts of old enemies still around her and the sleeping house. The cry had merged with the dream she had been having. In her dream, she had been reliving the long-ago swoop on her skimmer, handgun in fist, down into the first of the outlaw camps. It had been when Dorsai was new, and the camps, back in the mountains, had been bases for the out-of-work mercenaries. She had finally led the women of Foralie District against these men who had raided their homes for so long in the intervals when the professional soldiers of their own households were away fighting on other worlds.

The last thing the outlaws had expected from a bunch of women was a frontal assault in full daylight. Therefore, it was that that she had given them. In her dream she had been recalling the fierce bolts from the handgun slicing through makeshift walls and the bodies beyond, setting fire to dried wood and oily rags.

By the time she was in among the huts, some of the outlaws were already armed and out of their structures, and the rest of the fight had disintegrated into a blur of bodies and weapons. The outlaws were all veterans—but so, in their own way, were the women from the households. There were good shots on both sides. In her younger strength, then, she was a match for any out-of-condition mercenary. Also, she was carried along by a rage they could not match...

She blinked, pushing the images of the dream from her. The outlaws were gone now—as were the Eversills, who had tried to steal her land, and other enemies. They were all gone now, making way for new foes. She listened a moment longer, but about her the house of Fal Morgan was still.

After a moment she got up anyway, stepping for a second into the chill bath of night air as she reached for a robe from the chair by her bed. Strong moonlight, filtering through sheer curtains, gave back her ghost in a dim image from the tall armoire mirror. A ghost from sixty years past. For a second before the robe settled about her, the lean and still-erect shape in the mirror invented the illusion of a young, full-fleshed body. She went out.

Twenty steps down the long panelled corridor, with the familiar, silent, cone rifles and other combat arms standing like sentries in their racks on either wall, she became conscious of the fact that habit still kept the energy handgun in her grasp. She shelved it in the rack and went on to her great-granddaughter's door. She opened it and stepped in.

The moonlight shone through the curtains even more brightly on this side of the house. Betta still slept, breathing heavily, her swollen middle rising like a promise under the covering blankets. The concern about this child-to-be that had occupied Amanda all these past months came back on her with fresh urgency. She touched the rough, heavy cloth over the unborn life briefly and lightly with her fingertips. Then she turned and went back out. Down the corridor and around the corner, the Earth-built clock in the living room chimed the first quarter of an hour past 4:00 A.M.

She was fully awake now, and her mind moved purposefully. The birth was due at any time, and Betta was insistent about wanting to use the name Amanda if it was a girl. Was she wrong in withholding her name again? Her decision could not be put off much longer. In the kitchen, she made herself tea. Sitting at the table by the window, she drank it, gazing down over the green tops of the conifers, the pines and spruces on the slope that fell away from the side of the house and rose again to the close horizon of the ridge. She saw the mountain peaks beyond, overlooking Foralie Town and Fal Morgan alike, together with a dozen similar homesteads.

She could not put off any longer making up her mind. As soon as the baby was born, Betta would want to name her. On the surface, it did not seem such an important matter. Why should one name be particularly sacred? Except that Betta did not realize—none of them in the family seemed to realize—how much the name Amanda had come to be a talisman for them all.

The trouble was, time had caught up with her. There was no guarantee that she could wait around for more children to be born. With the trouble that was probably coming, the odds were against her being lucky enough to still be here for the official naming of Betta's child, when that took place. But there had been a strong reason behind her refusal all these years to let her name be given to anyone in the younger generations. True, it was not an easy reason to explain or defend. Its roots were in something as deep as a superstition—the feeling in her that Fal Morgan would only stand as long as that name in the family could stand like a pillar to which they could all anchor. And how could she tell ahead of time how a baby would turn out?

Once more, she had worn a new groove around the full circle of the problem. For a few moments, while she drank her tea, she let her thoughts slide off to the conifers below, which she had stretched herself to buy as seedlings when the Earth stock had finally been imported here to this world they called the Dorsai. They had grown until now they blocked the field of fire from the house in that direction. During the Outlaw Years, she would never have let them grow so high.

With what might be now coming in the way of trouble from Earth, they should probably be cut down completely—though the thought of it went against something deep in her. This house, this land, all of it, was what she had built for herself, her children and their children. It was the greatest of her dreams, made real; there was no part of it, once won, that she could give up easily.

Still seated by the window, slowly drinking the hot tea, her mind went off entirely from the threats of the present to her earliest dreams, back to Caernarvon and the Wales of her childhood, to her small room on a top floor with the ceiling all angles.

She remembered that now, as she sat in this house with only two lives presently stirring inside its walls. No—three, with the child waiting to be born, who would be having dreams of her own before long. How old had she herself been when she had first dreamed of running the wind?

That had been a very early dream of hers, a waking dream—also invoked as she was falling asleep, so that, with luck, sometimes it became a real dream. She had imagined herself being able to run at great speed along the breast of the rolling wind, above city speed and countryside. In her imagination she had run barefoot, and she had been able to feel the texture of the flowing air under her feet, that was like a soft, moving mattress. She had been very young. But it had been a powerful thing, that running.

In her imagination, she had run from Caernarvon and Cardiff clear to France and back again—not above great banks of solar collectors or clumps of manufactories, but over open fields and mountains and cattle, over flowers in fields where green things grew and where people were happy. She had gotten finally so that she could run, in her imagination, farther and faster than anyone.

None was so fleet as she. She ran to Spain and Norway. She ran across Europe as far as Russia; she ran south to the end of Africa and beyond that to the Antarctic and saw the great whales still alive. She ran west over America and south over South America. She saw the cowboys and gauchos as they once had been, and she saw the strange people at the tip of South America, where it was quite cold.

She ran west over the Pacific, over all the south Pacific and over the north Pacific. She ran over the volcanos of the Hawaiian islands, over Japan and China and Indo-China. She ran south over Australia and saw deserts and the great herds of sheep and the wild kangaroos hopping.

Then she went west once more and saw the steppes and the Ukraine and the Black Sea and Constantinople that was, and Turkey, and all the plains where Alexander marched his army to the east, and then back to Africa. She saw strange ships with lug sails on the sea east of Africa, and she ran across the Mediterranean where she saw Italy. She looked down on Rome, with all its history, and on the Swiss Alps, where people yodeled and climbed mountains when they were not working very hard; and all in all she saw many things, until she finally ran home and fell asleep on the breast of the wind and on her own bed. Remembering it all, now that she was ninety-two years old—which was a figure that meant nothing to her—she sat here, light years from it all, on the Dorsai, thinking of it all and drinking tea in the last of the moonlight, looking down at her conifers.

She stirred, pushed the empty cup from her, and rose. Time to begin the day—her control bracelet chimed with the note of an incoming call.

She thumbed the bracelet's com button. The cover over the phone screen on the kitchen wall slid back, and the screen itself lit up with the heavy face of Piers Lindhoven. That face looked out and down at her, the lines that time had cut into it deeper than she had ever seen them. A sound of wheezing whistled and sang behind the labor of his speaking.

"Sorry, Amanda," his voice was hoarse and slow with both age and illness. "Woke you, didn't I?"

"Woke me?" She felt a tension in him and was suddenly alert. "Piers, it's almost daybreak. You know me better than that. What is it?"

"Bad news, I'm afraid." His breathing, like the faint distant music of war-pipes, sounded between words. "The invasion from Earth is on its way. Word just came. Coalition first-line troops—to reach the planet here in thirty-two hours."

"Well, Cletus told us it would happen. Do you want me down in town?"

"No," he said.

Her voice took on an edge in spite of her best intentions.

"Don't be foolish, Piers," she said. "If they can take away the freedom we have here, then the Dorsai ceases to exist—except in name. We're all expendable."

"Yes," he said, wheezing, "but you're far down on the list. Don't be foolish, Amanda. You know what you're worth to us."

"Piers, what do you want me to do?"

He looked at her with a face carved by the same years that had touched her so lightly.

"Cletus just sent word to Eachan Khan to hold himself out from any resistance action here. That leaves us back where we were to begin with in a choice for a commander for the district. I know, Betta's about due—"

"That's not it," she broke in. "You know what it is. You ought to. I'm not that young anymore. Does the district want someone who might fold up on them?"

"They want you, at any cost. You know that," Piers said heavily. "Even Eachan only accepted because you asked someone else to take it. There's no one in the district, no matter what their age or name, who won't jump when you speak. No one else can say that. What do you think they care about the fact that you aren't what you were physically? They want you."

Amanda took a deep breath. She had a feeling in her bones about this. He was going on.

"I've already passed the word by Arvid Johnson and Bill Athyer—those two Cletus left behind to organize the planet's defense. With Betta as she is, we wouldn't have called on you if there was any other choice—but there isn't, now—"

"All right," said Amanda. There was no point in trying to dodge what had to be. Fal Morgan would have to be left empty and unprotected against the invaders. That was simply the way of it. No point, either, in railing against Piers. His exhaustion under the extended asthmatic attack was plain. "I'll be glad to if I'm really needed. You know that. You've already told Johnson and Athyer I'll do it?"

"I just said I'd ask you."

"No need for that. You should know you can count on me. Shall I call and tell them it's settled?"

"I think . . . they'll be contacting you." Amanda glanced at her bracelet. Sure enough, a tiny red phone light on it was blinking—signalling another call in waiting. It could have begun that blinking any time in the last minute or so, but she should have noticed it before this.

"I think they're on line now," she said. "I'll sign off. And I'll take care of things, Piers. Try and get some sleep."

"I'll sleep . . . soon," he said. "Thanks, Amanda."

"Nonsense." She broke the connection and touched the bracelet for the second call. The contrast was characteristic of this Dorsai world of theirs—sophisticated com equipment built into a house constructed by hand of native timber and stone. The screen grayed and then came back into color to show an office room all but hidden by the large-boned face of a blond-haired man in his middle twenties. The single-barred star of a vice-marshall glinted on the collar of his gray field uniform. Above it was a face that might have been boyish once, but now had a stillness to it, a quiet and waiting that made it old before its time.

"Amanda ap Morgan?"

"Yes," said Amanda. "You're Arvid Johnson?"

"That's right," he answered. "Piers suggested we ask you to take on the duty of commander of Foralie District."

"Yes, he just called."

"We understand," Arvid's eyes in the screen were steady on her, "your great-granddaughter's pregnant—"

"I've already told Piers I'd do it." Amanda examined Arvid minutely. He was one of the two people on which they must all depend—with Cletus Grahame gone. "If you know this district, you know there's no one else for the job. Eachan Khan could do it, but apparently that son-in-law of his just told him to keep himself available for other things."

"We know about Cletus's asking him to stay out of things," said Arvid. "I'm sorry it has to be you—"

"Don't be sorry," said Amanda. "I'm not doing it for you. We're all doing it for ourselves."

"Well, thanks anyway." He smiled a little wearily.

"As I say, it's not a matter for thanks."

"Whatever you like."

Amanda continued to examine him closely, across the gulf of the years separating them. What she was seeing, she decided, was that new certainty that was beginning to be noticeable in the Dorsai around Cletus. There was something about Arvid that was as immovable as a mountain.

"What do you want me to do first?" she asked.

"There's to be a meeting of all district commanders of this island at South Point, at 0900 this morning. We'd like you here. Also, since Foralie's the place Cletus is going to come back to—if he comes back— you can expect some special attention, and Bill and I would like to talk to you about that. We can arrange pick-up for you from the Foralie Town airpad, if you'll be waiting there in an hour."

Amanda thought swiftly.

"Make it two hours. I've got things to do first."

"All right. Two hours, then. Foralie Town airpad."

"Don't concern yourself," said Amanda. "I'll remember."

She broke the connection. For a brief moment more she sat, turning things over in her mind. Then she rang Foralie homestead, home of Cletus and Melissa Grahame.

There was a short delay, then the narrow-boned face of Melissa— Eachan Khan's daughter, now Cletus's wife—took shape on the screen. Melissa's eyelids were still heavy with sleep, her hair tousled.

"Who—oh, Amanda," she said.

"I've just been asked to take over district command, from Piers," Amanda said. "The invasion's on its way, and I've got to leave Fal Morgan in an hour for a meeting at South Point. I don't know when or if I'll be back. Can you take Betta?"

"Of course." Melissa's voice and face were coming awake as she spoke. "How close is she?"

"Any time."

"She can ride?"

"Not horseback. Just about anything else."

Melissa nodded.

"I'll be over in the skimmer in forty minutes." She looked out of the screen at Amanda. "I know—you'd rather I move in with her there. But I can't leave Foralie now. I promised Cletus."

"I understand," said Amanda. "Do you know yet when Cletus will be back?"

"No. Anytime—like Betta." Her voice thinned a little. "I'm never sure."

"No. Nor he, either, I suppose." Amanda watched the younger woman for a second. "I'll have Betta ready when you get here. Good-bye."

"Good-bye."

Amanda broke contact and set about getting Betta up and packed. this done, there was the house to be organized for a period of perhaps some days without inhabitants. Betta sat bundled in a chair in the kitchen, waiting as Amanda finished programming the automatic controls of the house for the interval.

"You can call me from time to time at Foralie," Betta said.

"When possible," said Amanda.

She glanced over and saw the normally open, friendly face of her great-granddaughter, now looking puffy and pale above the red cardigan sweater enveloping her. Betta was more than capable in ordinary times; it was only in emergencies like this that she had a tendency to founder. Amanda checked her own critical frame of mind. It was not easy for Betta, about to have a child with her husband, father, and brother all off-planet, in combat, and—the nature of war being what it was—the possibility existing that none of them might come back to her. There were only three men at the moment left in the house of ap Morgan, and only two women, now one of those two, Amanda, herself, was going off on a duty that could end in a hangman's rope or a firing squad. For she did not delude herself that the Earth-bred Alliance and Coalition military would fight with the same restraint toward civilians the soldiers of the younger worlds showed.

But it would not help to fuss over Betta now. It would help none of them. There was an approaching humming noise outside the house that crescendoed to a peak just beyond the kitchen door and stopped.

"Melissa," said Betta.

"Come on," Amanda said.

She led the way outside. Betta followed, a little clumsily, and Melissa with Amanda helped her into the open cockpit of the ducted fan skimmer.

"I'll check up on you when I have time," Amanda said, kissing her great-granddaughter briefly. Betta's arms tightened fiercely around her.

"*Mandy!*" The diminutive of her name which only the young children normally used and the sudden desperate appeal in Betta's voice sent a surge of empathy arcing between them. Over Betta's shoulder, Amanda saw the face of Melissa, calm and waiting. Unlike Betta, Melissa came into her own in a crisis—it was in ordinary times that the daughter of Eachan Khan fumbled and lost her way.

"Never mind me," said Amanda. I'll be all right. Take care of your own duties."

With strength, she freed herself and waved them off. For a second more she stood, watching their skimmer hum off down the slope. Betta's farewell had just woken a grimness in her that was still there. Melissa and Betta. Either way, being a woman who was useful half the time was no good. Life required you to be operative at all hours and seasons.

That was the problem with a talisman-name like her own. She who would own it must be operative in just that way—at all times. When someone of that capability should be born into the family, she could release the name of Amanda, which she had so far refused to every female child in the line. As she refused it to Betta for this child. And yet . . . and yet, it was not right to lock up the name forever. As each generation moved farther away from her own time, it and the happenings connected with it would then become more and more legendary, more and more unreal. . . .

She put the matter for the thousandth time from her mind and turned back to buttoning up Fal Morgan. Passing down the long hall, she let her fingers trail for a second on its dark wainscotting. Almost, she could feel a living warmth in the wood, the heart of the house beating. But there was nothing more she could do to protect it now. In the days to come, it, too, must take its chances.

Fifteen minutes later, she was on her own skimmer, heading downslope toward Foralie Town. At her back was an overnight bag, considerably smaller than the one they had packed for Betta. Under her belt was a heavy energy pistol on full charge and in perfect order. In the long-arm boot of the skimmer was an ancient blunderbus of a pellet shotgun, its clean and decent barrel replaced minutes before by one that was rusted and old, but workable. As she reached the foot of the slope and started the rise to the ridge, her gaze was filled by the mountains, and Fal Morgan moved for the moment into the back of her mind.

The skimmer hummed upslope, only a few feet above the ground. Out from under the spruce and pine, the highland sun was brilliant. The thin earth cover, broken by outcroppings of granite and quartz, was brown, sparsely covered by tough green grasses. The air was cold and light, unwarmed by the sun. She felt it deep in her lungs when she breathed. *The wine of the morning,* her own mother had called air like this, nearly a century ago.

She mounted to the crest of the ridge and the mountains stood up around her on all sides, shoulder to shoulder like friendly giants, as she topped the ridge and headed down the farther slope to Foralie, now visible, distant and small by the river bend far below. The sky was brilliantly clear with the new day. Only a small, stray cloud here and there graced its perfection. The mountains stood, looking down. There were people here who were put off by their bare rock, their remote and icy summits, but she herself found them honest—secure, strong, and holding, brothers to her soul.

A deep feeling moved in her, even after all these years. Even more than for the home she had raised, she had found in herself a love for this world. She loved it as she loved her children, her children's children, and her three husbands—each was different, each one unmatchable in its own way.

She had loved it, not more than but as much as she had loved her first-born, Jimmy, all the days of his life. But why should she love the Dorsai so much? There had been mountains in Wales—fine mountains. But when she first came here after her second husband's death, something about this land, this planet, had spoken to her and claimed her with a voice different from any she had ever heard before. She and it had strangely become joined, beyond separation. A strange, powerful, almost aching affection had come to bind her to it. Why should just a world, a place of ordinary water and land and wind and sky, be something to touch her so deeply?

But she was sliding swiftly now, down the gentler, longer curve of the slope that led to Foralie Town. She could see the brown track of the river road now, following the snake of blue water that wound away to the east and out between a fold in the mountains, and in its other direction from the town, west and up until it disappeared in the rocky folds above, where its source lay in the water of permanent ice sheets at seventeen thousand feet. Small clumps of the native softwood trees moved and passed like shutters between her and sight of the town below as she descended. But at this hour, she saw no other traffic about. Twenty minutes later, she came to the road and the river below the town and turned left, upstream toward the buildings that were now close.

She passed out from behind a clump of small softwoods and slid past the town manufactory and the town dump, which now separated her from the river and the wharf that let river traffic unload directly to the manufactory. The manufactory itself was silent and inactive at this early hour. The early sun winked on the rubble of refuse, broken metal and discarded material of all kinds, in the little hollow below the exhaust vent of the manufactory's power unit.

The Dorsai was a poor world in terms of arable land and most natural resources, but it did supply petroleum products from the drowned shorelines of the many islands that took the place of continents on the watery planet. So crude oil had been the fuel chosen for the power generator at the manufactory, which had been imported at great cost from Earth. The tools driven by that generator were as sophisticated as any found on Earth, while the dump was as primitive as any that pioneer towns had ever had. As primitive as her stone Fal Morgan, with the modern communications equipment hidden within, she thought.

She stopped the skimmer and got off, then walked a dozen feet or so back into the brush across the road from the dump. She took the heavy energy handgun from her belt and hung it low on the branch of a sapling, where the green leaves all about would hide it from anyone not standing within arm's reach of it. She made no further effort to protect it. The broad arrow stamped on its grip, mark of the ap Morgans, would identify it to anyone native to this world who might stumble across it.

She returned to the skimmer just as a metal door in the side of the manufactory slid back with a rattle and a bang. Jhanis Bins came out wheeling a dump carrier loaded with silvery drifts of fine metallic dust.

Amanda walked over to him as he wheeled the carrier to the dump and tilted its contents onto the rubble inches below the exhaust vent. He jerked the carrier back on to the roadway and winked at Amanda. Age and illness had wasted him to a near skeleton, but there was still strength in his body, if little endurance. Above the old knife-scar lying all the way across his nose, his eyes held a sardonic humor.

"Nickel grindings?" asked Amanda, nodding at what Jhanis had just dumped.

"Right," he said. There was a grim humor in his voice as well as in his eyes. "You're up early."

"So are you," she said.

"Lots to be done." He offered a hand. "Amanda."

She took it.

"Jhanis."

He let go and grinned again.

"Well, back to work. Luck Commander, ma'am."

He turned the carrier back toward the manufactory.

"News travels fast," she said.

"How else?" he replied over his shoulder. He went inside. The metal door rolled on its tracks and slammed shut behind him.

Amanda remounted the skimmer and slid it on into town. As she came to a street of houses just off the main street, she saw Bhaktabahadur Rais sweeping the path between the flowers in front of his house, holding the broom awkwardly but firmly in the clawed arthritic fingers of the one hand remaining to him. The empty sleeve of the other arm was pinned up neatly just below the shoulder joint. The small brown man smiled warmly as the skimmer settled to the ground when Amanda stopped its motors opposite him. He was no bigger than a twelve-year-old boy. In spite of his having almost as many years as Amanda, he moved as lightly as a child.

He carried the broom to the skimmer, leaned it against his shoulder and saluted. There was an impish sparkle about him.

"All right, Bhak," said Amanda. "I'm just doing what I'm asked. Did the young ones and their Ancients get out of town?"

He sobered.

"Piers sent them out two days ago," he said. "You didn't know?"

Amanda shook her head.

"I've been busy with Betta. Why two days ago?"

"Evidence they were out before we heard any Earth troops were coming." He shifted his broom back into his hand. "If nothing had happened, it would have been easy to have called them back after a few days. If you need me for anything, Amanda—"

"I'll ask, don't worry," she said. It would be easier at any time for Bhak to fight than it would be for him to wait. The kukri in its curved sheath still lay on his mantelpiece. "I've got to get on to the town hall."

She lifted the skimmer on the thrust of its fans. Their humming was loud in the quiet street.

"Where's Betta?" Bhak raised his voice.

"Foralie."

He smiled again.

"Good. Any news of Cletus?"

She shook her head and set the skimmer off down the street. On the main street, just past the last house back around the corner, she checked suddenly and went back. A heavy-bodied girl with long brown hair and a round somewhat bunched-up face was sitting on her front step. Amanda stopped the skimmer, got out and went up to the steps. The girl looked up at her.

"Marte," said Amanda, "what are you doing here? Why didn't you go out with the other boys and girls?"

Marte's face took on a slightly sullen look.

"I'm staying with Grandma."

"But you wanted to go with one of the teams," said Amanda gently. "You told me so just last week."

Marte did not answer. She merely stared hard at the concrete of the walk between her feet. Amanda went up the steps past her and into the house.

"Berthe?" she called as the door closed behind her.

"Amanda? I'm in the library." The voice that came back was deep enough to be male, but when Amanda followed it into a room off to her right, the old friend she found among the crowded bookshelves there, seated at a desk, writing on a sheet of paper, was a woman with even more years than herself.

"Hello, Amanda," Berthe Haugsrud said. "I'm just writing some instructions."

"Marte's still here," Amanda said.

Berthe pushed back in her chair and sighed.

"It's her choice. She wants to stay. I can't bring myself to force her to go if she doesn't want to."

"What have you told her?" Amanda heard the tone of her voice, sharper than she had intended.

"Nothing." Berthe looked at her. "You can't hide things from her,

Amanda. She's as sensitive as . . . anyone. She picked it up—from the air, from the other young ones. Even if she doesn't understand details, she knows what's likely to happen."

"She's young," said Amanda. "What is she—not seventeen yet?"

"But she's got no one but me," said Berthe. Her eyes were black and direct under the wrinkled lids. "Without me, she'd have nobody. Oh, I know everyone in town would look after her, as long as they could. But it wouldn't be the same. Here, in this house, with just the two of us, she can forget she's different. She can pretend she's just as bright as anyone. With that gone . . ."

They looked at each other for a moment.

"Well, it's your decision," said Amanda, turning away.

"And hers, Amanda. And hers."

"Yes. All right. Good-bye, Berthe."

"Good-bye, Amanda. Good luck."

"The same to you," said Amanda soberly. "The same to you."

She went out. She touched Marte's bowed head softly as she went by, but Marte did not stir or respond. Amanda remounted the skimmer and drove it around the farther corner, down the main street to the square concrete box that was the town hall.

"Hello, Jenna," she said, stepping into the outer office. "I'm here to be sworn in."

Jenna Chalk looked up from her desk behind the counter that bisected the front office. She was a pleasant, rusty-haired woman, small and in her mid-sixties, looking like anything in the universe but the ex-mercenary she was.

"Good," she said. "Piers has been waiting. I'll bring the papers, and we'll go back—"

"Still here?" said Amanda. "What's he doing waiting around?"

"He wanted to see you." Jenna slid her hands into the two wrist-crutches leaning against her desk and levered herself to her feet. Leaning on one crutch, she picked up the folder before her on her desk and turned, leading the way down the corridor behind the counter. The corridor led toward the back of the building and the other offices there. Amanda let herself through the swinging gate in the counter and caught up.

"How is he?" Amanda asked.

"Worn out—a little easier since the sun came up," said Jenna, hobbling along. Her bones over the years had become so fragile that they shattered at a touch, and her legs had broken so many times now that it was almost a miracle that she could walk at all. "I think he'll let himself risk some medication, after he sees you take over."

"He didn't need to wait for me," said Amanda. "That was foolish."

"It's his way," said Jenna. "The habits of seventy years don't change."

She stopped and pushed open the door they had come up against. Together they entered and found the massive, ancient shape of Piers propped up in a high-backed chair behind the wide desk of his office.

"Piers," said Amanda. "You didn't need to wait. Go home."

"I want to witness your signing-in," said Piers. Talking was still difficult for him, but Amanda noted that his breathing did seem to have eased slightly with the sunrise, in common asthmatic fashion. "Just in case the troops they drop here decide to check records."

"All right," said Amanda.

Jenna was already switching on the recording camera eye in the wall. They went through the ritual of signing papers and administering an oath to Amanda that gave her the official title of mayor of Foralie Town, which would be a cover for her secret rank of district commander.

"Now, for God's sake, go home!" said Amanda to Piers when they were done. "Take some of that medicine of yours and sleep."

"I will," said Piers. "Thank you for this, Amanda. And good luck. My skimmer's out back. Could you help me to it?"

Amanda put one hand under the heavy old man's right elbow and helped him to his feet. The years had taken much of her physical strength, but she still knew how to concentrate what she had at the point needed. She piloted Piers out the back way and helped him into the seat of his skimmer.

"Can you get down and take care of yourself by yourself when you get home?" she asked.

"No trouble," Piers grunted at her. He put the skimmer's power on, and it lifted. He glanced at her once more.

"Amanda."

"Piers." She laid a hand for a second on his shoulder.

"It's a good world, Amanda."

"I know. I think so, too."

"Good-bye."

"Good-bye," said Amanda, and she watched the skimmer take him away.

She turned back into the town hall.

"Marte's still here," she said to Jenna. "I guess we'll just have to let her stay, if that's what she wants."

"It is," said Jenna.

"Are there any others still around I don't know about?"

"No, the young ones are all gone—and their Ancients."

"Have you got a map for me?"

Jenna reached into her folder and came out with a map of the country about Foralie Town, including the mountains surrounding. Initials in red were scattered about it.

"Each team under the initials of its Ancient," Jenna said.

Amanda studied it.

"They're all out in position now, then?"

Jenna nodded.

"And they're all armed?"

"With the best we had to give them," Jenna said. She shook her head. "I can't help it, Amanda. It's bad enough for us at our age, but to give our young people hand weapons and ask them to stop—"

"Do you know an alternative?" said Amanda.

Jenna shook her head again, silent.

"An aircraft's due to pick me up from the pad here in three-quarters of an hour," Amanda said. "I'll be checking the situation out around the town otherwise, between now and then. Just in case I don't get back here before we're hit, are you going to have any trouble convincing the invaders that I'm a mayor and nothing more?"

Jenna snorted.

"I've been clerk in this town hall nine years—"

"All right," said Amanda. "I just wanted to put it in words. If the troops they send in won't billet in town, try and get them to camp close in on the upriver side."

"Of course," said Jenna. "I know. You don't have to tell me, Amanda. Anyway, there shouldn't be much trouble getting them there. It's a natural bivouac area."

"Yes. All right then," Amanda said. "Take care of yourself, too, Jenna."

"We both better take care of ourselves," said Jenna. "Luck, Amanda."

Amanda went out.

She was on the airpad, waiting, when a light, four-place gravity aircraft dropped suddenly out of the blue above and touched down lightly on the pad. A door swung open. She went forward, carrying her single piece of luggage, and climbed in. The craft took off. Amanda found herself seated next to Geoff Harbor, district commander of North Point.

"You both know each other, don't you?" asked the pilot, looking back over his shoulder.

"For sixteen years," said Geoff. "Hello, Amanda."

"Geoff," she said. "They bringing you in for this meeting, too? Are you all ready, up there at North Point?"

"Yes. All set," he answered both questions, looking at her curiously above his narrow nose and wedge-shaped chin. He was only in his forties, but twenty years of living with the after-effects of massive battle injuries had given his skin a waxy look. "I was expecting Eachan."

"Eachan was asked by Cletus Grahame to hold himself ready for something else," said Amanda. "Piers took charge, and I just replaced him this morning."

"Asthma getting him?"

"The pressure of all this thing pushed him into an attack, I think," said Amanda. "Have you met this Arvid Johnson, or the other one—Bill Athyer?"

"I've met Arvid," said Geoff. "He's what Cletus Grahame's now calling a "battle op"—a field tactician. Athyer's strategist, and they work as a team—but you must have heard all this."

"Yes," said Amanda. "But what I want to know is some first-hand opinions on what they're like."

"Arvid struck me as being damn capable," said Geoff. "If they work well together, then Bill Athyer can't be much less. And if Cletus put them in charge of the defense here . . . but you know Cletus, of course?"

"He's a neighbor," said Amanda. "I've met him a few times."

"And you've got doubts about him, too?"

"No," said Amanda. "But we're trying to make bricks without straw. A handful of adults with a force of half-grown teenagers to knock down an assault force of first-line troops. Miracles are going to have to be routine, and nothing's so good we shouldn't worry about whether it's good enough."

Geoff nodded.

A short while later they set down on the airpad outside the island government center at South Point. A lean, brown-skinned soldier wearing the collar tabs that showed Groupman's rank—one of the staff of a dozen or so combat-qualified Dorsai that Arvid Johnson and Bill Athyer had been allowed to keep for their defense of the planet—was waiting for them as they stepped out of the aircraft. He led them to a briefing room already half-full of district commanders from all over the island, then turned to the room at large.

"If you'll take seats—" he announced. The district commanders sorted themselves out on the folding chairs facing a platform at one end of the room. A minute or so later, two men came in and stepped up on the platform. One was Arvid Johnson. Seen at full-length, he was a tower of a man, with blond hair that, in this artificial light, looked so pale, that it seemed almost invisible. The unconquerability of him radiated to the rest of them in the room. The man beside him was of about the same age, but small, with a heavy beak of a nose—what Amanda had learned to call a "Norman nose" when she was a little girl. His eyes swept the room like gun muzzles.

The small man, Amanda thought, must be Bill Athyer, the strategist. At first glance, Bill might have appeared not only unimpressive, but sour—but Amanda's swift and experienced perceptions picked up something vibrant and brilliant in him. Literally, without losing whatever painful and inhibiting self-consciousness and self-doubt he was born with, he must somewhere have picked up the inner fire that now shone through his unremarkable exterior. He was all flame within—and that flame made him a strange contrast to the cool, almost remote competence of Arvid.

"Sorry to spring this on you," Arvid said when both men were standing on the platform facing the audience. "But it seems, after all, we can't wait for the district commanders who aren't here yet. We've just had word that whoever's navigating the invasion ships is either extremely lucky or very good. He's brought them out of their last phase shift right on top of the planet. They're in orbit overhead now and already dropping troops on our population centers."

He paused and looked around the room.

"The rest of the Dorsai's been notified, of course," he said. "Bill Athyer and myself, with the few line soldiers we've got, are going to have to start moving—and keep moving. Don't try to find us—we'll find you. Communication will be known-person to known-person. In short, if the word you get from us doesn't come through somebody you trust implicitly, disregard it."

"This is one of our strengths," said Bill Athyer, so swiftly it was almost as if he interrupted. His voice was harsh, but crackled with something like high excitement. "Just as we know the terrain, we know each other. These two things let us dispense with a lot the invader has to have. But be warned—our advantages are going to be of most use only during the first few days. As they get to know us, they'll begin to be able to guess what we can do. Now, you've each submitted operational plans for the defense of your particular district within the general guidelines Arvid and I drew up. We've reviewed these plans, and by now you've all seen our recommendations for emendations and additions. If, in any case, there's more to be said, we'll get in touch with you as necessary. So you'd probably all better head back to your districts as quickly as possible. We've enough aircraft waiting to get you all back—hopefully before the invasion forces hit your districts. Get moving—is Amanda Morgan here?"

"Here!" called Amanda.

"Would you step up here, please?"

With Bill Athyer's last words, all the seated commanders had gotten to their feet, and Amanda was hidden in the swarm of bodies. She pushed her way forward to the platform and looked up into the faces of the unusual pair standing there.

"I'm Amanda Morgan," she said.

"A word with you before you leave," said Bill. "Will you come along?"

He led the way out of the briefing room. Arvid and Amanda followed. They stepped into a small office, and Arvid shut the door behind them on the noise in the hall as the other commanders moved to their waiting aircraft.

"You took command of the Foralie District just this morning," Bill said. "Have you had any chance to look at the plans handed in by the man you replaced?"

"Piers Lindhoven checked with several of us when he drafted them," Amanda said. "But in any case, anyone in Foralie District over the age of nine knows how we're going to deal with whoever they send against us."

"All right," said Bill. Arvid nodded.

"You understand," Bill went on, "in Foralie there, you'll be at the pick-point for whatever's going to happen. You can probably expect, if our information's right, to see Dow deCastries himself, as well as extra troops and a rank-heavier staff of enemy officers than any of the other districts. They'll be zeroing in on Foralie homestead."

The thought of Betta and the unborn child there was a sudden twinge in Amanda's chest.

"There's no one at Foralie but Melissa Grahame and Eachan Khan, right now," she said. "Nobody to speak of."

"There's going to be. Cletus will be on his way back as soon as the information we're invaded hits the Exotics—and I think you know the Exotics get news faster than anyone else. He may be on his way right now. Dow deCastries will be expecting this. So you can also expect your district to be one of the first, if not the first, hit. Odds are good that you, at least, aren't going to get home before the first troops touch down in your district. But we'll do our best for you. We've got our fastest aircraft holding for you now. Any last questions, or needs?"

Amanda looked at them both. Young men both of them.

"Not now," she said. "In any case, we know what we have to do."

"Good." It was Arvid speaking again. "You'd better get going then."

The craft they were holding for her turned out to be a small, two-place, high-altitude gravity flyer, which rocketed to the ten-kilometer altitude, then back down toward Foralie on a flight path like the trajectory of a fired mortar shell. They were less than half an hour in the air. Nonetheless, as they plunged toward Foralie Town airpad, the com system inside the craft crackled.

"*Identify yourself. Identify yourself. This is Outpost Four-nine-three. Alliance-Coalition Expeditionary Force to the Dorsai. You are under our weapons. Identify yourself.*"

The pilot glanced briefly at Amanda and touched the transmit button on his control wheel.

"What'd you say?" he asked. "This is Mike Amery, on a taxi run from South Point just to bring the Foralie Town mayor home. Who did you say you were?"

Outpost Four-nine-three, Alliance-Coalition Expeditionary Force to the Dorsai. Identify the person you call the mayor of Foralie Town."

"Amanda Morgan," said Amanda clearly to the com equipment, "of the household ap Morgan, Foralie District."

"Hold. Do not attempt to land until we check your identification. Repeat. Hold. Do not attempt to land until given permission."

The speaker was abruptly silent again. The pilot checked the landing pattern for the craft. They waited. After several minutes, the order came to bring themselves in.

Two transport-pale, obviously Earth-native privates in Coalition uniforms were covering the aircraft hatch with cone rifles as Amanda preceded the pilot out on to the pad. A thin, serious-faced young Coalition lieutenant motioned the two of them to a staff car.

"Where do you think you're taking us?" Amanda demanded. "Who are you? What're you doing here, anyway?"

"It'll all be explained at your town hall, ma'am," said the lieutenant. "I'm sorry, but I'm not permitted to answer questions."

He got into the staff car with them and tapped the driver on the shoulder. They drove to town, through streets empty of any human figures not in uniforms. With the emptiness of the streets was a stillness. On the north edge of the town, on the upslope of the meadow that Amanda had mentioned to Jenna, Amanda glimpsed beehive-shaped cantonment huts of bubble plastic being blown into existence in orderly rows—and from this area alone came a sound, distant but real, of voices and activities. Amanda felt the prevailing wind from the south on the back of her neck, and scented the faint odors of the fresh riverwater and the dump, although the manufactory itself was silent.

The staff car reached the town hall. The pilot was left in the outer office, but Amanda was ushered in past guards to the office that had been Piers's and was now hers. There, a large map of the district had been imaged on one wall and several officers of grades between major and brigadier general were standing about in a discussion that seemed very close to argument. Only one person in the room wore civilian clothing, and this was a tall, slim man seated at Amanda's desk, tilted back in its chair, apparently absorbed in studying the map that was imaged.

He seemed oddly remote from the rest, isolated by position or authority and willing to concentrate on the map, leaving the officers to their talk. The expression on his face was thoughtful, abstract. Few men Amanda had met in her long life could have legitimately been called handsome, but this man was. His features were so regular as to approach unnaturalness. His dark hair was touched with gray only at the temples, and his high forehead seemed to shadow deep-set eyes, so dark that they appeared inherently unreadable. If it had not been for those eyes and an air of power that seemed to wrap him like light from some invisible source, he might have looked too pretty to be someone to reckon with. Watching him now, however, Amanda had few doubts as to his ability, or his identity.

"Sir—," began the lieutenant who had brought Amanda in, but the brigadier to whom he spoke, glancing up, interrupted him, speaking directly to Amanda.

"You're the mayor here? What were you doing away from the town? Where are all your townspeople?"

"General." Amanda spoke slowly. She did not have to invent the anger behind her words. "Don't ask me questions. I'll do the asking. Who're you? What made you think you could walk into this office without my permission? Where'd you come from? And what're you doing here, under arms, without getting authority first—from the island authorities at South Point and from us?"

"I think you understand all right—" began the general.

"I think I don't," said Amanda. "You're here illegally, and I'm still waiting for an explanation—and an apology for pushing yourself into my office without leave."

The brigadier's mouth tightened, and the skin wrinkled and puffed around his eyes.

"Foralie District's been occupied by the Alliance-Coalition authorities," he said. "That's all you need to know. Now, I want some answers—"

"I'll need a lot more of an explanation than that," broke in Amanda. "Neither the Alliance nor the Coalition, nor any Alliance-Coalition troops, has any right I know of to be below parking orbit. I want your authority for being here. I want to talk to your superior—and I want both those things now!"

"What kind of a farce do you think you're playing?" The words burst out of the brigadier. "You're under occupation—"

"General," said a voice from the desk, and every head in the room turned to the man who sat there. "Perhaps I ought to talk to the mayor."

"Yes, sir," muttered the brigadier. The skin around his eyes was still puffy, his face darkened now with blood-gorged capillaries. "Amanda Morgan, this is Dow deCastries, Supreme Commander of Alliance-Coalition forces."

"I didn't imagine he could be anyone else," said Amanda. She took a step that brought her to the outer edge of her desk and looked across it at Dow.

"You're sitting in my chair," she said.

Dow rose easily to his feet and stepped back, gesturing to the now-empty seat.

"Please...," he said.

"Just stay on your feet. That'll be good enough for now," said Amanda. She made no move to sit down herself. "You're responsible for this?"

"Yes, you could say I am." Dow looked at her thoughtfully. "General Amorine," he spoke without looking away from Amanda— "the mayor and I probably had better talk things over privately."

"Yes, sir, if that's what you want."

"It is. It is, indeed." Now, Dow did look at the brigadier, who stepped back.

"Of course, sir," Amorine turned on the lieutenant who had brought Amanda in. "You checked her for weapons, of course?"

"Sir...I—" The lieutenant was flustered. His stiff embarrassment pleaded that you did not expect a woman Amanda's age to go armed.

"I don't think we need worry about that, General." Dow's voice was still relaxed, but his eyes were steady on the brigadier.

"Of course, sir." Amorine herded his officers out. The door closed behind them, leaving Amanda and Dow standing face to face.

"You're sure you won't sit down?" asked Dow.

"This isn't a social occasion," said Amanda.

"No," said Dow. "Unfortunately, no it isn't. It's a serious situation, in which your whole planet has been placed under Alliance-Coalition control. Effectively, what you call the Dorsai no longer exists."

"Hardly," said Amanda.

"You have trouble believing that?" said Dow. "I assure you—"

"I've no intention of believing it, now or later," Amanda said. "The Dorsai isn't this town. It isn't any number of towns just like it. It's not even the islands and the sea—it's the people."

"Exactly," said Dow, "and the people are now under the control of the Alliance-Coalition. You brought it on yourself, you know. You've squandered your ordinary defensive force on a dozen other worlds, and you've got nothing but noncombatants left here. In short, you're helpless. But that's not my concern. I'm not interested in your planet, or your people, as people. It's just necessary we make sure they aren't led astray again by another dangerous madman like Cletus Grahame."

"Madman?" echoed Amanda dryly.

Dow raised his eyebrows.

"Don't you think he was mad in thinking he could succeed against the two richest powers on the most powerful human world in existence?" He shook his head. "But there's not much point in our arguing politics, is there? All I want is your cooperation."

"Or else what?"

"I wasn't threatening," Dow said mildly.

"Of course you were," said Amanda. She held his eyes with her own for a long second. "Do you know your Shakespeare?"

"I did once."

"Near the end of *Macbeth,* when Macbeth himself hears a cry in the night that signals the death of Lady Macbeth," Amanda said, "he says *'there was a time my senses would have cool'd to hear a night-shriek. . . .'* remember it? Well, that time passes for all of us, with the years. You'll probably have a few to go yet to find that out for yourself, but if and when you do, you'll discover that eventually you outlive fear, just as you outlive a lot of other things. You can't bully me, you can't scare me—or anyone else in Foralie District with enough seniority to take my place.

It was his turn now to consider her for a long moment without speaking.

"All right," he said. "I'll believe you. My only interest, as I say, is in arresting Cletus Grahame and taking him back to Earth with me."

"You occupy a whole world just to arrest one man?" Amanda said.

"Please." He held up one long hand. "I thought we were going to talk straightforwardly with each other. I want Cletus. Is he on the Dorsai?"

"Not as far as I know."

"Then I'll go to his home and wait for him to come to me," said Dow. He glanced at the map. "That'll be Foralie—the homestead marked there near your own Fal Morgan?"

"That's right."

"Then I'll move up there now. Meanwhile, I want to know what the situation is here, clearly. Your able fighting men are all off-planet. All right. But there's no one in this town who isn't crippled, sick, or over sixty. Where are all your healthy young women, your teenagers below military age, and anyone else who's effective?"

"Gone off out of town," said Amanda.

Dow's black eyes seemed to deepen.

"That hardly seems normal. I assume you had warnings of us, at least as soon as we were in orbit. I'd be very surprised if it wasn't news of our being in orbit that brought you back here in that aircraft just now. You wouldn't have messaged ahead, telling your children and able-bodied adults to scatter and hide?"

"No," said Amanda, "I didn't, and no one here gave any such direction."

"Then maybe you'll explain why they're all gone?"

"Do you want a few hundred reasons?" Amanda said. "It's the end of summer. The men are gone. This town is just a supply and government center. Who's young and wants to hang around here all day? The younger women living in town are up visiting at the various homesteads where they've got friends and there's some social life. The babies and younger children went with their mothers. The older children are off on team exercises."

"Team exercises?"

"Military team exercises," said Amanda bluntly and with grim humor, watching him. "Otherwise known as 'creeping and crawling'. This is a world where the main occupation, once you're grown, is being a mercenary soldier. So this is our version of field trips. It's good exercise, the youngsters get some academic credit for it when they go back to school in a few weeks, and it's a chance for them to get away from adult supervision and move around on their own, camping out."

Dow frowned.

"No adult supervision?"

"Not a lot," said Amanda. "There's one adult—called an "Ancient," with each team, in case of emergencies, but in most cases, the team makes its own decision about what kind of games it'll play with other teams in the same area, where it'll set up camp, and so forth."

"These children," Dow was still frowning, "are they armed?"

"With real weapons? They never have been."

"Are they likely to get any wild notions about doing something to our occupying forces—"

"Commander," said Amanda, "Dorsai children don't get wild notions about military operations. Not if they expect to stay Dorsai as adults."

"I see," said Dow. He smiled slowly at her. "All the same, I think we better get them and the able-bodied adults back into town here, where we can explain to them what the situation is and what they should or shouldn't do. Also there's a few of your other people who're conspicuous by their absence. For example, where are your medical people?"

"We've got one physician and three meds here in Foralie District," said Amanda. "They all ride circuit most of the time. You'll find them scattered out at various homesteads right now.

"I see," said Dow again. "Well, I think you better call them in as well, along with any other adult from the homesteads who's physically able to come."

"No," said Amanda.

He looked at her. His eyebrows raised.

"Courage, Amanda Morgan," he said, "is one thing. Stupidity, something else."

"And nonsense is nonsense wherever you find it," said Amanda. "I told you you couldn't bully me—or anyone else you'll find in this town. And you'll need one of us who's here to deal with the people of the district for you. I can bring the youngsters back in if necessary, and with them such adults from the homesteads who don't need to stay where they are. If the medical people are free to come in, I can get them, too. But in return, I'll want some things from you."

"I don't think you're in a position to bargain."

"Of course I am," said Amanda. "Let's not play games. It's much easier for you if you can get civilian cooperation—it's much faster. Difficulty with the populace means expense, when you're carrying the cost of enough troops to nail down a planet—even as sparsely settled a planet as this one. And you yourself said once you get Cletus you'll be taking off without another thought for the rest of us."

"That's not exactly what I said," Dow replied.

Amanda snorted.

"All right," he said, "what was it you had in mind?"

"First, get your troops out of our town unless you were thinking of billeting them in our homes here."

"I think you saw camp being set up just beyond the houses a street or two over."

"All right," Amanda said. "Then I want them to stay out of town unless they've got actual business here. When they do come in, they're to come in as visitors, remembering their manners. I don't want any of your officers, like that brigadier just now, trying to throw their weight around. Our people are to be free of any authority from yours, so we can get back to business as usual—and that includes putting the manufactory back into operation immediately. I noticed you'd had the power shut off. Don't you realize we've got contracts to fill—contracts for manufactured items, so that we can trade with the rest of Dorsai for the fish, the grain, and other things we have to have to live?"

"All right," said Dow. "I suppose we can agree to those things."

"I'm not finished," Amanda said swiftly. "Also, you and all the rest of your forces are to stay put, in your encampment. I don't want you upsetting and alarming the district while I go find the teams and get people back here from the homesteads. It'll take me a week anyway—"

"No," said Dow. "We'll be putting out patrols immediately, and I myself'll be leaving with an escort for Foralie homestead in a few hours."

"In that case—," Amanda was beginning, but this time it was Dow who cut her short.

"In that case—"—his voice was level— "you'll force me to take the more difficult and time-consuming way with your people. I didn't bargain with you on any of the other things you asked for. I'm not bargaining now. Go ahead and take back your town, start up your manufactory, and round up only those you feel can come in safely. But our patrols go out as soon as we're ready to send them, and I leave today, just as I said. Now, do we have an agreement?"

Amanda nodded slowly.

"We have," she said. "All right, you'd better get those officers of yours back in here. I'm not going to have to move to cover the district personally, even in a week. I'll go right now, but I want to hear that manufactory operating before I'm out of earshot of town. I suppose you've got Jhanis Bins closed up in his house, like everyone else."

"Whoever he is," said Dow. "He'd be under house quarantine, yes."

"All right, I'll call him," said Amanda. "But I want your General Amorine to send an officer to get him and take him safely to the man-ufactory, just in case some of your enlisted men may not have heard word of this agreement by that time."

"Fair enough," said Dow. He stepped to the desk and keyed the com system there. "General, will you and your staff step back into the office?"

"Yes, Mr. deCastries." The voice from the wall came promptly.

Twenty minutes later, Amanda reached the airpad in the same staff car that had brought her in from it. Under the eyes of the two enlisted men on duty there, her skimmer stood waiting for her.

"Thanks," she said to the young lieutenant who had brought her in. She climbed out of the staff car, walked across the pad, and got into her skimmer.

"Just a minute," called the lieutenant.

She looked back to see him standing up in his staff car. There was a shine to his forehead that told of perspiration.

"You've got a weapon there, ma'am," he said. "Just a minute. Sol-dier—you!" He pointed to one of the enlisted men guarding the pad. "Get that piece and bring it over to me."

"Lieutenant," said Amanda, "this is still a young planet, and we had lawless people roaming around our mountains as recently as just a few years back. We all carry guns here."

"Sorry, ma'am. I have to examine it. Soldier..."

The enlisted man came over to the skimmer, pulled the pellet shotgun from the scabbard beside her, and winked at her.

"Got to watch you dangerous outworlders," he said under his breath. He glanced over the pellet gun, turned it up to squint down its barrel, and chuckled, again under his breath.

He carried the weapon to the lieutenant and said something Amanda could not catch. The lieutenant also tilted the pellet gun up to look briefly into its barrel, then handed it back.

"Take it to her," he ordered. He lifted his head and called across to Amanda. "Be careful with it, ma'am."

"I will be," said Amanda.

She received the rifle, powered up the skimmer, and slid off through the fringe of trees around the pad.

She took her way toward the downriver side of town. As she went, the sudden throb of the engines in the manufactory erupted in her ear. She smiled, but she was suddenly conscious of the prevailing wind in her face. Sweating, she asked herself, at your age? She turned her scorn inward. Where was all that talk of yours to deCastries about having outlived fear?

She swung through town and around by the river road past the dump. The manufactory stood, noisily operating. There was no Coalition uniform in sight outside the building and the side looking in her direction was blank of windows. She stopped her skimmer long enough to walk back into the brush and retrieve the energy handgun she had hung on the tree. Then she remounted her skimmer and headed upslope, out of town.

Her mind was racing. Dow had intimated he would head out to Foralie homestead this afternoon. Which meant Amanda herself would have to go directly there to get there before him. She had hoped to come in there with evening and perhaps even stay overnight to see how Betta was doing. Now it would have to be a case of getting in and out in an hour at most. And, almost more important, either before or after she reached there, she had to reach the team which was holding the territory through which Dow and his escort would pass.

Who was Ancient for that team? So many things had happened so far this day that she had to search her memory for a moment before it came up with the name of Ramon Dye. Good. Ramon was one of the best of the Ancients, and, aside from the fact that he was legless, strong as a bull.

Thinking deeply, she slid the skimmer along under maximum power. She was burning up a month's normal expenditure of energy in a few days, with her present spendthrift use of the vehicle, but there was a time for thriftiness and a time to spend. Of her two choices, it would have to be a decision to contact Ramon's team first, before going to Foralie. Ramon's team would have to send runners to the other teams, since even visual signals would be too risky, with the Coalition troops at Foralie Town probably loaded with the latest in surveillance equipment. The more time she could give the runners, the better.

It was a stroke of bad luck, Dow's determination to send out patrols and go immediately to Foralie himself. Bad on two counts. Patrols out meant some of the troops away from the immediate area of the town at all times. It would have been much better to have them all concentrated there. Also, patrols out meant that sooner or later some of them would have to be taken care of by the teams—and that, while it would have to be faced if and when it came, was something not good to think about until then. There would be a heavy load thrown on the youngsters—not only to do what had to be done, but to do it with the coolheadedness and calculation of adults, without which they could not succeed, and their lives would be thrown away for nothing.

She reminded herself that up through medieval times, twelve- and fourteen-year-olds had been commonly found in armies. Ship's boys had been taken for granted in the navies of the eighteenth and nineteenth centuries. But these historical facts brought no comfort. The children who would be going up against Earth-made weapons here would be children she had known since their birth.

But she must not allow them to guess how she felt. Their faith in their seniors, well-placed or misplaced, was something they would need to hang on to as long as possible for their own sakes.

She came at last to a mountain meadow a full meter high with fall grass. The meadow was separated by just one ridge from Foralie homestead. Amanda turned her skimmer into the shade of a clump of native softwoods on the upslope edge of the meadow, below the ridge. On the relatively open ground beneath those trees, she put the vehicle down and waited.

It was all of twenty minutes before her ear picked up—not exactly a sound that should not have been there, but a sound that was misplaced in the rhythm of natural noises surrounding her. She lifted her voice.

"All right!" she called. "I'm in a hurry. Come on in!"

Heads emerged above the grasstops, as close as half a dozen meters from her and as far out as halfway across the meadow. Figures stood up—tanned, slim figures in flexible shoes, twill slacks strapped tight at the ankle, and long-sleeved, tight-wristed shirts, all of neutral color. One of the tallest, a girl about fifteen, put two fingers in her mouth and whistled.

A skimmer came over the ridge and hummed down toward Amanda until it sank to a stop beside her on the ground. The team members, ranging in age from eight years of age to sixteen, were already gathering around the two of them.

Amanda waited until they were all there, then nodded to the man on the other skimmer and looked around the closed arc of sun-browned faces, sun-bleached hair.

"The invaders are here, in Foralie Town," she said. "Coalition first-line troops under a brigadier and staff, with Dow deCastries."

The faces looked back at her in silence. Adults would have reacted with voice and feature. These looked at her with the same expressions they had shown before, but Amanda, knowing them all, could feel the impact of the news on them.

"Everyone's out?" the man on the other skimmer asked.

Amanda turned again to the Ancient. Perched on his skimmer the way he was, Ramon Dye might have forced a stranger to look twice before discovering that there were no legs below Ramon's hips. Strapped openly in the boot of his vehicle, behind him, were the two artificial legs he normally used in town, but out here, like the team members, he was stripped to essentials. His square, quiet face under its straight brown hair looked at her with concern.

"Everybody's out but those who're supposed to be there," said Amanda. "Except for Marte Haugsrud. She decided to stay with her grandmother."

Still there was that utter silence from the circle of faces, although more than half a dozen of them had grown up within a few doors of Berthe. It was not that they did not feel, Amanda reminded herself; it was that by instinct, like small animals, they were dumb under the whiplash of fate.

"But we've other things to talk about," she said—and felt the emotion she had evoked in them with her news relax under the pressure of her need for their attention. "DeCastries is taking an armed escort with him to Foralie to wait for Cletus, and he's also going to start sending out patrols immediately."

She looked about at them all.

"I want you to get runners out to the nearest other teams—nothing but runners, mind you, those troops will be watching for any recordable signalling—and tell them to pass other runners on to spread the word. Until you get further word from me, all patrols are to be left alone, completely alone, no matter what they do. Watch them, learn everything you can about them, but stay out of sight. Pass that word on to the homesteads, as well as to the other teams."

She paused, looking around, waiting for questions. None came.

"I've made an agreement with deCastries that I'll bring all the teams and all the able adults in from the homesteads to Foralie Town, to be told the rules of the occupation. I've told him it'll take me at least a week to round everyone up. So we've got that much time anyway."

"What if Cletus doesn't come home in a week?" asked the girl who had whistled for Ramon.

"Cross that bridge when we come to it," said Amanda. "But I think he'll be here. Whether he is or not, though, we've still got the district to defend. Word or an order from Arvid Johnson and Bill Athyer is to be trusted only if it comes through someone you trust personally—pass that along to the other teams and homesteads, too. Now, I'm going on up to Foralie to brief them on Dow's coming. Any questions or comments so far?"

"Betta hasn't had her baby yet," said a young voice.

"Thanks for telling me," said Amanda. She searched the circle with her eyes, but she was not able to identify the one who had just spoken. "Let's stick to business for the moment though. I've got a special job for your best infiltrator—unless one of the neighboring teams has someone better than you have. Have they?"

Several voices told her immediately that the others had not.

"Who've you got then?"

"Lexy—," the voices answered.

An almost white-haired twelve-year-old girl was pushed forward, scowling a little. Amanda looked at her—Alexandra Andrea, from Tormai homestead. Lexy, like the others, was slim by right of youth; but a squareness of shoulder and a sturdiness of frame were already evident. For no particular reason, Amanda suddenly remembered how her own hair, when she was a child, had been so blond as to be almost white.

The memory of her young self brought another concern to mind. She looked searchingly at Lexy. What she knew about Lexy included indications of a certain amount of independence and a flair for risk-taking. Even now, obviously uncomfortable at being shoved forward this way, Lexy was still broadcasting an impression of truculence and self-acknowledged ability. Character traits, Amanda thought, remembering her own childhood again, that could lead to a disregard of orders and to chance-taking.

"I need someone to go in close to the cantonments the occupation troops have set up at Foralie Town," she said aloud. "Someone who can listen, pick up information, and get back with it safely. Note—I said safely."

She locked eyes with Lexy.

"Do you take chances, Lexy?" she asked. "Can I trust you to get in and get out without taking risks?"

There was a sudden outbreak of hoots and laughter from the team.

"Send Tim with her!"

Lexy flushed. A slight boy, Lexy's age or possibly as much as a year or two younger, was pushed forward. With Lexy, he looked like a feather beside a rock.

"Timothy Royce," Amanda said, looking at him. "How good are you, Tim?"

"He's good," said Lexy. "That is, he's better than the rest of these elephants."

"Lexy won't take chances with Tim along," said the girl who had whistled. Amanda was vainly searching her memory for this one's name. Sometimes when they shot up suddenly, she lost track of who they were, and the tall girl was already effectively an adult.

"How about it, Tim?" Amanda asked the boy. Tim hesitated.

"He gets scared," a very young voice volunteered.

"No, he doesn't!" Lexy turned on the crowd. "He's cautious, that's all."

"No," said Tim, unexpectedly. "I do get scared. But with Lexy I can do anything you want."

He looked openly at Amanda.

Amanda looked at Ramon.

"I can't add anything," he said, shaking his head. "Lexy's good, and Tim's pretty good—and they work well together."

His eyes settled on Amanda's suddenly.

"But do you have to have someone from one of the teams?"

"Who else is there?"

"One of the older ones . . ." His voice trailed off. Amanda looked back at the faces ringed about.

"Team?" she asked.

There was a moment of almost awkward silence, and then the girl who had whistled—Rhea Abo, the name suddenly leaped into existence in Amanda's mind—spoke.

"Any of us'll go," she said. "But Lexy's the best."

"That's it then," said Amanda. She put the power to her skimmer and lifted it off the ground. "Lexy, Tim—I'll meet you after dark tonight, just behind the closest ridge above the meadow north of town. All of you—be careful. Don't let the patrols see you. And get those runners out as fast as you can."

She left them, the circle parted, and she hummed up and over the ridge. Foralie homestead lay on a small level space a couple of hundred meters beyond her, on a rise that commanded a clear view in all directions as far as the town itself.

Behind the long, low, timbered house there, she could see the oversized jungle gym that Cletus had caused to be constructed at Grahame House and then moved here, after his marriage to Melissa. It had been a device to help him build himself back physically after his knee operation, and there was no reason for it to evoke any particular feeling in her. But now, seeing its spidery and intricate structure casting its shadow on the roof of the long, plain-timbered house beneath it, she suddenly felt—almost as if she touched the cold metal of it with her hand—the hard, intricately woven realities that would be bringing Dow and Cletus to their final meeting beneath that shadow.

She slid the skimmer down to the house. Melissa, with the tall, gray-mustached figure of Eachan Khan beside her, came out of the front door, and they were standing, waiting for her as she brought the skimmer up to them and dropped it to the ground.

"Betta's fine, Amanda," said Melissa. "Still waiting. What's going on?"

"The occupation troops are down in Foralie Town."

"We know," said Eachan Khan in his brief, clipped British-accented speech. "Watched them drop in, using the scope on our roof."

"They've got Dow deCastries with them," Amanda said, getting down from the skimmer. "He's after Cletus, of course. He plans to come up here to Foralie right away. He may be right behind me—"

The ground under her feet seemed to rock suddenly. She found Eachan Khan holding her up.

"Amanda!" said Melissa, supporting her on the other side. "When did you eat last?"

"I don't remember . . ." She found that the words had difficulty coming out. Her knees trembled, and she felt close to fainting. A distant fury filled her. This was the aspect of her age that she resented most deeply. Rested and nourished, she could face down a deCastries. But let any unusual time pass without food and rest and she became just another frail oldster.

Her next awareness was of being propped up on a couch in the Foralie sitting room, with a pillow behind her back. Melissa was helping her sip hot, sweet tea that had the fiery taste of Dorsai whiskey in it. Her head began to clear. By the time the cup was empty, there was a plate of neatly cut sandwiches made by Eachan Khan on the coffee table beside her. She had forgotten how delicious sandwiches could be.

"What's the rest of the news then?" Eachan asked, when she had eaten. "What happened to you today?"

She told them.

". . . I must admit, Eachan," she said, as she wound up, looking at the stiff-backed ex-general, "I wasn't too pleased about Cletus's asking you to sit on your hands here—and even less pleased with you for agreeing. But I think I understand it better since I met deCastries himself. If any one of them's likely to suspect how we might defend ourselves, it'll be him, not those officers with him. And the one thing that'll go further to keep him from starting to suspect anything will be finding you puttering around here, keeping house right under his nose while he waits for Cletus. He knows your military reputation."

"Wouldn't call it puttering," said Eachan. "But you're right. Cletus does have a tendency to think around corners."

"Let alone the fact"—Amanda held his eye with her own—"that if something happens to me, you'll still be here to take over."

"Depends on circumstance."

"Nonetheless," said Amanda.

"Of course," Eachan said. "Naturally, if I'm free—and needed—I'd be available."

"Yes—" Amanda broke off suddenly. "But I've got to get out of here!"

She sat up abruptly on the couch, swinging her feet to the floor.

"DeCastries and his escort are probably right behind me. I'd just planned to drop by and brief you—"

She got to her feet, but lightheadedness took her again at the sudden movement, and she sat down again unexpectedly.

"Amanda, be sensible. You can't go anywhere until you've rested for a few hours," said Melissa.

"I tell you, deCastries—"

"Said he'd be up here yet today? I don't think so," said Eachan.

She turned, almost to glare at him.

"What makes you so sure?"

"Because he's no soldier. Bright of course—Lord yes, he's bright. But he's not a soldier. That means he's in the hands of those officers of his. Earth-bound types, still thinking in terms of large-unit movements. They might get patrols out, late in the day, but they won't get Dow off."

"What if he simply orders them to get him off?" Amanda demanded.

"They'll promise him, of course, but somehow everybody won't be together, the vehicles won't be set, with everything harnessed up and ready to go, before sundown, and even Dow'll see the sense of not striking out into unfamiliar territory with night coming on."

"How can you be that sure?" Melissa asked her father.

"That brigadier's got his own future to think of. Better to have Dow down on him over not getting off on time than to send someone like Dow out and turn out to be the officer who lost him. The day's more than half over. If Dow and his escort get bogged down for even a few hours by some harebrained locals fighting back—that's the way the brigadier'll be thinking—they could end up being caught out, unable to move, in the open at dark. Strange country, nighttime, and an open perimeter's chancy with a prize political package like Dow. No, no—he won't be here until tomorrow at the earliest."

Eachan cocked an eye on Amanda.

"But if you like," he said. "Melly and I'll take turns on the scope up on the roof. If anything moves out of Foralie, we can see it, and by the time we're sure it's definitely moving in this direction, we'll still have two hours before it can get here at column speed. Take a nap, Amanda. We'll call you if you need to move."

Amanda gave in. Stretched out on a large bed in one of the wide, airy bedrooms of Foralie, the curtains drawn against the sunlight, she fell into a heavy sleep from which she roused, it seemed, within minutes. But, blinking the numbness of slumber from her vision, she saw that beyond the closed curtains, there was now darkness, and the room around her was plunged in a deeper gloom than that of curtained daylight.

"What time is it?" she called out, throwing back the single blanket which she had been covered. No answer came. She sat on the edge of the bed summoning herself to awareness, then got to her feet and let herself out into the hall, where artificial lights were lit.

"What time is it?" she repeated, coming into the kitchen. Both Eachan Khan and Melissa looked up from the table there, and Melissa got to her feet.

"Two hours after sunset," she answered. But Amanda had already focused on the wall clock across the room, which displayed the figure 21:10. "Sit down, Amanda. You'll want some tea."

"No," said Amanda. "I was supposed to meet two of the youngsters from the local team just above Foralie Town before sunset—"

"We know," said Eachan. "We had a runner from that team when they saw you didn't leave here. The two you're talking about went, and Ramon went with them. He knows what you want in the way of information."

"I've got to get down there to meet them."

"Amanda—sit!" said Melissa from the kitchen unit. "Tea'll be ready for you in a second."

"I don't want any tea," said Amanda.

"Of course you do," said Melissa.

Of course, she did. It was another of her weaknesses of age. She could almost taste the tea in anticipation and her sleep-heavy body yearned for the internal warmth that would help it wake up. She sat down at the table opposite Eachan.

"Fine watch you keep," she said to him.

"Nothing came from Foralie Town in this direction before sunset," he said. "They're not starting out with Dow in the dark, as I said. So I came back inside, of course. You could stay the night, if you want."

"No, I've got to get there, and I've a lot of ground to cover—" She broke off as Melissa placed a steaming cup before her. "Thanks, Melissa."

"But why don't you stay the night?" Melissa asked, sitting back down at the table herself. "Betta's already asleep, but you could see her in the morning—"

"No. I've got to go."

Melissa looked at her father.

"Dad?"

"No," said Eachan. "I think perhaps she's right. But will you come back for the night, afterwards, Amanda?"

"No. I don't know where I'll light."

"If you change your mind," said Melissa, "just come to the door and ring. But I don't have to tell you that."

Amanda left Foralie homestead half an hour later. The moon, which had been full the night before, was just past full, but scattered clouds cut down the brilliant night illumination she had woken to early that morning. She made good time on the skimmer toward the ridge where she had arranged to meet Lexy and Tim. A hundred meters or so behind it, she found Ramon's skimmer, empty, and dropped her own beside it. No one was in sight. Ramon could not walk upright without his prosthetics, but he could creep-and-crawl as well as any other adult. Amanda was about to work her way up to the ridge herself, staying low so that any instruments in the cantonment below would not discover her, when a rustle in the shadows warned her of people returning. A few moments later, Ramon, Lexy, and Tim all rose from the ground at arm's length from her.

"Sorry," said Amanda, "I should have been here earlier."

"It wasn't necessary," said Ramon. His powerful arms hauled him up to his own skimmer, and he sat upright there.

"Yes, it was," said Amanda. "You didn't let these two go until things were shut down—"

"They didn't go down until full dark," said Ramon. "Not until the last of the patrols had left and the manufactory was shut down. The townsfolk were all inside, and the troops were all in their cantonment area. Tim stayed behind the perimeter there, and Lexy went up to just outside the outer line of huts, close enough so she could hear them talking, but with plenty of room to leave if she needed to."

Amanda transferred her attention to Lexy.

"What were they talking about?"

"Usual stuff," said Lexy. "The officers, and the equipment, how long they'd be here before they'd ship off again. Regular solider off-duty talk."

"Did they talk about when deCastries would be leaving for Foralie?"

"First thing in the morning. They'd stalled about getting ready, so he couldn't get off today," said Lexy. "They don't think much of those of our people who're left here, but still none of them I heard talking felt much like starting out with night coming on."

"What do they think of their officers?"

"Nothing great. There's a major they all like, but he's not on the general's staff. They really draw the line between enlisted and officer."

"Now you see for yourself how that is with Old World troops," commented Ramon to the two young ones.

"It's a pretty stupid way for them to be, all the same, out here in hostile territory," said Lexy. "But they've got a good pool of light vehicles. No armor. Vehicle-mounted light weapons and hand weapons. I could have brought you one of their cone rifles—"

"Oh, could you?"

There was a little silence in the darkness that betrayed Lexy's recognition of her slip of the tongue.

"The whole line of huts was empty. All I did was look in the last one in the line," said Lexy. "These Earth troops—they're worse than elephants, I could have gone in and picked their pockets and got out without their knowing about it."

The moon came from behind a cloud that had been hiding it, and in the pale light Amanda could see Lexy's face—tightmouthed.

"Ramon," said Amanda. "Didn't you tell them specifically not to go into the cantonment area?"

"I'm sorry, Amanda," said Ramon. "I didn't. Not specifically."

"Lexy, under no conditions, now or in the future, do you or anyone else go beyond the outer line of huts." Exasperation took her suddenly. "And don't bristle! If you have to resent an order, try to keep the fact to yourself."

Another cloud obscured the moon. Lexy's voice came unexpectedly out of the darkness.

"Why?"

"For one reason, because an hour later you may wish you had. For another, learn never to challenge automatically. No one's that good. Sit on your impulse until you know everything that's likely to happen when you act on it."

Silence out of the darkness. Amanda wondered whether Lexy was filing the information she had just received in the automatic discard file of her mind, or—just possibly—tucking it away for future reference.

"Now," Amanda said. "Anything else? Any talk of plans? Any talk of Cletus being on the way here?"

"No," said Lexy. "They did talk about relocation, after Cletus is tried back on Earth. And they even said something about changing the name of our planet. That doesn't make sense."

Amanda breathed deeply.

"I'm afraid it does," she said.

"Amanda?" It was Ramon asking. "I'm not sure I follow you."

"DeCastries tried to give me the impression that this whole invasion was designed only to arrest Cletus and take him back to Earth to stand trial. I let him think I went along with that. But of course they've got a lot more than that in mind, with the expense they've gone to here. What they really want to do is bury the Dorsai—and everyone in uniform bearing that name. Obviously what they've planned is to use Cletus's trial as a means to whip up Earth sentiment. Then, with a lot of public backing, they can raise the funds they'd need to spread our people out on other worlds and give this world a new name and a new breed of settler."

Amanda thought for a moment, while the moon continued to play peekaboo with the clouds.

"I'd better go back to Foralie tonight after all," she said. "Eachan will have to know this, in case he has to take over. Lexy—anything else?"

"Nothing, Amanda, really. Just off-duty talk."

"All right. I want this listening to go on—only at night, though, after the town and the cantonment's settled down. Ramon, will you stay on top of that? And also make sure neither Lexy nor anyone else goes into the cantonment area. Past the outer line sentries is all right, if they know what they're doing. But not, repeat not, into the cantonment streets, and never into the huts themselves. There's more here than just your personal risk to think about, Lexy. It's our whole world, and all of us, at stake."

Silence.

"All right, Amanda. We'll take care of it," said Ramon. "And we'll get word to you if anything breaks."

"The necessary thing," said Amanda, "is letting me know if there's any word of Cletus getting here. All right. I'll see you tomorrow evening."

She lifted her skimmer on minimum power to keep the sound of its motors down and swung away in the dirction of Foralie. Had she been unfairly hard on Lexy? The thought walked through her mind unbidden. It was not an unfamiliar thought nowadays; Betta, Melissa, Lexy . . . a number of them evoked it in her. How far was she justified in expecting them to react as she herself would? To what extent was it right of her to expect a future Amanda to react as she would?

No easy answer came to her. On the surface it was unfair. She was unfair. On the other hand there were the inescapable facts. There was the need that someone, at least, react as she did, and the reality that what she required of them was what experience had taught her life required of them all. Forcibly, she put the unresolved problem once again from her and made herself concentrate on the imperatives of the moment.

Midmorning of the following day she lay in tall grass, high on a slope, and watched the train that was the escort of Dow deCastries winding up through the folds of the hills toward Foralie. Around her were the members of Ramon's team. The train consisted of what looked like two platoons of enlisted men, under four officers and Dow himself, all sliding over the ground in aircushion staff cars, with a heavy energy rifle deck-mounted on every car but the one occupied by Dow. The vehicles moved with the slowness of prudence, and there were flankers out on skimmers, as well as two skimmers at point.

"They'll reach Foralie in another twenty minutes or so," Ramon said in Amanda's ear. "What should we do about getting runners in to Eachan and Melissa?"

"Don't send anyone in," Amanda said. "Eachan will come out to you if he wants contact. Or maybe Melissa will. At any rate, let them set it up. Tell them I've gone to look at the situation generally throughout the district. I need to know what the other patrols sent out are doing."

She waited until the train had disappeared over the ridge toward which it had been heading, then slid back down into the small slope behind her where her skimmer was hidden.

"You're fully powered?" asked Ramon, looking at the skimmer.

"Enough for nonstop operation for a week," said Amanda. "I'll see you this evening, down above the cantonments."

The rest of that day she was continually on the move. It was quite true, as she had told Dow, that it would take her a week to fully cover the homesteads of the Foralie District. But it was not necessary for what she had in mind to call at every homestead, since she had a communications network involving the teams and the people in the homesteads themselves. She needed only to call at those few homesteads where she needed personal contact with such as the medical personnel or such as Tosca Aras, invalided home and anchored in his house by age and a broken leg. Tosca, like Eachan, was an experienced tactical mind to whom the rest could turn in case anything took her out of action.

In any case, her main interest was in the patrols Dow had sent out. Eachan, watching with the scope on the Foralie rooftop, reported that two had gone out the evening before and this morning another four had taken their way on different bearings, out into the district. In each case, they seemed to be following a route taking them to the homesteads of a certain area of the district on a swing that looked like it might last twenty-four hours, and at the end of that time bring them back to Foralie Town and their cantonments.

"They don't seem to be out looking for trouble," Myron Lee, Ancient for one of the other teams, said to Amanda as they stood behind a thicket looking down on one of these patrols. Myron, lean to the point of emaciation and in his fifties, was hardly any stronger physically than Amanda, but radiated an impression of unconquerable energy.

"On the other hand," he went on, "they didn't exactly come out unprepared for trouble either."

The patrol they were watching, like all the others Amanda had checked, was a single platoon under a single commissioned officer. But its personnel were mounted on staff cars and skimmers, as the escort for Dow had been, and in this case, every staff car mounted a heavy energy rifle, while the soldiers riding both these and the skimmers carried both issue cone rifles and sidearms.

"What have they been doing when they reach a homestead?" Amanda asked.

"They take the names and images of the people there, and take images of the homestead itself. Census work, of a sort," said Myron.

Amanda nodded. She had been given the same description whenever she had asked that question about other patrols. It was not unusual military procedure to gather data about the people and structures in any area where a force was stationed—but the method of the particular survey seemed to imply that the people and buildings surveyed might need to be taken by force at some time in the future.

By evening she was back behind the ridge overlooking the meadow holding the cantonments. Lexy, Tim, and Ramon were waiting when she got there. They waited a little longer, together, while twilight gave way to full dark. The clouds were even thicker this night, and when the last of the light was gone, they could not see each other, even at arm's length.

"Go ahead," Amanda said to the two youngsters. "Remember, word of Cletus or any word of what's going on in town are the two things I particularly want to hear about."

There was the faintest rustle of grass, and she was alone with Ramon. A little over an hour later, the two team members were back.

"Nothing much of anything going on," Lexy reported. "Nothing about Cletus coming. They'd like some news themselves about how long they're going to be here and what they're going to do. All they say about the town is that it's dull—they say what good would it be if they could go in there? There's no place to drink or anything else going on. They did mention an old lady being sick, but they didn't say which one."

"Berthe Haugsrud's the oldest," said Ramon's voice, out of the darkness.

Amanda snorted.

"At their age," she said, "anyone over thirty's old. All right, we'll meet here again and try it once more, tomorrow night."

She left them and swung east to the Aras homestead to see if the district's single physician, Dr. Ekram Bayar, who had been reported there, had heard word of any sick in Foralie Town.

"He's gone over to Foralie," Tosca Aras's diminutive daughter told her. "Melissa phoned to say Mene Betta was going into labor. Ekram said he didn't expect any problems, but since he was closer than any of the medicians, he went himself. But he's coming back here. Do you want to phone over there now?"

Amanda hesitated.

"No," she said. "I've been staying off the air so that whatever listening devices they've got down in the troop area can't be sure where I am. I'll wait a bit here. Then, if he doesn't come soon, you could call for me and find out how things are."

"You could take a nap," said the small woman.

"No, I've got things to do," said Amanda.

But she ended up taking the nap. Mene called her awake on the intercom at what turned out to be an hour an a half later. She came in to the Aras sitting room to find Tosca himself up, with his broken leg stretched out stiffly on a couch, and both Mene and Ekram with the old general, having a drink before dinner.

"Amanda!" Mene said. "It was a false alarm about Betta."

"Uh!" Amanda found a chair and dropped heavily into it. "The pains stopped?"

"Before Ekram even got here."

Amanda looked across at the physician, a sturdy, brown-faced thirty-year-old with a shock of black, straight hair and a bushy black mustache.

"She probably doesn't need me at all," he said to Amanda. "I'd guess she'll have one of the easier births on record around here."

"You don't know that," said Amanda.

"Of course I don't," he said. "I'm just giving you my opinion."

It came to her suddenly that Ekram, like herself and everyone else, had been under an emotional strain since the invasion became a reality. She became aware suddenly of Tosca stretching out an arm in her direction.

"Here," he said. He was handing her a glass.

"What's this? Whisky? Tosca, I can't—"

"You aren't going any place else tonight," he said. "Drink it."

She became conscious that the others all had glasses in their hands.

"And then you can have dinner," said Tosca.

"All right." She took the glass and sipped cautiously at it. Tosca had diluted the pure liquor with enough water so that it was the sort of mixture she could drink with some comfort. She looked over the rim of her glass at the physician.

"Ekram," she said. "I had some of the team children listening outside the cantonments. They reported the soldiers had been mentioning some-one—an old woman, they said—was sick in town. . . ."

"Berthe." He put down his glass on the coffee table before the couch on which he sat, his face a little grim. "I should go down there."

"No," said Tosca.

"If you get in there, they may not let you out again," said Amanda. "They'll have military medicians."

"Yes. A full physician, a lieutenant colonel—there for the benefit of this Dow deCastries more than for the troops, I'd guess," Ekram said. "I've talked to him over the air. Something of a political appointee, I gather. Primarily a surgeon, but he seemed capable, and he said he'd take care of anyone in town when I wasn't there. He expects me to be available most of the time, of course."

"You told him you had your hands full up here?"

"Oh, yes," Ekram gnawed a corner of his moustache, something he almost never did. "I explained that with most of the mothers of young children being upcountry right now . . ."

He trailed off.

"He accepted that, all right?"

"Accepted it? Of course, he accepted it. I hope you realize, Amanda,"— he stared hard at her—"it's not my job to ignore people."

"Who're you ignoring? Berthe? You told the truth. You've got patients needing you all over the place up here."

"Yes," he said.

But his gaze was stony. It went off from her to the unlit, wide stone fireplace across the room, and he drank sparsely from his glass, in silence.

"I'll have dinner in a few minutes," said Mene, leaving them.

With dinner, Ekram became more cheerful. But by the following morning, the phone began to ring with calls from other households relaying word they had heard in conversations with people still in the town of now two or three of the older people there being ill.

"Not one of the ones who're supposed to be sick has called," Mene pointed out over the breakfast table.

"They wouldn't, of course. Noble—yes, damned noble, all of them! All of you. I'm sorry, Amanda—" He turned stiffly to Amanda. "I'm going down."

"All right," said Amanda.

She had meant to leave early, but she had stayed around, fearing just such a decision from Ekram. They would have to give, somewhat. But they need not give everything.

"All right," she said again. "But not until this evening. Not until things are shut down for the day."

"No," said Ekram. "I'm going now."

"Ekram," said Amanda. "Your duty's to everyone. Not just to those in the town. The real need for you may be yet to come. You're our only physician, and we may get to the equivalent of a field hospital before this is over."

"She's right," said Tosca.

"Damn it!" said Ekram. He got up from the table, slammed his chair back into place and walked out of the kitchen. "Damn this whole business!"

"It's hard for him, of course," said Tosca, "but you needn't worry, Amanda."

"All right," Amanda said. "Then I'll get going."

She spent the day out, tracking the patrols. In one or two instances, where the sweep was the third through a particular area, the majority, at least, of the soldiers in a particular patrol were those who had been out on the first sweep—not only to her eyes, but also to the sharper observation of the team members who had been keeping track of those patrols. She watched them closely through a scope, trying to see if there were any signs of sloppiness or inattention evident in the way they performed their duties, but she was unable to convince herself that she saw any.

She had a good deal more success, with the help of the team members, in identifying patterns of behavior that were developing in a way they made their sweeps. Their approach to a household, for one thing, had already begun to settle down to a routine. That was the best clue that the line soldiers had yet given as to their opinion of the dangerousness of those still left in Foralie District. She found herself wondering, briefly, how all the other districts in all the other cantons of the Dorsai were doing with their defense plans and their particular invaders. Some would have more success against the Earth troops, some less—that was inherent in the situation and in the nature of things.

She sent word to the households themselves to the effect that the people in them should, whenever possible, do and say the same thing each time to the patrols so as to build a tendency in these contacts toward custom and predictability.

It was midafternoon when a runner caught up with her with a message that had been passed by phone from homestead to homestead for her, in the guise of neighborly gossip.

"Ekram's left the upcountry for town," she was told. The runner, a fourteen-year-old boy, looked at her with the steady blue eyes of the D'Aurois family.

"Why?" Amanda asked. "Did whoever passed the message say why?"

"He was at the Kiempii homestead, and he got a call from the military doctor," the boy said. "The other doctor's worried about identifying whatever's making people sick in town."

"That's all?"

"That's all Reiko Kiempii passed on, Amanda."

"Thank you," she said.

"—Except that she said the latest word is nothing's happened yet with Betta."

"Thanks," Amanda said.

She was a good hour of skimmer time from the Kiempii homestead. It was not far out of her way on her route to meet Lexy, Tim, and Ramon once more above the meadow with the cantonment huts. She left her checking on the patrols and headed out.

When she got there, Reiko was outside waiting, having heard Amanda was on the way. Amanda slid the skimmer to a stop and spoke eye to eye with the calm, tall, bronzed young woman, without getting out of the vehicle.

"The call went to Foralie first," Reiko told her, "but Ekram had already moved on. It finally caught up with him here, about two hours ago."

"Then you don't know what the military doctor told him?"

"No, all Ekram said was that he had to go down, that he couldn't leave it all to the other physician any longer."

Amanda looked at Maru Kiempii's daughter bleakly.

"Three hours until dark," she said, "before I can get Lexy down to listen to what they're talking about in the cantonments."

"Eat something. Rest," said Reiko.

"I suppose so."

Amanda had never had less appetite or felt less like resting in her life. She could feel events building inexorably toward an explosion, as she had felt the long rollers of the Atlantic surf on the harsh seashores of her childhood, building to the one great wave that would drive spray clear to the high rocks on which she stood watching.

But it was common sense to eat and rest, with much of a long day behind her and possibly a long night ahead.

Just before sunset, she left the Kiempii homestead and arrived at the meeting place with Lexy, Tim, and Ramon before full dark. The clouds were thick, and the air that wrapped about them was heavy with the dampness of the impending weather.

"Ekram still in town?" she asked.

"Yes," said Ramon. "We've got a cordon circling the whole area outside the picket line the troops set up around the town. No one's gone out all day but patrols. If Ekram does, we'll get word as soon as he leaves."

"Good," said Amanda. "Lexy, Tim, be especially careful. A night like this their sentries could be in a mood to shoot first and check afterward. And the same thing applies to the soldiers in the cantonment area itself."

"All right," said Lexy.

They went off. Amanda did not offer to talk and Ramon did not intrude questions upon her. Now that she was at the scene of some actual action, she began to feel the fatigue of the day in spite of her rest up at Kiempii homestead, and she dozed lightly, sitting on her skimmer.

She roused at a touch on her arm.

"They're coming back," said Ramon's voice in her ear.

She sat up creakily and tried to blink the heavy obscurity out of her eyes. But it was almost solid around her. The only thing visible was the line of the ridgecrest, some thirty meters off, silhouetted against the lighter dark of the clouded sky. The clouds were low enough to reflect a faint glow from the lights of the town and the cantonment beyond the ridge.

"Amanda, we heard about Cletus—" It was Lexy's voice, right at her feet. She could see nothing of either youngster.

"What did you hear?"

"Well, not about Cletus himself, exactly—" put in Tim.

"Practically, it was," said Lexy. "They've got word from one of their transport ships in orbit. It picked up the signal of a ship phasing in, just outside our star system. They think it's Cletus coming. If it is, they figure that in a couple more short phase shifts he ought to be in orbit here; and he ought to be down on the ground at Foralie by early afternoon tomorrow, at the latest."

"Did they say anything about their transport trying to arrest him in orbit?"

"No," said Lexy.

"Did you expect them to, Amanda?" Ramon asked.

"No," said Amanda. "He's coming of his own choice, and it makes sense to let your prey all the way into a trap before you close it. Once in orbit, his ship wouldn't be able to get away without being destroyed by theirs anyway. But mainly, they want to be sure to get him alive for that full-dress trial back on Earth, so they can arrange to have the rest of us deported and scattered. So, I wouldn't expect they'll do anything until he's grounded. But there's always orders that get misunderstood, and commanders who jump the gun."

"Tomorrow afternoon," said Ramon musingly. "That's it then."

"That's it," said Amanda grimly. "Lexy, what else?"

"Lots of people in town are sick—" Lexy's voice was unaccustomedly hushed, as if it had finally come home to her what this situation was leading to, with people she had known all her life. "Both docs are working."

"How about the soldiers? Any of them sick?"

"Yes, lots," said Lexy. "Just this evening, a whole long line of them went on sick call."

Amanda turned in the direction of Ramon's flitter and spoke to the invisible Ancient.

"Ramon," she said, "how many hours was Ekram in town in the afternoon?"

"Not more than two."

"We've got to get him out of there. . . ." But her tone of voice betrayed the fact that she was talking to herself rather than to the other three, and no one answered.

"I want to know the minute he leaves," Amanda said. "If he isn't gone by morning . . . I'd better stay here tonight."

"If you want to move back beyond the next ridge, we can build you a shelter," Ramon said. "We can build it up over you and your skimmer and you can tap heat off the skimmer. That way you can be comfortable and maybe get some sleep."

Amanda nodded, then remembered they could not see her.

"Fine," she said.

In the shelter, with the back of her driver's seat laid down and the other seat cushions arranged to make a bed, Amanda lay thinking. Around her, a circle of cut and stripped saplings had been driven into the earth and bent together at their tops to make the frame. This sagged gently over her head under the weight of the leafy branches that interwove the saplings, the whole crowned and made waterproof by the groundsheet from the boot of the skimmer. In spite of the soft warmth filling the shelter from the skimmer, humming on minimum power to its heater unit, the slight weight of her old down jacket spread over her shoulders gave her comfort.

She felt a strange sadness and loneliness. Present concerns slid off and were lost in personal memories. She found herself thinking once more of Jimmy, her first-born—Betta's grandfather—whom she had loved more than any of her other children, though none of them had known it. Jimmy, whom she had cared for as child and adult through his own long life and all three of her own marriages, and brought at last with her here to the Dorsai to found a household. He was the Morgan from which all the ap Morgans since were named. He had lived sixty-four years, and ended up a good man and a good father—but all those years she had held the reins tight upon him.

Not his fault. As a six-month-old baby, he had been taken—legally stolen from her by her in-laws after his father's death, and the less than a short year and a half of their marriage. She had fought for four years after that, fought literally and legally, until finally she had worn her father- and mother-in-law down to where they were forced to allow her visiting rights, and then she had stolen him back. Stolen him, and fled off-Earth to the technologically-oriented new world of Newton, where she had married again, to give the boy a home and a father.

But when she had finally gotten him back, he had been damaged. Lying now, in this shelter in the Dorsai hills, she once more faced the fact that it might not have been her in-laws' handling of him alone that had been to blame. It could also have been something genetic in their ancestry and her first husband's. But whatever it was, she had lost a healthy, happy baby, and regained a boy given to sudden, near-psychotic outbursts of fury and ill-judgment.

But she had encompassed him, guarded him, controlled him—keeping him always with her and bringing him through the years to a successful life and a quiet death. Only—at a great cost. For she had never been free in all that time to let him know how much she loved him. Her sternness, her unyielding authority, had made up the emotional control he had required to supply the lack of it in himself. When he lay dying at last, in the large bedroom at Fal Morgan, she had been torn by the desire to let him know how she had always felt. But a knowledge of the selfishness of that desire had sustained her in silence. To put into plain words the role she had played for him all his life would have taken away what pride he had in the way he had lived, would have underlined the fact that without her he could never have stood alone.

So, she had let him go, playing her part to the last. At the very end he had tried to say something to her. He had almost spoken, and a small corner of her mind clung to the thought that there, in the last moment, he had been about to say that he understood, that he had always understood, that he knew how she loved him.

Now, lying in the darkness of the shelter, Amanda came as close as she ever had in her existence to crying out against whatever ruled the universe. Why had life always called upon her to be its disciplinarian, its executioner, as it was doing now, once again? Cheek pressed against the tough, smooth-worn leather of the skimmer seat cushion, she heard the answer in her own mind—it was because she would do the job and others would not.

She was too old for tears. She drifted off into sleep without feeling the tide that took her out, dry-eyed.

A rustle, the sound of the branches that completely enclosed her being pulled apart, brought her instantly awake. Gray daylight was leaking through the cover below the cap of the groundsheet, and there was the sound of a gust of rain pattering on the groundsheet itself.

"Amanda—" said Ramon, and crawled into the shelter. There was barely room for him to squat beside her skimmer. His face, under a rain-slick poncho hood, was on a level with hers.

She sat up.

"What time is it?"

"Nine hundred hours. It's been daylight for nearly three hours. Ekram's still in town. I thought you'd wanted to be wakened."

"Thanks."

"General Amorine—that brigadier in charge of the troops—has been phoning around the homesteads. He wants you to come in and talk to him."

"He can do without. Twelve hours," said Amanda. "How could I sleep twelve hours? Are the patrols out? How did the troops on them look?"

"A little sloppy in execution. Everybody hunched up—under rain gear of course. But they didn't look too happy, even aside from that. Some were coughing, the team members said."

"Any news from the homesteads—any news they've heard over the air, by phone from town?"

"Ekram and the military doc were up all night."

"We've got to get him out of there—" Amanda checked and corrected herself. "I've got to get him out of there. What's the weather for the rest of today?"

"Should clear by noon. Then cold, windy, and bright."

"By the time Cletus is here we should have good visibility?"

"We should, Amanda."

"Good. Pass the word. I want those patrols observed all the time. Let me know if you can how many of the men on them become unusually sick or fall out. And check with Dow's escort troops at Foralie. Chances are they're all in good shape, but it won't hurt to check. The minute Cletus arrives, pass the word for the four other teams closest to Foralie to move in and join up with your team. Ring Foralie completely with the teams—what's that?"

Ramon had just put a thermos jug and a small metal box on the deck of her skimmer.

"Tea and some food," Ramon said. "Mene sent it down."

"I'm not an invalid."

"No, Amanda," said Ramon, backing out through the opening in the shelter on hands and knees he wore. Outside, he pushed the branches back into place to seal the gap he had made entering. Left to herself, her mind busy, Amanda drank the hot tea and ate the equally hot stew and biscuits she found in the metal box.

Finished, she got up and donned her own poncho, dismantled the shelter, and put the ground cloth back in the boot, the seat-back and cushions, back in place. Outside, the wind was gusty and cold with occasional rain. She lifted her skimmer and slid it down to just behind the lower ridge, where the ponchoed figure of Ramon sat keeping a scope trained on the cantonments and town below.

"I've changed my mind about that commanding officer," Amanda told him. "I'm going in to talk to him—"

A gust of wind and rain made her duck her head.

"Amanda?" Ramon was frowning up at her. "What if he won't let you out again?"

"He'll let me out," Amanda said. "But whether I'm there or not, the teams are going to have to be ready to move against deCastries' escort and any troops they send up with Cletus, once Cletus gets to Foralie. Just as they want Cletus for trial, we want Cletus safe, and we want deCastries, alive—not dead. If most of the rest of the districts can't break loose, we want something to bargain with. Cletus'll know how to use deCastries that way."

"If you're not available and it's time to attack them, should we wait for Eachan to come out and take over?"

"If you think there's time—you and the other Ancients. If time looks tight, don't hesitate. Move on your own."

Ramon nodded.

"I'll look for you here when I come back," Amanda said, then lifted her skimmer, sending it off at a slant behind the cover of the ridge to approach the town from the opposite, down-river side.

She paused behind a ridge to drop off her handgun and then came up along the river road, where she encountered a Alliance-Coalition sentry in rain gear, about five hundred meters out behind the manufactory. She slid the skimmer directly at him and set it down, half a dozen meters from him. He held his cone rifle pointed toward her as he walked forward.

"Take that gun out of its scabbard, ma'am," he said, nodding at the pellet shotgun, "and hand it to me—butt first."

She obeyed.

He cradled the cone rifle in one arm to take the heavy weight of the pellet gun in both hands. He glanced at it, held it up to look into the barrel and handed it back to her.

"Not much of a weapon, ma'am."

"No?" Amanda, holding the recovered pellet gun in the crook of her arm, swung it around horizontally until its muzzle rested against the deckface between her and the boot, the deckface over the power unit. "What if I decide to pull the trigger right now?"

She saw his face go still, caught between shock and disbelief.

"You hadn't thought of that?" said Amanda. "The pellets from this weapon could add enough kinetic energy to the power core to blow it, you, and me to bits. In your motor pool, I could set off a chain explosion that would wipe out your full complement of vehicles. Had you thought of that?"

He stared at her for a second longer, then his face moved.

"Maybe you think you better impound it after all?"

"No," he said. "I don't think you're about to commit suicide, even if they'd let you anywhere near our motor pool—which they wouldn't."

He coughed.

"What's your business in town, ma'am?"

"I'm Amanda Morgan, mayor of Foralie Town," she said. "That's my business. And for that matter, your commanding officer's been asking to see me. Don't tell me they didn't give you an image and a description of me?"

"Yes," he said. He coughed, lowered his rifle, and wiped from his cheek some of the moisture that had just dripped from the edge of his rain hood. He had a narrow young face. "You're to go right on in."

"Then why all this nonsense?"

He sighed a little.

"Orders, ma'am."

"Orders!" She peered at him. "You don't look too well."

He shook his head.

"Nothing important, ma'am. Go ahead."

She lifted her skimmer and went past him. The sound of the manufactory grew in her ears. She checked the skimmer outside its sliding door, strongly tempted to look inside and see if Jhanis Bins was still at the control board. The town dump looked even less attractive than it ordinarily did. The nickel grindings, which Jhanis had dumped just the other day, had slumped into pockets and hollows, and now these were partially filled with liquid that in the gray day looked to have a yellowish tinge. She changed her mind about going in to look for Jhanis. Time was too tight. She touched the power control bar of the skimmer and headed on into town, feeling the wet, rain-studded wind on the back of her neck.

The streets were empty. Down a side alley she saw a skimmer that she recognized as Ekram's, behind the house of Marie Dureaux. She went on, past the city hall and up to the edge of the cantonment area, where she was again stopped, this time by two sentries.

"Your general wanted to see me," she said after identifying herself.

"If you'll wait a moment while we call in, ma'am..."

A moment later she was waved through and directed to a command building four times the size of the ordinary cantonment huts, but made of the same blown bubble plastic. Once again she was checked by sentries and ushered, eventually, into an office with a desk, a chair behind it, and one less-comfortable chair facing it.

"If you'll have a seat here," said the sergeant who brought her in.

She sat and waited for some ten or twelve minutes. At the end of that time a major came in, carrying a folder of record films, which he slipped into the desk viewer, punching up the first one.

"Amanda Morgan," he said, looking over the top of the viewer, which was slanted toward him, hiding the film on display from her.

"That's right," said Amanda. "And you're Major..."

He hesitated.

"Major Suel," he said after a second. "Now, about the situation here in town and in the district—"

"Just a second, Major," said Amanda. "I came in to talk to your general."

"He's busy. You can talk to me. Now, about the situation—"

He broke off. Amanda was already on her feet.

"You can tell the general for me, I don't have time to waste. Next time he can come and find me." Amanda turned toward the door.

"Just a minute—" There was the sound of the major's chair being pushed back. "Just a minute!"

"No minute," said Amanda. "I was asked to come in to talk to General Amorine. If he's not available, I've got my hands too full to wait around."

She reached for the door. It did not open for her.

"Major," she said, looking back over her shoulder. "Open this door."

"Come back and sit down," he said, standing behind his desk. "You can leave after we've talked. This is a military base—"

He broke off again. Amanda had come back to the desk and walked around it to face the desk viewer. She reached out to press his phone button and the document on the viewer vanished to show the face of the sergeant who had let her in here.

"Sir—" The sergeant broke off in confusion, seeing Amanda.

"Sergeant," said Amanda, "connect me with Dow deCastries up at Foralie homestead right away."

"Cancel that!" said the major. "Sergeant—cancel that."

He punched off the phone and walked to the door.

"Wait!" he threw back at Amanda and went out.

Amanda followed him to the door, but found it once more locked to her touch. She went back and sat down. Less than five minutes later, the major returned with the skin taut over the bones of his face. He avoided looking directly at her.

"This way, if you will," he said, holding the door open.

"Thank you, Major."

He brought her to a much larger and more comfortable office, with a tall window against which the rain was now gusting. There was a desk in the corner, but the rest of the furniture consisted of padded armchairs, with the single exception of a single armless straight-backed chair facing the desk. It was to this chair that Amanda was taken.

General Amorine, who had been standing by the window, walked over to seat himself behind the desk.

"I've been trying to get you for two days," he said.

Amanda, who had not been invited to sit, did so anyway.

"And I've been busy doing what I promised Dow deCastries I'd do," she said. "I still am busy at it, and this trip in to see you is delaying it."

He looked at her, stiff-faced. A cough took him by the throat.

"Mayor," he said, when the coughing was done, "you're in no position to push."

"General, I'm not pushing. You are."

"I'm the commanding officer of the occupying force here," he said. "It's my job to push when things don't work."

He checked, as if he would cough again, but did not. A gust of wind rattled loudly against the office window in the brief moment of silence between them. Amanda waited.

"I say," he repeated. "It's my job to push when things don't work."

"I heard you," said Amanda.

"They aren't working now," Amorine said. "They aren't working to

my satisfaction. We want a census of this district and all pertinent data—
and we want it without delay."

"There hasn't been any delay."

"I think there has."

Amanda sat looking at him.

"I know there has," Amorine said.

"For example?"

He looked at her for several seconds without saying anything.

"How long," he said, "has it been since you were on Earth?"

"Seventy years or so," said Amanda.

"I thought so," he said. "I thought it had been something like that
long. Out here on the new worlds, you've forgotten just what Earth is
like. Here, on wild planets with lots of space and only handfuls of people
even in your largest population centers, you tend to forget."

"The mess and the overcrowding?"

"The people and the power!" he said harshly—and broke off to cough
again. He wiped his mouth. "When you think in terms of people out
here, you think in terms of thousands—millions, at the most, when your
thinking is planet-wide. But on Earth those same figures are billions. You
think in terms of a few hundred thousand square meters of floor space
given over to manufactory on a whole world. On Earth that space is
measured in trillions of square meters. You talk about using a few million
kilowatt-hours of energy. Do you know how kilowatt-hours of used energy
are counted on Earth?"

"So?" said Amanda.

"So—" He coughed. "So, you forget the differences. Out here for
seventy years, you forget what Earth really is, in terms of wealth and
strength, and you begin to think that you can stand up against her. The
greatest power the human race has ever known looms over you like a
giant, and you let yourself dream that you can fight that power."

"Come into our backyard, and we can fight you," said Amanda. "You're
a long way from your millions and your trillions now, General."

"No," said Amorine, and he said it without coughing or heat. "That's
your self-delusion only. Earth's got the power to wipe clean every other
humanly-settled world whenever she wants to. When Earth moves, when
she decides to move, you'll vanish. And you people here are indeed going
to vanish. I want you to believe that—for your own sake. You'll save
yourself and all the people you love a great deal of pain if you can wake
yourself up to an understanding of what the facts are."

He looked at her. She looked back.

"You are all, all of you, already gone," he said. "For the moment
you've still got your town, and your homes, and your own name, but all
those things are going to go. You, yourself, in your old age, are going

to be moved to another place, a place you don't know, to die among strangers—all this because you've been foolish enough to forget what Earth is."

He paused. She still sat, not speaking.

"There's no reprieve, no choice," he said. "What I'm telling you is for your own information only. Our politicians haven't announced it yet— but the Dorsai is already a forgotten world, and everyone on it will soon be scattered individually through all the other inhabited planets. For you—for you, only—I've got an offer, that for you, only, will make things easier."

He waited, but still she gave him no assistance.

"You're being uncooperative with our occupation here," he said. "I don't care what Mr. deCastries' opinion of you is. I *know*. I know non-cooperation when I run into it. I'd be a failure in my job if I didn't. Bear in mind, we don't have to have your cooperation, but it'd help. It'd save paperwork, effort, and explanations. So, what I'm offering you is, co-operate and I'll promise this much for you: I'll ensure that whatever few years you have left can be lived here, on your own world. You'll have to watch everyone else being shipped off, but you, at least, won't have to end your days among strangers."

He paused.

"But you'll have to take me up on this now," he said, "or you'll lose the chance for good. Say yes now, and follow through, or the chance is gone. Well?"

"General," said Amanda. "I've listened to you. Now, you listen to me. You're the one who's dreaming. It's not us who are already dead and gone—it's you and your men. You're already defeated. You just don't know it."

"Mrs. Morgan," said Amorine heavily, "you're a fool. There's no way you can defeat Earth."

"Yes," said Amanda bleakly. Another gust of rain came and rattled against the window, like the tapping of the fingers of dead children. "Believe me, there is."

He stood up.

"All right," he said. "I tried. We'll do it our own way from now on. You can go."

Amanda also stood up.

"One thing, however," she said. "I want to see Cletus when he lands."

"Cletus? Cletus Grahame, you mean?" Amorine stared at her. "What makes you think he's going to land?"

"Don't talk nonsense, General," Amanda said. "You know as well as I do, he's due in by early afternoon."

"Who told you that?"

"Everyone knows it."

He stared at her.

"Damn!" he said softly. "No, you cannot see Grahame—now or in the future."

"I've got to be able to report to the local people that he's well and agreeable to being in your custody," Amanda said. "Or do you want the district to rise in arms spontaneously?"

He stared at her balefully. Staring, he began to cough again. When the fit was over, he nodded.

"He'll be down in a little over an hour. Shall we find you a place to wait?"

"If it's an hour, I'll go into town and get some things done. Will you leave word at the airpad, so I can get past your soldiers?"

He nodded.

"Ask for Lieutenant Estrange," he said.

She went out.

Back in town she found Ekram's skimmer still parked behind the house of Marie Dureaux. She parked her own skimmer beside his and let herself in the back door, into the kitchen.

Ekram was there, washing his hands at the sink. He looked back over his shoulder at her at the sound of her entrance.

"Marie?" Amanda said.

"Marie's dead." He turned his head back to the sink.

"And you're still in town here."

He finished washing and turned to face her, wiping his hands on a dishtowel.

"Berthe Haugsrud's dead," he said. "Bhaktabahadur Rais is dead. Fifteen more are dying. Young Marte Haugsrud's sick. There're five dead soldiers in the cantonments, thirty more dying and most of the rest sick."

"So you leave," she said.

"Leave? How can I leave? Their medical officer knows something's going on. There's just nothing he can do about it. He'd be an absolute incompetent idiot not to know that something's going on, particularly since they've been getting word from other occupation units—not from many, but even a few's enough—where the same thing's happening. All that's kept them blind this long is the fact it started hitting our people first. If I run now—"

He broke off. His face was lean with weariness, stubbled with beard.

"You go," Amanda said. "That's an order."

"To hell with orders!"

"Cletus is due to land in an hour. You've had three hours in town here during daylight hours. In three more hours we're going to have open war. Get out of here, get up in those hills and get ready to handle casualties."

"The kids..." He swayed a little on his feet. "Kids, kids and guns..."

"Will you go?"

"Yes." His voice was dull. He walked stiff-jointedly past her and out the back door. Following him, she saw him climb, still with the awkwardness of exhaustion, onto his skimmer, lift it, and head it out of town.

Amanda went back inside to see whether there was anything she could do for the remains of Marie. But there was nothing. She left and went to the Haugsrud house to see if Marte could be brought to leave town with her, now that Berthe was dead. But the doors were locked and Marte refused to answer, though Amanda could see her through a window, sitting on the living room couch. Amanda tried several ways to force her way in, but time began to grow short. She turned away at last and headed toward the airpad.

She was almost late getting there. By the time she had made contact with Lieutenant Estrange and been allowed to the airpad itself, a shuttleboat bearing the inlaid sunburst emblem of the Exotics was landed, and Cletus was stepping out onto the pad. A line of vehicles and an armed escort was already waiting for him.

He was wearing a sidearm, which was taken from him, and led toward the second of the waiting staff cars.

"I've got to speak to him!" said Amanda fiercely to Estrange. "Weren't you given orders I was to be able to speak to him?"

"Yes. Please—wait a minute. Wait here."

The lieutenant went forward and spoke to the colonel in charge of operation. After some little discussion, Estrange came back and got Amanda.

"If you'll come with me?" He brought her to Cletus, who was already seated in the staff car.

"Amanda!" Cletus looked out over the edge of the open window of the staff car. "Is everyone all right?"

"Fine," said Amanda. "I've taken over the post of mayor from Piers."

"Good," said Cletus urgently. His cheerful, lean face was a little thinner than when she had seen it last, marked a little more deeply by lines of tension. "I'm glad it's you. Will you tell everyone they must keep calm about all this? I don't want anyone getting excited and trying to do things. These occupying soldiers have behaved themselves, haven't they?"

"Oh, yes," said Amanda.

"Good. I thought they would. I'll leave matters in your hands then. They're taking me up to Grahame House—to Foralie, I mean. Apparently Dow deCastries is already there, and I'm sure once I've had a talk with him we can straighten this all out. So all anyone needs to do is just sit tight for a day or two, and everything will be all right. Will you see the district understands that?"

Out of the corners of her eyes, Amanda could see the almost-wondering contempt growing on the faces of the Coalition officers and men within hearing.

"I'll take care of it, Cletus."

"I know you will. Oh—how's Betta?"

"You'll see her when you get to Foralie," said Amanda. "She's due to have her baby any time now."

"Good. Good. Tell her I saw her brother David just a few days ago, and he's fine. No—wait. I'll tell her myself, since I'll be seeing her first. Talk to you shortly, Amanda."

"Yes, Cletus," said Amanda, stepping back from the staff car. The convoy got underway and moved out.

"And that's this military genius of theirs?" she heard one of the enlisted men muttering to another, as she turned away with Estrange.

Five minutes later she was on her way past the cordon of sentries enclosing the town, and twelve minutes after that, having stopped only to pick up her handgun, she stood beside Ramon, who was on his skimmer, looking down from cover on the more slow-moving convoy as it headed in the direction of Foralie.

"We'll want all the available teams in position around Foralie before they get there," she said. "But when they show up, let them through. We'll want them together with Dow's escort before we hit them."

"Most of the men in that convoy are sick," said Ramon.

"Yes," said Amanda, half to herself. "But the ones who've been up there with Dow all this time are going to be perfectly healthy. And they're front line troops. If we don't get them in the first few minutes, it's going to cost us—"

"Maybe not," said Ramon. She looked at him.

"What do you mean?"

"I mean, not all of them up at Foralie may be healthy. I haven't had a chance to tell you, but a patrol came up there early today and stayed for about two hours. They could have switched personnel."

"Not likely." Amanda frowned. "Dow's their prize package. Why would they take the healthy troops they have protecting him and replace them with cripples, just to get more of their able-bodied down at town?"

"They might have some reason we don't know about."

Amanda shook her head.

"I don't believe it," she said. "In fact, until I hear positively there's been a change of personnel at Foralie, I won't believe it. We'll continue on the assumption that they're all healthy troops there, and the only advantage we've got is surprise. Cletus, bless him, helped us with that as much as he could. He did everything possible to put their suspicions to sleep, down in town."

"He did?" Ramon stared at her. "What did he do?"

Amanda told him what Cletus had said from the staff car in the hearing of the convoy soldiery.

Ramon's face lengthened.

"But maybe he really means we shouldn't do anything until..."

His voice trailed at the look on Amanda's face.

"If a rooster came up to you and quacked," said Amanda sharply, "would you ignore everything else about it and decide it'd turned into a drake?"

She looked down her nose at him.

"Even if Cletus actually had taken leave of his senses, that wouldn't alter the situation for the rest of us," she went on. "We've still got to move in, rescue him, and take deCastries when he reaches Foralie. It's the one chance we've got. But don't concern yourself. Cletus understands the situation here."

She nodded at his skimmer.

"You go get the teams into position. I'll meet you at Foralie before they get there."

"Where will you be?" Ramon's face was a little pale.

"I'll be rounding up any adults capable of using a weapon—except the women with young children—from the near households. We'll need anyone we can get."

"What about the other patrols?"

"Once we've got deCastries, we shouldn't have much opposition from anyone else who's been in Foralie Town. A good half of them are going to be dead in a week, and the most of the rest won't be able to fight."

"They may fight even if they're not able."

"How can they—" She broke off, suddenly seeing the white look in Ramon's eyes. "What's the matter with you? You ought to know that."

"I didn't want to know," he said. "I didn't listen when they told us."

"Didn't you?" said Amanda. "Well, you'd better listen now then. Carbon monoxide passed over finely divided nickel gives you a liquid—nickel carbonyl, a volatile liquid that melts at twenty-five degrees centigrade, boils at forty-three degrees and evaporates at normal temperatures in the open. One part in a million of the vapors can be enough to cause allergic dermatitis and edema of the lungs—irreversible."

His face was stark. His mouth was open as if he gasped for breath.

"I don't mind the fighting," he said thickly. "It's just the thought of the casualties among the soldiers. If this war could only be stopped now, before it starts—"

"Casualties? Before it starts?" Amanda held him with her eyes. "What do you think Berthe Haugsrud and Bhak and the others have been, down in town?"

He did not answer.

"They're our casualties," she said, "already counted. The war you want to stop before it starts has been going for two days. Did you think it would all take place with no cost at all?"

"No, I..." He swayed a little on his skimmer, and the momentary gust of anger he had sparked off in her went away suddenly.

"I know," she said. "There're things that aren't easy for you to think about. They aren't easy for Ekram. Nor for me, nor any of us. Nor was it easy for those people like Berthe, down in town, who stayed there knowing what was going to happen to them. But do you have any more of it to face or live with than they did, or the boys and girls on the teams will?"

"No," he said. "But I can't help how I feel."

"No," she said. "No, of course you can't. Well, do the best you can anyway."

He nodded numbly and reached for the power bar of his skimmer. Amanda watched him lift and slide away, gazing for a long moment after his powerful shoulders, now slumped and weary. Then she mounted her own skimmer and took off at right angles to his route.

She reproached herself as she went for her outburst at him. He was still young and had not seen what people could do to people. He had no basis of experience from which to imagine what would happen to the dispossessed Dorsai, once they were scattered thinly among the populations of other worlds who had been educated to hold them in detestation and contempt. He could still cling to a hope that somehow an enemy could be defeated with such cleverness that neither friend nor foe need suffer.

She headed toward the Aras homestead to pick up Mene as the first of her adult recruits for the assault on Foralie.

Travelling there, even now, she found the mountains calming her spirit. The rain had topped, according to the weather predictions Ramon had given her, and a swift wind was tearing the cloud cover to tatters. The sky revealed was a high, hard blue, and the air, on the wings of a stiff breeze, piping with an invigorating cold. She felt stilled, concentrated and clear of mind.

For better or worse, they must now move into literal combat. There was no more time to worry whether individuals would measure up. There was no time for her cataloguing of the sort of lackings she had noted in Betta, in Melissa, in Lexy, and just now in Ramon. Time had run out on her decision of the name for Betta's child. She must leave word with others before the actual assault on Foralie about what she had decided, one way or another, so that it could be passed on to Betta if necessary. She would do just that. At the last minute, she would make up her mind one way or another and have done with it.

Forty-five minutes later, she swung her skimmer up to a fold in the hills, carrying Mene Aras with her. As she topped the rise and dipped down into the hidden hollow beyond, she saw the Ancients of five teams, together with a dozen or so of the team-leaders and runners from them, plus Jer Walker leaning on both his walking canes and a half-rifle slung from the shoulders of his frail, ninety-year-old body. Nine of the other women, most of them young and also armed, were already there. But most welcome of all was the sight of the unusual pair that were Arvid Johnson and Bill Athyer, together with six of the Dorsai they had been able to keep as staff.

Amanda slid her skimmer to a stop, stepped off, and walked up to Arvid and Bill.

"I was deliberately not counting on you," she said, "but I thought you might be here in time."

"You'll need us," Arvid said. "I take it you knew Swahili is now the officer in charge of Dow's escort? He came up here with replacement troops this morning."

"Swahili?" Amanda frowned, for the name had a familiar ring, but eluded identification.

"He's a major with these Coalition troops. But he was one of Eachan Khan's officers," Bill said. "A Dorsai once—but probably you've never seen him. He didn't like any place where there wasn't any fighting going on. He joined Eachan some years ago, out on one of the off-world contracts, and I think he was only here in this district briefly, once or twice. The only things that usually brought him to the Dorsai were short visits to that new training center Cletus set up on the other side of the world."

"The point is, though, he literally is a Dorsai—or was. One of the best we ever had, in fact," said Arvid. "If anyone's going to catch us moving in before we want them to know we're there, it'll be him."

There was a strange, almost sad note in Arvid's voice.

"Yes, he's that good. Some of us"—Bill glanced for a second at his tall companion—"thought he was the best we had . . . in some ways. At any rate, that's why Arvid and I'll be going in first, to secure the house."

"You're taking charge then?" said Amanda.

"We hadn't planned on it," said Arvid swiftly. "It's your district, of course—"

"Don't talk nonsense," said Amanda. "We'll do anything that works. Did you really think I'd be prickly about my authority?"

"No," said Arvid. "Not really. But I do think you should stay in overall command. These local people know you, not me. Just give us four minutes head start, then move in. We'll take the house. That'll leave you the compound area that was set up for the escort troops, beside the house. How do you plan to handle that?"

"The only way we can," said Amanda. "I'll go in first, with the other adults behind me—openly, like neighbors coming to visit—and I'll try to disarm the sentry. Then we'll take the compound—we adults—building by building. Meanwhile, the teams will lie out around with their weapons and try to see that, whatever happens, none of the soldiers break out of the compound area after we've gone in."

Arvid nodded.

"All right," he said. "Our word is that all the men in the convoy bringing Cletus in are pretty well sick and useless. I suppose you also have the information that most of the well troops that came up originally with Dow were traded back to town for the personnel of the patrol that came up with Swahili—a patrol of sick that were sent up this morning? That should make things easier for you."

Amanda scowled.

"I heard that from Ramon—one of my team Ancients," she said. "I don't believe it. Why trade good fighting men for bad around someone as important as Dow?"

"It checks out, all the same," said Arvid. "We hear Dow was called by their military physician late last night. He was the one who ordered the change."

"You monitored that call?"

"No. Just got a report on it, passed out through Foralie Town."

Amanda shook her head stubbornly.

"One further piece of evidence," said Arvid. "On the basis of the report, I had a couple of my staff check the patrol that went out and the patrol that came back. It was a completely different set of faces that returned."

Amanda sighed.

"All right. If that's right . . ." She swung away from him. "Take off any time you're ready."

"We're ready now," said Arvid. "Four minutes."

"Good luck," she said, and went over to her own group, the assorted gang of women, Jer, the five Ancients and the young team members, carrying their cone and energy rifles in the crook of their arms, muzzle down, like hunting weapons.

"All right," she said to them all. "You know what you're supposed to do, and you heard me talking just now with Arvid and Bill . . ."

She hesitated, finding herself strangely, uncharacteristically, at a loss for words. There was something that needed to be said, something that she had been working toward for a very long time, that she needed to tell them before they went where they were going. But whatever it was, it would not define itself for her. A skimmer topped the ridge opposite the one that overlooked Foralie and came sliding down to them under full power, carrying Reiko Kiempii, armed. Amanda saw the tall young woman's eyes slip past her for a second to Arvid. Then Reiko had reached the rest of them and jumped off her skimmer.

"I got word over the phone just before I left home," she said to Amanda. "Betta's in labor—the real thing this time."

"Thanks," said Amanda, hardly knowing she spoke.

Suddenly, as if a switch had been pulled, the words she had been looking for were ready to her tongue. With this news, everything abruptly fell into order—her silent, lifelong love for Jimmy and for Fal Morgan, the years of struggling to survive back when the outlaw mercenaries had prowled the new Dorsai settlements, the sending out of the men in each generation to be killed, to earn the necessary credits that alone would let them all continue to survive—just as they were and wished to be.

As they were.

Those were the magic words. They had a right to be as they were, and it was a right worth all it cost. This harsh world had been one that no one else had wanted. But they had taken it, she and the others like her. They had built it with their own hands and blood. It was theirs. *You love,* she thought suddenly, *what you give to—and in proportion as you give.*

That was all she had wanted to say. But now, looking around her at the adolescent faces of the young team members, as the other adult women, at old Jer Walker, she realized there had never been any need to tell the rest of them that. From the youngest to the oldest, they already knew it. It was in their bones and blood, as it was in hers. Perhaps not all of them had yet put it into words in their minds, as she had just done in hers—but they knew.

She looked at them. Mixed in among their living figures she thought she saw the presence of ghosts—of Berthe Haugsrud, of Bhaktabahadur Rais, of Jimmy himself and all those from other households who had died for the Dorsai, both here and on other worlds. Like the mountains, these stood up all around them, patiently waiting.

It came to her then like a revelation that none of it mattered—their individual weaknesses, the things that they seemed to lack that she herself either had innately, or that time had taught her. She had been guilty of *Amandamorphism*—thinking only someone exactly like herself could earn even passing marks to qualify for the role she had played here so long. But that idea was nonsense. The fact that no two people were exactly alike had nothing to do with the fact that two people could be equally useful.

There came a time when anyone had to face the leaving of ultimate decisions to others, and to time itself. A time when faith proved either to have been well-placed or misplaced, but when it was too late to do anything more about it. It was not up to her to leave Betta a last decision about the use of the Amanda name for Betta's child. Betta herself was the one to decide that, as Amanda had made necessary decisions in her own time, and all generations to come would have to make their own decisions in their time.

"What are you smiling at, Amanda?" said Reiko, looming beside and over her.

"Nothing," said Amanda. "Nothing at all."

She turned to the rest of them.

"I'll go in first," she said, "as soon as Arvid and Bill with their team have had their four minute lead. The rest of you, follow me, coming two to a skimmer, from different directions. We'll use Betta as an excuse for gathering at Foralie, as long as that's conveniently turned up. Actually, the excuse won't matter. . . ."

She looked around at their faces.

"Myself, first. Then Mene and Reiko. The rest team up as you wish. Team members, stay close and fire as needed, but don't move into the compound unless or until you're called in by one of us who've gone ahead. That includes Ancients. Ancients, stay with your teams. In case everything falls apart here, it'll be up to each of you to pull your team off, get it back into the mountains, and keep it alive. Everybody understand?"

They nodded or murmured their understanding.

"All right—" She was interrupted by a flicker of red, a cloth being waved briefly from just behind the crest of the ridge overlooking Foralie. "All right. Convoy in sight. It'll take it another five minutes or so to reach the house. Everybody up behind the ridge, ready to go."

Lying with the others, just behind the crest of the ridge, she looked through a screen of grass at the convoy. Even to her eye, its vehicle column seemed to move somewhat sluggishly. Evidently that part of Arvid's information—about the convoy troops all being sick—was correct. She crossed her fingers mentally upon the hope that the rest of what he had told her was also reliable—but with misgivings. Counting the team members, the Dorsai would outnumber the troops of the convoy and those already at Foralie nearly five to one—but children against experienced soldiers made that figure one of mockery. Experienced soldiers against civilians was bad enough.

The convoy was almost to the house. She pushed herself backwards and got to her feet below the crest of the ridge. Looking over, she saw the last of the Dorsai soldiers belonging to Bill and Arvid already disappearing—they would be crawling forward through the tall grass now to get as close as they could come to the house before making their move. She checked her watch, counting off the minutes. When four were gone, she waved to the other civilians, mounted her skimmer, and took it up over the ridge, directly down upon the single sentry standing in front of the compound of bubble plastic structures at the far end of the house. The convoy had pulled out of sight into the compound just moments before she reached him, and his head was still turned looking after it. She had set the skimmer down before he belatedly turned to the sound of her power unit. His cone rifle swung up hastily to cover her.

"Stay right there—" he began. She interrupted him.

"Oh, stop that nonsense! My great-granddaughter's having a baby. Where is she?"

"Where? She . . . oh, the house, of course, ma'am."

"All right, you go tell her I'll be right there. I've got to speak to whoever's in charge of that convoy—"

"I can't leave my post. I'm sorry, but—"

"What do you mean, you can't leave your post? Don't you recognize me? I'm the mayor of Foralie Town. You must have been shown an image of me as part of your briefing. Now, you get in there—"

"I'm sorry. I really can't—"

"Don't tell me can't—"

They argued, the sentry forgetting his weapon to the point where its barrel sagged off to one side. A new humming announced another skimmer that slid down upon them with Reiko and Mene Aras aboard.

"Halt—" said the soldier, swinging his rifle to command these new arrivals.

"Now what're you doing?" said Amanda, exasperatedly. Out of the corner of her eye, she saw Cletus being escorted into the house. The majority of the soldiers of the convoy should now be out of their vehicles and moving inside one or another of the cantonment buildings. There was still no sign of Arvid, Bill, and their team.

"Don't you understand that neighbors come calling when there's a birth?" she said sharply, interrupting another argument that was developing between the sentry and Reiko. "I know these neighbors well. I'll vouch for them . . ."

"In a second, ma'am . . ." the sentry threw over his shoulder at her and turned back to Reiko.

"No second," said Amanda.

The difference in the tone of her voice brought him around. He froze at the sight of Amanda's heavy handgun pointed at his middle. Ineffective as they were at ordinary rifle distance, the energy handguns were devastating at point-blank range like this. Even if Amanda's aim should be bad—and she held the gun too steadily to suggest bad aim—any pressure on its trigger would mean his being cut almost in two.

"Just keep talking," said Amanda softly. She held the gun low, so that the sentry's own body shielded any view of it from the compound or the house. "You and I are just going on with our conversation. Wave these two to the compound as if you were referring them to someone there. There'll be other skimmers coming—"

"Yes . . . two more. On the way now," Mene's voice almost hissed, close by her ear.

"—and after each one stops here for a moment, you'll wave them to the compound, too. Do you understand?" Amanda said.

"Yes. . . ." His eyes were on the steady muzzle of her handgun.

"Good. Mene, Reiko, go ahead. Wait until enough others catch up with you before you make a move though."

"Leave it to us," said Reiko. Their skimmer lifted and hummed toward the compound.

"Just stand relaxed," Amanda told the sentry. "Don't move your rifle."

She sat. The sentry's face showed the pallor of what was perhaps illness, now overlaid with a mute desperation. He did not move. He was not as youthful as some of the other soldiers, but from the relative standpoint of Amanda's years, they were all young. Other skimmers came and moved on to the compound, until all the adults had gone by her.

"Stand still," Amanda said to the sentry.

Off to one side, a movement caught her eye. It was a figure slipping around the corner of the house and entering the door. Then another. Arvid and Bill with their men—at last.

She turned her head slightly to look. Five . . . six figures flickered around the corner of the house and in through the door. Out of the other corner of her eyes she caught movement close to her. Looking back, she saw the sentry bringing up the barrel of his rifle to knock the energy weapon out of her hand. Twenty, even ten years before, she would have been able to move the handgun out of the way in time, but age had slowed her too much.

She felt the weight against her wrist as metal met metal and the energy gun was sent flying. But she was already stooping to the scabbard with the pellet shotgun as the sentry's cone rifle swung back to point at her. The stream of cones whistled over her bent head, then lowered. She felt a single heavy shock in the area of her left shoulder, but then the shotgun had, in its turn, batted the light frame of the cone rifle aside and the sentry was looking into the wide muzzle of the heavier gun.

"Drop it," said Amanda.

Her own words sounded distant in her own ears. There was a strange feeling all through her. The impact had been high enough so that possibly the single cone that struck her had not made a fatal wound, but shock was swift with missiles from that weapon.

The cone rifle dropped to the ground.

"Now lie down, face down," said Amanda. She was still hearing her voice as if from a long distance away, and the world about her had an unreal quality to it. "No, out of arm's reach of the rifle. . . ."

The sentry obeyed. She touched the power bar of her skimmer, lifted it and lowered it carefully on the lower half of his body. Then she killed the power and got off. Pinned down by the weight upon him, the sentry lay helpless.

"If you call or struggle, you'll get shot," she told him.

"I won't," said the sentry.

There was the whistling of cone rifle fire from the direction of the cantonment. She turned in that direction, but there was no one to be seen outside the buildings she faced. The vehicle park was behind them, however, screened by them from her sight.

She bent to pick up the handgun, then thought better of it. The pellet shotgun was operable in spite of the rust in its barrel, and uncertain as she was now, she was probably better off with a weapon having a wide shot pattern. She began to walk unsteadily toward the compound. Every step took an unbelievable effort and her balance was not good, so that she wavered as she went. She reached the first building and opened its door. A supply room—empty. She went on to the next and opened the door, too wobbly to take ordinary precautions in entering. The thick air of a sickroom took her nostrils as she entered. Tina Alchenso, one of the other women, stood with an energy rifle, covering a barracks-like interior in which all the soldiers there seemed sick or dying. The air seemed heavy as well with the scentless odor of resignation and defeat. Those who were able had evidently been ordered out of their beds. They lay face down on the floor in the central aisle, hands stretched out beyond their heads.

"Where's everybody?" Amanda asked.

"They went on to the other buildings," Tina said.

Amanda let herself out again and went on, trying doors as she went. She found two more buildings where one of the adults stood guard over ill soldiers. She was almost back to the vehicle parking area when she saw a huddled figure against the outside wall of a building.

"Reiko!" she said, and knelt clumsily beside the other woman.

"Stop Mene," Reiko barely whispered. She was bleeding heavily just above the belt of her jumper. "Mene's out of her head."

"All right," said Amanda. "You lie quiet."

With an effort, she rose and went on. There was the next building before her. She opened the door and found Mene holding her energy rifle on yet another room of sick and dying soldiers. Mene's face was white and wiped clean of expression. Her eyes stared, fixed, and her finger quivered on the firing button of the weapon. The gaze of all the men in the room were on her face, and there was not even the sound of breathing.

"Mene," said Amanda gently. Mene's gaze jerked around to focus on Amanda for a brief moment before returning to the soldiers.

"Mene...," said Amanda softly. "It's almost over. Don't hurt anyone now. It's just about over. Just hold them for a while longer. That's all, just hold them."

Mene said nothing.

"Do you hear me?"

Mene nodded jerkily, keeping her eyes on the men before her.

"I'll be back soon," said Amanda.

She went out. The world was even more unreal about her, and she felt as if she was walking on numb legs. But that was unimportant. Something large was wrong with the overall situation.

Something was very wrong. There were only two more huts shielding her from the vehicle park where the convoy had just unloaded. Those two buildings could not possibly hold all the rest of the original escort, plus the troops of the convoy. Nor should just those two huts be holding two or three of her adults. It did not matter what Arvid had told her. Something had gone astray—she could feel it like a cold weight in her chest below the weakness and unreality brought on by her wound.

She tried to think with a dulled mind. She could gamble that Arvid and Bill's team had already subdued the house, and go back there now, without checking further, to get help.... Her mind cleared a little. A move like that would be the height of foolishness. Even if Arvid and Bill had men to spare to come back here with her, going for assistance would waste time when there might be no time to waste.

She took a good grip on her pellet gun, which was becoming an intolerable weight in her hands, and started around the curved wall of one of the huts.

Possibly the sense of unreality that held her was largely to blame—but it seemed to her that there was no warning at all. Suddenly she found herself in the midst of a tight phalanx of vehicles, the front ones already loaded with weaponed and alert-looking soldiers, and the rear ones with other such climbing into them. But, if her appearance among them had seemed sudden to her, it had apparently seemed the same to them.

She was abruptly conscious that all movement around her had ceased. Soldiers were poised, half in, half out of their vehicles. Their eyes were on her.

Plainly, her fears had been justified. The apparent replacement of well soldiers by sick ones had been a trap, and these she faced now were about to move in for a counterattack. She felt the last of her energy and will slipping away, took one step forward, and jammed the muzzle of her pellet shotgun against the side panel shielding the power unit in the closest vehicle.

"Get down," she said to the officers and men facing her.

They stared at her as if she was a ghost risen out of the ground before them.

"I'll blow every one of you up if I have to—and be glad to," she said. "Get out. Lie down, face down, all of you!"

For a second more they merely sat frozen, staring. Then understanding seemed to go through them in an invisible wave. They began to move out of their seats.

"Hurry...," said Amanda, for her strength was going fast. "On the ground..."

They obeyed. Dreamily, remotely, she saw them climbing from the vehicles and prostrating themselves on the ground.

Now what do I do, Amanda thought? She had only a minute or two of strength left.

The answer came from the back of her head—the only answer. *Press the firing button of the pellet gun after all, and make sure no one gets away*—

Unexpectedly, there was the sound of running feet behind her. She started to glance back over her shoulder and found herself caught and upheld. She was surrounded by the field uniforms of four of the Dorsai staff members who had been with Arvid and Bill.

"Easy...," said the one holding her—almost carrying her, in fact. "We've got it. It's all over."

There succeeded a sort of blur, and then a large space of nothing at all. At last things cleared somewhat—but only somewhat—and she found herself lying under covers in one of the Foralie bedrooms. Like someone in a high fever, she was conscious of people moving all around her at what seemed like ungracious speed, and talking words she could not quite catch. Her shoulder ached. Small bits and phrases of dialogue came clear from moment to moment.

"...*shai Dorsai!*"

What was that? That ridiculous phrase that the children had made up only a few years back, and which was now beginning to be picked up by their elders as a high compliment? It was supposed to mean real *actual* Dorsai. Nonsense.

It occurred to her, as some minor statistic might, that she was dying, and she was vaguely annoyed with herself for not having realized this earlier. There were things she should think about, if that was the case. If Betta had been in labor before the attack began, she might well have her child by now.

If so, it was important that she tell Betta what she had decided just before they moved in on the troops, that the use of the name Amanda was her responsibility now, and the responsibility of succeeding generations. . . .

"Well," said a voice just above her, and she looked up into the face of Ekram. He stank of sweat and anesthetic. "Coming out of it, are you?"

"How long? . . ." It was incredibly hard to speak.

"Oh, about two days," he answered with abominable cheerfulness.

She thought of her need to tell Betta of her decision.

"Betta . . ." she said. It was becoming a little easier to talk, but the effort was still massive. She had intended to ask specifically for news of Betta and the child.

"Betta's fine. She's got a baby boy, all parts in good working order. Three point seven three kilograms."

Boy! A shock went through her.

Of course. But why shouldn't the child be a boy? No reason—except that, deluded by her own aging desires, she had fallen into the comfortable thought that it would not be anything but a girl.

A boy. That made the matter of names beside the point entirely.

For a moment, however, she teetered on the edge of self-pity. After all she had known, after all these years, why couldn't it have been a girl—under happier circumstances when she could have lived to know it, and find that it was a child who could safely take up her name?

She hauled herself back to common sense. What was all this foolishness about names anyway? The Dorsai had won, had kept itself independent. That was her reward, as well as the reward to all of them—not just the sentimental business of passing her name on to a descendant. But she should still tell Betta of her earlier decision, if Ekram would only let them bring the girl to her. It would be just like the physician to decide that her dying might be hurried by such an effort and refuse to let Betta come. She would have to make sure he understood this was not a decision for him to make. A deathbed wish was sacred, and he must understand that was what this was. . . .

"Ekram," she managed to say faintly. "I'm dying. . . ."

"Not unless you want to," said Ekram.

She stared at him aghast. This was outrageous. This was too much. After all she had been through. . . . Then the import of his words trickled through the sense of unreality wrapping her.

"Bring Betta here! At once!" she said, and her voice was almost strong.

"Later," said Ekram.

"Then I'll have to go to her," she said grimly.

She was only able to move one of her arms feebly sideways on top of the covers, in token of starting to get up from the bed. But it was enough.

"All right. All right!" said Ekram. "In just a minute."

She relaxed, feeling strangely luxurious. It was all right. The name of the game was survival, not how you did it. A boy! She almost laughed. Well, that sort of thing happened from time to time. In a few more years it could also happen that this boy could have a sister. It was worth waiting around to see. She would still have to die someday, of course—but in her own good time.

WARRIOR

EARTH, 2269

The spaceliner coming in from New Earth and Freiland, worlds under the Sirian sun, was delayed in its landing by traffic at the spaceport in Long Island Sound. The two police lieutenants, waiting on the bare concrete beyond the shelter of the terminal buildings, turned up the collars of their cloaks against the hissing sleet in this unweatherproofed area. The sleet was turning into tiny hailstones that bit and stung all exposed areas of skin. The gray November sky poured them down without pause or mercy; the vast, reaching surface of concrete seemed to dance with their white multitudes.

"Here it comes now," said Tyburn, the Manhattan Complex police lieutenant, risking a glance up into the hailstorm. "Let me do the talking when we take him in."

"Fine by me," answered Breagan, the spaceport officer. "I'm only here to introduce you—and because it's my bailiwick. You can have Kenebuck, with his hood connections and his millions. If it were up to me, I'd let the soldier get him."

"It's him," said Tyburn, "who's likely to get the soldier—and that's why I'm here. You ought to know that."

The great mass of the interstellar ship settled to the concrete like a cautious mountain two hundred yards off. It protruded a landing stair near its base like a metal leg, and the passengers began to disembark. The two policemen spotted their man immediately in the crowd.

"He's big," said Breagan, with the judicious appraisal of someone safely on the sidelines, as the two of them moved forward.

"They're all big, these professional military men off the Dorsai world," answered Tyburn, a little irritably, shrugging his shoulders under his cloak against the cold. "They breed themselves that way."

"I know they're big," said Breagan. "This one's bigger."

The first wave of passengers was rolling toward them now, their quarry among the mass. Tyburn and Breagan moved forward to meet him. When they got close they could see, even through the hissing sleet, every line of his dark, unchanging face looming above the lesser heights of the people around him, his military erectness molding the civilian clothes he wore until they might as well have been a uniform. Tyburn found himself staring fixedly at the tall figure as it came toward him. He had met such professional soldiers from the Dorsai before, and the stamp of their breeding had always been plain on them. But this man was somehow even more so than the others Tyburn had seen. In some way, he seemed to be the spirit incarnate of the Dorsai.

He was one of twin brothers, Tyburn remembered now from the dossier back at his office. Ian and Kensie were their names, of the Graeme family at Foralie, on the Dorsai. And the report was that Kensie had two men's likability, while his brother Ian, now approaching Tyburn, had a double portion of grim shadow and solitary darkness.

Staring at the man coming toward him, Tyburn could believe the dossier now. For a moment even, with the sleet and the cold taking possession of him, he found himself believing in the old saying that, if the born soldiers of the Dorsai ever cared to pull back to their own small, rocky world and challenge the rest of humanity, not all the thirteen other inhabited planets could stand against them. Once, Tyburn had laughed at that idea. Now, watching Ian approach, he could not laugh. A man like this would live for different reasons from those of ordinary men—and die for different reasons.

Tyburn shook off the wild notion. The figure coming toward him, he reminded himself sharply, was a professional military man—nothing more.

Ian was almost to them now. The two policemen moved in through the crowd and intercepted him.

"Commandant Ian Graeme?" said Breagan. "I'm Kaj Breagan of the spaceport police. This is Lieutenant Walter Tyburn of the Manhattan Complex Force. I wonder if you could give us a few minutes of your time?"

Ian Graeme nodded, almost indifferently. He turned and paced along with them, his longer stride making more leisurely work of what was for them a brisk walk. They led him away from the route of the disembarking passengers and in through a metal door at one end of the terminal marked Unauthorized Entry Prohibited. Inside, they took an elevator tube up to the offices of the terminal's top floor and ended up in chairs around a desk in one of the offices.

All the way in, Ian had said nothing. He sat in his chair now with the

same indifferent patience, gazing at Tyburn behind the desk and at Breagan seated back against the wall at the desk's right side. Tyburn found
himself staring back in fascination. Not at the granite face, but at the
massive, powerful hands of the man, hanging idly between the chair arms
that supported his forearms. Tyburn, with an effort, wrenched his gaze
from those hands.

"Well, Commandant," he said, forcing himself at last to look up into
the dark, unchanging features, "you're here on Earth for a visit, we
understand."

"To see the next-of-kin of an officer of mine." Ian's voice, when he
spoke at last, was almost mild compared to the rest of his appearance.
It was a deep, calm voice, but lightless—like a voice that had long
forgotten the need to be angry or threatening. Only . . . there was something sad about it, Tyburn thought.

"A James Kenebuck?" said Tyburn.

"That's right," answered the deep voice of Ian." His younger brother,
Brian Kenebuck, was on my staff in the recent campaign on Freiland.
He died three months back."

"Do you," asked Tyburn, "always visit your deceased officers' next
of kin?"

"When possible. Usually, of course, they die in the line of duty."

"I see," said Tyburn. The office chair in which he sat seemed hard
and uncomfortable underneath him. He shifted slightly. "You don't happen to be armed, do you, Commandant?"

Ian did not even smile.

"No," he said.

"Of course, of course," said Tyburn, uncomfortable. "Not that it makes
any difference." He was looking again, in spite of himself, at the two
massive, relaxed hands opposite him. "Your . . . extremities by themselves
are lethal weapons. We register professional karate and boxing experts
here, you know—or did you know?"

Ian nodded.

"Yes," said Tyburn. He wet his lips and then was furious with himself
for doing so. Damn my orders, he thought suddenly and whitely, I don't
have to sit here making a fool of myself in front of this man, no matter
how many connections and millions Kenebuck owns.

"All right, look here, Commandant," he said harshly, leaning forward.
"We've had a communication from the Freiland-North Police about you.
They suggest that you hold Kenebuck—James Kenebuck—responsible
for his brother Brian's death."

Ian sat looking back at him without answering.

"Well," demanded Tyburn raggedly, after a long moment, "do you?"

"Force-leader Brian Kenebuck," said Ian calmly, "led his Force, consisting of thirty-six men at the time, against orders, farther than was wise into enemy perimeter. His Force was surrounded and badly shot up. Only he and four men returned to the lines. He was brought to trial in the field under the Mercenaries Code for deliberate mishandling of his troops under combat conditions. The four men who had returned with him testified against him. He was found guilty and I ordered him shot."

Ian stopped speaking. His voice had been perfectly even, but there was so much finality about the way he spoke that after he finished there was a pause. Tyburn and Breagan stared at him as if they had both been tranced. Then the silence, echoing in Tyburn's ears, jolted him back to life.

"I don't see what all this has to do with James Kenebuck then," said Tyburn. "Brian committed some . . . military crime and was executed for it. You say you gave the order. If anyone's responsible for Brian Kenebuck's death then, it seems to me it'd be you. Why connect it with someone who wasn't even there at the time, someone who was here on Earth all the while—James Kenebuck?"

"Brian," said Ian, "was his brother."

The emotionless statement was calm and coldly reasonable in the silent, brightly-lit office. Tyburn found his open hands had shrunk themselves into fists on the desk top. He took a deep breath and began to speak in a flat, official tone.

"Commandant," he said, "I don't pretend to understand you. You're a man of the Dorsai, a product of one of the splinter cultures out among the stars. I'm just an old-fashioned Earthborn—but I'm a policeman in the Manhattan Complex, and James Kenebuck is . . . well, he's a taxpayer in the Manhattan Complex."

He found he was talking without meeting Ian's eyes. He forced himself to look at them—they were dark unmoving eyes.

"It's my duty to inform you," Tyburn went on, "that we've had intimations to the effect that you're to bring some retribution to James Kenebuck because of Brian Kenebuck's death. These are only intimations, and as long as you don't break any laws here on Earth, you're free to go where you want and see whom you like. *But this is Earth, Commandant.*"

He paused, hoping that Ian would make some sound, some movement. But Ian only sat there, waiting.

"We don't have any Mercenaries Code here, Commandant," Tyburn went on harshly. "We haven't any feud-right, no *droit-de-main*. But we do have laws. Those laws say that, though a man may be the worst murderer alive, until he's brought to book in our courts, under our process of laws, no one is allowed to harm a hair of his head. Now, I'm not here to argue whether this is the best way or not, just to tell you that that's the way things are." Tyburn stared fixedly into the dark eyes. "Now," he said bluntly, "I know that if you're determined to try to kill Kenebuck without counting the cost, I can't prevent it."

He paused and waited again. But Ian still said nothing.

"I know," said Tyburn, "that you can walk up to him like any other citizen, and once you're within reach you can try to kill him with your bare hands before anyone can stop you. *I* can't stop you in that case. But what I can do is catch you afterwards, if you succeed, and see you convicted and executed for murder. And you *will* be caught and convicted, there's no doubt about it. You can't kill James Kenebuck the way someone like you would kill a man and get away with it here on Earth—do you understand that, Commandant?"

"Yes," said Ian.

"All right," said Tyburn, letting out a deep breath. "Then you understand. You're a sane man and a Dorsai professional. From what I've been able to learn about the Dorsai, it's one of your military tenets that part of a man's duty to himself is not to throw his life away in a hopeless cause. And this cause of yours to bring Kenebuck to justice for his brother's death is hopeless."

He stopped. Ian straightened in a movement preliminary to getting up.

"Wait a second," said Tyburn.

He had come to the hard part of the interview. He had prepared his speech for this moment and rehearsed it over and over again—but now he found himself without faith that it would convince Ian.

"One more word," said Tyburn. "You're a man of camps and battlefields, a man of the military, and you must be used to thinking of yourself as a pretty effective individual. But here, on Earth, those special skills of yours are mostly illegal. And without them you're ineffective and helpless. Kenebuck, on the other hand, is just the opposite. He's got money—millions. And he's got connections, some of them nasty. And he was born and raised here in Manhattan Complex." Tyburn stared emphatically at the tall, dark man, willing him to understand. "Do you follow me? If you, for example, should suddenly turn up dead here, we just might not be able to bring Kenebuck to book for it. Where we absolutely could, and would, bring you to book if the situation were reversed. Think about it."

He sat, still staring at Ian. But Ian's face showed no change, or sign that the message had gotten through to him.

"Thank you," Ian said. "If there's nothing more, I'll be going."

"There's nothing more," said Tyburn, defeated. He watched Ian leave. It was only when Ian was gone and he turned back to Breagan that he recovered a little of his self-respect. For Breagan's face had paled.

* * *

Ian went down through the terminal and took a cab into Manhattan Complex to the John Adams Hotel. He registered for a room on the fourteenth floor of the transient section of that hotel and inquired about the location of James Kenebuck's suite in the resident section, then sent his card up to Kenebuck with a request to come by to see the millionaire. After that, he went on up to his own room, unpacked his luggage, which had already been delivered from the spaceport, and took out a small, sealed package. Just at that moment there was a soft chiming sound, and his card was returned to him from a delivery slot in the room wall. It fell into the salver below the slot and he picked it up, to read what was written on the face of it. The penciled note read:

Come on up—
K.

He tucked the card and the package into a pocket and left his transient room. And Tyburn, who had followed him to the hotel and who had been observing, through sensors placed in the walls and ceilings, all of Ian's actions from the second of his arrival, half rose from his chair in the room of the empty suite directly above Kenebuck's, which had been quietly taken over as a police observation post. Then, helplessly, Tyburn swore and sat down again to follow Ian's movements in the screen fed by the sensors. So far there was nothing the policeman could do legally— nothing but watch.

So he watched as Ian strode down the softly carpeted hallway to the elevator tube, rose in it to the eightieth floor, and stepped out to face the heavy, transparent door sealing off the resident section of the hotel. He held up Kenebuck's card and its message to a concierge screen beside the door, and with a soft sigh of air the door slid back to let him through. He passed on in, found a second elevator tube, and took it up thirteen more stories. Black doors opened before him—and he stepped one step forward into a small foyer to find himself surrounded by three men.

They were big men—one, a lantern-jawed giant, was even bigger than Ian—and they were vicious. Tyburn, watching through the sensor in the foyer ceiling that had been secretly placed there by the police the day before, recognized all of them from his files. They were underworld muscle hired by Kenebuck at word of Ian's coming—all armed, and brutal, and hair trigger—mad dogs of the lower city. After that first step into their midst, Ian stood still. And there followed a strange, unnatural cessation of movement in the room.

The three stood checked. They had been about to put their hands on Ian to search him for something, Tyburn saw, and probably to rough him up in the process. But something had stopped them, some abrupt change in the air around them. Tyburn, watching, felt the change as they did, but for a moment he felt it without understanding. Then understanding came to him.

The difference was in Ian, in the way he stood there. He was, Tyburn saw, simply . . . waiting. That same patient indifference Tyburn had seen in him in the terminal office was there again. In the split second of his single step into the room, he had discovered the men, had measured them, and stopped. Now, he waited, in his turn, for one of them to make a move.

A sort of black lightning had entered the small foyer. It was abruptly obvious to the watching Tyburn, as to the three below, that the first of them to lay hands on Ian would be the first to find the hands of the Dorsai soldier upon him—and those hands were death.

For the first time in his life, Tyburn saw the personal power of the Dorsai fighting man, made plain without words. Ian needed no badge upon him, standing as he stood now, to warn that he was dangerous. The men about him were mad dogs, but, patently, Ian was a wolf. There was a difference with the three, which Tyburn now recognized for the first time. Dogs—even mad dogs—fight, and the losing dog, if he can, runs away. But no wolf runs. For a wolf wins every fight but one, and in that one he dies.

After a moment, when it was clear that none of the three would move, Ian stepped forward. He passed through them without even brushing against one of them, to the inner door opposite, and opened it and went on through.

He stepped into a three-level living room stretching to a large, wide window, its glass rolled up, and black with the sleet-filled night. The living room was as large as a small suite in itself, and filled with people, men and women, richly dressed. They held cocktail glasses in their hands as they stood or sat, and talked. The atmosphere was heavy with the scents of alcohol and women's perfumes and cigarette smoke. It seemed that they paid no attention to his entrance, but their eyes followed him covertly once he had passed.

He walked forward through the crowd, picking his way to a figure before the dark window, the figure of a man almost as tall as himself, erect, athletic-looking, with a handsome, sharp-cut face under whitish-blond hair that stared at Ian with a sort of incredulity as Ian approached.

"Graeme . . . ?" said this man, as Ian stopped before him. His voice in this moment of off-guardedness betrayed its two levels, the semi-hoodlum whine and harshness underneath, the polite accents above. "My boys . . . you didn't—," he stumbled, "leave anything with them when you were coming in?"

"No," said Ian. "You're James Kenebuck, of course. You look like your brother." Kenebuck stared at him.

"Just a minute," Kenebuck said. He set down his glass, turned and went quickly through the crowd and into the foyer, shutting the door behind him. In the hush of the room, those there heard first silence, then a short, unintelligible burst of sharp voices, then silence again. Kenebuck came back into the room, two spots of angry color high on his cheekbones. He came back to face Ian.

"Yes," he said, halting before Ian. "They were supposed to . . . tell me when you came in." He fell silent, evidently waiting for Ian to speak, but Ian merely stood, examining him, until the spots of color on Kenebuck's cheekbones flared again.

"Well?" he said abruptly. "Well? You came here to see me about Brian, didn't you? What about Brian?" He added, before Ian could answer, in a tone suddenly brutal: "I know he was shot, so you don't have to break that news to me. I suppose you want to tell me he showed all sorts of noble guts—refused a blindfold and that sort of—"

"No," said Ian. "He didn't die nobly."

Kenebuck's tall, muscled body jerked a little at the words, almost as if the bullets of an invisible firing squad had poured into it.

"Well . . . that's fine!" he laughed angrily. "You come light-years to see me and then you tell me that! I thought you liked him—liked Brian."

"Liked him? No," Ian shook his head. Kenebuck stiffened, his face for a moment caught in a gape of bewilderment. "As a matter of fact," Ian went on, "he was a glory-hunter. That made him a poor soldier and a worse officer. I'd have transferred him out of my command if I'd had time before the campaign on Freiland started. Because of him, we lost the lives of thirty-two men in his Force that night."

"Oh." Kenebuck pulled himself together and looked sourly at Ian. "Those thirty-two men. You've got them on your conscience—is that it?"

"No," said Ian. There was no emphasis on the word as he said it, but somehow to Tyburn's ears above, the brief short negative dismissed Kenebuck's question with an abruptness like contempt. The spots of color on Kenebuck's cheeks flamed.

"You didn't like Brian and your conscience doesn't bother you— what're you here for then?" he snapped.

"My duty brings me," said Ian.

"Duty?" Kenebuck's face stilled and went rigid.

Ian reached slowly into his pocket as if he were surrendering a weapon under the guns of an enemy and did not want his move misinterpreted. He brought out the package from his pocket.

"I brought you Brian's personal effects," he said. He turned and laid the package on a table beside Kenebuck. Kenebuck stared down at the package. The color over his cheekbones faded until his face was nearly as pale as his hair. Then slowly, hesitantly, as if he were approaching a booby trap, he reached out and gingerly picked it up. He held it and turned to Ian, staring into Ian's eyes almost demandingly.

"It's in here?" said Kenebuck in a voice barely above a whisper, and with a strange emphasis.

"Brian's effects," said Ian, watching him.

"Yes . . . sure. All right," said Kenebuck. He was plainly trying to pull himself together, but his voice was still almost whispering. "I guess . . . that settles it."

"That settles it," said Ian. Their eyes held together. "Good-bye," said Ian. He turned and walked back through the silent crowd and out of the living room. The three musclemen were no longer in the foyer. He took the elevator tube down and returned to his own hotel room.

Tyburn, who with a key to the service elevators, had not had to change tubes on the way down as Ian had, was waiting for him when Ian entered. Ian did not seem surprised to see Tyburn there. He only glanced casually at the policeman as he crossed to a decanter of Dorsai whiskey that had since been delivered up to the room.

"That's that then!" burst out Tyburn in relief. "You got in to see him, and he ended up letting you out. You can pack up and go now. It's over."

"No," said Ian. "Nothing's over yet." He poured a few inches of the pungent, dark whisky into a glass and moved the decanter over another glass. "Drink?"

"I'm on duty," said Tyburn sharply.

"There'll be a little wait," said Ian calmly. He poured some whisky into the other glass, took up both glasses, and stepped across the room to hand one to Tyburn. Tyburn found himself holding it. Ian had walked on to stand before the ceiling-high window. Outside, night had fallen, but—faintly seen in the lights from the city levels below—the sleet here above the weather shield still beat like small, dark ghosts against the transparency.

"Hang it, man, what more do you want?" burst out Tyburn. "Can't you see it's you I'm trying to protect—as well as Kenebuck? I don't want *anyone* killed! If you stay around here now, you're asking for it. I keep telling you, here in Manhattan Complex you're the helpless one, not Kenebuck. Do you think he hasn't made plans to take care of you?"

"Not until he's sure," said Ian, turning from the ghost-sleet, beating like lost souls against the window glass, trying to get in.

"Sure about what? Look, Commandant," said Tyburn, trying to speak calmly. "Half an hour after we heard from the Freiland-North Police about you, Kenebuck called my office to ask for police protection." He broke off angrily. "Don't look at me like that! How do I know how he found out you were coming? I tell you he's rich, and he's got connections!

But the point is, the police protection he's got is just a screen—an excuse—for whatever he's got planned for you on his own. You saw those hoods in the foyer!"

"Yes," said Ian unemotionally.

"Well, think about it!" Tyburn glared at him. "Look, I don't hold any brief for James Kenebuck! All right—let me tell you about him! We knew he'd been trying to get rid of his brother since Brian was ten— but blast it, Commandant, Brian was no angel, either—"

"I know," said Ian, seating himself in a chair opposite Tyburn.

"All right, you know! I'll tell you anyway!" said Tyburn. "Their grand-father was a local kingpin—he was in every racket on the eastern sea-board. He was one of the mob, with millions he didn't dare count because of where they'd come from. In their father's time, those millions started to be fed into legitimate businesses. The third generation, James and Brian, didn't inherit anything that wasn't legitimate. Hell, we couldn't even make a jaywalking ticket stick against one of them, if we'd ever wanted to. James was twenty and Brian ten when their father died, and when he died, the last bit of tattletale gray went out of the family linen. But they kept their hoodlum connections, Commandant!"

Ian sat, glass in hand, watching Tyburn almost curiously.

"Don't you get it?" snapped Tyburn. "I tell you that, on paper, in law, Kenebuck's twenty-four-karat gilt-edge. But his family was hoodlum, he was raised like a hoodlum, and he thinks like a hood! He didn't want his young brother Brian around to share the crown prince position with him—so he set out to get rid of him. He couldn't just have him killed, so he set out to cut him down, show him up, break his spirit, until Brian took one chance too many trying to match up to his older brother and killed himself off."

Ian slowly nodded.

"All right!" said Tyburn. "So Kenebuck finally succeeded. He chased Brian until the kid ran off and became a professional soldier—something Kenebuck wouldn't leave his wine, women, and song long enough to shine at. And he can shine at most things he really wants to shine at, Commandant. Under that hood attitude and all those millions, he's got a good mind and a good body that he's made a hobby out of training. But, all right. So now it turns out Brian was still no good, and he took some soldiers along when he finally got around to doing what Kenebuck wanted—getting himself killed. All right! But what can you do about it? What can anyone do about it, with all the connections, and all the money, and all the law on Kenebuck's side of it? And, why should you think about doing something about it anyway?"

"It's my duty," said Ian. He had swallowed half the whiskey in his glass, absently, and now he turned the glass thoughtfully around, watching the brown liquor swirl under the forces of momentum and gravity. He looked up at Tyburn. "You know that, Lieutenant."

"Duty! Is duty that important?" demanded Tyburn. Ian gazed at him, then looked away, at the ghost-sleet beating vainly against the glass of the window that held it back in the outer dark.

"Nothing's more important than duty," said Ian, half to himself, his voice thoughtful and remote. "Mercenary troops have the right to care and protection from their own officers. When they don't get it, they're entitled to justice, so that the same thing is discouraged from happening again. That justice is a duty."

Tyburn blinked, and unexpectedly a wall seemed to go down in his mind.

"Justice for those thirty-two dead soldiers of Brian's!" he said, suddenly understanding. "That's what brought you here!"

"Yes." Ian nodded, and lifted his glass almost as if to the sleet-ghosts to drink the rest of the whisky.

"But," said Tyburn, staring at him, "You're trying to bring a civilian to justice. And Kenebuck has you out-gunned and out-maneuvered—"

The chiming of the communicator screen in one corner of the hotel room interrupted him. Ian put down his empty glass, went over to the screen, and depressed a stud. His wide shoulders and back hid the screen from Tyburn, but Tyburn heard his voice.

"Yes?"

The voice of James Kenebuck sounded in the hotel room.

"Graeme—listen!"

There was a pause.

"I'm listening," said Ian calmly.

"I'm alone now," said the voice of Kenebuck. It was tight and harsh. "My guests have gone home. I was just looking through that package of Brian's things . . ." He stopped speaking and the sentence seemed to Tyburn to dangle unfinished in the air of the hotel room. Ian let it dangle for a long moment.

"Yes?" he finally said.

"Maybe I was a little hasty . . ." said Kenebuck. But the tone of his voice did not match the words. The tone was savage. "Why don't you come up, now that I'm alone, and we'll . . . talk about Brian after all?"

"I'll be up," said Ian.

He snapped off the screen and turned around.

"Wait!" said Tyburn, starting up out of his chair. "You can't go up there!"

"Can't?" Ian looked at him. "I've been invited, Lieutenant."

The words were like a damp towel slapping Tyburn in the face, waking him up.

"That's right . . ." he stared at Ian. "Why? Why'd he invite you back?"

"He's had time," said Ian, "to be alone. And to look at that package of Brian's."

"But . . ." Tyburn scowled. "There was nothing important in that package. A watch, a wallet, a passport, some other papers . . . Customs gave us a list. There wasn't anything unusual there."

"Yes," said Ian. "And that's why he wants to see me again."

"But what does he want?"

"He wants me," said Ian. He met the puzzlement of Tyburn's gaze. "He was always jealous of Brian," Ian explained, almost gently. "He was afraid Brian would grow up to outdo him in things. That's why he tried to break Brian, even to kill him. But now Brian's come back to face him."

"Brian . . . ?"

"In me," said Ian. He turned toward the hotel door.

Tyburn watched him turn, then suddenly, like a man coming out of a daze, he took three hurried strides after him as Ian opened the door.

"Wait!" snapped Tyburn. "He won't be alone up there! He'll have hoods covering you through the walls. He'll definitely have traps set for you . . ."

Easily, Ian lifted the policeman's grip from his arm.

"I know," he said. And went.

Tyburn was left in the open doorway, staring after him. As Ian stepped into the elevator tube, the policeman moved. He ran for the service elevator that would take him back to the police observation post above the sensors in the ceiling of Kenebuck's living room.

When Ian stepped into the foyer the second time, it was empty. He went to the door to the living room of Kenebuck's suite, found it ajar, and stepped through it. Within, the room was empty, with glasses and overflowing ashtrays still on the tables; the lights had been lowered. Kenebuck rose from a chair with its back to the far, large window at the end of the room. Ian walked toward him and stopped when they were little more than an arm's length apart.

Kenebuck stood for a second, staring at him, the skin of his face tight. Then he made a short, almost angry gesture with his right hand. The gesture gave away the fact that he had been drinking.

"Sit down!" he said. Ian took a comfortable chair, and Kenebuck sat down in the one from which he had just risen. "Drink?" said Kenebuck. There was a decanter and glasses on the table beside and between them. Ian shook his head. Kenebuck poured part of a glass for himself.

"That package of Brian's things," he said abruptly, the whites of his eyes glinting as he glanced up under his lids at Ian. "There was just personal stuff. Nothing else in it!"

"What else did you expect would be in it?" asked Ian calmly.

Kenebuck's hands clenched suddenly on the glass. He stared at Ian, and then burst out into a laugh that rang a little wildly against the emptiness of the large room.

"No, no . . ." said Kenebuck loudly. "I'm asking the questions, Graeme. I'll ask them! What made you come all the way here, to see me, anyway?"

"My duty," said Ian.

"Duty? Duty to whom—Brian?" Kenebuck looked as if he would laugh again, then thought better of it. There was the white, wild flash of his eyes again. "What was something like Brian to you? You said you didn't even like him."

"That was beside the point," said Ian quietly. "He was one of my officers."

"One of your officers! He was my brother! That's more than being one of your officers!"

"Not," answered Ian in the same voice, "where justice is concerned."

"Justice?" Kenebuck laughed. "Justice for Brian? Is that it?"

"And for thirty-two enlisted men."

"Oh—" Kenebuck snorted laughingly. "Thirty-two men . . . those thirty-two men!" He shook his head. "I never knew your thirty-two men, Graeme, so you can't blame me for them. That was Brian's fault; him and his idea—what was the charge they tried him on? Oh, yes, that he and his thirty-two or thirty-six men could raid enemy headquarters and come back with the enemy commandant. Come back . . . covered with glory." Kenebuck laughed again. "But it didn't work. Not my fault."

"Brian did it," said Ian, "to show you. You were what made him do it."

"Me? Could I help it if he never could match up to me?" Kenebuck stared down at his glass and took a quick swallow from it, then went back to cuddling it in his hands. He smiled a little to himself. "Never could even *catch* up to me." He looked whitely across at Ian. "I'm just a better man, Graeme. You better remember that."

Ian said nothing. Kenebuck continued to stare at him; slowly, Kenebuck's face grew more savage.

"Don't believe me, do you?" said Kenebuck softly. "You better believe me. I'm not Brian, and I'm not bothered by Dorsais. You're here, and I'm facing you—alone."

"Alone?" said Ian. For the first time Tyburn, above the ceiling over the heads of the two men, listening and watching through hidden sensors, thought he heard a hint of emotion—contempt—in Ian's voice. Or had he imagined it?

"Alone—Well!" James Kenebuck laughed again, but a little cautiously. "I'm a civilized man, not a hick frontiersman. But I don't have to be a fool. Yes, I've got men covering you from behind the walls of the room here. I'd be stupid not to. And I've got this..." He whistled, and something about the size of a small dog, but made of smooth, black metal, slipped out from behind a sofa nearby and slid on an aircushion over the carpeting to their feet.

Ian looked down. It was a sort of satchel with an orifice in the top from which two metallic tentacles protruded slightly.

Ian nodded slightly.

"A medical mech," he said.

"Yes," said Kenebuck, "cued to respond to the heartbeat of anyone in the room with it. So you see, it wouldn't do you any good, even if you somehow knew where all my guards were and beat them to the draw. Even if you killed me, this could get to me in time to keep it from being permanent. So, I'm unkillable. Give up!" He laughed and kicked at the mech. "Get back," he said to it. It slid back behind the sofa.

"So you see..." he said. "Just sensible precautions. There's no trick to it. You're a military man—and what's that mean? Superior strength. Superior tactics. That's all. So I outpower your strength, outnumber you, make your tactics useless—and what are you? Nothing." He put his glass carefully aside on the table with the decanter. "But I'm not Brian. I'm not afraid of you. I could do without these things if I wanted to."

Ian sat watching him. On the floor above, Tyburn had stiffened.

"Could you?" asked Ian.

Kenebuck stared at him. The white face of the millionaire contorted. Blood surged up into it, darkening it. His eyes flashed whitely.

"What're you trying to do—test me?" he shouted suddenly. He jumped to his feet and stood over Ian, waving his arms furiously. It was, recognized Tyburn overhead, the calculated, self-induced hysterical rage of the hoodlum world. But how would Ian Graeme below know that? Suddenly, Kenebuck was screaming. "You want to try me out? You think I won't face you? You think I'll back down like that brother of mine, that..." he broke into a flood of obscenity in which the name of Brian was freely mixed. Abruptly, he whirled about to the walls of the room, yelling at them. "Get out of there! All right, out! Do you hear me? All of you! Out—"

Panels slid back, bookcases swung aside and four men stepped into the room. Three were those who had been in the foyer earlier when Ian had entered for the first time. The other was of the same type.

"Out!" screamed Kenebuck at them. "Everybody out. Outside, and lock the door behind you. I'll show this Dorsai, this..." Almost foaming at the mouth, he lapsed into obscenity again.

Overhead, above the ceiling, Tyburn found himself gripping the edge of the table below the observation screen so hard his fingers ached.

"It's a trick!" he muttered between his teeth to the unhearing Ian. "He planned it this way! Can't you see that?"

"Graeme armed?" inquired the police sensor technician at Tyburn's right. Tyburn jerked his head around momentarily to stare at the technician.

"No," said Tyburn. "Why?"

"Kenebuck is." The technician reached over and tapped the screen, just below the left shoulder of Kenebuck's jacket image. "Slug-thrower."

Tyburn made a fist of his aching right fingers and softly pounded the table before the screen in frustration.

"All right!" Kenebuck was shouting below, turning back to the still-seated form of Ian and spreading his arms wide. "Now's your chance. Jump me! The door's locked. You think there's anyone else near to help me? Look!" He turned and took five steps to the wide, knee-high to ceiling window behind him, punched the control button, and watched as it swung wide. A few of the whirling sleet-ghosts outside drove from out of ninety stories of vacancy into the opening—and fell dead in little drops of moisture on the windowsill as the automatic weather shield behind the glass blocked them out.

He stalked back to Ian, who had neither moved nor changed expression through all this. Slowly, Kenebuck sank back down into his chair, his back to the night, the blocked-out cold, and the sleet.

"What's the matter?" he asked slowly, acidly. "You don't do anything? Maybe *you* don't have the nerve, Graeme?"

"We were talking about Brian," said Ian.

"Yes, Brian . . ." Kenebuck said, quite slowly. "He had a big head. He wanted to be like me, but no matter how he tried—how I tried to help him—he couldn't make it." He stared at Ian. "That's just the way, he never could make it—the way he decided to go into enemy lines when there wasn't a chance in the world. That's the way he was—a loser."

"With help," said Ian.

"What? What's that you're saying?" Kenebuck jerked upright in his chair.

"You helped him lose," Ian's voice was matter of fact. "From the time he was a young boy, you built him up to want to be like you—to take long chances and win. Only your chances were always on safe bets, and his were as unsafe as you could make them."

Kenebuck drew in an audible, hissing breath.

"You've got a big mouth, Graeme!" he said in a low, slow voice.

"You wanted," said Ian, almost conversationally, "to have him kill himself off. But he never quite did. And each time he came back for more, because he had it stuck into his mind, carved into his mind, that he wanted to impress you—even though by the time he was grown, he saw what you were up to. He knew, but he still wanted to make you admit that he wasn't a loser. You'd twisted him that way while he was growing up, and that was the way he grew."

"Go on," hissed Kenebuck. "Go on, big mouth."

"So, he went off-Earth and became a professional soldier," went on Ian steadily and calmly. "Not because he was drafted like someone from Newton or a born professional from the Dorsai, or hungry like one of the ex-miners from Coby, but to show you you were wrong about him. He found one place where you couldn't compete with him, and he must have started writing back to you to tell you about it—half rubbing it in, half asking for the pat on the back you never gave him."

Kenebuck sat in the chair and breathed. His eyes were all one glitter.

"But you didn't answer his letters," said Ian. "I suppose you thought that'd make him desperate enough to finally do something fatal. But he didn't. Instead, he succeeded. He went up through the ranks. Finally, he got his commission and made Force-leader, and you began to be worried. It wouldn't be long, if he kept on going up, before he'd be above the field officer grades and out of most of the actual fighting."

Kenebuck sat perfectly still, leaning a little forward. He looked almost as if he were praying, or putting all the force of his mind to willing that Ian finish what he had started to say.

"And so," said Ian, "on his twenty-third birthday—which was the day before the night on which he led his men against orders into the enemy area—you saw that he got this birthday card..." He reached into a side pocket of his civilian jacket and took out a white, folded card that showed signs of having been savagely crumpled but was now smoothed out again. Ian opened it and laid it beside the decanter on the table between their chairs, the sketch and legend facing Kenebuck. Kenebuck's eyes dropped to look at it.

The sketch was a crude outline of a rabbit, with a combat rifle and battle helmet discarded at its feet, engaged in painting a broad yellow stripe down the center of its own back. Underneath this picture was printed in block letters the question—"WHY FIGHT IT?"

Kenebuck's face slowly rose from the sketch to face Ian, and the millionaire's mouth stretched at the corners and went on stretching into a ghastly version of a smile.

"Was that all...?" whispered Kenebuck.

"Not all," said Ian. "Along with it, glued to the paper by the rabbit, there was this—"

He reached almost casually into his pocket.

"No you don't!" screamed Kenebuck triumphantly. Suddenly he was on his feet, jumping behind his chair, backing away toward the darkness of the window behind him. He reached into his jacket and his hand came out holding the slug-thrower, which cracked loudly in the room. Ian had not moved, and his body jerked to the heavy impact of the slug.

Suddenly, Ian had come to life. Incredibly, after being hammered by a slug, the shock of which should have immobilized an ordinary man, Ian was out of the chair, on his feet, and moving forward. Kenebuck screamed again—this time with pure terror—and began to back away, firing as he went.

"Die, you—! Die!" he screamed. But the towering Dorsai figure came on. Twice it was hit and spun clear around by the heavy slugs, but like a football fullback shaking off the assaults of tacklers, it plunged on, with great strides narrowing the distance between it and the retreating Kenebuck.

Screaming finally, Kenebuck came up with the back of his knees against the low sill of the open window. For a second his face distorted itself out of all human shape in a grimace of its terror. He looked to right and to left but there was no place left to run. He had been pulling the trigger of his slug-thrower all this time, but now the firing pin clicked at last upon an empty chamber. Gibbering, he threw the weapon at Ian, and it flew wide of the driving figure of the Dorsai, now almost upon him, great hands outstretched.

Kenebuck jerked his head away from what was rushing toward him. Then, with a howl like a beaten dog, he turned and flung himself through the window before those hands could touch him, into ninety-odd stories of unsupported space. And his howl carried away, down into silence.

Ian halted. For a second he stood before the window, his right hand still clenched about whatever it was he had pulled from his pocket. Then, like a toppling tree, he fell—

—as Tyburn and the technician with him finished burning through the ceiling above and came dropping through the charred opening into the room. They almost landed on the small object that had come rolling from Ian's now lax hand. An object that was really two objects glued together. A small paint-brush and a transparent tube of glaringly yellow paint.

"I hope you realize, though," said Tyburn two weeks later on an icy, bright December day as he and the recovered Ian stood just inside the terminal waiting for the boarding signal from the spaceliner about to take off for the Sirian worlds, "what a chance you took with Kenebuck. It was just luck it worked out for you the way it did."

"No," said Ian. He was apparently as emotionless as ever—a little more gaunt from his stay in the Manhattan hospital, but he had mended with the swiftness allowed by virtue of his Dorsai constitution. "There was no luck. It all happened the way I planned it."

Tyburn gazed in astonishment.

"Why..." he said, "if Kenebuck hadn't had to send his hoods out of the room to make it seem necessary for him to shoot you himself when you put your hand into your pocket that second time—or if you hadn't had the card in the first place—" He broke off, suddenly thoughtful. "You mean...?" he stared at Ian. "Having the card, you planned to have Kenebuck get you alone...?"

"It was a form of personal combat," said Ian. "And personal combat is my business. You assumed that Kenebuck was strongly entrenched, facing my attack. But it was the other way around."

"But you had to come to him—"

"I had to appear to come to him," said Ian, almost coldly. "Otherwise he wouldn't have believed that he had to kill me—before I killed him. By his decision to kill me, he put himself in the attacking position."

"But he had all the advantages!" said Tyburn, his head whirling. "You had to fight on his ground, here where he was strong..."

"No," said Ian. "You're confusing the attack position with the defensive one. By coming here, I put Kenebuck in the position of finding out whether I actually had the birthday card, and the knowledge of why Brian had gone against orders into enemy territory that night. Kenebuck planned to have his men in the foyer shake me down for the card—but they lost their nerve."

"I remember," murmured Tyburn.

"Then, when I handed him the package, he was sure the card was in it. But it wasn't," went on Ian. "He saw his only choice was to give me a situation where I might feel it was safe to admit having the card and the knowledge. He had to know about that, because Brian had called his bluff by going out and risking his neck after getting the card. The fact that Brian was tried and executed later made no difference to Kenebuck. That was a matter of law—something apart from hoodlum guts, or lack of guts. If no one knew that Brian was braver than his older brother, that was all right. But if I knew, he could only save face under his own standards by killing me."

"He almost did," said Tyburn. "Any one of those slugs—"

"There was the medical mech," said Ian calmly. "A man like Kenebuck would be bound to have something like that around, to play safe—just as he would be bound to set an amateur's trap." The boarding horn of the spaceliner sounded. Ian picked up his luggage bag. "Good-bye," he said, offering his hand to Tyburn.

"Good-bye..." he muttered. "So you were just going along with Kenebuck's trap. All of it. I can't believe it..." He released Ian's hand and watched as the big man swung around and took the first two strides away toward the bulk of the ship, shining in the winter sunlight. Then, suddenly, the numbness broke clear from Tyburn's mind. He ran after Ian and caught at his arm. Ian stopped and swung half-around, frowning slightly.

"I can't believe it!" cried Tyburn. "You mean you went up there *knowing* Kenebuck was going to pump you full of slugs and maybe kill you—all just to square things for thirty-two enlisted soldiers under the command of a man you didn't even like? I don't believe it—you can't be that cold-blooded! I don't care how much of a man of the military you are!"

Ian looked down at him. And it seemed to Tyburn that the Dorsai face had gone away from him, somehow become as remote and stony as a face carved high up on some icy mountaintop.

"But I'm not just a man of the military," Ian said. "That was the mistake Kenebuck made, too. That was why he thought that, stripped of military elements, I'd be easy to kill."

Tyburn, looking at him, felt a chill run down his spine as icy as wind off a glacier.

"Then, in heaven's name," cried Tyburn, "what are you?"

Ian looked from his far distance down into Tyburn's eyes and the sadness rang as clear in his voice, finally, as iron-shod heels on barren rock.

"I am a man of war," said Ian softly.

With that, he turned and went on. Tyburn saw him black against the winter-bright sky, looming over all the other departing passengers, on his way to board the spaceship.

LOST DORSAI

CETA, 2273

I am Corunna El Man.

I brought the little courier vessel down at last at the spaceport of Nahar City on Ceta, the large world around Tau Ceti. I had made it from the Dorsai in six phase shifts to transport, to the stronghold of Gebel Nahar, our Amanda Morgan—she whom they call the second Amanda.

Normally I am far too senior in rank to act as a courier pilot. But I was home on leave at the time. The courier vessels owned by the Dorsai Cantons are too expensive to risk lightly, but the situation required a contracts expert at Nahar more swiftly than one could safely be gotten there. They asked me to take on the problem, and I solved it by stretching the possibilities on each of the phase shifts, coming here.

The risks I took had not seemed to bother Amanda. That was not surprising, since she was Dorsai. but neither did she talk to me much on the trip, and that was a thing that had come to be, with me, a little unusual.

For things had been different for me after Baunpore. In the massacre there following the siege, when the North Freilanders finally overran the town, they cut up my face for the revenge of it, and they killed Else, for no other reason than that she was my wife. There was nothing left of her but incandescent gas, dissipating throughout the universe, and since there could be no hope of a grave, nothing to come back to, nor any place where she could be remembered, I rejected surgery and chose to wear my scars as a memorial to her.

It was a decision I never regretted. But it was true that with those scars came an alteration in the way other people reacted to me. With some I found that I became almost invisible, and nearly all seemed to relax their natural impulse to keep private their personal secrets and concerns.

It was almost as if they felt that somehow I was now beyond the point where I would stand in judgment of their pains and sorrows. No, on second thought, it was something even stronger than that. It was as if I was a burnt-out candle in the dark room of their inner selves—a lightless but safe companion whose presence reassured them that their privacy was still unbreached. I doubt very much that Amanda and those I was to meet on this trip to Gebel Nahar would have talked to me as freely as they did if I had met them back in the days when I had had Else alive.

We were lucky on our incoming. The Gebel Nahar is more a mountain fortress than a palace or government center, and for military reasons, Nahar City, near it, has a spaceport capable of handling deep-space ships. We debarked, expecting to be met in the terminal the minute we entered through its field doors. But we were not.

The principality of Nahar Colony lies in tropical latitudes on Ceta, and the main lobby of the terminal was small, but high-ceilinged and airy; its floor and ceiling were tiled in bright colors, plants were growing in planter areas all about, and bright, enormous, heavily-framed paintings hung on all the walls. We stood in the middle of all this, and foot traffic moved around us. No one looked directly at us, although neither I with my scars nor Amanda—who bore a remarkable resemblance to those pictures of the first Amanda in our Dorsai history books—was easy to ignore.

I went over to check with the message desk and found nothing there for us. Coming back, I had to hunt for Amanda, who had stepped away from where I had left her.

"El Man—," her voice said without warning, behind me. "Look!"

Her tone had warned me, even as I turned. I caught sight of her and the painting she was looking at, all in the same moment. It was high up on one of the walls, and she stood just below it, gazing.

Sunlight through the transparent front wall of the terminal flooded her and the picture alike. She was in all the natural colors of life—as Else had been—tall, slim, in light blue cloth jacket and short cream-colored skirt, with white-blond hair and that incredible youthfulness that her namesake ancestor had also owned. In contrast, the painting was rich in garish pigments, gold leaf and alizarin crimson, the human figures it depicted caught in exaggerated, melodramatic attitudes.

Leto de muerte, the large brass plate below it read. *Hero's Death-Couch,* as the title would roughly translate from the bastard, archaic Spanish spoken by the Naharese. It showed a great, golden bed set out on an open plain in the aftermath of the battle. All about were corpses and bandaged officers standing in gilt-encrusted uniforms. The living surrounded the bed and its occupant, the dead hero, who, powerfully muscled yet emaciated, hideously wounded and stripped to the waist, lay upon a thick pile of velvet cloaks, jewelled weapons, marvelously wrought tapestries, and golden utensils, all of which covered the bed.

The body lay on its back, chin pointing at the sky, face gaunt with the agony of death, still firmly holding in one large hand to its naked chest, the hilt of an oversized and ornate sword, its massive blade darkened with blood. The wounded officers standing about and gazing at the corpse were posed in dramatic attitudes. In the foreground, on the earth beside the bed, a single ordinary soldier in battle-torn uniform, dying, stretched forth one arm in tribute to the dead man.

Amanda looked at me for a second as I moved up beside her. She did not say anything. It was not necessary to say anything. In order to live, for two hundred years we on the Dorsai have exported the only commodity we owned—the lives of our generations—to be spent in wars for others' causes. We live with real war, and to those who do that, a painting like this is close to obscenity.

"So that's how they think here," said Amanda.

I looked sideways and down at her. Along with the appearance of her ancestor, she had inherited the first Amanda's incredible youthfulness. Even I, who knew she was only a half-dozen years younger than myself— and I was now in my mid-thirties—occasionally forgot that fact, and was jolted by the realization that she thought like my generation rather than like the stripling she seemed to be.

"Every culture has its own fantasies," I said. "And this culture's Hispanic, at least in heritage."

"Less than ten percent of the Naharese population's Hispanic nowadays, I understand," she answered. "Besides, this is a caricature of Hispanic attitudes."

She was right. Nahar had originally been colonized by immigrants— Gallegos from the northwest of Spain who had dreamed of large ranches in a large open territory. Instead, Nahar, squeezed by its more industrial and affluent neighbors, had become a crowded, small country that had retained a bastard version of the Spanish language as its native tongue and a medley of half-remembered Spanish attitudes and customs as its culture. After the first wave of immigrants, those who came to settle here were of anything but Hispanic ancestry, but still they had adopted the language and ways they found here.

The original ranchers had become enormously rich, for though Ceta was a sparsely populated planet, it was food-poor. The later arrivals swelled the cities of Nahar, and stayed poor—very poor.

"I hope the people I'm to talk to are going to have more than ten percent of ordinary sense," Amanda said. "This picture makes me wonder if they don't prefer fantasy. If that's the way it is at Gebel Nahar . . ."

She left the sentence unfinished, shook her head, and then—apparently pushing the picture from her mind—smiled at me. The smile lit up her face, in something more than the usual sense of that phrase. With her, it was something different, an inward lighting deeper and greater than those words usually indicate. I had only met her for the first time, three days earlier, and Else was all I had ever or would ever want, but now I could see what people had meant on the Dorsai, when they had said she inherited the first Amanda's abilities both to command others and to make them love her.

"No message for us?" she said.

"No—," I began. But then I turned, for out of the corner of my eye I saw someone approaching us.

She also turned. Our attention was caught because the man striding toward us on long legs was a Dorsai. He was big. Not the size of the Graeme twins, Ian and Kensie, who were in command at Gebel Nahar on the Naharese contract, but close to that size and noticeably larger than I was. Dorsai, however, come in all shapes and sizes. What had identified him to us—and obviously, us to him—was not his size, but a multitude of small signals, too subtle to be catalogued. He wore a Naharese army bandmaster's uniform, with warrant officer tabs at the collar, and he was blond-haired, lean-faced, and no more than in his early twenties. I recognized him.

He was the third son of a neighbor from my own canton of High Island, on the Dorsai. His name was Michael de Sandoval, and little had been heard of him for six years.

"Sir—Ma'am," he said, stopping in front of us. "Sorry to keep you waiting. There was a problem getting transport."

"Michael," I said. "Have you met Amanda Morgan?"

"No, I haven't." He turned to her. "An honor to meet you, ma'am. I suppose you're tired of having everyone say they recognize you from your great-grandmother's pictures?"

"Never tire of it," said Amanda cheerfully, and gave him her hand. "But you already know Corunna El Man?"

"The El Man family are High Island neighbors," said Michael. He smiled at me for a second, almost sadly. "I remember the Captain from when I was only six years old and he was first home on leave. If you'll come along with me, please? I've already got your luggage in the bus."

"Bus?" I said, as we followed him toward one of the window-wall exits from the terminal.

"The band bus for Third Regiment. It was all I could get."

We emerged onto a small parking pad scattered with a number of atmosphere flyers and ground vehicles. Michael de Sandoval led us to a stubby-framed, powered lifting body that looked as if it could hold about thirty passengers. Inside, one person saved the vehicle from being completely empty. It was an Exotic in a dark blue robe, an Exotic with white hair and a strangely ageless face. He could have been anywhere between thirty and eighty years of age, and he was seated in the lounge area at the front of the bus, just before the compartment wall that divided off the control area in the vehicle's nose. He stood up as we came in.

"Padma, Outbond to Ceta," said Michael. "Sir, may I introduce Amanda Morgan, contracts adjuster, and Corunna El Man, senior ship captain, both from the Dorsai? Captain El Man just brought the adjuster in by courier."

"Of course, I know about their coming," said Padma.

He did not offer a hand to either of us. Nor did he rise. But, like many of the advanced Exotics I have known, he did not seem to need to. As with those others, there was a warmth and peace about him that the rest of us were immediately caught up in, and any behavior on his part seemed natural and expected.

We sat down together. Michael ducked into the control compartment, and a moment later, with a soft vibration, the bus lifted from the parking pad.

"It's an honor to meet you, Outbond," said Amanda. "But it's even more of an honor to have you *meet* us. What rates us that sort of attention?"

Padma smiled slightly.

"I'm afraid I didn't come just to meet you," he said to her. "Although Kensie Graeme's been telling me all about you, and"—he looked over at me—"even I've heard of Corunna El Man."

"Is there anything you Exotics don't hear about?" I said.

"Many things," he shook his head gently but seriously.

"What was the other reason that brought you to the spaceport then?" Amanda asked.

He looked at her thoughtfully.

"Something that has nothing to do with your coming," he said. "It happens I had a call to make to elsewhere on the planet, and the phones at Gebel Nahar are not as private as I like. When I heard Michael was coming to get you, I rode along to make my call from the terminal here."

"It wasn't a call on behalf of the Conde of Nahar then?" I asked.

"If it was—or if it was for anyone but myself"—he smiled—"I wouldn't want to betray a confidence by admitting it. I take it you know about El Conde? The titular ruler of Nahar?"

"I've been briefing myself on the colony and on Gebel Nahar ever since it turned out I needed to come here," Amanda answered.

I could see her signalling me to leave her alone with him. It showed in the way she sat and the angle at which she held her head. Exotics are perceptive, but I doubt that Padma picked up that subtle, private message.

"Excuse me," I told them. "I think I'll go have a word with Michael."

I got up and went through the door into the control section, closing it behind me. Michael sat relaxed, one hand on the control rod, and I sat down myself in the copilot's seat.

"How are things at home, sir?" he asked without turning his head from the sky ahead of us.

"I've only been back this once since you'd have left yourself," I said. "But it hasn't changed much. My father died last year."

"I'm sorry to hear that."

"Your father and mother are well—and I hear your brothers are all right, out among the stars," I said. "But, of course, you know that."

"No," he said, still watching the sky ahead. "I haven't heard for quite a while."

A silence threatened.

"How did you happen to end up here?" I asked. It was almost a ritual question between Dorsais away from home.

"I heard about Nahar. I thought I'd take a look at it."

"Did you know it was as fake Hispanic as it is?"

"Not fake," he said. "Something . . . but not that."

He was right, of course.

"Yes," I said. "I guess I shouldn't use the word fake. Situations like the one here come out of natural causes, like all others."

He looked directly at me. I had learned to read such looks since Else died. He was very close in that moment to telling me something more than he would probably have told anyone else. But the moment passed and he looked back out the windshield.

"You know the situation here?" he said.

"No. That's Amanda's job," I said. "I'm just a driver on this trip. Why don't you fill me in?"

"You must know some of it already," he said, "and Ian or Kensie Graeme will be telling you the rest. But in any case . . . the Conde's a figurehead. Literally. His father was set up with that title by the first Naharese immigrants, who're all now rich ranchers. They had a dream of starting their own hereditary aristocracy here, but that never really worked. Still, on paper, the Conde's the hereditary sovereign of Nahar, and in theory, the army belongs to him as commander in chief. But the army's always been drawn from the poor of Nahar—the city poor and the *campesinos*,—and they hate the rich first-immigrants. Now there's a revolution brewing, and the army doesn't know which way it'll jump."

"I see," I said. "So a violent change of government is on the way, and our contract here's with a government that may be out of power tomorrow. Amanda's got a problem."

"It's everyone's problem," Michael said. "The only reason the army hasn't declared itself for the revolutionaries is because its parts don't work together too well. Coming from the outside, the way you have, the ridiculousness of the locals' attitudes may be what catches your notice first. But actually those attitudes are all the nonrich have, here, outside of a bare existence—this business of the flags, the uniforms, the music, the duels over one wrong glance, and the idea of dying for your regiment—or being ready to go at the throat of any other regiment at the drop of a hat."

"But," I said, "what you're describing isn't any practical, working sort of military force."

"No. That's why Kensie and Ian were contracted in here, to do something about turning the local army into something like an actual defensive force. The other principalities around Nahar all have their eyes on the ranchlands here. Given a normal situation, the Graemes'd already be making progress—you know Ian's reputation for training troops. But the way it's turned out, the common soldiers here think of the Graemes as tools of the ranchers, the revolutionaries preach that they ought to be thrown out, and the regiments are noncooperating with them. I don't think they've got a hope of doing anything useful with the army under present conditions, and the situation's been getting more dangerous daily—for them, and now for you and Amanda as well. The truth is, I think Kensie and Ian'd be wise to take their loss on the contract and get out."

"If accepting loss and leaving was all there was to it, someone like Amanda wouldn't be needed here," I said. "There has to be more than that to involve the Dorsai in general."

He said nothing.

"How about you?" I said. 'What's your position here? You're Dorsai, too."

"Am I?" he said to the windshield in a low voice.

I had at last touched on what had been going unspoken between us. There was a name for individuals like Michael, back home. They were called "lost Dorsai." The name was not used for those who had chosen something other than a military vocation. It was reserved for those of Dorsai heritage who seemed to have chosen their life work, whatever it was, and then—suddenly and without explanation—abandoned it. In Michael's case, as I knew, he had graduated from the Academy with honors, but after graduation, he had abruptly withdrawn his name from assignment and left the planet, with no explanation even to his family.

"I'm bandmaster of the Third Naharese Regiment," he said now. "My regiment likes me. The local people don't class me with the rest of you, generally—" He smiled a little sadly again. "Except that I don't get challenged to duels."

"I see," I said.

"Yes." He looked over at me now. "So, while the army is still technically obedient to the Conde, as its commander in chief, actually just about everything's come to a halt. That's why I had trouble getting transportation from the vehicle pool to pick you up."

"I see—," I repeated. I had been about to ask him some more, but just then the door to the control compartment opened behind us and Amanda stepped in.

"Well, Corunna," she said, "how about giving me a chance to talk with Michael?"

She smiled past me at him, and he smiled back. I did not think he had been strongly taken by her—whatever was hidden in him was a barrier to anything like that. But her very presence, with all it implied of home, was plainly warming to him.

"Go ahead," I said, getting up. "I'll go say a word or two to the Outbond."

"He's worth talking to," Amanda spoke after me as I went.

I stepped out, closed the door behind me, and rejoined Padma in the lounge area. He was looking out the window beside him and down at the plains that lay between the town and the small mountain from which Gebel Nahar took its name. The city we had just left was on a small rise west of that mountain, with suburban and planted areas in between. Around and beyond that mountain—for the fortlike residence that was Gebel Nahar faced east—the actual, open grazing land of the cattle plains began. Our bus was one of those vehicles designed to fly ordinarily at about treetop level—though of course it could go right up to the limits of the atmosphere in a pinch—but right now we were about three hundred meters up. As I stepped out of the control compartment, Padma took his attention from the window and looked back at me.

"Your Amanda's amazing," he said as I sat down facing him, "for someone so young."

"She said something like that about you," I told him. "But in her case, she's not quite as young as she looks."

"I know," Padma smiled. "I was speaking from the viewpoint of my own age. To me, even you seem young."

I laughed. What I had had of youth had been far back, some years before Baunpore. But it was true that, in terms of years, I was not even middle-aged.

"Michael's been telling me that a revolution seems to be brewing here in Nahar," I said to him.

"Yes." He sobered.

"That wouldn't be what brings someone like you to Gebel Nahar?"

His hazel eyes were suddenly amused.

"I thought Amanda was the one with the questions," he said.

"Are you surprised I ask?" I said. "This is an out-of-the-way location for the Outbond to a full planet."

"True." He shook his head. "But the reasons that bring me here are Exotic ones. Which means, I'm afraid, that I'm not free to discuss them."

"But you know about the local movement toward a revolution?"

"Oh, yes." He sat in perfectly relaxed stillness, his hands loosely together in the lap of his robe, light brown against the dark blue. His face was calm and unreadable. "It's part of the overall pattern of events on this world."

"Just this world?"

He smiled back at me.

"Of course," he said gently, "our Exotic science of ontogenetics deals with the interaction of all known human and natural forces, on all the inhabited worlds. But the situation here in Nahar, and specifically the situation at Gebel Nahar, is primarily a result of local, Cetan forces."

"International planetary politics."

"Yes," he said. "Nahar is surrounded by five other principalities, none of which have cattle-raising land like this. They'd all like to have a part or all of this colony in their control."

"Which ones are backing the revolutionaries?"

He gazed out the window for a moment without speaking. It was a presumptuous thought on my part to imagine that my strange geas, which made people want to tell me private things, would work on an Exotic. But for a moment I had had the familiar feeling that he was about to open up to me.

"My apologies," he said at last. "It may be that in my old age I'm falling into the habit of treating everyone else like—children."

"How old are you then?"

He smiled.

"Old—and getting older."

"In any case," I said, "you don't have to apologize to me. It'll be an unusual situation when bordering countries don't take sides in a neighbor's revolution."

"Of course," he said. "Actually, all of the five think they have a hand in it on the side of the revolutionaries. Bad as Nahar is now, it would be a shambles after a successful revolution, with everybody fighting everybody else for different goals. The other principalities all look for a situation in which they can move in and gain. But you're quite right. International politics is always at work, and it's never simple."

"What's fueling this situation then?"

"William," Padma looked directly at me, and for the first time, I felt the remarkable effect of his hazel eyes. His face held such a calmness that all his expression seemed to be concentrated in those eyes.

"William?" I asked.

"William of Ceta."

"That's right," I said, remembering. "He owns this world, doesn't he?"

"It's not really correct to say he owns it," Padma said. "He controls most of it—and a great many parts of other worlds. Our present-day version of a merchant prince, in many ways. But he doesn't control everything, even here on Ceta. For example, the Naharese ranchers have always banded together tightly to deal with him, and his best efforts to split them apart and gain a direct authority in Nahar haven't worked. He controls after a fashion, but only by manipulating the outside conditions that the ranchers have to deal with."

"So he's the one behind the revolution?"

"Yes."

It was plain enough to me that it was William's involvement here that had brought Padma to this backwater section of the planet. The Exotic science of ontogenetics, which was essentially a study of how humans interacted, both as individuals and societies, was something they took very seriously, and William, as one of the movers and shakers of our time, would always have his machinations closely watched by them.

"Well, it's nothing to do with us, at any rate," I said, "except as it affects the Graemes' contract."

"Not entirely," he said. "William, like most gifted individuals, knows the advantage of killing two, or even fifty, birds with one stone. He hires a good many mercenaries, directly and indirectly. It would benefit him if events here could lower the Dorsai reputation and the market value of its military individuals."

"I see—," I began, and broke off as the hull of the bus rang suddenly— as if to a sharp blow.

"Down!" I said, pulling Padma to the floor of the vehicle and away from the window beside which we had been sitting. One good thing about Exotics—they trust you to know your own line of work. He obeyed me instantly and without protest. We waited . . . but there was no repetition of the sound.

"What was it?" he asked after a moment, but without moving from where I had brought him.

"Solid projectile slug. Probably from a heavy hand weapon," I told him. "We've been shot at. Stay down, if you please, Outbond."

I got up myself, staying low and to the center of the bus, and went through the door into the control compartment. Amanda and Michael both looked around at me as I entered, their faces alert.

"Who's out to get us?' I asked Michael.

He shook his head.

"I don't know," he said. "Here in Nahar, it could be anything or anybody. It could be the revolutionaries or simply someone who doesn't like the Dorsai—or someone who doesn't like Exotics—or even someone who doesn't like me. Finally, it could be someone drunk, drugged, or just in a macho mood."

"—who also has a military hand weapon."

"There's that," Michael said. "But everyone in Nahar is armed, and most of them, legitimately or not, own military weapons."

He nodded at the windscreen.

"Anyway, we're almost down," he said.

I looked out. The interlocked mass of buildings that was the government seat called Gebel Nahar was sprawled halfway down from the top of the small mountain, just below us. In the tropical sunlight, it looked like a resort hotel, built on terraces that descended the steep slope. The only difference was that each terrace terminated in a wall, and the lowest of the walls were ramparts of solid fortifications, with heavy weapons emplaced along them. Gebel Nahar, properly garrisoned, should have been able to dominate the countryside against surface troops all the way out to the horizon, at least on this side of the mountain.

"What's the other side like?" I asked.

"Mountaineering cliff—there's heavy weapon emplacements cut out of the rock there, too, and reached by tunnels going clear through the mountain," Michael answered. "The ranchers spared no expense when they built this place. Gallego thinking. They and their families might all have to hole up here one day."

But a few moments later we were on the poured concrete surface of a vehicle pool. The three of us went back into the body of the bus to rejoin Padma, and Michael let us out of the vehicle. Outside, the parking area was abnormally silent.

"I don't know what's happened—," said Michael as we set foot outside. We three Dorsai had checked, instinctively, ready to retreat back into the bus and take off again if necessary.

A voice shouting from somewhere beyond the ranked flyers and surface vehicles brought our heads around. There was the sound of running feet, and a moment later a soldier wearing an energy sidearm, but dressed in the green and red Naharese army uniform with band tabs, burst into sight and slid to a halt, panting before us.

"Sir—," he wheezed, in the local dialect of archaic Spanish. "Gone—"

We waited for him to get his breath; after a second, he tried again.

"They've deserted, sir!" he said to Michael, trying to pull himself to attention. "They've gone—all the regiments—everybody!"

"When?" asked Michael.

"Two hours past. It was all planned. Certainly, it was planned. In each group, at the same time, a man stood up. He said that now was the time to desert, to show the *ricones* where the army stood. They all marched out, with their flags, their guns, everything. Look!"

He turned and pointed. We looked. The vehicle pool was on the fifth or sixth level down from the top of the Gebel Nahar. It was possible to see, from this as from any of the other levels, straight out for miles over the plains. Looking now we saw, so far off no other sign was visible, the tiny, occasional twinkles of reflected sunlight, seemingly right on the horizon.

"They are camped out there, waiting for an army they say will come from all the other countries around to reinforce them and accomplish the revolution."

"Everyone's gone?" Michael's words in Spanish brought the soldier's eyes back to him.

"All but us. The soldiers of your band, sir. We are the Conde's Elite Guard now."

"Where are the two Dorsai commanders?"

"In their offices, sir."

"I'll have to go to them right away," said Michael to the rest of us. "Outbond, will you wait in your quarters, or will you come along with us?"

"I'll come," said Padma.

The five of us went across the parking area between the crowded vehicles and into a maze of corridors. Through these at last we found our way to a large suite of offices, where the outward wall of each room was all window. Through the window of the one we were in, we looked out on the plain below, where the distant and all but invisible Naharese regiments were now camped. We found Kensie and Ian Graeme together in one of the inner offices, standing talking before a massive desk large enough to serve as a conference table for a half-dozen people.

They turned as we came in—and once again I was hit by the curious illusion that I usually experienced on meeting these two. It was striking enough whenever I approached one of them, but when the twins were together, the effect was enhanced.

In my own mind I had always laid it to the fact that in spite of their size—and either one is nearly a head taller than I am—they are so evenly proportioned physically that their true dimensions do not register on you until you have something to measure them by. From a distance, it is easy to take them for not much more than ordinary height. Then, having unconsciously underestimated them, you or someone else whose size you know approaches them, and it is that individual who seems to change in size as he, or she, or you get close. If it is you, you are very aware of the change. But if it is someone else, you can still seem to shrink somewhat, along with that other person. To feel yourself become smaller in relationship to someone else is a strange sensation, if the phenomenon is entirely subjective.

In this case, the measuring element turned out to be Amanda, who ran to the two brothers the minute we entered the room. Her home, Fal Morgan, was the homestead closest to the Graeme home of Foralie, and the three of them had grown up together. As I said, she was not a small woman, but by the time she had reached them and was hugging Kensie, she seemed to have become not only tiny, but fragile, and suddenly— again, as it always does—the room seemed to orient itself about the two Graemes.

I followed her and held out my hand to Ian.

"Corunna!" he said. He was one of the few who still called me by the first of my personal names. His large hand wrapped around mine. His face—so different from, yet so like his twin brother's—looked down into mine. In truth, they were identical, and yet there was all the difference in the universe between them. Only it was not a physical difference, for all its powerful effect on the eye. Literally, it was that Ian was lightless, and all the bright element that might have been in him was instead in his brother, so that Kensie radiated double the human normal amount of sunny warmth. Dark and light. Night and day. Brother and brother.

And yet, there was a closeness, an identity, between them of a kind that I have never seen in any other two human beings.

"Do you have to go back right away?" Ian was asking me. "Or will you be staying to take Amanda back?"

"I can stay," I said. "My leave-time to the Dorsai wasn't that tight. Can I be of use here?"

"Yes," Ian said. "You and I should talk. Just a minute, though—"

He turned to greet Amanda in his turn and tell Michael to check and see if the Conde was available for a visit. Michael went out with the soldier who had met us at the vehicle pool. It seemed that Michael and his bandsmen, plus a handful of servants and the Conde himself, added up to the total present population of Gebel Nahar, outside of those in this room. The ramparts were designed to be defended by a handful of people, if necessary, but we had barely more than a handful in the forty members of the regimental band Michael had led, and they were evidently untrained in anything but marching.

We left Kensie with Amanda and Padma. Ian led me into an adjoining office, waved me to a chair, and took one himself.

"I don't know the situation on your present contract—," he began.

"There's no problem. My contract's to a space force leased by William of Ceta. I'm leader of Red Flight under the overall command of Hendrik Galt. Aside from the fact that Galt would understand, as any other Dorsai would, if a situation like this warranted it, his forces aren't doing anything at the moment. Which is why I was on leave in the first place, along with half his other senior officers. I'm not William's officer. I'm Galt's."

"Good," said Ian. He turned his head to look past the high wing of the chair he was sitting in and out over the plain where the little flashes of light were visible. His arms lay relaxed upon the arms of the chair, his massive hands loosely curved about the ends. There was, as there always had been, something utterly lonely but utterly invincible about Ian. Most non-Dorsais seem to draw a noticeable comfort from having a Dorsai around in times of physical danger, as if they assumed that any one of us would know the right thing to do and do it. It may sound fanciful, but I have to say that in somewhat the same way as the non-Dorsai reacted to the Dorsai, so did most of the Dorsai I've known always react to Ian.

But not all of us. Kensie never had, of course. Nor, come to think of it, had any of the other Graemes, to my knowledge. But then, there had always been something—not solitary, but independent and apart—about each of the Graemes. Even Kensie. It was a characteristic of the family. Only, Ian had that double share of it.

"It'll take them two days to settle in out there," he said now, nodding at the nearly invisible encampments on the plain. "After that, they'll either have to move against us, or they'll start fighting among themselves. That means we can expect to be overrun here in two days."

"Unless what?" I asked. He looked back at me.

"There's always an unless," I said.

"Unless Amanda can find us an honorable way out of the situation," he said. "As it now stands, there doesn't seem to be any way out. Our only hope is that she can find something in the contract or the situation that the rest of us have overlooked. Drink?"

"Thanks."

He got up and went to a sideboard, poured a couple of glasses half-full of dark brown liquor, and brought them back. He sat down once more, handing a glass to me, and I sniffed at its pungent darkness.

"Dorsai whiskey," I said. "You're provided for here."

He nodded. We drank.

"Isn't there anything you think she might be able to use?" I asked.

"No," he said. "It's a hope against hope. An honor problem."

"What makes it so sensitive that you need an adjuster from home?" I asked.

"William. You know him, of course. But how much do you know about the situation here in Nahar?"

I repeated to him what I had picked up from Michael and Padma.

"Nothing else?" he asked.

"I haven't had time to find out anything else. I was asked to bring Amanda here on the spur of the moment, so on the way out I had my hands full. Also, she was busy studying the available data on this situation herself. We didn't talk much."

"William—," he said, putting his glass down on a small table by his chair. "Well, it's my fault we're into this, rather than Kensie's. I'm the strategist, he's the tactician on this contract. The large picture was my job, and I didn't look far enough."

"If there were things the Naharese government didn't tell you when the contract was under discussion, then there's your out, right there."

"Oh, the contract's challengeable, all right," Ian said. He smiled. I know there are those who like to believe that he never smiles, and that notion is nonsense. But his smile is like all the rest of him. "It wasn't the information they held back that's trapped us, it's this matter of honor. Not just our personal honor—the reputation and honor of all Dorsai. They've got us in a position where whether we stay and die or go and live, it'll tarnish the planetary reputation."

I frowned at him.

"How can they do that? How could you get caught in that sort of trap?"

"Partly"—Ian lifted his glass, drank, and put it back down again—"because William's an extremely able strategist himself—again, as you know. Partly because it didn't occur to me, or Kensie, that we were getting into a three-party rather than a two-party agreement."

"I don't follow you."

"The situation in Nahar," he said, "was always one with its built-in termination clause—I mean, for the ranchers, the original settlers. The type of country they tried to set up was something that could only exist under uncrowded, near-pioneering conditions. The principalities around their grazing area got settled in some fifty Cetan years ago. After that, the neighboring countries got built up and industrialized, and the semi-feudal notion of open plains and large individual holdings of land got to be impractical on the international level of this world. Of course, the first settlers, those Gallegos from Galicia in northwest Spain, saw that coming from the start. That was why they built this place we're sitting in."

His smile came again.

"But that was back when they were only trying to delay the inevitable," he said. "Sometime in more recent years they evidently decided to come to terms with it."

"Bargain with the more modern principalities around them, you mean?" I said.

"Bargain with the rest of Ceta, in fact," he said. "And the rest of Ceta, nowadays, is William—for all practical purposes."

"There again, if they had an agreement with William that they didn't tell you about," I said, "you've every excuse, in honor as well as on paper, to void the contract. I don't see the difficulty."

"Their deal they've got with William isn't a written or even a spoken contract," Ian answered. "What the ranchers did was let him know that he could have the control he wanted here in Nahar—as I said, it was obvious they were going to lose it eventually, anyway—if not to him, to someone or something else—if he'd meet their terms."

"And what were they after in exchange?"

"A guarantee that their lifestyle and this pocket culture they'd developed would be maintained and protected."

He looked under his dark brows at me.

"I see," I said. "How did they think William could do that?"

"They didn't know. But they didn't worry about it. That's the slippery part. They just let the fact be known to William that if they got what they wanted, they'd stop fighting his attempts to control Nahar directly. They left it up to him to find the ways to meet their price. That's why there's no other contract we can cite as an excuse to break this one."

I drank from my own glass.

"It sounds like William. If I know him," I said, "he'd even enjoy engineering whatever situation was needed to keep this country fifty years behind the times. But it sounded to me earlier as if you were saying that he was trying to get something out of the Dorsai at the same time. What good does it do him if you have to make a penalty payment for breaking this contract? It won't bankrupt you Graemes to pay it, will it? And even if you had to borrow from general Dorsai contingency funds, it wouldn't be more than a pinprick against those funds. Also, you still haven't explained this business of your being trapped here, not by the contract, but by the general honor of the Dorsai."

Ian nodded.

"William's taken care of both things," he said. "His plan was for the Naharese to hire Dorsai to make their army a working unit. Then his revolutionary agents would cause a revolt of that army. Then, with matters out of hand, he could step in with his own non-Dorsai officers to control the situation and bring order back to Nahar."

"I see," I said.

"He then would mediate the matter," Ian went on, "the revolutionary people would be handed some limited say in the government—under his outside control, of course—and the ranchers would give up their absolute local authority, but little of anything else. They'd stay in charge of their ranches, as his managers, with all his wealth and forces to back them against any real push for control by the real revolutionary faction, which would eventually be tamed and brought in line, also—the way he's tamed and brought in line all the rest of this world, and some good-sized chunks of other worlds."

"So," I said thoughtfully, "what he's after is to show that his military people can do things Dorsai can't?"

"You follow me," said Ian. "We command the price we do now only because military like ourselves are in limited supply. If they want Dorsai results—military situations dealt with at either no cost or a minimum cost, in life and material—they have to hire Dorsai. That's as it stands now. But if it looks like others can do the same job as well or better, our price has to go down, and the Dorsai will begin to starve."

"It'd take some years for the Dorsai to starve. In that time we could live down the results of this, maybe."

"But it goes farther than that. William isn't the first to dream of being able to hire all the Dorsai and use them as a personal force to dominate the worlds. We've never considered allowing all our working people to end up in one camp. But if William can depress our price below what we need to keep the Dorsai free and independent, then he can offer us wages better than the market—survival wages, available from him alone— and we'll have no choice but to accept."

"Then you've got no choice yourself," I said. "You've got to break this contract, no matter what it costs."

"I'm afraid not," he answered. "The cost looks right now to be the one we can't afford to pay. As I said, we're damned if we do, damned if we don't—caught in the jaws of this nutcracker unless Amanda can find us a way out—"

The door to the office where we were sitting opened at that moment, and Amanda herself looked in.

"It seems some local people calling themselves the Governors have just arrived—" Her tone was humorous, but every line of her body spoke of serious concern. "Evidently, I'm supposed to go and talk with them right away. Are you coming, Ian?"

"Kensie is all you'll need," Ian said. "We've trained them to realize that they don't necessarily get both of us on deck every time they whistle. You'll find it's just another step in the dance anyway—there's nothing to be done with them."

"All right." She started to withdraw, stopped. "Can Padma come with us?"

"Check with Kensie. I'd say it's best not to ruffle the Governors' feathers by asking to let him sit in right now."

"That's all right," she said. "Kensie already thought not, but he said I should ask you."

She went out.

"Sure you don't want to be there?" I asked him.

"No need." He got up. "There's something I want to show you. It's important you understand the situation here thoroughly. If Kensie and myself should both be knocked out, Amanda would only have you to help her handle things—and if you're certain about being able to stay?"

"As I said," I repeated, "I can stay."

"Fine. Come along then. I wanted you to meet the Conde de Nahar. But I've been waiting to hear from Michael as to whether the Conde's receiving right now. We won't wait any longer. Let's go see how the old gentleman is."

"Won't he—the Conde, I mean—be at this meeting with Amanda and the Governors?"

Ian led the way out of the room.

"Not if there's serious business to be talked about. On paper, the Conde controls everything but the Governors. They elect him. Of course, aside from the paper, they're the ones who really control everything."

We left the suite of offices and began to travel the corridors of Gebel Nahar once more. Twice we took lift tubes and once we rode a motorized strip down one long corridor, but at the end, Ian pushed open a door and we stepped into what was obviously the orderly room fronting a barracks section.

The soldier bandsman seated behind the desk there came to his feet immediately at the sight of us—or perhaps it was just at the sight of Ian.

"Sirs!" he said in Spanish.

"I ordered Mr. de Sandoval to find out for me if the Conde would receive Captain El Man and myself," Ian said in the same language. "Do you know where the bandmaster is now?"

"No, sir. He has not come back. Sir—it is not always possible to contact the Conde quickly—"

"I'm aware of that," said Ian. "Rest easy. Mr. de Sandoval's due back here shortly then?"

"Yes, sir. Any minute now. Would the sirs care to wait in the bandmaster's office?"

"Yes," said Ian.

The orderly turned aside, lifting his hand in a decidedly nonmilitary gesture to usher us past his desk through a farther entrance into a larger room, very orderly and with a clean desk, but crowded with filing cabinets and with its walls hung with musical instruments.

Most of these were ones I had never seen before, although they were all variants on string or wind musicmakers. There was one that looked like an early Scottish bagpipe. It had only a single drone, some seventy centimeters long, and a chanter about half that length. Another was obviously a keyed bugle of some sort, but with most of its central body length wrapped with red cord ending in dependent tassels. I moved about the walls, examining each as I came to it, while Ian took a chair and watched me. I came back at length to the deprived bagpipe.

"Can you play this?" I asked Ian.

"I'm not a piper," said Ian. "I can blow a bit, of course—but I've never played anything but regular highland pipes. You'd better ask Michael if you want a demonstration. Apparently, he plays everything—and plays it well."

I turned away from the walls and took a seat myself.

"What do you think?" asked Ian. I was gazing around the office.

I looked back at him and saw his gaze curiously upon me.

"It's . . . strange," I said.

And the room was strange, for reasons that would probably never strike someone not a Dorsai. No two people keep an office the same way, but just as there are subtle characteristics by which one born to the Dorsai will recognize another, so there are small signals about the office of anyone on military duty and from that world. I could tell at a glance, as could Ian or any one of us, if the officer into whose room we had just stepped was Dorsai or not. The clues lie, not so much with what was in the room, as in the way the things there and the room itself was arranged. There is nothing particular to Dorsai-born individuals about such a recognition. Almost any veteran officer is able to tell you whether the owner of the office he has just stepped into is also a veteran officer, Dorsai or not. But in that case, as in this, it would be easier to give the answer than to list the reasons why the answer was what it was.

So, Michael de Sandoval's office was unmistakably the office of a Dorsai. At the same time, it owned a strange difference from any other Dorsai's office that almost shouted at us. The difference was a basic one, underneath any comparison of this place with the office of a Dorsai who had his walls hung with weapons, or with one who kept a severely clean desktop and message baskets and preferred no weapon in sight.

"He's got these musical instruments displayed as if they were fighting tools," I said.

Ian nodded. It was not necessary to put the implication into words. If Michael had chosen to hang a banner from one of the walls testifying to the fact that he would absolutely refuse to lay his hands upon a weapon, he could not have announced himself more plainly to Ian and myself.

"It seems to be a strong point with him," I said. "I wonder what happened?"

"His business, of course," said Ian.

"Yes," I said.

But the discovery hurt me—because suddenly I identified what I had felt in young Michael from the first moment I had met him, here on Ceta. It was pain, a deep and abiding pain, and you cannot have known someone since he was in childhood and not be moved by that sort of pain.

The orderly stuck his head into the room.

"Sirs," he said, "the bandmaster comes. He'll be here in one minute."

"Thank you," said Ian.

A moment later, Michael came in.

"Sorry to keep you waiting—," he began.

"Perfectly all right," Ian said. "The Conde made you wait yourself before letting you speak with him, didn't he?"

"Yes, sir."

"Well, is he available now, to be met by me and Captain El Man?"

"Yes, sir. You're both most welcome."

"Good."

Ian stood up and so did I. We went out, followed by Michael to the door of his office.

"Amanda Morgan is seeing the Governors at the moment," Ian said to him as we left him. "She may want to talk to you after that's over. You might keep yourself available to her."

"I'll be right here," said Michael. "Sir—I wanted to apologize for my orderly's making excuses about my not being here when you came." He glanced over at the orderly, who looked embarrassed. "My men have been told not to—"

"It's all right, Michael," said Ian. "You'd be an unusual Dorsai if they didn't try to protect you."

"Still—," said Michael.

"Still," said Ian. "I know they've trained only as bandsmen. They may be line troops at the moment—all the line troops we've got to hold this place with—but I'm not expecting miracles."

"Well," said Michael. "Thank you, Commander."

"You're welcome."

We went out. Once more, Ian led me through a maze of corridors and lifts.

"How many of his band decided to stay with him when the regiments moved out?" I asked as we went.

"All of them," said Ian.

"And no one else stayed?"

Ian looked at me with a glint of humor.

"You have to remember," he said, "Michael did graduate from the Academy, after all."

A final short distance down a wide corridor brought us to a massive pair of double doors. Ian touched a visitor's button on the right-hand door and spoke to an annunciator panel in Spanish.

"Commander Ian Graeme and Captain El Man are here with permission to see the Conde."

There was a pause of a moment and then one of the doors opened to show us another of Michael's bandsmen.

"Be pleased to come in, sirs," he said.

"Thank you," Ian said as we walked past. "Where's the Conde's major-domo?"

"He is gone, sir. Also most of the other servants."

"I see."

The room we had just been let into was a wide lobby filled with enormous and magnificently kept furniture, but lacking any windows. The bandsman led us through two more rooms like it, also without windows, until we were finally ushered into a third, window-walled room, with the same unchanging view of the plains below. A stick-thin old man dressed in black was standing with the help of a silver-headed cane before the center of the window.

The soldier faded out of the room. Ian led me to the old man.

"El Conde," he said, still in Spanish, "may I introduce Captain Corunna El Man. Captain, you have the honor of meeting El Conde de Nahar, Macias Francisco Ramón Manuel Valentin y Compostela y Abente."

"You are welcome, Captain El Man," said the Conde. He spoke a more correct, if more archaic, Spanish than that of the other Naharese I had so far met, and his voice was the thin remnant of what once must have been a remarkable bass. "We will sit down now, if you please. If my age produces a weakness, it is that it is wearisome to stand for any length of time."

We settled ourselves in heavy, overstuffed chairs with massively padded arms—more like thrones than chairs.

"Captain El Man," said Ian, "happened to be on leave, back on the Dorsai. He volunteered to bring Amanda Morgan here to discuss the present situation with the Governors. She's talking to them now."

"I have not met . . ." The Conde hesitated over her name. ". . . Amanda Morgan."

"She is one of our experts of the sort that the present situation calls for."

"I would like to meet her."

"She's looking forward to meeting you."

"Possibly this evening? I would have liked to have had all of you to dinner, but you know, I suppose, that most of my servants have gone."

"I just learned that," said Ian.

"They may go," said the Conde. "They will not be allowed to return. Nor will the regiments who have deserted their duty be allowed to return to my armed forces."

"With the Conde's indulgence," said Ian, "we don't yet know all the reasons for their leaving. It may be that some leniency is justified."

"I can think of none." The Conde's voice was thin with age, but his back was as erect as a flagstaff and his dark eyes did not waver. "But if you think there is some reason for it, I can reserve judgment momentarily."

"We'd appreciate that," Ian said.

"You are very lenient." The Conde looked at me. His voice took on an unexpected timbre. "Captain, has the commander here told you? Those deserters out there"—he flicked a finger toward the window and the plains beyond—"under the instigation of people calling themselves revolutionaries, have threatened to take over Gebel Nahar. If they dare to come here, I and what few loyal servants remain will resist. To the death!"

"The Governors—," Ian began.

"The Governors have nothing to say in the matter!" the Conde turned fiercely on him. "Once, they—their fathers and grandfathers, rather—chose my father to be El Conde. I inherited that title and neither they, nor anyone else in the universe has the authority to take it from me. While I live, I will be El Conde, and the only way I will cease to be El Conde will be when death takes me. I will remain, I will fight—alone if need be—as long as I am able. But I will retreat, never! I will compromise, *never*!"

He continued to talk, for some minutes, but although his words changed, the message of them remained the same. He would not give an inch to anyone who wished to change the governmental system in Nahar. If he had been obviously uninformed or ignorant of the implications of what he was saying, it would have been easy to let his words blow by unheeded. But this was obviously not the case. His frailty was all in the thin old body. His mind was not only clear, but fully aware of the situation. What he announced was simply an unshakable determination never to yield in spite of reason or the overwhelming odds against him.

After a while he ran down. He apologized graciously for his emotion, but not for his attitude, and, after a few minutes more of meaninglessly polite conversation on the history of Gebel Nahar itself, let us leave.

"So you see part of our problem," said Ian to me when we were alone again, walking back to his offices.

We went a little distance together in silence.

"Part of that problem," I said, "seems to lie in the difference between our idea of honor and theirs, here."

"And William's complete lack of it," said Ian. "You're right. With us, honor's a matter of the individual's obligation to himself and his community—which can end up being to the human race in general. To the Naharese, honor's an obligation only to one's own soul."

I laughed involuntarily.

"I'm sorry," I said as he looked at me. "But you hit it almost too closely. Did you ever read Calderon's poem about the mayor of Zalamea?"

"I don't think so. Calderon?"

"Pedro Calderon de la Barca, seventeenth century Spanish poet. He wrote a poem called *El Alcalde de Zalamea*."

I gave him the lines he had reminded me of.

> *Al Rey la hacienda y la vida*
> *Se ha de dar; pero el honor*
> *Es patrimonio del alma*
> *Y el alma soló es de Dios.*

"'Fortune and life we owe to the King,'" murmured Ian, "'but honor is patrimony of the soul and the soul belongs to God alone.' I see what you mean."

I started to say something, then decided it was too much effort. I was aware of Ian glancing sideways at me as we went.

"When did you eat last?" he asked.

"I don't remember," I said. "But I don't particularly need food right now."

"You need sleep then," said Ian. "I'm not surprised, after the way you made it here from the Dorsai. When we get back to the office, I'll call one of Michael's men to show you your quarters, and you'd better sleep in. I can make your excuses to the Conde if he still wants us all to get together tonight."

"Yes. Good," I said. "I'd appreciate that."

Now that I had admitted to tiredness, it was an effort even to think. For those who have never navigated between the stars, it is easy to forget the implications of the fact that the danger increases rapidly with the distance moved in a single shift—beyond a certain safe amount of light-years. We had exceeded safe limits as far as I had dared push them on each of the six shifts that had brought Amanda and myself to Ceta.

It's not just that danger—the danger of finding yourself with so large an error in navigation that you cannot recognize any familiar star patterns from which to navigate. It is the fact that even when you emerge in known space, a large error factor requires infinitely more recalculation to locate your position. It is vital to locate yourself to a fine enough point so that your error on the next shift will not be compounded and you will find yourself lost beyond repair.

For three days I had had no more than catnaps between periods of
calculation. I was numb with a fatigue I had held at bay until this moment
with the body adrenaline that can be evoked to meet an emergency.

When the bandsman supplied by Ian had shown me at last to a suite
of rooms, I found I wanted nothing more than to collapse on the enormous
bed in the bedroom. But years of instinct made me prowl the quarters
first and check them out. My suite consisted of three rooms and bathroom,
and it had the inevitable plains-facing window wall—with one difference.
This one had a door in it to let me out onto a small balcony running the
length of this particular level. It was divided into a semi-private outdoor
area for each suite by tall plants in pots. These acted as screens at each
division point.

I checked the balcony area and the suite, locked the doors to the hall
and to the balcony, and slept.

It was sometime after dark when I suddenly awoke. I was awake and
sitting up on the edge of the bed in one reflex movement before it
registered that what had roused me had been the sound of the call chime
at the front door of my suite.

I reached over and keyed on the annunciator circuit.

"Yes?" I said. "Who is it?"

"Michael de Sandoval," said Michael's voice. "Can I come in?"

I touched the stud that unlocked the door. It swung open, letting a
knife-blade sharp swath of light from the corridor into the darkness of
my sitting room, as seen through the entrance from my bedroom. I was
up on my feet now and moving to meet him in the sitting room. He
entered and the door closed behind him.

"What is it?" I asked.

"The ventilating system is out on this level," he said, and I realized
that the air in the suite was now perfectly motionless—motionless and
beginning to be a little warm and stuffy. Evidently, Gebel Nahar had been
designed to be sealed against outside atmosphere.

"I wanted to check the quarters of everyone on this level," Michael
said. "Interior doors aren't so tight that you would have asphyxiated, but
the breathing could have gotten a little heavy. Maybe by morning we can
locate what's out of order and fix it. This is part of the problem of the
servant staff taking off when the army did. I'd suggest that I open the
door to the balcony for you, sir."

He was already moving across the room toward the door he had mentioned.

"Thanks," I said. "What was the situation with the servants? Were they
revolutionary sympathizers, too?"

"Not necessarily." He unlocked the door and propped it open to the
night air, which came coolly and sweetly through the aperture. "They

just didn't want their throats cut along with the Conde's, when the army stormed its way back in here."

"I see," I said.

"Yes." He came back to me in the center of the sitting room.

"What time is it?" I asked. "I've been sleeping as if I was under drugs."

"A little before midnight."

I sat down in one of the chairs of the unlighted lounge. The glow of the soft exterior lights spaced at ten-meter intervals along the outer edge of the balcony came through the window wall and dimly illuminated the room.

"Sit for a moment," I said. "Tell me. How did the meeting with the Conde go this evening?"

He took a chair facing me.

"I should be getting back soon," he said. "I'm the only one we've got available for a duty officer at the moment. But—the meeting with the Conde went like a charm. He was so busy being gracious to Amanda, he almost forgot to breathe defiance against the army deserters."

"How did Amanda do with the Governors, do you know?"

I sensed, rather than saw, a shrug of his shoulders in the gloom.

"There was nothing much to be done with them," he said. "They talked about their concern over the desertion of the regiments and wanted reassurances that Ian and Kensie could handle the situation. Effectively, it was all choreographed."

"They've left then?"

"That's right. They asked for guarantees for the safety of the Conde. Both Ian and Kensie told them that there was no such thing as a guarantee, but that we'd protect the Conde, of course, with every means at our disposal. Then they left."

"It sounds," I said, "as if Amanda could have saved her time and effort."

"No. She said she wanted to get the feel of them." He leaned forward. "You know, she's something to write home about. I think if anyone can find a way out of this, she can. She says herself that there's no question that there is a way out—it's just that finding it in the next twenty-four to thirty-six hours is asking a lot."

"Has she checked with you about these people? You seem to be the only one around who knows them at all well."

"She talked with me when we flew in—you remember. I told her I'd be available any time she needed me. So far, however, she's spent most of her time either working by herself, or with Ian or Padma."

"I see," I said. "Is there anything I can do? Would you like me to spell you on the duty officer bit?"

"You're to rest, Ian says. He'll need you tomorrow. I'm getting along fine with my duties." He moved toward the front door of the suite. "Goodnight."

"Goodnight," I said.

He went out, the knife of light from the corridor briefly cutting across the carpeting of my sitting room and vanishing again as the door opened, then latched behind him.

I stayed where I was in the sitting room chair, enjoying the gentle night breeze through the propped-open door. I may have dozed. At any rate, I came to suddenly to the sound of voices from the balcony. Not from my portion of the balcony, but from the portion next to it, beyond my bedroom window to the left.

". . . yes," a voice was saying. Ian had been in my mind, and for a second I thought I was hearing Ian speak. But it was Kensie. The voices were identical, only, there was a difference in attitude that distinguished them.

"I don't know . . ." It was Amanda's voice answering, a troubled voice.

"Time goes by quickly," Kensie said. "Look at us. It was just yesterday we were in school together."

"I know," she said. "You're talking about it being time to settle down. But maybe I never will."

"How sure are you of that?"

"Not sure, of course." Her voice changed as if she had moved some little distance from him. I had an unexpected mental image of him standing back by the door in a window wall through which they had just come out together, and of her, having just turned and walked to the balcony railing, where she now stood with her back to him, looking out at the night and the starlit plain.

"Then you could take the idea of settling down under consideration."

"No," she said. "I know I don't want to do that."

Her voice changed again, as if she had turned and come back to him. "Maybe I'm ghostridden, Kensie. Maybe it's the old spirit of the first Amanda that's ruling out the ordinary things for me."

"She married—three times."

"But her husbands weren't important to her that way. Oh, I know she loved them. I've read her letters and what her children wrote down about her after they were adults themselves. But she really belonged to everyone, not just to her husbands and children. Don't you understand? I think that's the way it's going to have to be for me, too."

He said nothing. After a long moment she spoke again. Her voice was lowered and drastically altered.

"Kensie? Is it that important?"

His voice was lightly humorous, but the words came a fraction more slowly than they had before.

"It seems to be."

"But it's something we both just fell into, as children. It was just an assumption on both our parts. Since then, we've grown up. You've changed. I've changed."

"Yes."

"You don't need me. Kensie, you don't need *me*—" Her voice was soft. "Everybody loves you."

"Could I trade?" The humorous tone persisted. "Everybody for you?"

"Kensie, don't!"

"You ask a lot," he said. Now the humor was gone, but there was still nothing in the way he spoke that reproached her. "I'd probably find it easier to stop breathing."

There was another silence.

"Why can't you see? I don't have any other choice," she said. "I don't have any more choice than you do. We're both what we are, and stuck with what we are."

"Yes," he said.

The silence this time lasted a long time. But they did not move, either of them. By this time my ear was sensitized to sounds as light as the breathing of a sparrow. They had been standing a little apart, and they stayed standing apart.

"Yes," he said again finally—and this time it was a long, slow *yes*, a tired *yes*. "Life moves. And all of us move with it, whether we like it or not."

She moved to him now. I heard her steps on the concrete floor of the balcony.

"You're exhausted," she said. "You and Ian both. Get some rest before tomorrow. Things'll look different in the daylight."

"That sometimes happens." The touch of humor was back, but there was effort behind it. "Not that I believe it for a moment, in this case."

They went back inside.

I sat where I was, wide awake. There had been no way for me to get up and get away from their conversation without letting them know I was there. Their hearing was at least as good as mine, and like me they had been trained to keep their senses always alert. But knowing all that did not help. I still had the ugly feeling that I had been intruding where I should not have been.

There was no point in moving now. I sat where I was, trying to talk sense to myself and get the ugly feeling under control. I was so concerned with my own feelings that for once I did not pay close attention to the sounds around me. The first warning I had was a small noise in my own entrance to the balcony area. I looked up to see the dark silhouette of a woman in the doorway.

"You heard," Amanda's voice said.

There was no point in denying it.

"Yes," I told her.

She stayed where she was, standing in the doorway.

"I happened to be sitting here when you came out on the balcony," I said. "There was no chance to shut the door or move away."

"It's all right," she came in. "No, don't turn on the light."

I dropped the hand I had lifted toward the control studs in the arm of my chair. With the illumination from the balcony behind her, she could see me better than I could see her. She sat down in the chair Michael had occupied a short while before.

"I told myself I'd step over and see if you were sleeping all right," she said. "Ian has a lot of work in mind for you tomorrow. But I think I was really hoping to find you awake."

Even through the darkness, the signals came loud and clear. My geas was at work again.

"I don't want to intrude," I said.

"If I reach out and haul you in by the scruff of the neck, are you intruding?" Her voice had the same sort of lightness overlying pain that I had heard in Kensie's. "I'm the one who's thinking of intruding—of intruding my problems on you."

"That's not necessarily an intrusion," I said.

"I hoped you'd feel that way," she said. It was strange to have her voice coming in such everyday tones from a silhouette of darkness. "I wouldn't bother you, but I need to have all my mind on what I'm doing here, and personal matters have ended up getting in the way."

She paused.

"You don't really mind people spilling all over you, do you?" she said.

"No," I said.

"I thought so. I got the feeling you wouldn't. Do you think of Else much?"

"When other things aren't on my mind."

"I wish I'd known her."

"She was someone to know."

"Yes. Knowing someone else is what makes the difference. The trouble is, often we don't know. Or we don't know until too late." She paused. "I suppose you think, after what you heard just now, that I'm talking about Kensie?"

"Aren't you?"

"No. Kensie and Ian—the Graemes are so close to us Morgans that we might as well all be related. You don't usually fall in love with a relative—or you don't think you will, at least, when you're young. The kind of person you imagine falling in love with is someone strange and exciting—someone from fifty light-years away."

"I don't know about that," I said. "Else was a neighbor, and I think I grew up being in love with her."

"I'm sorry." Her silhouette shifted a little in the darkness. "I'm really just talking about myself. But I know what you mean. In sober moments, when I was younger, I more or less just assumed that some day I'd wind up with Kensie. You'd have to have something wrong with you not to want someone like him."

"And you've got something wrong with you?" I said.

"Yes," she said. "That's it. I grew up, that's the trouble."

"Everybody does."

"I don't mean I gew up physically. I mean, I matured. We live a long time, we Morgans, and I suppose we're slower growing up than most. But you know how it is with young anythings—young animals as well as young humans. Did you ever have a wild animal as a pet as a child?"

"Several," I said.

"Then you've run into what I'm talking about. While the wild animal's young, it's cuddly and tame, but when it grows up, the day comes it bites or slashes at you without warning. People talk about that being part of their wild nature. But it isn't. Humans change just exactly the same way. When anything young grows up, it becomes conscious of itself, its own wants, its own desires, its own moods. Then the day comes when someone tries to play with it and it isn't in a playing mood—and it reacts with *'Back off! What I want is just as important as what you want!'* And all at once, the time of its being young and cuddly is over forever."

"Of course," I said. "That happens to all of us."

"But to us—to our people—it happens too late!" she said. "Or rather, we start life too early. By the age of seventeen on the Dorsai we have to be out and working like an adult, either at home or on some other world. We're pitchforked into adulthood. There's never any time to take stock, to realize what being adult is going to turn us into. We don't realize we aren't cubs anymore until one day we slash or bite someone without warning—and then we realize that we've changed—and they've changed. But it's too late for us to adjust to the change in the other person because we've already been trapped by our own change."

She stopped. I sat, not speaking, waiting. From my experience with this sort of thing since Else died, I assumed that I no longer needed to talk. She would carry the conversation now.

"No, it wasn't Kensie I was talking about when I first came in here, and I said the trouble is you don't know someone else until too late. It's Ian."

"Ian?" I said, for she had stopped again, and now I felt with equal instinct that she needed some help to continue.

"Yes," she said. "When I was young, I didn't understand Ian. I do now. Then, I thought there was nothing to him—or else he was simply solid all the way through, like a piece of wood. But he's not. Everything you can see in Kensie is there in Ian, only there's no light to see it by. Now I know. And now it's too late."

"Too late?" I said. "He's not married, is he?"

"Married? Not yet. But you didn't know? Look at the picture on his desk. Her name's Leah. She's on Earth. He met her when he was there, four years ago. But that's not what I mean by too late. I mean—it's too late for me. What you heard me tell Kensie is the truth. I've got the curse of the first Amanda. I'm born to belong to a lot of people first; and only to any single person second. As much as I'd give for Ian, that equation's there in me, ever since I grew up. Sooner or later, it'd put even him in second place for me. I can't do that to him, and it's too late for me to be anything else."

"Maybe Ian'd be willing to agree to those terms."

She did not answer for a second. Then I heard a slow intake of breath from the darker darkness that was her.

"You shouldn't say that," she said.

There was a second of silence. Then she spoke again, fiercely.

"Would you suggest something like that to Ian if our positions were reversed?"

"I didn't suggest it," I said. "I mentioned it."

Another pause.

"You're right," she said. "I know what I want and what I'm afraid of in myself, and it seems to me so obvious I keep thinking everyone else must know, too."

She stood up.

"Forgive me, Corunna," she said. "I've got no right to burden you with all this."

"It's the way the world is," I said. "People talk to people."

"And to you, more than most." She went toward the door to the balcony and paused in it. "Thanks again."

"I've done nothing," I said.

"Thank you anyway. Goodnight. Sleep if you can."

She stepped out through the door; and through the window wall I watched her, very erect, pass to my left until she walked out of my sight beyond the sitting room wall.

I went back to bed, not really expecting to fall asleep again easily. But I dropped off and slept like a log.

When I woke it was morning, and my bedside phone was chiming. I flicked it on and Michael looked at me out of the screen.

"I'm sending a man up with maps of the interior of Gebel Nahar," he said, "so you can find your way around. Breakfast's available in the general staff lounge, if you're ready."

"Thanks," I told him.

I got up and was ready when the bandsman he had sent arrived with a small display cube holding the maps. I took it with me and the bandsman showed me to the lounge—which, it turned out, was not a lounge for the staff of Gebel Nahar in general, but one for the military commanders of that establishment. Ian was the only other person present when I got there, and he was just finishing his meal.

"Sit down," he said.

I sat.

"I'm going ahead on the assumption that I'll be defending this place in twenty-four hours or so," he said. "What I'd like you to do is familarize yourself with its defenses, particularly the first line of walls and its weapons, so that you can either direct the men working them or take over the general defense, if necessary."

"What have you got in mind for a general defense?" I asked as a bandsman came out of the kitchen area to see what I would eat. I told him and he went.

"We've got just about enough of Michael's troops to man that first wall and have a handful in reserve," he said. "Most of them have never touched anything but a hand weapon in their life, but we've got to use them to fight with the emplaced energy weapons against foot attack up the slope. I'd like you to get them on the weapons and drill them. Michael should be able to help you, since he knows which of them are steady and which aren't. Get breakfast in you, and I'll tell you what I expect the regiments to do on the attack and what I think we might do when they try it."

He went on talking while my food came and I ate. Boiled down, his expectations—based on what he had learned of the Naharese military while he had been here, and from consultation with Michael—were for a series of infantry wave attacks up the slope until the first wall was overrun. His plan called for a defense of the first wall until the last safe moment, destruction of the emplaced weapons, so they could not be turned against us, and a quick retreat to the second wall with its weapons—and so, step by step retreating up the terraces. It was essentially the sort of defense that Gebel Nahar had been designed for by its builders. The problem would be getting absolutely green and excitable troops like the Naharese bandsmen to retreat cool-headedly on order. If they could not be brought to do that, and lingered behind, then the first wave over the ramparts could reduce their numbers to the point where there would not be enough of them to make any worthwhile defense of the second terrace, to say nothing of the third, the fourth, and so on, and still have men left for a final stand within the fortress-like walls of the top three levels.

Given an equal number of veteran, properly trained troops, to say nothing of Dorsai-trained ones, we might even have held Gebel Nahar in that fashion and inflicted enough casualties on the attackers to eventually make them pull back. But unspoken between Ian and myself as we sat in the lounge was the fact that the most we could hope to do with what we had was inflict a maximum of damage while losing.

Again unspoken between us, however, was the fact that the stiffer our defense of Gebel Nahar, even in a hopeless situation, the more difficult it would be for the Governors and William to charge the Dorsai officers with incompetence of defense.

I finished eating and got up to go.

"Where's Amanda?" I asked.

"She's working with Padma—or maybe I should put it that Padma's working with her," Ian said.

"I didn't know Exotics took sides."

"He isn't," Ian said. "He's just making knowledge—his knowledge—available to someone who needs it. That's standard Exotic practice, as you know as well as I do. He and Amanda are still hunting some political angle to bring us and the Dorsai out of this without prejudice."

"What do you really think their chances are?"

Ian shook his head.

"But," he said, shuffling together the papers he had spread out before him on the table, "of course, where they're looking is away out, beyond the areas of strategy I know. We can hope."

"Did you ever stop to think that possibly Michael, with his knowledge of these Naharese, could give them some insights they wouldn't otherwise have?" I asked.

"Yes," he said. "I told them both that, and told Michael to make himself available to them if they thought they could use him. So far, I don't think they have."

He got up, holding his papers, and we went out—I to the band quarters and Michael's office, he to his own office and the overall job of organizing our supplies and everything else necessary for the defense.

Michael was not in his office. The orderly directed me to the first wall, where I found him already drilling his men on the emplaced weapons there. I worked with him for most of the morning, and then we stopped, not because there was not a lot more practice needed, but because his untrained troops were exhausted and beginning to make mistakes simply out of fatigue.

Michael sent them to lunch. He and I went back to his office and had sandwiches and coffee brought in by his orderly.

"What about this?" I asked after we were done, getting up and going to the wall where the archaic-looking bagpipe hung. "I asked Ian about it, but he said he'd only played highland pipes and that if I wanted a demonstration, I should ask you."

Michael looked up from his seat behind his desk and grinned. The drill on the guns seemed to have done something for him in a way he was not really aware of himself. He looked younger and more cheerful than I had yet seen him, and obviously he enjoyed any attention given to his instruments.

"That's a *gaita gallega,*" he said. "Or, to be correct, it's a local imitation of the *gaita gallega* you can still find occasionally being made and played in the province of Galicia in Spain, back on Earth. It's a perfectly playable instrument to anyone who's familiar with the highland pipes. Ian could have played it—I'd guess he just thought I might prefer to show it off myself."

"He seemed to think you could play it better," I said.

"Well..." Michael grinned again. "Perhaps, a bit."

He got up and came over to the wall with me.

"Do you really want to hear it?" he asked.

"Yes, I do."

He took it down from the wall.

"We'll have to step outside," he said. "It's not the sort of instrument to be played in a small room like this."

We went back out onto the first terrace, by the deserted weapon emplacements. He swung the pipe up in his arms, the long single drone with its fringe tied at the two ends of the drone, resting on his left shoulder and pointing up into the air behind him. He took the mouthpiece between his lips and laid his fingers across the holes of the chanter. Then he blew up the bag and began to play.

The music of the pipes is like Dorsai whiskey. People either cannot stand it, or they feel that there's nothing comparable. I happen to be of those who love the sound—for no good reason, I would have said until that trip to Gebel Nahar, since my own heritage is Spanish rather than Scottish and I had never before realized that it was also a Spanish instrument.

Michael played something Scottish and standard—"The Flowers of the Forest," I think—pacing slowly up and down as he played. Then,

abruptly he swung around and stepped out—almost strutted, in fact—
and played something entirely different.

I wish there were words in me to describe it. It was anything but
Scottish. It was Hispanic, right down to its backbones—a wild, barbaric,
musically ornate challenge of some sort that heated the blood in my veins
and threatened to raise the hair on the back of my neck.

He finished at last with a sort of dying wail as he swung the deflating
bag down from his shoulder. His face was not young anymore; it was
changed. He looked drawn and old.

"What was that?" I demanded.

"It's got a polite name for polite company," he said. "But nobody uses
it. The Naharese call it "Su Madre.""

"Your Mother?" I echoed. Then, of course, it hit me. The Spanish
language has a number of elaborate and poetically insulting curses to
throw at your enemy about his ancestry; and the words *su madre* are
found in most of them.

"Yes," said Michael. "It's what you play when you're daring the enemy
to come out and fight. It accuses him of being less than a man in all the
senses of that phrase—and the Naharese love it."

He sat down on the rampart of the terrace suddenly, like someone very
tired and discouraged by a long and hopeless effort, resting the *gaita
gallega* on his knees.

"And they like me," he said, staring blindly at the wall of the barracks
area behind me. "My bandsmen, my regiment—they like me."

"There're always exceptions," I said, watching him. "But usually the
men who serve under them like their Dorsai officers."

"That's not what I mean." He was still staring at the wall. "I've made
no secret here of the fact I won't touch a weapon. They all knew it from
the day I signed on as bandmaster."

"I see," I said. "So that's it."

He looked up at me abruptly.

"Do you know how they react to cowards—as they consider them—
people who are able to fight but won't, in this particular, crazy splinter
culture? They encourage them to get off the face of the earth. They show
their manhood by knocking cowards around here. But they don't touch
me. They don't even challenge me to duels."

"Because they don't believe you," I said.

"That's it." His face was almost savage. "They don't. Why won't they
believe me?"

"Because you only *say* you won't use a weapon," I told him bluntly.
"In every other language you speak, everything you say or do, you
broadcast just the opposite information. That tells them that not only can

you use a weapon, but that you're so good at it none of them who'd challenge you would stand a chance. You could not only defeat someone like that, you could make him look foolish in the process. And no one wants to look foolish, particularly a macho-minded individual. That message is in the very way you walk and talk. How else could it be, with you?"

"That's not true!" He got suddenly to his feet, holding the *gaita*. "I live what I believe in. I have, ever since—"

He stopped.

"Maybe we'd better get back to work," I said as gently as I could.

"No!" The word burst out of him. "I want to tell someone. The odds are we're not going to be around after this. I want someone to—"

He broke off. He had been about to say "someone to understand" and he had not been able to get the words out. But I could not help him. As I've said, since Else's death, I've grown accustomed to listening to people. But there is something in me that tells me when to speak and when not to help them with what they wish to say. And now I was being held silent.

He struggled with himself for a few seconds, and then calm seemed to flow over him.

"No," he said, as if talking to himself. "What people think doesn't matter. We're not likely to live through this, and I want to know how you react."

He looked at me.

"That's why I've got to explain it to someone like you," he said. "I've got to know how they'd take it back home, if I'd explained it to them. And your family is the same as mine, from the same canton, the same neighborhood, the same sort of ancestry..."

"Did it occur to you that you might not owe anyone an explanation?" I asked. "When your parents raised you, they only paid back the debt they owed their parents for raising them. If you've got any obligation to anyone—and even that's a moot point, since the idea behind our world is that it's a planet of free people—it's to the Dorsai in general, to bring in interstellar exchange credits by finding work off-planet. And you've done that by becoming bandmaster here. Anything beyond that's your own private business."

It was quite true. The vital currency between worlds was not wealth, as every schoolchild knows, but the exchange of interplanetary work credits. The inhabited worlds trade special skills and knowledge, packaged in human individuals, and the exchange credits earned by a Dorsai on Newton enables the Dorsai to hire a geophysicist from Newton—or a physician from Kultis. In addition to his personal pay, Michael had been earning exchange credits ever since he had come here. True, he might have earned these at a higher rate if he had chosen work as a mercenary combat officer, but the exchange credits he did earn as band-master more than justified the expense of his education and training.

"I'm not talking about that—," he began.

"No," I said. "You're talking about a point of obligation and honor not very much removed from the sort of thing these Naharese have tied themselves up with."

He stood for a second, absorbing that. But his mouth was tight and his jaw set.

"What you're telling me," he said at last, "is that you don't want to listen. I'm not surprised."

"Now," I said, "you really are talking like a Naharese. I'll listen to anything you want to say, of course."

"Then sit down," he said.

He gestured to the rampart and sat down himself. I came and perched there, opposite him.

"Do you know I'm a happy man?" he demanded. "I really am. Why not? I've got everything I want. I've got a military job, I'm in touch with all the things that I grew up feeling made the kind of life one of my family ought to have. I'm one of a kind. I'm better at what I do and everything connected with it than anyone else they can find—and I've got my other love, which was music, as my main duty. My men like me, my regiment is proud of me. My superiors like me."

I nodded.

"But then there's this other part. . . ." His hands closed on the bag of the *gaita,* and there was a faint sound from the drone.

"Your refusal to fight?"

"Yes." He got up from the ramparts and began to pace back and forth, holding the instrument, talking a little jerkily. "This feeling against hurting anything. . . . I had it, too, just as long as I had the other—all the dreams I made up as a boy from the stories the older people in the family told me. When I was young, it didn't seem to matter to me that the feeling and the dreams hit head-on. It just always happened that, in my own personal visions, the battles I won were always bloodless, the victories always came with no one getting hurt. I didn't worry about any conflict in me then. I thought it was something that would take care of itself later, as I grew up. You don't kill anyone when you're going through the Academy, of course. You know as well as I do that the better you are, the less of a danger you are to your fellow students. But what was in me didn't change. It was there with me all the time, not changing."

"No normal person likes the actual fighting and killing," I said. "What sets us Dorsai off in a class by ourselves is the fact that most of the time we *can* win bloodlessly, where someone else would have dead bodies piled all over the place. Our way justifies itself to our employers by saving them money, but it also gets us away from the essential brutality of combat and keeps us human. No good officer pins medals on himself in proportion to the people he kills and wounds. Remember what Cletus says about that? He hated what you hate, just as much."

"But he could do it when he had to." Michael stopped and looked at me, the skin of his face drawn tight over the bones. "So can you, now. Or Ian. Or Kensie."

That was true, of course. I could not deny it.

"You see," said Michael, "that's the difference between out on the worlds and back at the Academy. In life, sooner or later, you get to the killing part. Sooner or later, if you live by the sword, you kill with the sword. When I graduated and had to face going out to the worlds as a fighting officer, I finally had to make that decision. And so I did. I can't hurt anyone. I won't hurt anyone—even to save my own life, I think. But at the same time, I'm a soldier and nothing else. I'm bred and born a soldier. I don't want any other life, I can't conceive of any other life—and I love it."

He broke off abruptly. For a long moment he stood staring out over the plains at the distant flashes of light from the camp of the deserted regiments.

"Well, there it is," he said.

"Yes," I said.

He turned to look at me.

"Will you tell my family that?" he asked. "If you should get home and I don't?"

"If it comes to that, I will," I said. "But we're a long way from being dead yet."

He grinned unexpectedly, a sad grin.

"I know," he said.

"It's just that I've had this on my conscience for a long time. You don't mind?"

"Of course not."

"Thanks," he said.

He hefted the *gaita* in his hands as if he had just suddenly remembered that he held it.

"My men will be back out here in about fifteen minutes," he said. "I can carry on with the drilling myself, if you've got other things you want to do."

I looked at him a little narrowly.

"What you're trying to tell me," I said, "is that they'll learn faster if I'm not around."

"Something like that." He laughed. "They're used to me, but you make them self-conscious. They tighten up and keep making the same mistakes over and over again, and then they get into a fury with themselves and do even worse. I don't know if Ian would approve, but I do know these people, and I think I can bring them along faster alone...."

"Whatever works," I said. "I'll go and see what else Ian can find for me to do."

I turned and went to the door that would let me back into the interior of Gebel Nahar.

"Thank you again," he called after me. There was a note of relief in his voice that moved me more strongly than I had expected, so that instead of telling him that what I had done in listening to him was nothing at all, I simply waved at him and went inside.

I found my way back to Ian's office, but he was not there. It occurred to me suddenly that Kensie, Padma, or Amanda might know where he had gone—and they should all be at work in other offices of that same suite.

I went looking and found Kensie with his desk covered with large-scale printouts of terrain maps.

"Ian?" he said. "No, I don't know. But he ought to be back in his office soon. I'll have some work for you tonight, by the way. I want to mine the approach slope. Michael's bandsmen can do the actual work, after they've had some rest from the day, but you and I are going to need to go out first and make a sweep to pick up any observers they've sent from the regiments to camp outside our walls. Then, later, before dawn, I'd like some of us to do a scout of that camp of theirs on the plains and get some hard ideas as to how many of them there are, what they have to attack with, and so on...."

"Fine," I said. "I'm all slept up now. Call on me when you want me."

"You could try asking Amanda or Padma if they know where Ian is."

"I was just going to."

Amanda and Padma were in a conference room two doors down from Kensie's office, seated at one end of a long table covered with text printouts and with an activated display screen built flat into its top. Amanda was studying the screen, and they both looked up as I put my head in the door. But while Padma's eyes were sharp and questioning, Amanda's were abstract, like the eyes of someone refusing to be drawn all the way back from whatever was engrossing her.

"Just a question...," I said.

"I'll come," Padma said to me. He turned to Amanda. "You go on."

She went back to her contemplation of the screen without a word. Padma got up and came to me, stepping into the outside room and shutting the door behind him.

"I'm trying to find Ian."

"I don't know where he'd be just now," said Padma. "Around Gebel Nahar somewhere—but saying that's not much help."

"Not with the size of this establishment." I nodded toward the door he had just shut.

"It's getting rather late, isn't it," I asked, "for Amanda to hope to turn up some sort of legal solution?"

"Not necessarily." The outer office we were standing in had its own window wall, and next to that window wall were several of the heavily overstuffed armchairs that were a common article of furniture in the place. "Why don't we sit down there? If he comes in from the corridor, he's got to go through this office, and if he comes out on the terrace of this level, we can see him through the window."

We went over and took chairs.

"It's not exact, actually, to say that there's a legal way of handling this situation that Amanda's looking for. I thought you understood that?"

"Her work is something I don't know a thing about," I told him. "It's a specialty that grew up as we got more and more aware that the people we were making contracts with might have different meanings for the same words, and different notions of implied obligations, than we had. So we've developed people like Amanda, who steep themselves in the differences of attitudes and ideas we might run into with the splinter cultures we deal with."

"I know," he said.

"Yes, of course you would, wouldn't you?"

"Not inevitably," he said. "It happens that as an Outbond, I wrestle with pretty much the same sort of problems that Amanda does. My work is with people who aren't Exotics, and my responsibility most of the time is to make sure we understand them—and they us. That's why I say that what we have here goes far beyond legal matters."

"For example?" I found myself suddenly curious.

"You might get a better word picture if you said that what Amanda is searching for is a *social* solution to the situation."

"I see," I said. "This morning Ian talked about Amanda saying that there always was a solution, but the problem here was to find it in so short a time. Did I hear that correctly—that there's always a solution to a tangle like this?"

"There's always any number of solutions," Padma said. "The problem is to find the one you'd prefer—or maybe just the one you'd accept. Human situations, being human-made, are always mutable at human hands, if you can get to them with the proper pressures before they happen. Once they happen, of course, they become history—"

He smiled at me.

"And history, so far at least, is something we aren't able to change. But changing what's about to happen simply requires getting to the base of the forces involved in time, with the right sort of pressures exerted in the right directions. What takes time is identifying the forces, finding what pressures are possible and where to apply them."

"And we don't have time."

His smile went.

"No. In fact, you don't."

I looked squarely at him.

"In that case, shouldn't you be thinking of leaving yourself?" I said. "According to what I gather about these Naharese, once they overrun this place, they're liable to kill anyone they come across here. Aren't you too valuable to Mara to get your throat cut by some battle-drunk soldier?"

"I'd like to think so," he said. "But you see, from our point of view, what's happening here has importance that goes entirely beyond the local, or even the planetary, situation. Ontogenetics identifies certain individuals as possibly being particularly influential on the history of their time. Ontogenetics, of course, can be wrong—it's been wrong before this. But we think the value of studying such people as closely as possible at certain times is important enough to take priority over everything else."

"Historically influential? Do you mean William?" I asked. "Who else— not the Conde? Someone in the revolutionary camp?"

Padma shook his head.

"If we tagged certain individuals publicly as being influential men and women of their historic time, we would only prejudice their actions and the actions of the people who knew them and muddle our own conclusions about them—even if we could be sure that ontogenetics had read their importance rightly. And we can't be sure."

"You don't get out of it that easily," I said. "The fact that you're physically here probably means that the individuals you're watching are right here in Gebel Nahar. I can't believe it's the Conde. His day is over, no matter how things go. That leaves the rest of us. Michael's a possibility, but he's deliberately chosen to bury himself. I know I'm not someone to shape history. Amanda? Kensie and Ian?"

He looked at me a little sadly.

"All of you, one way or another, have a hand in shaping history. But who shapes it largely and who only a little is something I can't tell you. As I say, ontogenetics isn't that sure. As to whom I may be watching, I watch everyone."

It was a gentle but impenetrable shield he opposed me with. I let the matter go. I glanced out the window, but there was no sign of Ian.

"Maybe you can explain how Amanda or you go about looking for a solution," I said.

"As I said, it's a matter of looking for the base of the existing forces at work—"

"The ranchers—and William?"

He nodded.

"Particularly William—since he's the prime mover. To get the results he wants, William or anyone else had to set up a structure of cause and effect, operating through individuals. So, for anyone else to control the forces already set to work and bend them to different results, it's necessary to find where William's structure is vulnerable to cross-pressures and arrange for those to operate—again through individuals."

"And Amanda hasn't found a weak point yet?"

"Of course she has. Several." He frowned at me, but with a touch of humor. "I don't have any objection to telling you all this. You don't need to draw me with leading questions."

"Sorry," I said.

"It's all right. As I say, she's already found several. But none that can be implemented between now and sometime tomorrow, if the regiments attack Gebel Nahar then."

I had a strange sensation. As if a gate was slowly but inexorably being closed in my face.

"It seems to me," I said, "the easiest thing to change would be the position of the Conde. If he'd just agree to come to terms with the regiments, the whole thing would collapse."

"Obvious solutions are usually not the easiest," Padma said. "Stop and think. Why do you suppose the Conde would never change his mind?"

"He's a Naharese," I said. "More than that, he's honestly Hispanic. *El honor* forbids him from yielding an inch to soldiers who were supposedly loyal to him and now are threatening to destroy him and everything he stands for."

"But tell me," said Padma, watching me. "Even if *el honor* was satisfied, would he want to treat with the rebels?"

I shook my head.

"No," I said. It was something I had recognized before this, but only in the back of my mind. As I spoke to Padma now, it was like something emerging from the shadows to stand in the full light of day. "This is the great moment of his life. This is the chance for him to substantiate that paper title of his, to make it real. This way, he can prove to himself he is a real aristocrat. He'd give his life—in fact, he can hardly wait to give his life—to win that."

There was a little silence.

"So you see," said Padma. "Go on then. What other ways do you see a solution being found?"

"Ian and Kensie could void the contract and make the penalty payment. But they won't. Aside from the fact that no responsible officer from our world would risk giving the Dorsai the sort of bad name that could give, under these special circumstances, neither of those two brothers would abandon the Conde as long as he insisted on fighting. It's as impossible for a Dorsai to do that as it is for the Conde to play games with *el honor*. Like him, their whole life has been oriented against any such thing."

"What other ways?"

"I can't think of any," I said. "I'm out of suggestions—which is probably why I was never considered for anything like Amanda's job in the first place."

"As a matter of fact, there are a number of other possible solutions," Padma said. His voice was soft, almost pedantic. "There's the possibility of bringing economic counter pressure upon the ranchers, and there's the possibility of disrupting the control of the revolutionaries who've come in from outside Nahar to run this rebellion. In each case, none of these solutions are of the kind that can very easily be made to work in the short time we've got."

"In fact, there isn't any such thing as a solution that can be made to work in time. Isn't that right?" I said bluntly.

He shook his head.

"No. Absolutely wrong. If we could stop the clock at this second and take the equivalent of some months to study the situation, we'd undoubtedly find not only one, but several solutions that would abort the attack of the regiments in the time we've got to work with. What you lack isn't time in which to act, since that's merely something specified for the solution. What you lack is time in which to discover the solution that will work in the time there is to act."

"So you mean," I said, "that we're to sit here tomorrow with Michael's forty or so bandsmen—and face the attack of something like six thousand line troops, even though they're only Naharese line troops, all the time knowing that there is absolutely a way in which that attack doesn't have to happen, if only we had the sense to find it?"

"The sense—and the time," said Padma. "But yes, you're right. It's a harsh reality of life, but the sort of reality that history has turned on since history began."

"I see," I said. "Well, I find I don't accept it that easily."

"No." Padma's gaze was level and cooling upon me. "Neither does Amanda. Neither does Ian or Kensie. Nor, I suspect, even Michael. But then, you're all Dorsai."

I said nothing. It is a little embarrassing when someone plays your own top card against you.

"In any case," Padma went on, "none of you are being called on to merely accept it. Amanda's still at work. So is Ian. So are all the rest of you. Forgive me, I didn't mean to sneer at the reflexes of your culture. I envy you—a great many people envy you—that inability to give in. My point is that the fact that we know there's an answer makes no difference. You'd all be doing the same thing anyway, wouldn't you?"

"True enough," I said—and at that moment we were interrupted.

"Padma?" It was the general office annunciator speaking from the walls around us with Amanda's voice. "Could you give me some help, please?"

Padma got to his feet.

"I've got to go," he said.

He went out. I sat where I was, held by that odd little melancholy that had caught me up—and I think does the same with most Dorsai away from home—at moments all through my life. It is not a serious thing, just a touch of loneliness and sadness and the facing of the fact that life is measured, that there are only so many things that can be accomplished in it, try how you may.

I was still in this mood when Ian's return to the office suite by the corridor woke me out of it.

I got up.

"Corunna!" he said, and led the way into his private office. "How's the training going?"

"As you'd expect," I said. "I left Michael alone with them, at his suggestion. He thinks they might learn faster without my presence to distract them."

"Possible," said Ian.

He stepped to the window wall and looked out. My height was not enough to let me look over the edge of the parapet on this terrace and see down to the first where the bandsmen were drilling, but I guessed that his was.

"They don't seem to be doing badly," he said.

He was still on his feet, of course, and I was standing next to his desk. I looked at it now and found the cube holding the image Amanda had talked about. The woman pictured there was obviously not Dorsai, but there was something not unlike our people about her. She was strong-boned and dark-haired, the hair sweeping down to her shoulders, longer than most Dorsais out in the field would have worn it, but not long according to the styles of Earth.

I looked back at Ian. He had turned away from the window and his contemplation of the drill going on two levels below. But he had stopped partway in his turn, and his face was turned toward the wall beyond which Amanda would be working with Padma. I saw him in three-quarters face, with the light from the window wall striking that quarter of his features that was averted from me. I noticed tiredness about him. Not that it showed anywhere specifically in the lines of his face. He was, as always, like a mountain of granite, untouchable. But something about the way he stood spoke of a fatigue—perhaps a fatigue of the spirit rather than of the body.

"I just heard about Leah here," I said, nodding at the image cube, speaking to bring him back to the moment.

He turned as if his thoughts had been a long way away.

"Leah? Oh, yes." His own eyes went absently to the cube and away again. "Yes, she's Earth. I'll be going to get her after this is over. We'll be married in two months."

"That soon?" I said. "I hadn't even heard you'd fallen in love."

"Love?" he said. His eyes were still on me, but their attention had gone away again. He spoke more as if to himself than to me. "No, it was years ago I fell in love. . . ."

His attention focused suddenly. He was back with me.

"Sit down," he said, dropping into the chair behind his desk. I sat. "Have you talked to Kensie since breakfast?"

"Just a little while ago, when I was asking around to find you," I said.

"He's got a couple of runs outside the walls he'd like your hand with tonight after dark's well settled in."

"I know," I said. "He told me about them. A sweep of the slope in front of this place to clear it before laying mines there, and a scout of the regimental camp for whatever we can learn about them before tomorrow."

"That's right," Ian said.

"Do you have any solid figures on how many there are out there?"

"Regimental rolls," said Ian, "give us a total of a little over five thousand of all ranks. Fifty-two hundred and some. But something like this invariably attracts a number of Naharese who scent personal glory, or at least the chance for personal glory. Then there're perhaps seven or eight hundred honest revolutionaries in Nahar, Padma estimates, individuals who've been working to loosen the grip of the rancher oligarchy for some time. Plus a hundred or so agents provocateurs from outside."

"In something like this, those who aren't trained soldiers we can probably discount, don't you think?"

Ian nodded.

"How many of the actual soldiers'll have had any actual combat experience?" I asked.

"Combat experience in this part of Ceta," Ian said, "means having been involved in a border clash or two with the armed forces of the surrounding principalities. Maybe one in ten of the line soldiers has had that. On the other hand, every male, particularly in Nahar, has dreamed of a dramatic moment like this."

"So they'll all come on hard with the first attack," I said.

"That's as I see it," said Ian, "and Kensie agrees. I'm glad to hear it's your thought, too. Everyone out there will attack in that first charge, not merely determined to do well, but dreaming of outdoing everyone else around them. If we can throw them back even once, some of them won't come again. And that's the way it ought to go. They won't lose heart as a group. Just each setback will take the heart out of some, and we'll work them down to the hard core that's serious about being willing to die if only they can get over the walls and reach us."

"Yes," I said, "and how many of those do you think there are?"

"That's the problem," said Ian calmly. "At the very least, there's going to be one in fifty we'll have to kill to stop. Even if half of them are already out by the time we get down to it, that's sixty of them left. And we've got to figure by that time we'll have taken at least thirty percent casualties ourselves—and that's an optimistic figure, considering the fact that these bandsmen are the next thing to noncombatants. Man to man, on the kind of hard-core attackers that are going to be making it over the walls, the bandsmen that're left will be lucky to take care of an equal number of attackers. Padma, of course, doesn't exist in our defensive table of personnel. That leaves you, me, Kensie, Michael, and Amanda to handle about thirty bodies. Have you been keeping yourself in condition?"

I grinned.

"That's good," said Ian. "I forgot to figure that scar-face of yours. Be sure to smile like that when they come at you. It ought to slow them down for a couple of seconds at least, and we'll need all the help we can get."

I laughed.

"If Michael doesn't want you, how about working with Kensie for the rest of the afternoon?"

"Fine," I said.

I got up and went out. Kensie looked up from his printouts when he saw me again.

"Find him?" he asked.

"Yes. He suggested you could use me."

"I can. Join me."

We worked together the rest of the afternoon. The so-called large-scale terrain maps the Naharese army library provided were hardly more useful than tourist brochures, from our point of view. What Kensie needed to know was what the ground was like meter by meter from the front walls

on out over perhaps a couple of hundred meters of plain beyond where
the slope of the mountain met it. Given that knowledge, it would be
possible to make reasonable estimates as to how a foot attack might
develop, how many attackers we might be likely to have on a front, and
on which parts of that front, because of vegetation, or the footing, or the
terrain, attackers might be expected to fall behind their fellows during a
rush.

The Naharese terrain maps had never been made with such a detailed
information of the ground in mind. To correct them, Kensie had spent
most of the day before taking telescopic pictures of three-meter-square
segments of the ground, using the watch cameras built into the ramparts
of the first wall. With these pictures as reference, we now proceeded to
make notes on blown-up versions of the clumsy Naharese maps.

It took us the rest of the afternoon, but by the time we were finished,
we had a fairly good working knowledge of the ground before the Gebel
Nahar, from the viewpoint not only of someone storming up it, but from
the viewpoint of a defender who might have to cover it on his belly—
as Kensie and I would be doing that night. We knocked off, with the job
done, finally, about the dinner hour.

In spite of having finished at a reasonable time, we found no one else
at dinner but Ian. Michael was still up to his ears in the effort of teaching
his bandsmen to be fighting troops, and Amanda was still with Padma,
hard at the search for a solution, even at this eleventh hour.

"You'd both probably better get an hour of sleep, if you can spare the
time," Ian said to me. "We might be able to pick up an hour or two more
of rest just before dawn, but there's no counting on it."

"Yes," said Kensie. "And you might grab some sleep yourself."

Brother looked at brother. They knew each other so well, they were
so complete in their understanding of each other, that neither one bothered
to discuss the matter further. It had been discussed silently in that one
momentary exchange of glances, and now they were concerned with
other things.

As it turned out, I was able to get a full three hours of sleep. It was
just after ten o'clock local time when Kensie and I came out from Gebel
Nahar. On the reasonable assumption that the regiments would have
watchers keeping an eye on our walls—that same watch Kensie and I
were to silence so that the bandsmen could mine the slope—I had guessed
we would be doing something like going out over a dark portion of the
front wall on a rope. Instead, Michael was to lead us, properly outfitted
and with our faces and hands blackened, through some cellarways and
along a passage that would let us out into the night a good fifty meters
beyond the wall.

"How did you know about this?" I asked as he took us along the passage. "If there're more secret ways like this, and the regiments know about them—"

"There aren't and they don't," said Michael. We were going almost single file down the concrete-walled tunnel as he answered me. "This is a private escape hatch that's the secret of the Conde and no one else. His father had it built thirty-eight local years ago. Our Conde called me in to tell me about it when he heard the regiments had deserted.

I nodded. There was plainly a sympathy and a friendship between Michael and the old Conde that I had not had time to ask about. Perhaps it had come of their each being the only one of their kind in Gebel Nahar.

We reached the end of the tunnel and the foot of a short wooden ladder leading up to a circular metal hatch. Michael turned out the light in the tunnel and we were suddenly in absolute darkness. I heard him cranking something well-oiled, for it turned almost noiselessly. Above us the circular hatch lifted slowly to show starlit sky.

"Go ahead," Michael whispered. "Keep your heads down. The bushes that hide this spot have thorns at the end of their leaves."

We went up; I led, as being the more expendable of the two of us. The thorns did not stab me, although I heard them scratch against the stiff fabric of the black combat overalls I was wearing as I pushed my way through the bushes, keeping level to the ground. I heard Kensie come up behind me and the faint sound of the hatch being closed behind us. Michael was due to open it again in two hours and fourteen minutes.

Kensie touched my shoulder. I looked and saw his hand held up, to silhouette itself against the stars. He made the hand signal for *move out*, touched me again lightly on the shoulder, and disappeared. I turned away and began to move off in the opposite direction, staying close to the ground.

I had forgotten what a sweep like this was like. As with all our people, I had been raised with the idea of always being in effective physical condition. Of course, in itself, this is almost a univeral idea nowadays. Most cultures emphasize keeping the physical vehicle in shape so as to be able to deliver the mental skills wherever the market may require them. But, because in our case the conditions of our work are so physically demanding, we have probably placed more emphasis on it. It has become an idea that begins in the cradle and becomes almost an ingrained reflex, like washing or brushing teeth.

This may be one of the reasons we have so many people living to advanced old age—apart from those naturally young for their years, like the individuals in Amanda's family. Certainly, I think, it is one of the reasons why we tend to be active into extreme old age, right up to the moment of death. But, with the best efforts possible, even our training does not produce the same results as practice.

Ian had been right to needle me about my condition, gently as he had done it. The best facilities aboard the biggest space warships do not compare to the reality of being out in the field. My choice of work lies between the stars, but there is no denying that those like myself who spend the working years in ships grow rusty in the area of ordinary body skills. Now, at night, out next to the earth, on my own, I could feel a sort of self-consciousness of my body. I was too aware of the weight of my flesh and bones, the effort my muscles made, and the awkwardness of the creeping and crawling positions in which I had to cover the ground.

I worked to the right as Kensie worked left, covering the slope segment by segment, clicking off these chunks of Cetan surface in my mind according to the memory pattern in which I had fixed them. It was all sand and gravel and low brush, most with built-in defenses in the form of thorns or burrs. The night wind blew like an invisible current around me in the darkness, cooling me under a sky where no clouds hid the stars.

The light of a moon would have been welcome, but Ceta has none. After about fifteen minutes I came to the first of nine positions that we had marked in my area as possible locations for watchers from the enemy camp. Picking such positions is a matter of simple reasoning. Anyone but the best trained of observers, given the job of watching something like the Gebel Nahar, from which no action is really expected to develop, would find the hours long. Particularly when the hours in question are cool nighttime hours out in the middle of a plain where there is little to occupy the attention. Under those conditions, the watcher's certainty that he is simply putting in time grows steadily, and with the animal instinct in him, he drifts automatically to the most comfortable or sheltered location from which to do his watching.

But there was no one at the first of the positions I came to. I moved on.

It was just about this time that I began to be aware of a change in the way I was feeling. The exercise, the adjustment of my body to the darkness and the night temperature had begun to have their effects. I was no longer physically self-conscious. Instead, I was beginning to enjoy the action.

Old habits and reflexes had awakened in me. I flowed over the ground now, not an intruder in the night of Nahar, but part of it. My eyes had adjusted to the dim illumination of the starlight, and I had the illusion that I was seeing almost as well as I might have in the day.

Just so, with my hearing. What had been a confusion of dark sounds had separated and identified itself as a multitude of different auditory messages. I heard the wind in the bushes without confusing it with the distant noise-making of some small, wild plains animal. I smelled the different and separate odors of the vegetation. Now I was able to hold the small sounds of my own passage—the scuff of my hands and body upon the ground—separate from the other noises that rode the steady stream of the breeze. In the end, I was not only aware of them all, I was aware of being one with them—one of the denizens of the Cetan night.

There was an excitement to it, a feeling of naturalness and rightness in my quiet search through this dim-lit land. I felt not only at home here, but as if in some measure I owned the night. The wind, the scents, the sounds I heard, all entered into me, and I recognized suddenly that I had moved completely beyond an awareness of myself as a physical body separate from what surrounded me. I was pure observer, with the keen involvement that a wild animal feels in the world he moves through. I was disembodied—a pair of eyes, a nose, and two ears, sweeping invisibly through the world. I had forgotten Gebel Nahar. I had almost forgotten to think like a human. Almost—for a few moments—I had forgotten Else.

Then a sense of duty came and hauled me back to my obligations. I finished my sweep. There were no observers at all, either at any of the likely positions Kensie and I had picked out or anywhere else in the area I had covered. Unbelievable as it seemed from a military standpoint, the regiments had not even bothered to keep a token watch on us. For a second I wondered if they had never had any intention at all of attacking, as Ian had believed they would, and as everyone else, including the Conde and Michael's bandsmen, had taken for granted.

I returned to the location of the tunnel and met Kensie there. His hand signal showed that he had also found his area deserted. There was no reason why Michael's men should not be moved out as soon as possible and put to work laying the mines.

Michael opened the hatch at the scheduled time and we went down the ladder by feel in the darkness. With the hatch once more closed overhead, the light came on again.

"What did you find?" Michael asked as we stood squinting in the glare.

"Nothing," said Kensie. "It seems they're ignoring us. You've got the mines ready to go?"

"Yes," said Michael. "If it's safe out there, do you want to send the men out by one of the regular gates? I promised the Conde to keep the secret of this tunnel."

"Absolutely," said Kensie. "In any case, the fewer people who know about this sort of way in and out of a place like Gebel Nahar, the better. Let's go back inside and get things organized."

We went. Back in Kensie's office, we were joined by Amanda, who had temporarily put aside her search for a social solution to the situation.

We sat around in a circle and Kensie and I reported on what we had found.

"The thought occurred to me," I said, "that something might have come up to change the mind of the Naharese about attacking here."

Kensie and Ian shook their heads so unanimously and immediately it was as if they had reacted by instinct. The small hope in the back of my mind flickered and died. Experienced as the two of them were, if they were that certain, there was little room for doubt.

"I haven't waked the men yet," said Michael, "because after that drill on the weapons today they needed all the sleep they could get. I'll call the orderly and tell him to wake them now. We can be outside and at work in half an hour, and except for my rotating them in by groups for food and rest breaks, we can work straight through the night. We ought to have all the mines placed by a little before dawn."

"Good," said Ian.

I sat watching him and the others. My sensations, outside of having become one with the night, had left my senses keyed to an abnormally sharp pitch. I was feeling now like a wild animal brought into the artificial world of indoors. The lights overhead in the office seemed harshly bright. The air itself was full of alien, mechanical scents, little trace odors carried on the ventilating system of oil and room dust, plus all the human smells that result when our race is cooped up within a structure.

And part of this sensitivity was directed toward the other four people in the room. It seemed to me that I saw, heard, and smelled them with an almost painful acuity. I read the way each of them was feeling to a degree I had never been able to before.

They were all deadly tired—each in his or her own way, very tired, with a personal, inner exhaustion that had finally been exposed by the physical tiredness to which the present situation had brought all of them except me. It seemed what that physical tiredness had accomplished had been to strip away the polite covering that before had hidden the private exhaustion, and it was now plain on every one of them.

". . . Then there's no reason for the rest of us to waste any more time," Ian was saying. "Amanda, you and I'd better dress and equip for that scout of their camp. Knife and sidearm only."

His words brought me suddenly out of my separate awareness.

"You and Amanda?" I said. "I thought it was Kensie and I, Michael and Amanda who were going to take a look at the camp?"

"It was," said Ian. "One of the Governors who came in to talk to us yesterday is on his way in by personal aircraft. He wants to talk to Kensie again, privately. He won't talk to anyone else."

"Some kind of a deal in the offing?"

"Possibly," says Kensie. "We can't count on it, though, so we go ahead. On the other hand we can't ignore the chance. So I'll stay and Ian will go."

"We could do it with three," I said.

"Not as well as it could be done by four," said Ian. "That's a good-sized camp to get into and look over in a hurry. If anyone but Dorsai could be trusted to get in and out without being seen, I'd be glad to take half a dozen more. It's not like most military camps, where there's a single overall headquarters area. We're going to have to check the headquarters of each regiment, and there're six of them."

I nodded.

"You'd better get something to eat, Corunna," Ian went on. "We could be out until dawn."

It was good advice. When I came back from eating, the other three who were to go were already outfitted and in Ian's office. On his right thigh, Michael was wearing a knife—which was, after all, more tool than weapon—but he wore no sidearms, and I noticed Ian did not object. With her hands and face blacked, wearing the black stocking cap, overalls, and boots, Amanda looked taller and more square-shouldered than she had in her daily clothes.

"All right," said Ian. He had the plan of the camp laid out according to our telescopic observation of it through the rampart watch cameras, combined with what Michael had been able to tell us of Naharese habits.

"We'll go by field experience," he said. "I'll take two of the six regiments—the two in the center. Michael, because he's more recently from his academy training and because he knows these people, will take two regiments—the two on the left wing that includes the far left one that was his own Third Regiment. You'll take the Second Regiment, Corunna, and Amanda will take the Fourth. I mention this now in case we don't have a chance to talk outside the camp."

"It's unlucky you and Michael can't take regiments adjoining each other," I said. "That'd give you a chance to work together. You might need that with two regiments apiece to cover."

"Ian needs to see the Fifth Regiment for himself, if possible," Michael said. "That's the Guard Regiment, the one with the best arms. And since my regiment is a traditional enemy of the Guard Regiment, the two have deliberately been separated as far as possible—that's why the Guards are in the middle and my Third's on the wing."

"Anything else? Then we should go," said Ian.

We went out quietly by the same tunnel by which Kensie and I had gone for our sweep of the slope, leaving the hatch propped a little open against our return. Once in the open we spread apart at about a ten-meter interval and began to jog toward the lights of the regimental camp in the distance.

We were a little over an hour coming up on it. We began to hear it when we were still some distance from it. It did not resemble a military camp on the eve of battle half so much as it did a large, open-air party.

The camp was laid out in a crescent. The center of each regimental area was made up of the usual beehive-shaped buildings of blown bubble plastic that could be erected so easily on the spot. Behind and between the clumpings of these were ordinary tents of all types and sizes. There was noise and steady traffic between these tents and the plastic buildings, as well as between the plastic buildings themselves.

We stopped a hundred meters out, opposite the center of the crescent, and checked off. We were able to stand talking, quite openly. Even if we had been without our black accoutrements, the general sound and activity going on just before us ensured as much privacy and protection as a wall between us and the camp would have afforded.

"All back here in forty minutes," Ian said.

We checked chronometers and split up, going in. My target, the Second Regiment, was between Ian's two regiments and Michael's two. It was a section that had few tents, these seeming to cluster most thickly either toward the center of the camp or out on both wings. I slipped between the first line of buildings, moving from shadow to shadow. It was foolishly easy. Even if I had not already loosened myself up on the scout across the slope before Gebel Nahar, I would have found it easy. It was very clear that even if I had come not in scouting blacks but wearing ordinary local clothing, and obviously mispronouncing the local Spanish accent, I could have strolled freely and openly wherever I wanted. Individuals in all sorts of civilian clothing were intermingled with the uniformed military, and it became plain almost immediately that few of the civilians were known by name and face to the soldiers. Ironically, my night battle dress was the one outfit that would have attracted unwelcome attention—if they had noticed me.

But there was no danger that they would notice me. Effectively, the people moving between the buildings and among the tents had neither eyes nor ears for what was not directly under their noses. Getting about unseen under such conditions boils down simply to the fact that you move quietly—which means moving all of you in a single rhythm, including your breathing, and that when you stop, you become utterly still—which means being completely relaxed in whatever bodily position you have stopped in.

Breathing is the key to both, of course, as we learn back home in childhood games even before we are school age. Move in rhythm and stop utterly and you can sometimes stand in plain sight of someone who does not expect you to be there and go unobserved. How many times has everyone had the experience of being looked "right through" by someone who does not expect to see them at a particular place or moment?

So, there was no difficulty in what I had to do, and as I say, my experience on the slope had already keyed me. I fell back into my earlier feeling of being nothing but senses—eyes, ears, and nose, drifting invisibly through the scenes of the Naharese camp. A quick circuit of my area told me all we needed to know about this particular regiment.

Most of the soldiers were between their late twenties and early forties. Under other conditions, this might have meant a force of veterans. In this case, it indicated just the opposite, time-servers who liked the uniform, the relatively easy work, and the authority and freedom of being in the military. I found a few field energy weapons—light, three-man pieces that were not only out-of-date, but impractical to bring into action in open territory like that before Gebel Nahar. The heavier weapons we had emplaced on the ramparts would be able to take out such as these almost as soon as the rebels could try to put them into action, and long before they could do any real damage to the heavy defensive walls.

The hand weapons varied, ranging from the best of newer energy guns, cone rifles, and needle guns—in the hands of the soldiers—to the strangest assortment of ancient and modern hunting tools and slug-throwing sport pieces—carried by those in civilian clothing. I did not see any crossbows or swords, but it would not have surprised me if I had. The civilian and the military hand weapons alike, however, had one thing in common that surprised me, in the light of everything else I saw—they were clean, well cared for, and handled with respect.

I decided I had found out as much as necessary about this part of the camp. I headed back to the first row of plastic structures and the darkness of the plains beyond, having to detour slightly to avoid a drunken brawl that had spilled out of one of the buildings into the space between it and the next. In fact, there seemed to be a good deal of drinking and drugging going on, although none of those I saw had got themselves to the edge of unconsciousness yet.

It was on this detour that I became conscious of someone quietly moving parallel to me. In this place and time, it was highly unlikely that there was anyone who could do so with any secrecy and skill except one of us who had come out from Gebel Nahar. Since it was on the side of my segment that touched the area given to Michael to investigate, I guessed it was he. I went to look, and found him.

I've got something to show you, he signalled me. Are you done here?

Yes, I nodded.

Come on then.

He led me into his area, to one of the larger plastic buildings in the territory of the second regiment he had been given to investigate. He brought me to the building's back. The curving sides of such structures are not difficult to climb quietly if you have had some practice doing so. He led me to the top of the roof curve and pointed at a small hole.

I looked in and saw six men with the collar tabs of regimental commanders sitting together at a table, apparently having sometime since finished a meal. Also present were some officers of lesser rank, but none of these were at the table. Bubble plastic, in addition to its other virtues, is a good sound baffle; and since the table and those about it were not directly under the observation hole, but over against one of the curving walls some distance off, I could not make out their conversation. It was just below comprehension level. I could hear their words, but could not understand them.

But I could watch the way they spoke and their gestures, and tell how they were reacting to each other. It became evident, after a few minutes, that there were a great many tensions around that table. There was no open argument, but they sat and looked at each other in ways that were next to open challenges and the rumble of their voices bristled with the electricity of controlled anger.

I felt my shoulder tapped and took my attention from the hole to the night outside. It took a few seconds to adjust to the relative darkness on top of the structure, but when I did, I could see that Michael was again talking to me with his hands.

"Look at the youngest of the commanders—the one on your left, with the very black mustache. That's the commander of my regiment."

I looked, identified the man, and lifted my gaze from the hole briefly to nod.

"Now look across the table and as far down from him as possible. You see the somewhat heavy commander with the gray sideburns and the lips that almost pout?"

I looked, raised my head, and nodded again.

"That's the commander of the Guard Regiment. He and my commander are beginning to wear on each other. If not, they'd be seated side by side and pretending that anything that ever was between their two regiments has been put aside. It's almost as bad with the junior officers, if you know the signs to look for in each one's case. Can you guess what's triggered it off?"

"No," I told him, "but I suppose you do, or you wouldn't have brought me here."

"I've been watching for some time. They had the maps out earlier, and it was easy to tell what they were discussing. It's the position of each regiment in the line of battle tomorrow. They've agreed what it's to be, at last, but no one's happy with the final decision."

I nodded.

"I wanted you to see it for yourself. They're all ready to go at each other's throats, and it's an explosive situation. Maybe Amanda can find something in it she can use. I brought you here because I was hoping that when we go back to rendezvous with the others, you'll support me in suggesting that she come and see this for herself."

I nodded again. The brittle emotions betrayed by the commanders below had been obvious, even to me, the moment I had first looked through the hole.

We slipped quietly back down the curve of the building to the shadowed ground at its back and moved out together towards the rendezvous point.

We had no trouble making our way out through the rest of the encampment and back to our meeting spot. It was safely beyond the illumination of the lights that the regiments had set up amongst their buildings. Ian and Amanda were already there, and we stood together, looking back at the activity in the encampment as we compared notes.

"I called Captain El Man in to look at something I'd found," Michael said. "In my alternate area, there was a meeting going on between the regimental commanders—"

The sound of a shot from someone's antique explosive firearm cut him short. We all turned toward the encampment and saw a lean figure, wearing a white shirt brilliantly reflective in the lights, running toward us, while a gang of men poured out of one of the tents, stared about, and then started in pursuit.

The one they chased was running directly for us in his obvious desire to get away from the camp. It would have been easy to believe that he had seen us and was running to us for help, but the situation did not support that conclusion. Aside from the unlikeliness of his seeking aid from strangers dressed and equipped as we were, it was obvious that with his eyes still dilated from the lights of the camp and staring at black-dressed figures like ours, he was completely unable to see us.

All of us dropped flat into the sparse grass of the plain. But he still came straight for us. Another shot sounded from his pursuers.

It only seems, of course, that the luck in such situations is always bad. It is not so, of course. Good and bad balance out. But knowing this does not help when things seem freakishly determined to do their worst. The fugitive had all the open Naharese plain into which to run. He came toward us instead, as if drawn on a cable. We lay still. Unless he actually stepped on one of us, there was a chance he could run right through us and not know we were there.

He did not step on one of us, but he did trip over Michael, stagger on a step, check, and glance down to see what had interrupted his flight. He looked directly at Amanda and stopped, staring down in astonishment. A second later, he had started to swing around to face his pursuers, his mouth open to shout to them.

Whether he had expected the information of what he had found to soothe their anger toward him, or whether he had simply forgotten at that moment that they had been chasing him, was beside the point. He was obviously about to betray our presence, and Amanda did exactly the correct thing—even if it produced the least desirable results. She uncoiled from the ground like a spring released from tension, one fist taking the fugitive in the Adam's apple to cut off his cry, and the other going into him just under the breastbone to take the wind out of him and put him down without killing him.

She had been forced to rise between him and his pursuers. But, all black as she was in contrast to the brilliant whiteness of his shirt, she would well have flickered for a second before their eyes without being recognized. With the man down, we could have slipped away from the pursuers without their realizing until too late that we had been there. But the incredible bad luck of that moment was still with us.

As she took the man down, another shot sounded from the pursuers, clearly aimed at the new-stationary target of the fugitive—and Amanda went down with him.

She was up again in a second.

"Fine—I'm fine," she said. "Let's go!"

We went, fading off into the darkness at the same steady trot at which we had come to the camp. Until we were aware of specific pursuit, there was no point in burning up our reserves of energy. We moved steadily away, back toward Gebel Nahar, while the pursuers finally reached the fugitive, surrounded him, got him on his feet and talking.

By that time we could see them flashing around them the lights some of them had been carrying, searching the plain for us. But we were well away by that time, and drawing farther off every second. No pursuit developed.

"Too bad," said Ian, as the sounds and lights of the camp dwindled behind us. "But no great harm done. What happened to you, 'Manda?"

She did not answer. Instead, she went down again, stumbling and dropping abruptly. In a second we were all back and squatting around her.

She was plainly having trouble breathing.

"Sorry . . . ," she whispered.

Ian was already cutting away the clothing over her left shoulder.

"Not much blood," he said.

The tone of his voice said he was very angry with her. So was I. It was entirely possible that she might have killed herself by trying to run with a wound that should not have been excited by that kind of treatment. She had acted instinctively to hide the knowledge that she had been hit by that last shot, so that the rest of us would not hesitate in getting away safely. It was not hard to understand the impulse that had made her do it—but she should not have.

"Corunna," said Ian, moving aside. "This is more in your line."

He was right. As a captain, I was the closest thing to a physician aboard most of the time. I moved in beside her and checked the wound as best I could. In the general but faint starlight, it showed as merely a small patch of darkness against a larger, pale patch of exposed flesh. I felt it with my fingers and put my cheek down against it.

"Small caliber slug," I said. Ian breathed a little harshly out through his nostrils. He had already deduced that much. I went on. "Not a sucking wound. High up, just below the collarbone. No immediate pneumothorax, but the chest cavity'll be filling with blood. Are you very short of breath, Amanda? Don't talk, just nod or shake your head."

She nodded.

"How do you feel. Dizzy? Faint?"

She nodded again. Her skin was clammy to my touch.

"Going into shock," I said.

I put my ear to her chest again.

"Right," I said. "The lung on this side's not filling with air. She can't run. She shouldn't do anything. We'll need to carry her."

"I'll do that," said Ian. He was still angry—irrationally, emotionally angry, but trying to control it. "How fast do we have to get her back, do you think?"

"Her condition ought to stay the same for a couple of hours," I said. "Looks like no large blood vessels were hit, and the smaller vessels tend to be self-sealing. But the pleural cavity on this side has been filling up with blood and she's collapsed a lung. That's why she's having trouble breathing. No blood around her mouth, so it probably didn't nick an airway going through. . . ."

I felt around behind her shoulder but found no exit wound.

"It didn't go through. If there're MASH med-mech units back at Gebel Nahar and we get her back in the next two hours, she should be all right— if we carry her."

Ian scooped her into his arms. He stood up.

"Head down," I said.

"Right," he answered, and put her over one shoulder in a fireman's carry. "No, wait—we'll need some padding for my shoulder."

Michael and I took off our jerseys and made a pad for his other shoulder. He transferred her to that shoulder, with her head hanging down his back. I sympathized with her. Even with the padding, it was not a comfortable way to travel, and her wound and shortness of breath would make it a great deal worse.

"Try it at a slow walk first," I said.

"I'll try it. But we can't go slow walk all the way," said Ian. "It's nearly three klicks from where we are now."

He was right, of course. To walk her back over a distance of three kilometers would take too long. I went behind him to watch her as well as could be done. The sooner I got her to a med-mech unit the better. We started off, and he gradually increased his pace until we were moving smoothly but briskly.

"How are you?" he asked her, over his shoulder.

"She nodded," I reported from my position behind him.

"Good," he said, and began to jog.

We travelled. She made no effort to speak, and none of the rest of us spoke. From time to time, I moved up closer behind Ian to watch her at close range, and as far as I could tell, she did not lose consciousness once on that long, jolting ride. Ian forged ahead, something made of steel rather than of ordinary human flesh, his gaze fixed on the lights of Gebel Nahar, far off across the plain.

There is something that happens under those conditions where the choice is either to count the seconds, or disregard time altogether. In the end we all—and I think Amanda, too, as far as she was capable of controlling how she felt—went off a little way from ordinary time and did not come back to it until we were at the entrance to the Conde's secret tunnel, leading back under the walls of Gebel Nahar.

By the time I got Amanda laid out in the medical section of Gebel Nahar, she looked very bad indeed and was only semiconscious. Anything else, of course, would have been surprising indeed. It does not improve the looks of even a very healthy person to be carried head down for over thirty minutes. Luckily, the medical section had everything necessary in the way of med-mechs. I was able to find a portable unit that could be rigged for bed rest—vacuum pump, power unit, drainage bag. It was a matter of inserting a tube between Amanda's lung and chest wall—and this I left to the med-mech, which was less liable to human mistakes than I was on a day in which luck seemed to be running so badly—so that the unit could exhaust the blood from the pleural space into which it had drained.

It was also necessary to rig a unit to supply her with reconstituted whole blood while this draining process was going on. However, none of this was difficult, even for a part-trained person like myself, once we got her safely to the medical section. I finally got her fixed up and left her to rest. She was in no shape to do much else.

I went off to the offices to find Ian and Kensie. They were both there, and they listened without interrupting to my report on Amanda's treatment and my estimate of her condition.

"She should rest for the next few days, I take it," said Ian when I was done.

"That's right," I said.

"There ought to be some way we could get her out of here, to safety and a regular hospital," said Kensie.

"How?" I asked. "It's almost dawn now. The Naharese would zero in on any vehicle that tried to leave this place, by ground or air. It'd never get away."

Kensie nodded soberly.

"They should," said Ian, "be starting to move now, if this dawn was to be the attack moment."

He turned to the window, and Kensie and I turned with him. Dawn was just breaking. The sky overhead was white-blue and hard, and the brown stretch of the plain looked also stony and hard and empty between the Gebel Nahar and the distant line of the encampment. It was very obvious, even without vision amplification, that the soldiers and others in the encampment had not even begun to form up in battle positions, let alone begin to move toward us.

"After all their parties last night, they may not get going until noon," I said.

"I don't think they'll be that late," said Ian absently. He had taken me seriously. "At any rate, it gives us a little more time. Are you going to have to stay with Amanda?"

"I'll want to look in on her from time to time—in fact, I'm going back down now," I said. "I just came up to tell you how she is. But in between visits, I can be useful."

"Good," said Ian. "As soon as you've had another look at her, why don't you go see if you can help Michael. He's been saying he's got his doubts about those bandsmen of his."

"All right." I went out.

When I got back to the medical section, Amanda was asleep. I was going to slip out and leave her to rest, when she woke and recognized me.

"Corunna," she said, "how am I?"

"You're fine," I said, going back to the side of the bed where she lay. "All you need now is to get a lot of sleep and do a good job of healing."

"What's the situation outside?" she said. "Is it day yet?"

We were in one of the windowless rooms in the interior of Gebel Nahar.

"Just dawn," I said. "Nothing happening so far. In any case, you forget about all that and rest."

"You'll need me up there."

"Not with a tube between your ribs," I said. "Lie back and sleep."

Her head moved restlessly on the pillow.

"It might have been better if that slug had been more on target."

I looked down at her.

"According to what I've heard about you," I said, "you of all people ought to know that when you're in a hospital bed it's not the best time in the world to be worrying over things."

She started to speak, interrupted herself to cough, and was silent for a little time until the pain of the tube, rubbing inside her with the disturbance of her coughing, subsided. Even a deep breath would move that tube now and pain her. There was nothing to be done about that, but I could see how shallowly she breathed.

"No," she said. "I can't want to die. But the situation as it stands is impossible, and every way out of it there is is impossible, for all three of us. Just like our situation here in Gebel Nahar with no way out."

"Kensie and Ian are able to make up their own minds."

"It's not a matter of making up minds. It's a matter of impossibilities."

"Well, I said, "is there anything you can do about that?"

"I ought to be able to."

"Ought to, maybe, but can you?"

She breathed shallowly. Slowly she shook her head on the pillow.

"Then let it go. Leave it alone," I said. "I'll be back to check on you from time to time. Wait and see what develops."

"How can I wait?" she said. "I'm afraid of myself. Afraid I might throw everything overboard and do what I want most—and so ruin everyone."

"You won't do that."

"I might."

"You're exhausted," I told her. "You're in pain. Stop trying to think. I'll be back in an hour or two to check on you. Until then, rest!"

I went out.

I took the corridors that led me to the band section. I saw no other bandsmen in the corridors as I approached their section, but an orderly was on duty as usual in Michael's outer office, and Michael himself was in his own office, standing beside his desk with a sheaf of printed records in hand.

"Captain!" he said when he saw me.

"I've got to look in on Amanda from time to time," I said. "But in between, Ian suggested you might find me useful."

"I'd always find you useful, sir," he said with the ghost of a smile. "Do you want to come along to stores with me? I need to check a few items of supply, and we can talk as we go."

"Of course."

We left the offices and he led me down other corridors and into a supply section. What he was after, it developed, was not the supplies themselves, but the automated delivery system that would keep feeding them, on command—or at regular intervals, without command, if the communications network was knocked out—to various sections of Gebel Nahar. It was a system of a sort I had never seen before.

"Another of the ways the ranchers who designed this looked ahead to having to hole up here," Michael explained as we looked at the supply bins for each of the various sections of the fortress, each bin already stocked with the supplies it would deliver as needed. He was going from bin to bin, checking the contents of each and testing each delivery system to make sure it was working.

The overhead lights were very bright, and their illumination reflected off solid concrete walls painted a utilitarian, flat white. The effect was at once blinding and bleak, and the feeling of bleakness was reinforced by the stillness of the air. The ventilators must have been working here as in other interior parts of the Gebel Nahar, but with the large open space of the supply section and its high ceilings, the air felt as if there was no movement to it at all.

"Lucky for us," I said.

Michael nodded.

"Yes, if ever a place was made to be defended by a handful of people, this is it. Only, they didn't expect the defense to be by such a small handful as we are. They were thinking in terms of a hundred families, with servants and retainers. Still, if it comes to a last stand for us in the inner fort, on the top three levels, they're going to have to pay one hell of a price to get at us."

I watched his face as he worked. There was no doubt about it. He looked much more tired, much leaner and older than he had appeared to me only a few days before when he had met Amanda and me at the spaceport terminal of Nahar City. But the work he had been doing and what he had gone through could not alone have been enough to cut him down so visibly, at his age.

He finished checking the last of the delivery systems and the last of the bins. He turned away.

"Ian tells me you've got some concern as to how your bandsmen may stand up to the attack," I said.

His mouth thinned and straightened.

"Yes," he said. There was a little pause, and then he added: "You can't blame them. If they'd been real soldier types they would have been in one of the line companies. There's security, but no chance of promotion to speak of, in a band."

Then humor came back to him, a tired but real smile.

"Of course, for someone like myself," he said, "that's ideal."

"On the other hand," I said. "They're here with us. They stayed."

"Well . . ." He sat down a little heavily on a short stack of boxes and waved me to another. "So far it hasn't cost them anything but some hard work. And they've been paid off in excitement. I think I said something to you about that when we were flying out from Nahar City. Excitement— drama—is what most Naharese live for—and die for, for that matter, if the drama is big enough."

"You don't think they'll fight when the time comes?"

"I don't know." His face was bleak again. "I only know I can't blame them—I can't, of all people—if they don't."

"Your attitude's a matter of conviction."

"Maybe theirs is, too. There's no way to judge any one person by another. You never know enough to make a real comparison."

"True," I said. "But I still think that if they don't fight, it'll be for somewhat lesser reasons than yours for not fighting."

He shook his head slowly.

"Maybe I'm wrong, all wrong." His tone was almost bitter. "But I can't get outside myself to look at it. I only know I'm afraid."

"Afraid?" I looked at him. "Of fighting?"

"I wish it was of fighting," he laughed briefly. "No, I'm afraid that I don't have the will *not* to fight. I'm afraid that at the last moment, it'll all come back, all those early dreams and all the growing up and all the training—and I'll find myself killing, even though I'll know that it won't make any difference in the end and that the Naharese will take Gebel Nahar anyway."

"I don't think it'd be Gebel Nahar you'd be fighting for," I said slowly. "I think it'd be out of a natural, normal instinct to stay alive yourself as long as you can—or to help protect those who are fighting alongside you."

"Yes," he said. His nostrils flared as he drew in an unhappy breath. "The rest of you. That's what I won't be able to stand. It's too deep in me. I might be able to stand there and let myself be killed. But can I stand there when they start to kill someone else—like Amanda, and she already wounded?"

There was nothing I could say to him. But the irony of it rang in me just the same. Both he and Amanda, afraid that their instincts would lead them to do what their thinking minds had told them they should not do. He and I walked back to his office in silence. When we arrived, there was a message that had been left with Michael's orderly for me to call Ian.

I did. His face looked out of the phone screen at me, as unchanged as ever.

"The Naharese still haven't started to move," he said. "They're so unprofessional I'm beginning to think that perhaps we can get Padma, at least, away from here. He can take one of the small units from the vehicle pool and fly out toward Nahar City. My guess is that once they stop him and see he's an Exotic, they'll simply wave him on."

"It could be," I said.

"I'd like you to go and put that point to him," said Ian. "He seems to want to stay, for reasons of his own, but he may listen if you make him see that by staying here, he simply increases the load of responsibility on the rest of us. I'd like to order him out of here, but he knows I don't have the authority for that."

"What makes you think I'm the one to talk him into going?"

"It'd have to be one of the senior officers here to get him to listen," said Ian. "Both Kensie and I are too tied up to take the time. While even if either one was capable, Michael's a bad choice and Amanda's flat in bed."

"All right," I said. "I'll go talk to him right now. Where is he?"

"In his quarters, I understand. Michael can tell you how to find them."

I reached Padma's suite without trouble. In fact, it was not far from the suite of rooms that had been assigned to me. I found Padma seated at his desk making a recording. He broke off when I stepped into his sitting room in answer to his invitation, which had followed my knock on his door.

"If you're busy, I can drop back in a little while," I said.

"No, no." He swung his chair around, away from the desk. "Sit down. I'm just doing up a report for whoever comes out from the Exotics to replace me."

"You won't need to be replaced if you'll leave now," I said. It was a blunt beginning, but he had given me the opening and time was not plentiful.

"I see," he said. "Did Ian or Kensie ask you to talk to me, or is this the result of an impulse of your own?"

"Ian asked me," I said. "The Naharese are delaying their attack, and he thinks that they're so generally disorganized and unmilitary that there's a chance for you to get safely away to Nahar City. They'll undoubtedly stop whatever vehicle you'd take, when they see it coming out of Gebel Nahar. But once they see you're an Exotic—"

His smile interrupted me.

"All right," I said. "Tell me. Why shouldn't they let you pass when they see you're an Exotic? All the worlds know Exotics are noncombatants."

"Perhaps," he said. "Unfortunately, William has made a practice of identifying us as the machiavellian practitioners at the roots of whatever trouble and evil there is to be found anywhere. At the moment, most of the Naharese have an image of me that's half-demon, half-enemy. In their present mood of license, most of them would probably welcome the chance to shoot me on sight."

I stared at him. He was smiling.

"If that's the case, why didn't you leave days ago?" I asked him.

"I have my duty, too. In this instance, it's to gather information for those on Mara and Kultis." His smile broadened. "Also, there's the matter of my own temperament. Watching a situation like the one here is fascinating. I wouldn't leave now if I could. In short, I'm as chained here as the rest of you, even if it is for different reasons."

I shook my head at him.

"It's a fine argument," I said. "But if you'll forgive me, it's a little hard to believe."

"In what way?"

"I'm sorry," I told him, "but I don't seem to be able to give any real faith to the idea that you're being held here by patterns that are essentially the same as mine, for instance."

"Not the same," he said. "Equivalent. The fact that others can't match you Dorsai in your own particular area doesn't mean those others don't have equal areas in which equal commitments apply to them. The physics of life works in all of us. It simply manifests itself differently with different people."

"With identical results?"

"With comparable results—could I ask you to sit down?" Padma said mildly. "I'm getting a stiff neck looking up at you."

I sat down facing him.

"For example," he said. "In the Dorsai ethic, you and the others here have something that directly justifies your natural human hunger to do things for great purposes. The Naharese here have no equivalent ethic, but they feel the hunger just the same. So they invent their own customs, their *leto de muerte* concepts. But can you Dorsais, of all people, deny that their concepts can lead them to as true a heroism, or as true a keeping of faith, as your ethic leads you to?"

"Of course I can't deny that," I said. "But my people can at least be counted on to perform as expected. Can the Naharese?"

"No. But note the dangers of the fact that Dorsais are known to be

trustworthy, Exotics known to be personally nonviolent, the church soldiers of the Friendly Worlds known to be faith-holders. That very knowledge tends too often to lead one to take for granted that trustworthiness
is the exclusive property of the Dorsai, that there are no truly nonviolent
individuals not wearing Exotic robes, and that the faith of anyone not a
Friendly must be weak and unremarkable. We are all human and struck
with the whole spectrum of the human nature. For clear thinking, it's
necessary to first assume that the great hungers and responses are there
in everyone—then simply go look for them in all people—including the
Naharese."

"You sound a little like Michael when you get on the subject of the
Naharese." I got up. "All right, have it your way and stay if you want.
I'm going to leave now, myself, before you talk me into going out and
offering to surrender before they even get here."

He laughed. I left.

It was time again for me to check Amanda. I went to the medical
section. But she was honestly asleep now. Apparently she had been able
to put her personal concerns aside enough so that she could exercise a
little of the basic physiological control we are all taught from birth. If
she had, it could be that she would spend most of the next twenty-four
hours sleeping, which would be the best thing for her. If the Naharese
did not manage, before that time was up, to break through to the inner
fort where the medical section was, she would have taken a large stride
toward healing herself. If they did break through she would need whatever
strength she could gain between now and then.

It was a shock to see the sun as high in the sky as it was when I
emerged from the blind walls of the corridors once more, onto the first
terrace. The sky was almost perfectly clear and there was a small, steady
breeze. The day would be hot. Ian and Kensie were each standing at one
end of the terrace and looking through watch cameras at the Naharese
front.

Michael, the only other person in sight, was also at a watch camera,
directly in front of the door I had come out. I went to him. He looked
up as I reached him.

"They're on the move," he said, stepping back from the watch camera.
I looked into its rectangular viewing screen, bright with the daylight
scene it showed under the shadow of the battle armor hooding the camera.
He was right. The regiments had finally formed for the attack and were
now moving toward us with their portable field weapons at the pace of
a slow walk across the intervening plain.

I could see their regimental and company flags spaced out along the
front of the crescent formation and whipping in the morning breeze. The
Guard Regiment was still in the center and Michael's Third Regiment

out on the right wing. Behind the two wings, I could see the darker
swarms that were the volunteers and the revolutionaries in their civilian
clothing.

The attacking force had already covered a third of the distance to us.
I stepped away from the screen of the camera, and all at once the front
of men I looked at became a thin line with little bright flashes of reflected
sunlight and touches of color all along it, still distant under the near-
cloudless sky and the climbing sun.

"Another thirty or forty minutes before they reach us," said Michael.

I looked at him. The clear daylight showed him as pale and wire-tense.
He looked as if he had been whittled down until nothing but nerves were
left. He was not wearing weapons, although at either end of the terrace,
Ian and Kensie both had sidearms clipped to their legs, and behind us
there were racks of cone rifles ready for use.

The rifles woke me to something I had subconsciously noted but not
focused upon. The bays with the fixed weapons were empty of human
figures.

"Where're your bandsmen?" I asked Michael.

He gazed at me.

"They're gone," he said.

"Gone?"

"Decamped. Run off. Deserted, if you want to use that word."

I stared at him.

"You mean they've joined—"

"No, no." He broke in on me as if the question I was just about to
ask was physically painful to him. "They haven't gone over to the enemy.
They just decided to save their own skins. I told you—you remember,
I told you they might. You can't blame them. They're not Dorsai, and
staying here meant certain death for them."

"If Gebel Nahar is overrun," I said.

"Can you believe it won't be?"

"It's become hard to," I said, "now that there's just us. But there's
always a chance as long as anyone's left to fight. At Baunpore, I saw
men and women firing from hospital beds when the North Freilanders
broke in."

I should not have said it. I saw the shadow cross his eyes and knew
he had taken my reference to Baunpore personally, as if I had been
comparing his present weaponless state with the last efforts of the de-
fenders I had seen then. There were times when my scars became more
curse than blessing.

"That's a general observation only," I told him. "I don't mean to
accuse—"

"It's not what you accuse me of, it's what I accuse me of," he said in a low voice, looking out at the oncoming regiments. "I knew what it meant when my bandsmen took off. But I also understand how they could decide to do it."

There was nothing more I could say. We both knew that without his forty men we could not even make a pretense of holding the first terrace past the moment when the first line of Naharese would reach the base of the ramparts. There were just too few of us and too many of them to stop them from coming over the top.

"They're probably hiding just out beyond the walls," he said. He was still talking about his former bandsmen. "If we do manage to hold out for a day or two, there's a slight chance they might trickle back—"

He broke off, staring past me. I turned and saw Amanda.

How she had managed to do it by herself, I do not know. But clearly she had gotten herself out of her hospital bed and strapped the portable drainage unit onto her. It was not heavy or much bigger than a thick book, and it was designed for wearing by an ambulatory patient, but it must have been hell for her to rig it by herself with that tube rubbing inside her at every deep breath.

Now she was here, looking as if she might collapse at any time, but on her feet with the unit slung from her right shoulder and strapped to her left side. She had a sidearm clipped to her left thigh, over the cloth of the hospital gown; and the gown itself had been ripped up the center so that she could walk in it.

"What the hell are you doing up here?" I snarled at her. "Get back to bed!"

"Corunna—" She gave me the most level and unyielding stare I have ever encountered from anyone in my life. "Don't give me orders. I rank you."

I blinked at her. It was true I had been asked to be her driver for the trip here, and in a sense that put me under her orders. But for her to presume to tell a captain of a full flight of fighting ships, with an edge of half a dozen years in seniority and experience, that in a combat situation like this, she ranked him—it was raving nonsense. I opened my mouth to explode—and found myself bursting out in laughter instead. The situation was too ridiculous. Here we were, five people even counting Michael, facing six thousand, and I was about to let myself get trapped into an argument over who ranked who. Aside from the fact that only the accident of her present assignment gave her any claim to superiority over me, relative rank between Dorsai had always been a matter of local conditions and situations, tempered with a large pinch of common sense.

But obviously she was out here on the terrace to stay, and obviously I was not going to make any real issue of it under the circumstances. We both understood what was going on. Which did not change the fact that she should not have been on her feet. Like Ian out on the plain, and in spite of having been forced to see the funny side of it, I was still angry with her.

"The next time you're wounded, you better hope I'm not your medico," I told her. "What do you think you can do up here, anyway?"

"I can be with the rest of you," she said.

I closed my mouth again. There was no arguing with that answer. Out of the corner of my eyes, I saw Kensie and Ian approaching from the far ends of the terrace. In a moment they were with us.

They looked down at her, but said nothing, and we all turned to look again out cross the plain.

The Naharese front had been approaching steadily. It was still too far away to be seen as a formation of individuals. It was still just a line of a different shade than the plain itself, touched with flashes of light and spots of color. But it was a line with a perceptible thickness now.

We stood together, the five of us, looking at the slow, ponderous advance upon us. All my life, as just now with Amanda, I had been plagued by a sudden awareness of the ridiculous. It came on me now. What mad god had decided that an army should march against a handful— and that the handful should not only stand to be marched upon, but should prepare to fight back? But then the sense of the ridiculousness passed. The Naharese would continue to come on because all their lives had oriented them against Gebel Nahar. We would oppose them when they came because all our lives had been oriented to fighting for even lost causes, once we had become committed to them. In another time and place, it might be different for those of us on both sides. But this was the here and now.

With that, I passed into the final stage that always came on me before battle. It was as if I stepped down into a place of private peace and quiet. What was coming would come, and I would meet it when it came. I was aware of Kensie, Ian, Michael, and Amanda standing around me, and aware that they were experiencing much the same feelings. Something like a telepathy flowed among us, binding us together in a feeling of particular unity. In my life there has been nothing like that feeling of unity, and I have noticed that those who have once felt it never forget it. It is as it is, as it always has been, and we who are there at that moment are together. Against that togetherness, odds no longer matter.

There was a faint scuff of a foot on the terrace floor, and Michael was gone. I looked at the others, and the thought was unspoken between us. He had gone to put on his weapons. We turned once more to the plain and saw the approaching Naharese now close enough so that they were recognizable as individual figures. They were almost close enough for the sound of their approach to be heard by us.

We moved forward to the parapet of the terraces and stood watching. The day breeze, strengthening, blew in our faces. There was time now to appreciate the sunlight, the not-yet-hot temperature of the day and the moving air. Another few hundred meters and they would be within the range of maximum efficiency for our emplaced weapons—and we, of course, within range of their portables. Until then, there was nothing urgent to be done.

The door opened behind us. I turned, but it was not Michael. It was Padma, supporting El Conde, who was coming out to us with the help of a silver-headed walking stick. Padma helped him out to where we stood at the parapet, and for a second he ignored us, looking instead out at the oncoming troops. Then he turned to us.

"Gentlemen and lady," he said in Spanish, "I have chosen to join you."

"We're honored," Ian answered him in the same tongue. "Would you care to sit down?"

"Thank you, no. I will stand. You may go about your duties."

He leaned on the cane, watching across the parapet and paying no attention to us. We stepped back away from him, and Padma spoke in a low voice.

"I'm sure he won't be in the way," Padma said. "But he wanted to be down here, and there was no one but me left to help him."

"It's all right," said Kensie. "But what about you?"

"I'd like to stay, too," said Padma.

Ian nodded. A harsh sound came from the throat of the count, and we looked at him. He was rigid as some ancient dry spearshaft, staring out at the approaching soldiers, his face carved with the lines of fury and scorn.

"What is it?" Amanda asked.

I had been as baffled as the rest. Then a faint sound came to my ear. The regiments were at last close enough to be heard, and what we were hearing were their regimental bands—except Michael's band, of course— as a faint snatch of melody on the breeze. It was barely audible, but I recognized it, as El Conde obviously already had.

"They're playing the *te guelo*," I said. "Announcing 'no quarter.'"

The *te guelo* is a promise to cut the throat of anyone opposing. Amanda's eyebrows rose.

"For us?" she said. "What good do they think that's going to do?"

"They may think Michael's bandsmen are still with us, and perhaps they're hoping to scare them out," I said. "But probably they're doing it just because it's always done when they attack."

The others listened for a second. The *te guelo* is an effectively chilling piece of music, but as Amanda had implied, it was a little beside the point to play it to Dorsai who had already made their decision to fight.

"Where's Michael?" she asked now.

I looked around. It was a good question. If he had indeed gone for weapons, he should have been back out on the terrace by this time. But there was no sign of him.

"I don't know," I said.

"They stopped their portable weapons," Kensie said, "and they're setting them up to fire. Still out of effective range, against walls like this."

"We'd probably be better down behind the armor of our own embayments and ready to fire back when they get a little closer," said Ian. "They can't hurt the walls from where they are. They might get lucky and hurt some of us."

He turned to El Conde.

"If you'd care to step down into one of the weapon embayments, sir—" he said.

El Conde shook his head.

"I shall watch from here," he announced.

Ian nodded. He looked at Padma.

"Of course," said Padma. "I'll come in with one of you—unless I can be useful in some other way?"

"No," said Ian. A shouting from the approaching soldiers that drowned out the band music turned him and the rest of us once more toward the plain.

The front line of the attackers had broken into a run toward us. They were only a hundred meters or so now from the foot of the slope leading to the walls of Gebel Nahar. Whether it had been decided that they should attack from that distance, or—more likely—someone had gotten carried away and started forward early, did not matter. The attack had begun.

For a moment, all of us who knew combat recognized immediately this development had given us a temporary respite from the portable weapons. With their own soldiers flooding out ahead, it would be difficult for the gunners to fire at Gebel Nahar without killing their own men. It was the sort of small happenstance that can sometimes be turned to an advantage—but, as I stared out at the plain, I had no idea of what we might do that in that moment would make any real difference to the battle's outcome.

"Look!"

It was Amanda calling. The shouting of the attacking soldiers had stopped suddenly. She was standing right at the parapet, pointing out and down. I took one step forward, so that I could see the slope below close by the foot of the first wall, and I saw what she had seen.

The front line of the attackers was full of men trying to slow down against the continued pressure of those behind who had not yet seen what those in front had. The result was effectively a halting of the attack as more and more of them stared at what was happening on the slope.

What was happening there was that the lid of El Conde's private exit from Gebel Nahar was rising. To the Naharese military it must have looked as if some secret weapon was about to unveil itself on the slope— and it would have been this that had caused them to have sudden doubts and their front line of men to dig in their heels. They were still a good two or three hundred meters from the tunnel entrance, and the first line of attackers, trapped where they were by those behind them, must have suddenly conceived of themselves as sitting ducks for whatever field-class weapon would elevate itself through this unexpected opening and zero in on them.

But of course no such weapon came out. Instead, what emerged was what looked like a head wearing a regimental cap, with a stick tilted back by its right ear . . . and slowly, up onto the level of the ground and out to face them all, came Michael.

He was still without weapons. But he was now dressed in his full parade regimentals as band officer, and the *gaita gallega* was resting in his arms and on his shoulder, the mouthpiece between his lips, the long drone over his shoulder. He stepped out onto the slope of the hill and began to march down it, toward the Naharese.

The silence was deadly, and into that silence, striking up, came the sound of the *gaita gallega* as he started to play it. Clear and strong it came to us on the wall, and clearly it reached as well to the now-silent and motionless ranks of the Naharese. He was playing "Su Madre."

He went forward at a march step, shoulders level, the instrument held securely in his arms, and his playing went before him, throwing its challenge directly into their faces. A single figure marching against six thousand.

From where I stood, I had a slight angle on him, and with the help of the magnification of the screen on the watch camera next to me, I could get just a glimpse of his face from the side and behind him. He looked peaceful and intent. The exhausted leanness and tension I had seen in him earlier seemed to have gone out of him. He marched as if on parade, with the intentness of a good musician in performance, and all the time "Su Madre" was hooting and mocking at the armed regiments before him.

I touched the controls of the camera to make it give me a closeup look at the men in the front of the Naharese force. They stood as if paralyzed, as I panned along their line. They were saying nothing, doing nothing, only watching Michael come toward them as if he meant to march right through them. All along their front, they were stopped and watching.

But their inaction was something that could not last—a moment of shock that had to wear off. Even as I watched, they began to stir and speak. Michael was between us and them, and with the incredible voice of the bagpipe, his notes came almost loudly to our ears. But rising behind them, we now began to hear a low-pitched swell of sound like the growl of some enormous beast.

I looked in the screen. The regiments were still not advancing, but none of the figures I now saw as I panned down the front were standing frozen with shock. In the middle of the crescent formation, the soldiers of the Guard Regiment, who held a feud with Michael's own Third Regiment, were shaking weapons and fists at him and shouting. I had no way of knowing what they were saying, at this distance, and the camera could not help me with that, but I had no doubt that they were answering challenge with challenge, insult with insult.

All along the line, the front boiled, becoming more active every minute. They had all seen that Michael was unarmed, and for a few moments this held them in check. They threatened, but did not offer to fire on him. But even at this distance, I could feel the fury building up in them. It was only a matter of time, I thought, until one of them lost his self-control and used the weapon he carried.

I wanted to shout at Michael to turn around and come back to the tunnel. He had broken the momentum of their attack and thrown them into confusion. With troops like this, they would certainly not take up their advance where they had halted it. It was almost a certainty that after this challenge, this emotional shock, their senior officers would pull them back and reform them before coming on again. A valuable breathing space had been gained. It could be some hours, it could be not until tomorrow, before they would be able to mount a second attack, and in that time, internal tensions or any number of developments might work to help us further. Michael still had them between his thumb and forefinger. If he turned his back on them now, their inaction might well hold until he was back in safety.

But there was no way I could reach him with that message. And he showed no intention of turning back on his own. Instead he went steadily forward, scorning them with his music, taunting them for attacking in their numbers an opponent so much less than themselves.

Still the Naharese soldiery only shook their weapons and shouted insults at him, but now in the screen I began to see a difference. On the wing occupied by the Third Regiment, there were uniformed figures beginning to wave Michael back. I moved the view of the screen farther out along that wing and saw individuals in civilian clothes, some of those from the following swarm of volunteers and revolutionaries, who were pushing their way to the front, kneeling down, and putting weapons to their shoulders.

The Third Regiment soldiers were pushing these others back and jerking their weapons away from them. Fights were beginning to break out, but on that wing, those who wished to fire on Michael were being held back. It was plain that the Third Regiment was torn now between its commitment to join in the attack on Gebel Nahar and its impulse to protect their former bandmaster in his act of outrageous bravery. Still, I saw one civilian with the starved face of a fanatic who had literally to be tackled and held on the ground by three of the Third Regiment before he could be stopped from firing on Michael.

A sudden cold suspicion passed through me. I swung the view of the screen to the opposite wing, and there I saw the same situation. From behind the uniformed soldiers there, volunteers and civilian revolutionaries were trying to stop Michael with their weapons. Some undoubtedly were from the neighboring principalities where a worship of drama and acts of flamboyant courage was not part of the culture, as it was here. On this wing, also, the soldiers were trying to stop those individuals who attempted to shoot Michael. But here, the effort to prevent that firing was scattered and ineffective.

I saw a number of weapons of all types leveled at Michael. No sound could reach me, and only the sport guns and ancient explosive weapons showed any visible sign that they were being fired, but it was clear that death was finally in the air around Michael.

I switched the view hastily back to him. For a moment he continued to march forward in the screen as if some invisible armor was protecting him. Then he stumbled slightly, caught himself, went forward, and fell.

For a second time—for a moment only—the voice of the attackers stopped, cut off as if a multitude of invisible hands had been clapped over the mouths of those there. I lifted the view on the screen from the fallen shape of Michael and saw soldiers and civilians alike standing motionless, staring at him, as if they could not believe that he had at last been brought down.

Then, on the wing opposite to that held by the Third Regiment, the civilians that had been firing began to dance and wave their weapons in the air—and suddenly the whole formation seemed to collapse inward, the two wings melting back into the main body as the soldiers of the Third Regiment charged across the front to get at the rejoicing civilians, and the Guard Regiment swirled out to oppose them. The fighting spread as individual attacked individual. In a moment, they were all embroiled. A wild mob without direction or purpose of any kind, except to kill whoever was closest, took the place of the military formation that had existed only five minutes before.

As the fighting became general, the tight mass of bodies spread out like butter rapidly melting, and the struggle spread out over a larger and larger area, until at last it covered even the place where Michael had fallen. Amanda turned away from the parapet, and I caught her as she staggered. I held her upright and she leaned heavily against me.

"I have to lie down, I guess," she murmured.

I led her towards the door and the bed that was waiting for her back in the medical section. Ian, Kensie, and Padma turned and followed, leaving only El Conde, leaning on his silver-headed stick and staring out at what was taking place on the plain, his face lighted with the fierce satisfaction of a hawk perched above the body of its kill.

It was twilight before all the fighting had ceased, and with the dark there began to be heard the small sounds of the annunciator chimes at the main gate. One by one Michael's bandsmen began to slip back to us in Gebel Nahar. With their return, Ian, Kensie, and I were able to stop taking turns at standing watch, as we had up until then. But it was not until after midnight that we felt it was safe to leave long enough to go out and recover Michael's body.

Amanda insisted on going with us. There was no reason to argue against her coming with us and a good deal of reason in favor of it. She was responding very well to the drainage unit, and a further eight hours of sleep had rebuilt her strength to a remarkable degree. Also, she was the one who suggested we take Michael's body back to the Dorsai for burial.

The cost of travel between the worlds was such that few individuals could afford it, and few Dorsai who died in the course of their duties off-planet had their bodies returned for interment in native soil. But we had adequate space to carry Michael's body with us in the courier vessel, and it was Amanda's point that Michael had solved the problem by his action—something for which the Dorsai world in general owed him a debt. Both Padma and El Conde agreed, after what had happened today, that the Naharese would not be brought back to the idea of revolution again for some time. William's machinations had fallen through. Ian and Kensie could now either make it their choice to stay and execute their contract or legitimately withdraw from it for the reason that they had been faced with situations beyond their control.

In the end, all of us except Padma went out to look for Michael's body, leaving the returned bandsmen to stand duty. It was full night by the time we emerged once more onto the plain through the secret exit.

"El Conde will have to have another of these made for him," commented Kensie as we came out under the star-brilliant sky. "This passage is more a national monument than a secret now."

The night was one very much like the one before when Kensie and I had made our sweep in search of observers from the other side. But this time we were looking only for the dead—and that was all we found.

During the afternoon, all the wounded had been taken away by their friends, but there were bodies to be seen as we moved out to the spot where we had seen Michael go down. Not many of them. It had been possible to mark the location exactly using the surveying equipment built into the watch cameras. The fighting had been more a weaponed brawl than a battle. Which did not alter the fact that those who had died were dead. They would not come to live again, any more than Michael would. A small night breeze touched our faces from time to time as we walked. It was too soon after the fighting for the odors of death to have taken possession of the battlefield. For the present, under the stars, the scene we saw, including the dead bodies, had all the neatness and antiseptic quality of a stage setting.

We came to the place where Michael's body should have been, but it was gone. Ian switched on a pocket lamp, and he, with Kensie, squatted to examine the ground. I waited with Amanda. Ian and Kensie were the experienced field officers, with Hunter Team practice. I could spend several hours looking, to see what they would take in at a glance.

After a few minutes, they stood up again and Ian switched off the lamp. There were a few seconds while our eyes readjusted, and then the plain became real around us once more, replacing the black wall of darkness that the lamplight had instantly created.

"He was here, all right," Kensie said. "Evidently quite a crowd came to carry his body off someplace else. It'll be easy enough to follow the way they went."

We followed the trail of scuffed earth and broken vegetation left by the footwear of those who had carried away Michael's body. The track they had left was plain enough so that I myself had no trouble picking it out, even by starlight, as we went along at a walk. It led farther away from Gebel Nahar, toward where the center of the Naharese formation had been when the general fighting broke out. As we went, bodies became more numerous. Eventually, at a spot that must have been close to where the Guard Regiment had stood, we found Michael.

The mound on which his body lay was visible as a dark mass in the starlight, well before we reached it. But it was only when Ian switched on his pocket lamp again that we saw its true identity and purpose. It was a pile nearly a meter high and a good two meters long and broad. Most of what made it up was clothes, but there were many other things mixed in—belts and ornamental chains, ancient weapons, so old that they us must have been heirlooms, bits of personal jewelry, even shoes and boots.

But, as I say, the greater part of what made it up was clothing—in particular uniform jackets or shirts, although a fair number of detached sleeves or collars bearing insignia of rank had evidently been deliberately torn off by their owners and added as separate items.

On top of all this, lying on his back with his dead face turned toward the stars, was Michael. I did not need an interpretation of what I was seeing here, after my earlier look at the painting in the Nahar City Spaceport Terminal. Michael lay not with a sword, but with the *gaita gallega* held to his chest; and beneath him was the *leto de muerte*—the real *leto de muerte*, made up of everything that those who had seen him there that day, and who had fought for and against him after it was too late, considered the most valuable thing they could give from what was in their possession at the time.

Each had given the best he could, to build up a bed of state for the dead hero—a bed of triumph, actually, for in winning here Michael had won everything, according to their rules and their ways. After the supreme victory of his courage, as they saw it, there was nothing left for them but the offering of tribute—their possessions or their lives.

We stood, we three, looking at it all in silence. Finally, Kensie spoke.

"Do you still want to take him home?"

"No," said Amanda. The word was almost as a sigh from her as she stood looking at the dead Michael. "No. This is his home now."

We went back to Gebel Nahar, leaving the corpse of Michael with its honor guard of the other dead around him.

The next day Amanda and I left Gebel Nahar to return to the Dorsai. Kensie and Ian had decided to complete their contract, and it looked as if they should be able to do so without difficulty. With dawn, individual soldiers of the regiments had begun pouring back into Gebel Nahar, asking to be accepted once more into their duties. They were eager to please, and for Naharese, remarkably subdued.

Padma was also leaving. He rode into the spaceport with us, as did Kensie and Ian, who had come along to see us off. In the terminal, we stopped to look once more at the *leto de muerte* painting.

"Now I understand," said Amanda after a moment. She turned from the painting and lightly touched both Ian and Kensie who were standing on either side of her.

"We'll be back," she said, and led the two of them off.

I was left with Padma.

"Understand?" I said to him. "The *leto de muerte* concept?"

"No," said Padma softly. "I think she meant that now she understands what Michael came to understand, and how it applies to her. How it applies to everyone, including me and you."

I felt coldness on the back of my neck.

"To me?" I said.

"You have lost part of your protection, the armor of your sorrow and loss," he answered. "To a certain extent, when you let yourself become concerned with Michael's problem, you let someone else in to touch you again."

I looked at him, a little grimly.

"You think so?" I put the matter aside. "I've got to get out and start the checkover on the ship. Why don't you come along? When Amanda and the others come back and don't find us here, they'll know where to look."

Padma shook his head.

"I'm afraid I'd better say good-bye now," he replied. "There are other urgencies that have been demanding my attention for some time, and I've put them aside for this. Now it's time to pay them some attention. So I'll say good-bye now, and you can give my farewells to the others."

"Good-bye then," I said.

As when we had met, he did not offer me his hand, but the warmth of him struck through to me, and for the first time I faced the possibility that perhaps he was right. That Michael, or he, or Amanda—or perhaps the whole affair—had either worn thin a spot, or chipped off a piece, of that shell that had closed around me when I watched them kill Else.

"Perhaps we'll run into each other again," I said.

"With people like ourselves," he said, "it's very likely."

He smiled once more, turned, and went.

I crossed the terminal to the security section, identified myself, and went out to the courier ship. It was no more than half an hour's work to run the checkover—these special vessels are practically self-monitoring. When I finished, the others had still not yet appeared. I was about to go in search of them when Amanda pulled herself through the open entrance port and closed it behind her.

"Where's Kensie and Ian?" I asked.

"They were paged. The Board of Governors showed up at Gebel Nahar without warning. They both had to hurry back for a full-dress confrontation. I told them I'd say good-bye to you for them."

"All right. Padma sends his farewells by me to the rest of you."

She laughed and sat down in the copilot's seat beside me.

"I'll have to write Ian and Kensie to pass Padma's on," she said. "Are we ready to lift?"

"As soon as we're cleared for it. That port sealed?"

She nodded. I reached out to the instrument bank before me, keyed Traffic Control and asked to be put in sequence for lift-off. Then I gave my attention to the matter of warming the bird to life.

Thirty-five minutes later we lifted, and another ten minutes after that saw us safely clear of the atmosphere. I headed out for the legally requisite number of planetary diameters before making the first phase shift. Then, finally, with mind and hands free, I was able to turn my attention again to Amanda.

She was lost in thought, gazing deep into the pinpoint fires of the visible stars in the navigation screen above the instrument bank. I watched her without speaking for a moment, thinking again that Padma had possibly been right. Earlier, even when she had spoken to me in the dark of my room of how she felt about Ian, I had touched nothing of her. But now, I could feel the life in her as she sat beside me.

She must have sensed my eyes on her, because she roused from her private consultation with the stars and looked over.

"Something on your mind?" she asked.

"No," I said. "Or rather, yes. I didn't really follow your thinking, back in the terminal when we were looking at the painting and you said that now you understood."

"You didn't?" She watched me for a fraction of a second. "I meant that now I understood what Michael had."

"Padma said he thought you'd meant you understood how it applied to you—and to everyone."

She did not answer for a second.

"You're wondering about me—and Ian and Kensie," she said.

"It's not important what I wonder," I said.

"Yes, it is. After all, I dumped the whole matter in your lap in the first place, without warning. It's going to be all right. They'll finish up their contract here and then Ian will go to Earth for Leah. They'll be married and she'll settle in Foralie."

"And Kensie?"

"Kensie." She smiled sadly. "Kensie'll go on . . . his own way."

"And you?"

"I'll go mine." She looked at me very much as Padma had looked at me as we stood below the painting. "That's what I meant when I said I'd understood. In the end, the only way is to be what you are and do what you must. If you do that, everything works. Michael found that out."

"And threw his life away putting it into practice."

"No," she said swiftly. "He threw nothing away. There were only two things he wanted. One was to be the Dorsai he was born to be, and the other was never to use a weapon. It seemed he could have either one but not the other. Only, he was true to both and it worked. In the end, he was Dorsai and unarmed—and by being both he stopped an army."

Her eyes held me so powerfully that I could not look away.

"He went his way and found his life," she said, "and my answer is to go mine. Ian, his. And Kensie, his—"

She broke off so abruptly I knew what she had been about to say.

"Give me time," I said, and the words came a little more thickly than I had expected. "It's too soon yet. Still too soon since she died. But give me time, and maybe ... maybe, even me."

BROTHERS

STE. MARIE, 2280

Physically, he was big, very big. The professional soldiers of several generations from that small, harsh world called the Dorsai are normally larger than men from other worlds, but the Graemes are large even among the Dorsai. At the same time, like his twin brother, Ian, Commander Kensie Graeme was so well-proportioned in spite of his size that it was only at moments like this, when I saw him standing next to a fellow Dorsai like his executive officer, Colonel Charley ap Morgan, that I could realize how big he actually was. He had the black, curly hair of the Graemes, the heavy-boned face and brilliant gray-green eyes of his family, as well as that utter stillness at rest and that startling swiftness in motion that was characteristic of the several generations Dorsai.

So, too, had Ian, back in Blauvain, for physically the twins were the image of each other. But otherwise, temperamentally, their difference was striking. Everybody loved Kensie. He was like some golden god of the sunshine. While Ian was dark and solitary as the black ice of a glacier in a land where it was always night.

"...Blood," Pel Sinjin had said to me on our drive out here to the field encampment of the Expedition. "You know what they say, Tom. Blood and ice water, half-and-half in his veins, is what makes a Dorsai. But something must have gone wrong with those two when their mother was carrying them. Kensie got all the blood. Ian..."

He had let the sentence finish itself. Like Kensie's own soldiers, Pel had come to idolize the man and downgrade Ian in proportion. I had let the matter slide.

Now Kensie was smiling at us as if there was some joke we were not yet in on.

"A welcoming committee?" he said. "Is that what you are?"

"Not exactly," I said. "We came out to talk about letting your men into Blauvain City for rest and relaxation, now that you've got those invading soldiers from the Friendly Worlds all rounded up, disarmed, and ready for shipment home—what's the joke?"

"Just," said Charley ap Morgan, "that we were on our way into Blauvain to see you. We just got a repeater message that you and other planetary officials here on Ste. Marie are giving Ian and Kensie, with their staffs, a surprise victory dinner in Blauvain this evening."

"Hells bells!" I said.

"You hadn't been told?" Kensie asked.

"Not a damn word," I said.

It was typical of the fumbling of the so-called government-of-mayors we had here on our little world of Ste. Marie. Here was I, superintendent of police in Blauvain—our capital city—and here was Pel, commanding general of our planetary militia, which had been in the field with the Exotic Expedition sent to rescue us from the invading puritan fanatics from the Friendly Worlds, and no one had bothered to tell either one of us about a dinner for the two commanders of that expedition.

"You're going in then?" Pel asked Kensie. Kensie nodded. "I've got to call my HQ."

Pel went out. Kensie laughed.

"Well," he said, "this gives us a chance to kill two birds at once. We'll ride back with you and talk on the way. Is there some difficulty about Blauvain absorbing our men on leave?"

"Not that way," I said. "But even though the Friendlies have all been rounded up, the Blue Front is still with us in the shape of a good number of political outlaws and terrorists that want to pull down our present government. They lost the gamble they took when they invited in the Friendly troops, but now they may take advantage of any trouble that can be stirred up around your soldiers while they're on their own in the city."

"There shouldn't be any." Kensie reached for a dress gunbelt of black leather and began to put it on over the white dress uniform he was already wearing. "But we can talk about it, if you like—You'd better be doing some dressing yourself, Charley."

"On my way," said Charley ap Morgan, and went out.

So fifteen minutes later, Pel and I found ourselves headed back the way we had come, this time with three passengers. I was still at the controls of the police car as we slid on its aircushion across the rich grass of our Ste. Marie summer toward Blauvain, but Kensie rode with me in front, making me feel small beside him—and I am considered a large man among our own people on Ste. Marie. Beside Kensie, I must have looked like a fifteen-year-old boy. Pel was equally small in back between

Charley and a Dorsai senior commandant named Chu Van Moy—a heavy-bodied, black Mongol, if you can imagine such a man, from the Dorsai South Continent.

". . . No real problem," Kensie was saying as we left the grass at last for the vitreous road surface leading us in among the streets and roads of the city—in particular, the road curving in between the high office buildings of Blauvain's West Industrial Park, now just half a kilometer ahead. "We'll turn the men loose in small groups if you say. But there shouldn't be any need to worry. They're mercenaries, and a mercenary knows that civilians pay his wages. He's not going to make any trouble that would give his profession a bad name."

"I don't worry about your men," I said. "It's the Blue Front fabricating some trouble in the vicinity of some of your men and then trying to pin the blame on them that worries me. The only way to guard against that is to have your troops in small enough numbers so that my policemen can keep an eye on the civilians around them."

"Fair enough," said Kensie. He smiled down at me. "I hope, though, you don't plan on having your men holding our men's hands all through their evenings in town—"

Just then we passed between the first of the tall office buildings. A shadow from the late morning sun fell across the car, and the high walls around us gave Kensie's last words a flat echo. Right on the heels of those words—in fact, mixed in with them—came a faint sound as of multiple whistlings about us, and Kensie fell forward, no longer speaking, until his forehead against the front windowscreen stopped him from movement.

The next thing I knew I was flying through the air, literally. Charley ap Morgan had left the police car on the right side, dragging me along with a hand like a steel clamp on my arm, until we ended up against the front of the building on our right. We crouched there, Charley with his dress handgun in his fist and looking up at the windows of the building opposite. Across the narrow way, I could see Chu Van Moy with Pel beside him, a dress gun also in Chu's fist. I reached for my own police beltgun and remembered I was not wearing it.

About us there was utter silence. The narrow little projectiles from one or more sliver rifles that had fluted about us did not come again. For the first time, I realized there was no one on the streets and no movement to be seen behind the windows about us.

"We've got to get him to a hospital," said Pel on the other side of the street. His voice was strained and tight. He was staring fixedly at the still figure of Kensie, still slumped against the windscreen.

"A hospital," he said again. His face was as pale as a sick man's.

Neither Charley nor Chu paid any attention. Silently they were continuing to scan the windows of the building opposite them.

"A hospital!" shouted Pel suddenly.

Abruptly, Charley got to his feet and slid his weapon back into its holster. Across the street, Chu was also rising. Charley looked at the other Dorsai.

"Yes," said Charley, "where is the nearest hospital?"

But Pel was already behind the controls of the police car. The rest of us had to move or be left behind. He swung the car toward Blauvain's Medical Receiving, West, only three minutes away.

He drove the streets like a madman, switching on the warning lights and siren as he went. Screaming, the vehicle careened through traffic and signals alike to jerk to a stop behind the ambulance entrance at Medical West. Pel jumped from the car.

"I'll get a life support system—a medician—" he said, and ran inside.

I got out, and then Charley and Chu got out, more slowly. The two Dorsais were on opposite sides of the car.

"Find a room," Charley said. Chu nodded and went after Pel through the ambulance entrance.

Charley turned to the car. Gently, he picked up Kensie in his arms the way you pick up a sleeping child, holding Kensie to his chest so that Kensie's head fell in to rest on Charley's left shoulder. Carrying his field commander, Charley turned and went into the medical establishment. I followed.

Inside, there was a long corridor with hospital personnel milling about. Chu stood by a doorway a few meters down the hall to the left, half a head taller than the people between us. With Kensie in his arms, Charley went toward the other commandant.

Chu stood aside as Charley came up. The door swung back automatically, and Charley led the way into a room with surgical equipment in sterile cases along both its sides and an operating table in its center. Charley laid Kensie softly on the table, which was almost too short for his tall body. He put the long legs together, picked up the arms and laid their hands on the upper thighs. There was a line of small, red stains across the front of his jacket, high up, but no other marks. Kensie's face, with its eye closed, looked blindly to the white ceiling overhead.

"All right," said Charley. He led the way back out into the hall. Chu came last and turned to click the lock on the door into place, drawing his handgun.

"What's this?" somebody shouted at my elbow, pushing toward Chu. "That's an emergency room. You can't do that—"

Chu was using his handgun on low aperture to slag the lock of the door. A crude but effective way to make sure that the room would not be opened by anyone with anything short of an industrial, heavy-duty torch. The man who was talking was middle-aged, with a gray mustache and the short green jacket of a senior surgeon. I intercepted him and held him back from Chu.

"Yes, he can," I said, as he turned to stare furiously in my direction. "Do you recognize me? I'm Tomas Velt, the superintendent of police."

He hesitated, and then calmed slightly—but only slightly.

"I still say—" he began.

"By the authority of my office," I said, "I do now deputize you as a temporary police assistant. —That puts you under my orders. You'll see that no one in this hospital tries to open that door or get into that room until police authorization is given. I make you responsible. Do you understand?"

He blinked at me. But before he could say anything, there was a new outburst of sound and action, and Pel broke into our group, literally dragging along another man in a senior surgeon's jacket.

"Here!" Pel was shouting. "Right in here. Bring the life support—"

He broke off, catching sight of Chu.

"What?" he said. "What's going on? Is Kensie in there? We don't want the door sealed—"

"Pel," I said. I put my hand on his shoulder. "Pel!"

He finally felt and heard me. He turned a furious face in my direction.

"Pel," I said quietly, but slowly and clearly to him. He's dead. Kensie. Kensie is dead."

Pel stared at me.

"No," he said irritably, trying to pull away from me. I held him. *"No!"*

"Dead," I said, looking him squarely in the eyes. "Dead, Pel."

His eyes stared back at me, then seemed to lose their focus and stare off at something else. After a little, they focused back on mine again, and I let go of him.

"Dead?" he repeated. It was hardly more than a whisper.

He walked over and leaned against one of the white-painted corridor walls. A nurse moved toward him, and I signalled her to stop.

"Just leave him alone for a moment," I said. I turned back to the two Dorsai officers who were now testing the door to see if it was truly sealed.

"If you'll come to police headquarters," I said, "we can get the hunt going for whoever did it."

Charley looked at me briefly. There was no more friendly humor in his face now, but neither did it show any kind of shock or fury. The expression it showed was only a businesslike one.

"No," he said briefly. "We have to report."

He went out, followed by Chu, moving so rapidly that I had to run to keep up with their long strides. Outside the door, they climbed back into the police car, Charley taking the controls. I scrambled in behind them and felt someone behind me. It was Pel.

"Pel," I said. "You'd better stay—"

"No. Too late," he said.

And it was too late. Charley already had the police car in motion. He drove no less swiftly than Pel had driven, but without madness. For all that, though, I made most of the trip with my fingers tight on the edge of my seat, for with the faster speed of Dorsai reflexes he went through available spaces and openings in traffic where I would have sworn we could not get through.

We pulled up before the office building attached to the Exotic Embassy as space for Expeditionary Base Headquarters. Charley led the way in past a guard, whose routine challenge broke off in midsentence as he recognized the two of them.

"We have to talk to the base commander," Charley said to him. "Where's Commander Graeme?"

"With the Blauvain mayor, and the Outbond." The guard, who was no Dorsai, stammered a little. Charley turned on his heel. "Wait—sir, I mean the Outbond's with *him*, here in the commander's office."

Charley turned again.

"We'll go on in. Call ahead," Charley said.

He led the way without waiting to watch the guard obey, down a corridor and up an escalator ramp to an outer office where a young Force-leader stood up behind his desk at the sight of us.

"Sir—" The Force-leader said to Charley, "the Outbond and the mayor will only be with the commander another few minutes—"

Charley brushed past him, and the Force-leader spun around to punch at his desk phone. Heels clicking on the polished stone floor, Charley led us toward a farther door and opened it, stepping into the office beyond. We followed him there—into a large, square room with windows overlooking the city and our own broad-shouldered mayor, Moro Spence, standing there with a white-haired, calm-faced, hazel-eyed man in a blue robe. Both faced a desk at which sat the mirror image of Kensie that was his twin brother, Ian Graeme.

Ian spoke to his desk as we came in.

"It's all right," he said. He punched a button and looked up at Charley, who went forward with Chu beside him, to the very edge of the desk, and then both saluted.

"What is it?" asked Ian.

"Kensie," said Charley. His voice became formal. "Field Commander Kensie Graeme has just been killed, sir, as we were on our way into the city."

For perhaps a second—no longer—Ian sat without speaking. But his face—so like Kensie's and yet so different—did not change expression.

"How?" he asked then.

"By assassins we couldn't see," Charley answered. "Civilians, we think. They got away."

Moro Spence swore.

"The Blue Front!" he said. "Ian . . . Ian, listen—"

No one paid any attention to him. Charley was briefly recounting what had happened from the time the message about the invitation had reached the encampment—

"But there wasn't any celebration like that planned!" protested Moro Spence to the deaf ears around him. Ian sat quietly, his harsh, powerful face half in shadow from the sunlight coming in the high window behind him, listening as he might have listened to a thousand other reports. There was still no change visible in him, except perhaps that he, who had always been remote from everyone else, seemed even more remote now. His heavy forearms lay on the desktop, and the massive hands that were trained to be deadly weapons in their own right lay open and still on the papers beneath them. Almost, he seemed to be more legendary character than ordinary man. That impression was not mine alone. Behind me I heard Pel hiss on a breath of sick fury indrawn between his teeth, and I remembered how he had talked of Ian being only ice and water, Kensie only blood.

The white-haired man in the blue robe, who was the Exotic, Padma, Outbond to Ste. Marie for the period of the Expedition, was also watching Ian steadily. When Charley was through with his account, Padma spoke.

"Ian," he said, and his calm, light baritone seemed to linger and re-echo strangely on the ear, "I think this is something best handled by the local authorities."

Ian glanced at him.

"No," he answered. He looked at Charley. "Who's duty officer?"

"Ng'kok," said Charley.

Ian punched the phone button on his desk.

"Get me Colonel Waru Ng'kok, encampment HQ," he said to the desk.

"No?" echoed Moro. "I don't understand, Commander. We can handle it. It's the Blue Front, you see. They're an outlawed political—"

I came up behind him and put my hand on his shoulder. He broke off, turning around.

"Oh, Tom!" he said on a note of relief. "I didn't see you before. I'm glad you're here—"

I put my finger to my lips. He was politician enough to recognize that there are times to shut up. He shut up now, and we both looked back at Ian.

". . . Waru? This is Base Commander Ian Graeme," Ian was saying to his phone. "Activitate our four best Hunter Teams, and take three Forces from your on-duty troops to surround Blauvain. Seal all entrances to the city. No one allowed in or out without our authority. Tell the involved troops briefing on these actions will be forthcoming."

As professional, freelance soldiers under the pattern of the Dorsai contract—which the Exotic employers honored for all their military employees—the mercenaries were entitled to know the aim and purpose of any general orders for military action they were given. By a ninety-six percent vote among the enlisted men concerned, they could refuse to obey the order. In fact, by a hundred percent vote, they could force their officers to use them in an action they themselves demanded. But a hundred percent vote was almost unheard of. The phone grid in Ian's desktop said something I could not catch.

"No," replied Ian, "that's all."

He clicked off the phone and reached down to open a drawer in his desk. He took out a gunbelt—a working, earth-colored gunbelt unlike the dress one Kensie had put on earlier—with sidearm already in its holster, and, standing up, began to strap it on. On his feet, he dominated the room, towering over us all.

"Tom," he said, looking at me, "put your police to work finding out what they can. Tell them all to be prepared to obey orders by any one of our soldiers, no matter what his rank."

"I don't know if I've got the authority to tell them that," I said.

"I've just given you the authority," he answered calmly. "As of this moment, Blauvain is under martial law."

Moro cleared his throat, but I jerked a hand at him to keep him quiet. There was no one in this room with the power to deal with Ian's authority now, except the gentle-faced man in the blue robe. I looked appealingly at Padma, and he turned from me to Ian.

"Naturally, Ian, measures will have to be taken, for the satisfaction of the soldiers who knew Kensie," Padma said softly, "but perhaps finding the guilty men would be better done by the civilian police without military assistance?"

"I'm afraid we can't leave it to them," said Ian briefly. He turned to the other two Dorsai officers. "Chu, take command of the Forces I've just ordered to cordon the city. Charley, you'll take over as acting field commander. Have all the officers and men in the encampment held there, and gather back any who are off post. You can use the office next to this one. We'll brief the troops in the encampment this afternoon. Chu can brief his forces as he posts them around the city."

The two turned and headed toward the door.

"Just a minute, gentlemen!"

Padma's voice was raised only slightly. But the pair of officers paused and turned for a moment.

"Colonel ap Morgan, Commandant Moy," said Padma, "as the official representative of the Exotic government, which is your employer, I relieve you from the requirement of following any further orders of Commander Ian Graeme."

Charley and Chu looked past the Exotic to Ian.

"Go ahead," said Ian. They went. Ian turned back to Padma. "Our contracts provide that officers and men are not subject to civilian authority while on active duty, engaged with an enemy."

"But the war—the war with the Friendly invaders—is over," said Moro.

"One of our soldiers has just been killed," said Ian. "Until the identity of the killers is established, I'm going to assume we're still engaged with an enemy."

He looked again at me.

"Tom," he said. "You can contact your police headquarters from this desk. As soon as you've done that, report to me in the office next door, where I sent Charley."

He came around the desk and went out. Padma followed him. I went to the desk and put in a phone call to my own office.

"For God's sake, Tom!" said Moro to me as I punched phone buttons for the number of my office and started to get the police machinery rolling. "What's going on here?"

I was too busy to answer him. Someone else was not.

"He's going to make them pay for killing his brother," said Pel savagely from across the room. "That's what's going on!"

I had nearly forgotten Pel. Moro must have forgotten him absolutely, because he turned around to him now as if Pel had suddenly appeared on the scene in a cloud of fire and brimstone-odorous smoke.

"Pel?" he said. "Oh, Pel—get your militia together and under arms, right away. This is an emergency—"

"Go to hell!" Pel answered him. "I'm not going to lift a finger to keep Ian from hunting down those assassins. And no one else in the militia who knew Kensie Graeme is going to lift a finger, either."

"But this could bring down the government!" Moro was close to the idea of tears, if not to the actual article. "This could throw Ste. Marie back into anarchy, and the Blue Front will take over by default!"

"That's what the planet deserves," said Pel, "when it lets men like Kensie be shot down like dogs—men who came here to risk their lives to save our government!"

"You're crazier than these mercenaries are!" said Moro, staring at him.

Then a touch of hope lifted Moro's drawn features. "Actually, Ian seems calm enough. Maybe he won't—"

"He'll take this city apart if he has to," said Pel savagely. "Don't blind yourself."

I had finished my phoning. I punched off and straightened up, looking at Pel.

"I thought you told me there was nothing but ice and water to Ian?" I said.

'There isn't," Pel answered. "But Kensie's his twin brother. That's the one thing he can't sit back from and shuffle off. You'll see."

"I hope and pray I don't," I said, and I left the office for the one next door where Ian was waiting for me. Pel and Moro followed, but when we came to the doorway of the other office, there was a soldier there who would let only me through.

". . . We'll want a guard on that hospital room, and a Force guarding the hospital itself," Ian was saying slowly and deliberately to Charley ap Morgan as I came in. He was standing over Charley, who was seated at a desk. Back against a wall stood the silent figure in a blue robe that was Padma. Ian turned to face me.

"The troops at the encampment are being paraded in one hour." he said. "Charley will be going out to brief them on what's happened. I'd like you to go with him and be on the stand with him during the briefing."

I looked back at him, up at him. I had not gone along with Pel's ice-and-water assessment of the man. But now for the first time I began to doubt myself and to believe Pel. If ever there had been two brothers who seemed to be opposite halves of a single egg, Kensie and Ian had been those two. But here was Ian with Kensie dead—perhaps the only living person on the eleven human-inhabited worlds among the stars who had loved or understood him—and Ian had so far shown no more emotion at his brother's death than he might have on discovering an incorrect Order of the Day.

It occurred to me then that perhaps he was in emotional shock—and this was the cause of his unnatural calmness. But the man I looked at now had none of the signs of a person in shock. I found myself wondering if any man's love for his brother could be hidden so deep that not even that brother's violent death could cause a crack in the frozen surface of the one who went on living.

If Ian was repressing emotion that was due to explode sometime soon, then we were all in trouble. My Blauvain police and the planetary militia together were toy soldiers compared to these professionals. Without the Exotic control to govern them, the whole planet was at their mercy. But there was no point in admitting that—even to ourselves—while even the shadow of independence was left to us.

"Commander," I said. "General Pel Sinjin's planetary militia were closely involved with your brother's forces. He would like to be at any such briefing. Also, Moro Spence, Blauvain's mayor and *pro tem* president of the Ste. Marie Planetary Government, would want to be there. Both these men, Commander, have as deep a stake in this situation as your troops."

Ian looked at me.

"General Sinjin," he said after a moment. "Of course. But we don't need mayors."

"Ste. Marie needs them," I said. "That's all our Ste. Marie World Council is, actually—a collection of mayors from our largest cities. Show that Moro and the rest mean nothing, and what little authority they have will be gone in ten minutes. Does Ste. Marie deserve that from you?"

He could have answered that Ste. Marie had been the death of his brother—and it deserved anything he wished to give it. But he did not. I would have felt safer with him if he had. Instead, he looked at me as if from a long, long distance for several seconds, then over at Padma.

"You'd favor that?" he asked.

"Yes," said Padma. Ian looked back at me.

"Both Moro and General Sinjin can go with you then," he said. "Charley will be leaving from here by air in about forty minutes. I'll let you get back to your own responsibilities until then. You'd better appoint someone as liaison from your police, to stand by here in this office."

"Thanks," I said. "I will."

I turned and went out. As I left, I heard Ian behind me, dictating.

"... All travel by the inhabitants of the city of Blauvain will be restricted to that which is absolutely essential. Military passes must be obtained for such travel. Inhabitants are to stay off the streets. Anyone involved in any gathering will be subject to investigation and arrest. The city of Blauvain is to recognize the fact that it is now under martial, not civil, law. ..."

The door closed behind me. I saw Pel and Moro waiting in the corridor.

"It's all right," I told them. "You haven't been shut out of things—yet."

We took off from the top of that building forty minutes later, Charley and myself up in the control seats of a military eight-man liaison craft, with Pel and Moro sitting back among the passenger seats.

"Charley," I asked him, in the privacy of our isolation together up front in the craft, once we were air-borne. "What's going to happen?"

He was looking ahead through the forward vision screen and did not answer for a moment. When he did, it was without turning his head.

"Kensie and I," he said softly, almost absently, "grew up together. Most of our lives we've been in the same place, working for the same employers."

I had thought I knew Charley ap Morgan. In his cheerfulness, he had seemed more human, less of a half-god of war than other Dorsai like Kensie or Ian—or even lesser Dorsai officers like Chu. But now he had moved off with the rest. His words took him out of my reach, into some cold, high distant country where only Dorsai lived. It was a land I could not enter, the rules of which I would never understand. But I tried again anyway.

"Charley," I said, after a moment of silence, "that doesn't answer what I asked you."

He looked at me then, briefly.

"I don't know what's going to happen," he said.

He turned his attention back to the controls. We flew the rest of the way to the encampment without talking.

When we landed, we found the entire Expedition drawn up in formation. They were grouped by Forces into battalion and arm groups, and their dun-colored battle dress showed glints of light in the late afternoon sunlight. It was not until we mounted the stand facing them that I recognized the glitter for what it was. They had come to the formation under arms, all of them—although that had not been in Ian's orders. Word of Kensie had preceded us. I looked at Charley, but he was paying no attention to the weapons.

The sun struck at us from the southwest at a lowered angle. The troops were in formation with their backs to the old factory, and when Charley spoke, the amplifiers caught up his voice and carried it out over their heads.

"Troops of the Exotic Expeditionary Force in relief of Ste. Marie," he said. "By order of Commander Ian Graeme, this briefing is ordered for the hundred and eighty-seventh day of the Expedition on Ste. Marie soil."

The brick walls slapped his words back with a flat echo over the still men in uniform. I stood a little behind him, in the shadow of his shoulder, listening. Pel and Moro were behind me.

"I regret to inform you," Charley said, "that sniper activity within the city of Blauvain, this day, about thirteen hundred hours, cost us the life of Commander Kensie Graeme."

There was no sound from the men.

"The snipers have not yet been captured or killed. Since they remain unidentified, Commander Ian Graeme has ordered that the condition of hostilities, which was earlier assumed to have ended, is still in effect. Blauvain has been placed under martial law, sufficient force has been sent to seal the city against any exit or ingress, and all persons under

Exotic contract to the Expedition have been recalled to this encamp-ment. . . ."

I felt the heat of a breath on my ear and Pel's voice whispered to me.

"Look at them!" he said. "They're ready to march on Blauvain right now. Do you think they'll let Kensie be killed on some stinking little world like this of ours and not see that somebody pays for it?"

"Shut up, Pel," I murmured out of the corner of my mouth at him. But he went on.

"Look at them!" he said. "It's the order to march they're waiting for—the order to march on Blauvain. And if Charley doesn't end up giving it, there'll be hell to pay. You see how they've all come armed?"

"That's right, Pel, Blauvain's not your city!" It was a bitter whisper from Moro. "If it was Castelmaine they were itching to march on, would you feel the same way about it?"

"Yes!" hissed Pel fiercely. "If men come here to risk their lives for us, and we can't do any better than let them be gunned down in the streets, what do we deserve? What does anyone deserve?"

"Stop making a court case out of it!" whispered Moro harshly. "It's Kensie you're thinking of—that's all. Just like it's only Kensie they're thinking of, out there. . . ."

I tried again to quiet them, then realized that actually it did not make any difference. For all practical purposes, the three of us were invisible there behind Charley. The attention of the armed men ranked before us was all on Charley, and only on him. As Pel had said, they were waiting for one certain order—and only that order mattered to them.

It was like standing facing some great, dun-colored, wounded beast that must charge at any second now, if only because in action would there be relief from the pain it was suffering. Charley's expressionless voice went on, each word coming back like a slapping of dry boards together, in the echo from the factory wall. He was issuing a long list of commands having to do with the order of the camp and its transition back to a condition of battle-alert.

I could feel the tension rising as he approached the end of his list of orders without one that might indicate action by the Expedition against the city in which Kensie had died. Then, suddenly, the list was at an end.

". . . That concludes," said Charley, in the same unwarying tones, "the present orders dealing with the situation. I would remind the personnel of this Expedition that at present the identity of the assassins of Com-mander Graeme is unknown. The civilian police are exerting every effort to investigate the matter, and it is the opinion of your officers that nothing else can be done for the moment but to give them our complete cooperation. A suspicion exists that a native, outlawed political party known as the Blue Front may have been responsible for the assassination. If this should be so, we must be careful to distinguish between those of this world who are actually guilty of Commander Graeme's death and the great majority of innocent bystanders."

He stopped speaking.

There was not a sound from the thousands of men ranked before him.

"All right, Brigade-Major," said Charley, looking down from the stand at the ranking officer in the formation. "Dismiss your troops."

The brigade-major, who had been standing like all the rest facing the stand, wheeled about.

"*Atten-shun!*" he snapped, and the amplifier sensors of the stand picked his voice up and threw it out over the men in formation as they had projected Charley's voice. "*Dis-miss!*"

The formation did not disperse. Here and there a slight wavering in the ranks showed itself, and then the lines of standing figures were motionless again. For a long second, it seemed that nothing more was going to happen, that Charley and the mercenary soldiers before him would stand facing each other until the day of Judgment . . . and then somewhere among the ranks, a solitary and off-key bass voice began to sing.

> "*They little knew of brotherhood . . .*"
> Other voices rapidly picked it up.
> "*. . . The faith of fighting men—*
> "*Who once to prove their lie was good*
> "*Hanged Colonel Jacques Chrétien. . . .*"

And suddenly they were all singing in the ranks facing us. It was a song of the young colonel who had been put to death one hundred years before, when the Dorsai were just in their beginning. A New Earth city had employed a force of Dorsai with the secret intention of using them against an enemy force so superior as to surely destroy them utterly— so rendering payment for their services unnecessary while at the same time doing considerable damage to the enemy. Then the Dorsai had defeated the enemy instead, and the city faced the necessity of paying after all. To avoid this, the city authorities came up with the idea of charging the Dorsai commanding officer with dealing with the enemy, taking a bribe to claim victory for a battle never fought at all. It was the technique of the big lie, and it might even have worked if they had not made the mistake of arresting the commanding officer to back up their story.

It was not a song to which I would have had any objection, ordinarily. But now—suddenly—I found it directed at me. It was at Pel, Moro, myself, that the soldiers of the Expedition were all singing it. Before, I had felt almost invisible on the stand behind Charley ap Morgan. Now, we three civilians were the focus of every pair of eyes on the field—we civilians who were like the civilians that had hanged Jacques Chrétien; we who were Ste. Marians, like whoever had shot Kensie Graeme. It was like facing into the roaring maw of some great beast ready to swallow us up. We stood facing it, frozen.

Nor did Charley ap Morgan interfere.

He stood silent himself, waiting while they went through all the verses of the song to its end:—

> *. . . One-fourth of Rochmont's fighting strength—*
> *One battalion of Dorsai—*
> *Were sent by Rochmont forth alone,*
> *To bleed Helmuth, and die.*
>
> *But look, look down from Rochmont's heights*
> *Upon the Helmuth plain.*
> *At all of Helmuth's armored force*
> *By Dorsai checked, or slain.*
>
> *Look down, look down, on Rochmont's shame*
> *To hide the wrong she'd done,*
> *Made claim Helmuth had bribed Dorsais—*
> *No battle had been won.*
>
> *To prove that lie, the Rochmont Lords*
> *Arrested Jacques Chrétien,*
> *On charge he dealt with Helmuth's Chiefs*
> *For payment to his men.*
>
> *Commandant Arp Van Din sent word:*
> *'You may not judge Dorsai,*
> *'Return our Colonel by the dawn,*
> *'Or Rochmont town will die.'*
>
> *Strong-held behind her walls, Rochmont*
> *Scorned to answer them,*
> *Condemned, and at the daybreak, hanged,*
> *Young Colonel Jacques Chrétien.*

Bright, bright, the sun that morning rose
Upon each weaponed wall.
But when the sun set in the west,
Those walls were leveled all.

Then soft and white the moon arose
On streets and roofs unstained,
But when the moon was
   down once more
No street nor roof remained.

No more is there a Rochmont town
No more are Rochmont's men.
But stands a Dorsai monument
To Colonel Jacques Chrétien.

So pass the word from world to world,
Alone still stands Dorsai.
But while she lives, no one of hers,
By foreign wrong shall die.

They little knew of brotherhood
—The faith of fighting men—
Who once to prove their lie was good
Hanged Colonel Jacques Chrétien!

It ended. Once more they were silent—utterly silent. On the platform, Charley moved. He took half a step forward and the sensors picked up his voice once more and threw it out over the heads of the waiting men.

"Officers! Front and center. Face your men!"

From the end of each rank, figures moved. The commissioned and noncommissioned officers stepped forward, turned, and marched to a point opposite the middle of the rank they had headed, turned once more, and stood at attention.

"Prepare to fire."

The weapons in the hands of the officers came up to waist level, their muzzles pointing at the men directly before them. The breath in my chest was suddenly a solid thing. I could not have inhaled or exhaled if I had tried. I had heard of something like this, but I had never believed it, let alone dreamed that I would be there to see it happen. Out of the corner of my eye, I could see the angle of Charley ap Morgan's face, and it was a Dorsai face in all respects now. He spoke again.

"The command to dismiss has been given," Charley's voice rang and re-echoed over the silent men, "and not obeyed. The command will be repeated, under the stricture of the Third Article of the Professional Soldier's Covenant. Officers will open fire on any refusing to obey."

There was something like a small sigh that ran through all the standing men, followed by the faint rattle of safeties being released on the weapons of the men in ranks. They stood facing their officers and noncommissioned officers now—fellow soldiers and old friends. But they were all professionals. They would not simply stand and be executed if it came to the final point. The breath in my chest was now so solid it hurt, like something jagged and heavy pressing against my ribs. In ten seconds we could all be dead.

"Brigade-Major," said the level voice of Charley. "Dismiss your troops."

The brigade-major, who had turned once more to face Charley when Charley spoke to him, turned back again to the parade ground of men.

"Dis—" No more than in Charley's voice was there perceptible change in the brigade-major's command from the time it had been given before. "—miss!"

The formations dissolved. All at once the ranks were breaking up, the men in them turning away, the officers and noncoms lowering the weapons they had lifted to ready position at Charley's earlier command. The long-held breath tore itself out of my lungs so roughly it ripped at my throat. I turned to Charley, but he was halfway down the steps from the platform, as expressionless as he had been all through the last few minutes. I had to half-run to catch up to him.

"Charley!" I said, reaching him.

He turned to look at me as he walked along. Suddenly I felt how pale and sweat-dampened I was. I tried to laugh.

"Thank God that's over," I said.

"Over!" He shook his head. "It's not over, Tom. The enlisted men will be voting now. It's their right."

"Vote?" The world made no sense to me for a second. Then suddenly it made too much sense. "You mean—they might vote to march on Blauvain, or something like that?"

"Perhaps—something like that," he said.

I stared at him.

"And then?" I said. "You wouldn't . . . if their vote should be to march on Blauvain—what would you do?"

He looked at me almost coldly.

"Lead my troops," he said.

I stopped. Standing there, I watched him walk away from me. A hand tugged at my elbow, and I turned around to see that Pel and Moro had caught up to me. It was Moro who had his hand on my arm.

"Tom," said Moro, "what do we do now?"

"See Padma," I said. "If he can't do something, I don't know anybody who can."

Charley was not flying directly back to Blauvain. He was already in a staff meeting with his fellow officers, who were barred from the voting of the enlisted men by the Covenant. We three civilians had to borrow a land car from the encampment motor pool.

It was a silent ride, most of the way back into town. Once again I was at the controls, with Pel beside me. Sitting behind us, just before we reached the west area of the city, Moro leaned forward to put his head between us.

"Tom," he said. "You'll have to put your police on special duty. Pel, you've got to mobilize the militia—right now."

"Moro," I answered—and I suddenly felt dog-tired, weary to the point of exhaustion. "I've got less than three hundred men, ninety-nine percent of them without anything more exciting in the way of experience than filling out reports or taking charge at a fire, an accident, or a family quarrel. They wouldn't face those mercenaries even if I ordered them to."

"Pel," he said, turning away from me, "your men are soldiers. They've been in the field with these mercenaries—"

Pel laughed at him.

"Over a hundred years ago, a battalion of Dorsais took a fortified city—Rochmont—with nothing heavier than light field pieces. This is a *brigade*—six battalions—armed with the best weapons the Exotics can buy them—facing a city with no natural or artificial defenses at all. And you want my two thousand militiamen to try to stop them? There's no force on Ste. Marie that could stop those professional soldiers."

"At Rochmont they were all Dorsai—" Moro began.

"For God's sake!" cried Pel. "These are Dorsai-officered, the best mercenaries you can find. Elite troops—the Exotics don't hire anything else for fear they might have to touch a weapon themselves and damage their enlightenment—or whatever the hell it is! Face it, Moro! If Kensie's troops want to chew us up, they will. And there's nothing you or I can do about it!"

Moro said nothing for a long moment. Pel's last words had hit a near-hysterical note. When the mayor of Blauvain did speak again, it was softly.

"I just wish to God I knew why you want just that to happen so badly," he said.

"Go to hell!" said Pel. "Just go—"

I slammed the car into retro and we skidded to a halt, thumping down on the grass as the aircushion quit. I looked at Pel.

"That's something I'd like to know, too," I said. "All right, you liked

Kensie. So did I. But what we're facing is anything from the leveling of a city to a possible massacre of a couple of hundred thousand people. All that for the death of just one man?"

Pel's face looked bitter and sick.

"We're no good, we Ste. Marians," he said thickly. "We're a fat little farm world that's never done anything since it was first settled but yell for help to the Exotics every time we got into trouble. And the Exotics have bailed us out every time, only because we're in the same solar system with them. What're we worth? Nothing! At least the Dorsal and the Exotics have got some value—some use!"

He turned away from Moro and myself, and we could not get another word out of him.

We drove on into the city, where to my great relief, I finally got rid of Pel and Moro both and was able to get to police headquarters and take charge of things.

As I had expected, things badly needed taking care of there. As I should also have expected, I had very much underestimated how badly they needed it. I had planned to spend two or three hours getting the situation under control and then be free to seek out Padma. But, as it ended up, it took me nearly seven straight hours to damp down the panic, straighten out the confusion, and put some purpose and order back into the operations of all my people, off-duty and otherwise, who had reported for emergency service. Actually, it was little enough we were required to do—merely patrol the streets and see that the town's citizens stayed off the streets and out of the way of the mercenaries. Still, that took seven hours to put into smooth operation, and at the end of that time I was still not free to go hunting for Padma, but had to respond to a series of calls for my presence by the detective crew assigned to work with the mercenaries in tracking down the assassins.

I drove through the empty nighttime streets slowly, with my emergency lights on and the official emblem on my police car clearly illuminated. Three times, however, I was stopped and checked by teams of three to five mercenaries, in battle dress and fully weaponed, that appeared unexpectedly. The third time, the groupman—a noncommissioned officer—in command of the team stopping me, joined me in the car. When twice after that we encountered military teams, he leaned out the right window to show himself, and we were waved through.

We came at last to a block of warehouses on the north side of the city, and to one warehouse in particular. Within, the large, echoing structure was empty except for a few hundred square feet of crated harvesting machinery on the first of its three floors. I found my men on the second floor in the transparent cubicles that were the building's offices, apparently doing nothing.

"What's the matter?" I said when I saw them. They were not only idle, but they looked unhappy as well.

"There's nothing we can do, Superintendent," said the senior detective lieutenant present—Lee Hall, a man I'd known for sixteen years. "We can't keep up with them, even if they'd let us."

"Keep up?" I asked.

"Yes sir," Lee said. "Come on, I'll show you. They let us watch, anyway."

He led me out of the offices up to the top floor of the warehouse, a great, bare space with a few empty crates scattered between piles of unused packing materials. At one end, portable floodlights were illuminating an area with a merciless blue-white light that made the shadows cast by men and things look solid enough to stub your toe on. He led me toward the light until a groupman stepped forward to bar our way.

"Close enough, Lieutenant," he said to Lee. He looked at me.

"This is Tomas Velt, Blauvain superintendent of police."

"Honored to meet you, sir," said the groupman to me. "But you and the lieutenant will have to stand back here if you want to see what's going on."

"What is going on?" I asked.

"Reconstruction," said the groupman. "That's one of our Hunter Teams."

I turned to watch. In the white glare of the light were four of the mercenaries. At first glance they seemed engaged in some odd ballet or mime acting. They were at little distances from one another and first one, then another of them would move a short distance—perhaps as if he had gotten up from a nonexistent chair and walked across to any equally nonexistent table, then turned to face the others. Following which another man would move in and apparently do something at the same invisible table with him.

"The men of our Hunter Teams are essentially trackers, Superintendent," said the groupman quietly in my ear. "But some teams are better in certain surroundings than others. These are men of a team that works well in interiors."

"But what are they doing?" I said.

"Reconstructing what the assassins did when they were here," said the groupman. "Each of three men on the team takes the track of one of the assassins, and the fourth man watches them all as coordinator."

I looked at him. He wore the sleeve emblem of a Dorsai, but he was as ordinary-looking as myself or one of my detectives. Plainly, a first-generation immigrant to that world, which explained why he was wearing the patches of a noncommissioned, rather than a commissioned officer along with that emblem.

"But what kind of signs are they tracking?" I asked.

"Little things, mostly." He smiled. "Tiny things—some things you or I wouldn't be able to see if they were pointed out to us. Sometimes there's nothing and they have to go on guess—that's where the coordinator helps." He sobered. "Looks like black magic, doesn't it? It does, even to me sometimes, and I've been a Dorsai for fourteen years."

I stared at the moving figures.

"You said—three," I said.

"That's right," answered the groupman. "There were three snipers. We've tracked them from the office in the building they fired from, to here. This was their headquarters—the place they moved from, to the office, just before the killing. There's signs they were here a couple of days, at least, waiting."

"Waiting?" I asked. "How do you know there were three and they were waiting?"

"Lots of repetitive sign. Habitual actions. Signs of camping beds set up. Food signs for a number of meals. Metal lubricant signs showing weapons had been disassembled and worked over here. Signs of a portable, private phone—they must have waited for a phone call from someone telling them the commander was on his way in from the encampment."

"But how do you know there were only three?"

"There's signs for only three," he said. "Three—all big for your world, all under thirty. The biggest man had black hair and a full beard. He was the one who hadn't changed clothes for a week—" The groupman sniffed the air. "Smell him?"

I sniffed hard and long.

"I don't smell a thing," I said.

"Hmmm," the groupman looked grimly pleased. "Maybe those fourteen years have done me some good after all. The stink of him's in the air, all right. It's one of the things our Hunter Teams followed to this place."

I looked aside at Lee Hall, then back at the soldier.

"You don't need my detectives at all, do you?" I said.

"No sir," he looked me in the face. "But we assume you'd want them to stay with us. That's all right."

"Yes," I said. And I left there. If my men were not needed, neither was I, and I had no time to stand around being useless. There was still Padma to talk to.

But it was not easy to locate the Outbond. The Exotic Embassy either could not or would not tell me where he was, and the Expedition headquarters in Blauvain also claimed not to know. As a matter of ordinary police work, my own department kept track of important outworlders like the Graeme brothers and the Outbond as they moved around our city. But in this case, there was no record of Padma ever leaving the room in which I had last seen him with Ian Graeme, early in the day. I finally took my determination in both hands and called Ian himself to ask if Padma was with him.

The answer was a blunt No. That settled it. If Padma was with him, a Dorsai like Ian would have refused to answer rather than lie outright. I gave up. I was lightheaded with fatigue, and I told myself I would go home, get at least a few hours of sleep, and then try again.

So, with one of the professional soldiers in my police car to vouch for me at roadblocks, I returned to my own dark apartment, and when, alone at last, I came into the living room and turned on the light, there was Padma, waiting for me in one of my own chair-floats.

The jar of finding him there was solid—more like an emotional explosion than I would have thought. It was like seeing a ghost in reality, the ghost of someone from whose funeral you have just returned. I stood staring at him.

"Sorry to startle you, Tom," he said. "I know, you were going to have a drink and forget about everything for a few hours. Why don't you have a drink, anyway?"

He nodded toward the bar built into a corner of the apartment living room. I never used the thing unless there were guests on hand, but it was always stocked—that was part of the maintenance agreement in the lease. I went over and punched the buttons for a single brandy and water. I knew there was no use offering Padma alcohol.

"How did you get in here?" I said, with my back to him.

"I told your supervisor you were looking for me," Padma said. "He let me in. We Exotics aren't so common on your world here that he didn't recognize me."

I swallowed half the glass at a gulp, carried the drink back, and sat down in a chair opposite him. The background lighting in the apartment had gone on automatically when night darkened the windows. It was a soft light, pouring from the corners of the ceiling and from little random apertures and niches in the walls. Under it, in his blue robe, with his ageless face, Padma looked like the image of a Buddah, beyond all the human and ordinary storms of life.

"What are you doing here?" I asked. "I've been looking all over for you."

"That's why I'm here," Padma said. "The situation being what it is, you would want to appeal to me to help you with it. So I wanted to see you away from any place where you might blame my refusal to help on outside pressures."

"Refusal?" I said. It was probably my imagination, but the brandy and water I had swallowed seemed to have gone to my head already. I felt lightminded and unreal. "You aren't even going to listen to me first before saying no?"

"My hope," said Padma, "is that you'll listen to me first, Tom, before rejecting what I've got to tell you. You're thinking that I could bring pressure to bear on Ian Graeme to move his soldiers half a world away from Blauvain, or otherwise take the situation out of its critical present phase. But the truth is, I could not, and even if I could, I would not."

"Would not," I echoed muzzily.

"Yes. Would not. But not just because of personal choice. For four centuries now, Tom, we students of the Exotic sciences have been telling other men and women that our human race was committed to a future, to the workings of history as it is. It's true we Exotics have a calculative technique now, called ontogenetics, that helps us to resolve any present or predicted moment into its larger historical factors. We've made no secret of having such techniques. But that doesn't mean we can control what will happen, particularly while other men still tend to reject the very thing we work with—the concept of a large, shifting pattern of events that involves all of us and our lives."

"I'm a Catholic, I said. "I don't believe in predestination."

"Neither do we on Mara and Kultis," said Padma. "But we do believe in a physics of human action and interaction, which we believe works in a certain direction, toward a certain goal which we now think is less than a hundred years off—if, in fact, we haven't already reached it. Movement toward that goal has been building up for at least the last thousand years, and by now the momentum of its forces is massive. No single individual or group of individuals at the present time has the mass to oppose or turn that movement from its path. Only something greater than a human being as we know a human being might do that."

"Sure," I said. The glass in my hand was empty. I did not remember drinking the rest of its contents, but the alcohol was bringing me a certain easing of weariness and tension. I got up, went back to the bar, and came back with a full glass, while Padma waited silently. "Sure, I understand. You think you've spotted a historical trend here, and you don't want to interfere for fear of spoiling it. A fancy excuse to do nothing."

"Not an excuse, Tom," Padma said, and there was something different, like a deep gong-note in his voice, that blew the fumes of the brandy clear from my wits for a second and made me look at him. "I'm not telling you I won't do anything about the situation. I'm telling you that I can't do anything about it. Even if I tried to do something, it would be no use. It's not for you alone that the situation is too massive; it's that way for everyone."

l be all right, Force-leader," he said to the officer behind us.
n glad you're here. Mr. Mayor, though, if you don't mind
utside, I'll see you in a few minutes."

ad little choice but to go out again. The door shut behind him.
d me to a chair beside Pel and sat down again himself.

ead, General," he said to Pel. "Repeat what you'd started to
or the benefit of Tom, here."

nced savagely at me for a second out of the edge of his eyes
swering.

loesn't have anything to do with the police commissioner of
" he said, "or anyone else of Ste. Marie."

t," said Ian again. He did not raise his voice. The word was
iron door dropped in Pel's way, forcing him to turn back. Pel
nce more, grimly, at me.

just saying," he said, "if Commander Graeme would go to the
ent and speak to the enlisted men there, he could probably get
ote unanimously."

nanimously for what?" I asked.

house-to-house search of the Blauvain area," Ian answered.

ty's been cordoned," Pel said quickly. "A search like that would
e assassins in a matter of hours, with the whole expeditionary
ching."

I said, "and with the actual assassins, there'd be a few hundred
assassins, or people who fought or ran for the wrong reason,
wounded by the searchers. Even if the Blue Front didn't take
of the opportunity—which they certainly would—to start gun-
h the soldiers in the city streets."

of it?" said Pel, talking to Ian rather than to me. "Your troops
e any Blue Front people. And you'd be doing Ste. Marie a
vipe them out."

whole thing didn't develop into a wiping out of the whole
opulation of the city," I said.

e implying, Tom," said Pel, "that the Exotic troops can't be
by—"

him short.

uggestion, General," he said, "is the same one I've been getting
r quarters. Someone else is here with it right now. I'll let you
he answer I give him."

ed toward his desk annunciator.

n Groupman Whallo," he said.

ightened up and turned back to us as the door to his office
d in came the mercenary noncom I had brushed past out there.

"How do you know if you don't try?" I said. "Let me see you try, and it not work. Then maybe I'd believe you."

"Tom," he said, "can you lift me out of this chair?"

I blinked at him. I am no Dorsai, as I think I have said, but I am large for my world, which meant in this case that I was a head taller than Padma and perhaps a quarter again the weight. Also I was undoubtedly younger, and I had worked all my life to stay in good physical condition. I could have lifted someone my own weight out of that chair with no trouble, and Padma was less than that.

"Unless you're tied down," I said.

"I'm not." He stood up briefly, and then sat again. "Try and lift me, Tom."

I put my glass down, stepped over to his float and stood behind him. I wrapped my arms around his body under his armpits and lifted—at first easily, then with all my strength.

But not only could I not lift him, I could not budge him. If he had been a life-sized statue of stone, I would have expected to feel more reaction and movement in response to my efforts.

I gave up finally, panting, and stood back from him.

"What do you weigh?" I demanded.

"No more than you think. Sit down again, Tom—"

I did.

"Don't let it bother you. It's a trick, of course. No, not a mechanical trick, a physiological one—but a trick just the same, that's been shown on stage at times, at least during the last four hundred years."

"Stand up," I said. "Let me try again."

He did. I did. He was still immovable.

"Now," he said, when I had given up a second time. "Try once more, and you'll find you can lift me."

I wiped my forehead, put my arms around him, and heaved upward with all my strength. I almost threw him against the ceiling overhead. Numbly I set him down again.

"You see?" he said, reseating himself. "Just as I knew you could not lift me until I let you, I know that there is nothing I can do to alter present events here on Ste. Marie from their present direction. But you can."

"*I* can?" I stared at him, then exploded. "Then for God's sake tell me how?"

He shook his head, slowly.

"I'm sorry, Tom," he said. "But that's just what I can't do. I only know that, resolved to ontogenetic terms, the situation here shows you as a pivotal character. On you, as a point, the bundle of human forces that were concentrated here and bent toward destruction by another such pivotal character may be redirected back into the general historical pattern with a minimum of harm. I tell you this so that being aware of it, you can be watching for opportunities to redirect. That's all I can do."

Incredibly, with those words, he got up and went toward the door of the apartment.

"Hold on!" I said, and he stopped, turning back momentarily. "This other pivotal character. Who's he?"

Padma shook his head again.

"It would do you no good to know," he said. "I give you my word he is now far away from the situation and will not be coming back to it. He is not even on the planet."

"One of the assassins of Kensie!" I said. "And they've gotten away, off-planet!"

"No," said Padma. "No. The men who assassinated Kensie are only tools of events. If none of them had existed, three others would have been there in their place. Forget this other pivotal character, Tom. He was no more in charge of the situation he created than you are in charge of the situation here and now. He was simply, like you, in a position that gave him freedom of choice. Goodnight."

With those last words, he was suddenly out the door and gone. To this day I cannot remember if he moved particularly swiftly, or whether for some reason I now can't remember, I simply let him go. Just—all at once I was alone.

Fatigue rolled over me like the heavy waves of some ocean of mercury. I stumbled into the bedroom, fell on my sleeping float, and that was all I remembered until—only a second later, it seemed—I woke to the hammering of my telephone's chimes on my ears.

I reached out, fumbled at the bedside table, and pushed the *on* button.

"Velt here," I said thickly.

"Tom—this is Moro. Tom? Is that you, Tom?"

I licked my lips, swallowed, and spoke more understandably.

"It's me," I said. "What's the call for?"

"Where've you been?"

"Sleeping," I said. "What's the call for?"

"I've got to talk to you. Can you come—"

"You come here," I said. "I've got to get up and dress and get some coffee in me before I go anyplace. You can talk to me while I'm doing it."

I punched off. He was still saying something at the other end of the line, but just then I did not care what it was.

I pushed my dead-heavy body out of bed and began to move. I was dressed and at the coffee when he came.

"Have a cup." I pushed it at him as he [...] with me. He took it automatically.

"Tom—" he said. The cup trembled in h[...] sipped hastily from it before putting it dow[...] the Blue Front once, weren't you?"

"Weren't we all?" I said. "Back when w[...] and it was an idealistic outfit aimed at pu[...] into our world government?"

"Yes, yes, of course," Moro said. "But [...] member once, maybe you know who to c[...]

I began to laugh. I laughed so hard I had [...] spilling it.

"Moro, don't you know better than that[...] present leaders of the Blue Front were, th[...] police commissioner—the head law enforcer[...] is the last man the Blue Front would be in [...] come to you first. You were a member on[...] remember?"

"Yes," he said miserably. "But I don't [...] you're saying. I thought you might have [...] couldn't prove, or—"

"None of them," I said. "All right. Why [...] running the Blue Front now?"

"I thought I'd make an appeal to them [...] Kensie Graeme—to save the Blauvain peop[...] at me. "Just an hour ago the enlisted men [...] on whether to demand that their officers [...] voted over ninety-four percent, in favor. [...] bilized his militia, but I don't think he mea[...] to get in to talk to Ian all day."

"All day?" I glanced at the time on my w[...] P.M. *now*?"

"Yes," said Moro, staring at me. "I tho[...]

"I didn't mean to sleep like this!" I ca[...] toward the door. "Pel's trying to see Ian? [...] see him ourselves, the better."

So we went. But we were too late. By [...] Headquarters and past the junior officers t[...] Ian was, Pel was already with Ian. I brushed [...] our way and walked in, followed by Moro [...] who sat at a desk surrounded by stacks of [...] as Moro and I appeared.

"That [...]
"Tom, [...]
waiting [...]
Moro [...]
Ian wav[...]
"Go [...]
tell me, [...]
Pel gl[...]
before a[...]
"This [...]
Blauvai[...]
"Repe[...]
simply [...]
glanced [...]
"I wa[...]
encamp[...]
them to [...]
"Vote[...]
"For [...]
"The [...]
turn up [...]
force se[...]
"Sure [...]
suspecte[...]
killed o[...]
advantag[...]
fights w[...]
"Wha[...]
can han[...]
favor to [...]
"If th[...]
civilian [...]
"You'[...]
controlle[...]
Ian cu[...]
"Your[...]
from oth[...]
listen to [...]
He tu[...]
"Send[...]
He st[...]
opened t[...]

In the light, I saw it was the immigrant Dorsai of the Hunter Team I had encountered—the man who had been a Dorsai fourteen years.

"Sir!" he said, stopping a few steps before Ian and saluting. Uncovered himself, Ian did not return the salute.

"You've got a message for me?" Ian said. "Go ahead, I want these gentlemen to hear it, and my answer."

"Yes sir," said Whallo. I could see him glance at and recognize me out of the corner of his eyes. "As representative of the enlisted men of the Expedition, I have been sent to convey to you the results of our latest vote on orders. By unanimous vote, the enlisted men of this command have concurred in the need for a single operation."

"Which is?"

"That a house-to-house search of the Blauvain city area be made for the assassins of Field Commander Graeme," said Whallo. He nodded at Ian's desk and for the first time I saw solidigraphs there—artists' impressions, undoubtedly, but looking remarkably lifelike of three men in civilian clothes. "There's no danger we won't recognize them when we find them."

Whallo's formal and artificial delivery was at odds with the way I had heard him speak when I had run into him at the Hunter Team site. There was, it occurred to me suddenly, probably a military protocol even to matters like this—even to the matter of a man's death and the possible death of a city. It came as a little shock to realize it, and for the first time I began to feel something of what Padma had meant in saying that the momentum of forces involved here was massive. For a second it was almost as if I could feel those forces like great winds, blowing on the present moment. —But Ian was already answering him.

"Any house-to-house search involves possible military errors and danger to the civilian population," he was saying. "The military record of my brother is not to be marred after his death by any intemperate order from me."

"Yes sir," said Whallo. "I'm sorry, sir, but the enlisted men of the Expedition had hoped that the action would be ordered by you. Their decision calls for six hours in which you may consider the matter before our Enlisted Men's Council takes the responsibility for the action upon itself. Meanwhile, the Hunter Teams will be withdrawn—this is part of the voted decision."

"That, too?" said Ian.

"I'm sorry, sir. But you know," said Whallo, "they've been at a dead end for some hours now. The trail was lost in traffic, and the men might be anywhere in the central part of the city."

"Yes," said Ian. "Well, thank you for your message, Groupman."

"Sir!" said Whallo. He saluted again and went out.

As the door closed behind him, Ian's head turned back to face Pel and myself.

"You heard, gentlemen," he said. "Now, I've got work to do."

Pel and I left. In the corridor outside, Whallo was already gone and the young Force-leader was absent. Only Moro stood waiting for us. Pel turned on me furiously.

"Who asked you to show up here?" he demanded.

"Moro," I answered. "And a good thing, too. Pel, what's got into you? You act as if you had some personal axe to grind in seeing the Exotic mercenaries level Blauvain—"

He spun away from me.

"Excuse me!" he snapped. "I've got things to do. I've got to phone my headquarters."

Puzzled, I watched him take a couple of long strides away from me and out of the outer office. Suddenly, it was as if the winds of those massive forces I had felt for a moment just past in Ian's office had blown my head strangely clean, clear and empty, so that the slightest sound echoed with importance. All at once, I was hearing the echo of Pel saying those identical words as Kensie was preparing to leave the mercenary encampment for the nonexistent victory dinner, and a half-recognized but long-held suspicion in me flared into a raging certainty.

I took three long strides after him and caught him. I whirled him around and rammed him up against a wall.

"It was you!" I said. "You called from the encampment of the city just before we drove in. It was you who told the assassins we were on the way and to move into position to snipe at our car. You're Blue Front, Pel; and you set Kensie up to be murdered!"

My hands were on his throat and he could not have answered if he had wanted to. But he did not need to. Then I heard the click of bootheels on the floor of the polished stone corridor flagging outside the office and let go of him, slipping my hand under my uniform jacket to my beltgun.

"Say a word," I whispered to him, "or try anything . . . and I'll kill you before you can get the first syllable out. You're coming along with us!"

The Force-leader entered. He glanced at the three of us curiously.

"Something I can do for you gentlemen?" he asked.

"No," I said, "No, we're just leaving."

With one arm through Pel's and the hand of my other arm under my jacket on the butt of my beltgun, we went out as close as the old friends we had always been, Moro bringing up the rear. Out in the corridor, with the office door behind us, Moro caught up with me on the opposite side from Pel.

"How do you know if you don't try?" I said. "Let me see you try, and it not work. Then maybe I'd believe you."

"Tom," he said, "can you lift me out of this chair?"

I blinked at him. I am no Dorsai, as I think I have said, but I am large for my world, which meant in this case that I was a head taller than Padma and perhaps a quarter again the weight. Also I was undoubtedly younger, and I had worked all my life to stay in good physical condition. I could have lifted someone my own weight out of that chair with no trouble, and Padma was less than that.

"Unless you're tied down," I said.

"I'm not." He stood up briefly, and then sat again. "Try and lift me, Tom."

I put my glass down, stepped over to his float and stood behind him. I wrapped my arms around his body under his armpits and lifted—at first easily, then with all my strength.

But not only could I not lift him, I could not budge him. If he had been a life-sized statue of stone, I would have expected to feel more reaction and movement in response to my efforts.

I gave up finally, panting, and stood back from him.

"What do you weigh?" I demanded.

"No more than you think. Sit down again, Tom—"

I did.

"Don't let it bother you. It's a trick, of course. No, not a mechanical trick, a physiological one—but a trick just the same, that's been shown on stage at times, at least during the last four hundred years."

"Stand up," I said. "Let me try again."

He did. I did. He was still immovable.

"Now," he said, when I had given up a second time. "Try once more, and you'll find you can lift me."

I wiped my forehead, put my arms around him, and heaved upward with all my strength. I almost threw him against the ceiling overhead. Numbly I set him down again.

"You see?" he said, reseating himself. "Just as I knew you could not lift me until I let you, I know that there is nothing I can do to alter present events here on Ste. Marie from their present direction. But you can."

"*I* can?" I stared at him, then exploded. "Then for God's sake tell me how?"

He shook his head, slowly.

"I'm sorry, Tom," he said. "But that's just what I can't do. I only know that, resolved to ontogenetic terms, the situation here shows you as a pivotal character. On you, as a point, the bundle of human forces that were concentrated here and bent toward destruction by another such pivotal character may be redirected back into the general historical pattern with a minimum of harm. I tell you this so that being aware of it, you can be watching for opportunities to redirect. That's all I can do."

Incredibly, with those words, he got up and went toward the door of the apartment.

"Hold on!" I said, and he stopped, turning back momentarily. "This other pivotal character. Who's he?"

Padma shook his head again.

"It would do you no good to know," he said. "I give you my word he is now far away from the situation and will not be coming back to it. He is not even on the planet."

"One of the assassins of Kensie!" I said. "And they've gotten away, off-planet!"

"No," said Padma. "No. The men who assassinated Kensie are only tools of events. If none of them had existed, three others would have been there in their place. Forget this other pivotal character, Tom. He was no more in charge of the situation he created than you are in charge of the situation here and now. He was simply, like you, in a position that gave him freedom of choice. Goodnight."

With those last words, he was suddenly out the door and gone. To this day I cannot remember if he moved particularly swiftly, or whether for some reason I now can't remember, I simply let him go. Just—all at once I was alone.

Fatigue rolled over me like the heavy waves of some ocean of mercury. I stumbled into the bedroom, fell on my sleeping float, and that was all I remembered until—only a second later, it seemed—I woke to the hammering of my telephone's chimes on my ears.

I reached out, fumbled at the bedside table, and pushed the *on* button.

"Velt here," I said thickly.

"Tom—this is Moro. Tom? Is that you, Tom?"

I licked my lips, swallowed, and spoke more understandably.

"It's me," I said. "What's the call for?"

"Where've you been?"

"Sleeping," I said. "What's the call for?"

"I've got to talk to you. Can you come—"

"You come here," I said. "I've got to get up and dress and get some coffee in me before I go anyplace. You can talk to me while I'm doing it."

I punched off. He was still saying something at the other end of the line, but just then I did not care what it was.

I pushed my dead-heavy body out of bed and began to move. I was dressed and at the coffee when he came.

"Have a cup." I pushed it at him as he sat down at the porch table with me. He took it automatically.

"Tom—" he said. The cup trembled in his hand as he lifted it, and he sipped hastily from it before putting it down again. "Tom, you were in the Blue Front once, weren't you?"

"Weren't we all?" I said. "Back when we and it were young together, and it was an idealistic outfit aimed at putting some order and system into our world government?"

"Yes, yes, of course," Moro said. "But what I mean is, if you were a member once, maybe you know who to contact now—"

I began to laugh. I laughed so hard I had to put my cup down to avoid spilling it.

"Moro, don't you know better than that?" I said. "If I knew who the present leaders of the Blue Front were, they'd be in jail. The Blauvain police commissioner—the head law enforcement man of our capital city— is the last man the Blue Front would be in touch with nowadays. They'd come to you first. You were a member once, too, back in college days, remember?"

"Yes," he said miserably. "But I don't know anything now, just as you're saying. I thought you might have informers, or suspicions you couldn't prove, or—"

"None of them," I said. "All right. Why do you want to know who's running the Blue Front now?"

"I thought I'd make an appeal to them, to give up the assassins of Kensie Graeme—to save the Blauvain people. Tom—" He stared directly at me. "Just an hour ago the enlisted men of the mercenaries took a vote on whether to demand that their officers lead them on the city. They voted over ninety-four percent, in favor. And Pel ... Pel's finally mobilized his militia, but I don't think he means to help *us*. He's been trying to get in to talk to Ian all day."

"All day?" I glanced at the time on my wrist unit. "4:25—it's not 4:25 P.M. *now*?"

"Yes," said Moro, staring at me. "I thought you knew."

"I didn't mean to sleep like this!" I came out of the chair, moving toward the door. "Pel's trying to see Ian? The sooner we get down and see him ourselves, the better."

So we went. But we were too late. By the time we got to Expedition Headquarters and past the junior officers to the door of the office where Ian was, Pel was already with Ian. I brushed aside the Force-leader barring our way and walked in, followed by Moro. Pel was standing facing Ian, who sat at a desk surrounded by stacks of filmprints. He got to his feet as Moro and I appeared.

"That'll be all right, Force-leader," he said to the officer behind us. "Tom, I'm glad you're here. Mr. Mayor, though, if you don't mind waiting outside, I'll see you in a few minutes."

Moro had little choice but to go out again. The door shut behind him. Ian waved me to a chair beside Pel and sat down again himself.

"Go ahead, General," he said to Pel. "Repeat what you'd started to tell me, for the benefit of Tom, here."

Pel glanced savagely at me for a second out of the edge of his eyes before answering.

"This doesn't have anything to do with the police commissioner of Blauvain," he said, "or anyone else of Ste. Marie."

"Repeat," said Ian again. He did not raise his voice. The word was simply an iron door dropped in Pel's way, forcing him to turn back. Pel glanced once more, grimly, at me.

"I was just saying," he said, "if Commander Graeme would go to the encampment and speak to the enlisted men there, he could probably get them to vote unanimously."

"Vote unanimously for what?" I asked.

"For a house-to-house search of the Blauvain area," Ian answered.

"The city's been cordoned," Pel said quickly. "A search like that would turn up the assassins in a matter of hours, with the whole expeditionary force searching."

"Sure," I said, "and with the actual assassins, there'd be a few hundred suspected assassins, or people who fought or ran for the wrong reason, killed or wounded by the searchers. Even if the Blue Front didn't take advantage of the opportunity—which they certainly would—to start gun-fights with the soldiers in the city streets."

"What of it?" said Pel, talking to Ian rather than to me. "Your troops can handle any Blue Front people. And you'd be doing Ste. Marie a favor to wipe them out."

"If the whole thing didn't develop into a wiping out of the whole civilian population of the city," I said.

"You're implying, Tom," said Pel, "that the Exotic troops can't be controlled by—"

Ian cut him short.

"Your suggestion, General," he said, "is the same one I've been getting from other quarters. Someone else is here with it right now. I'll let you listen to the answer I give him."

He turned toward his desk annunciator.

"Send in Groupman Whallo," he said.

He straightened up and turned back to us as the door to his office opened and in came the mercenary noncom I had brushed past out there.

In the light, I saw it was the immigrant Dorsai of the Hunter Team I had encountered—the man who had been a Dorsai fourteen years.

"Sir!" he said, stopping a few steps before Ian and saluting. Uncovered himself, Ian did not return the salute.

"You've got a message for me?" Ian said. "Go ahead, I want these gentlemen to hear it, and my answer."

"Yes sir," said Whallo. I could see him glance at and recognize me out of the corner of his eyes. "As representative of the enlisted men of the Expedition, I have been sent to convey to you the results of our latest vote on orders. By unanimous vote, the enlisted men of this command have concurred in the need for a single operation."

"Which is?"

"That a house-to-house search of the Blauvain city area be made for the assassins of Field Commander Graeme," said Whallo. He nodded at Ian's desk and for the first time I saw solidigraphs there—artists' impressions, undoubtedly, but looking remarkably lifelike of three men in civilian clothes. "There's no danger we won't recognize them when we find them."

Whallo's formal and artificial delivery was at odds with the way I had heard him speak when I had run into him at the Hunter Team site. There was, it occurred to me suddenly, probably a military protocol even to matters like this—even to the matter of a man's death and the possible death of a city. It came as a little shock to realize it, and for the first time I began to feel something of what Padma had meant in saying that the momentum of forces involved here was massive. For a second it was almost as if I could feel those forces like great winds, blowing on the present moment. —But Ian was already answering him.

"Any house-to-house search involves possible military errors and danger to the civilian population," he was saying. "The military record of my brother is not to be marred after his death by any intemperate order from me."

"Yes sir," said Whallo. "I'm sorry, sir, but the enlisted men of the Expedition had hoped that the action would be ordered by you. Their decision calls for six hours in which you may consider the matter before our Enlisted Men's Council takes the responsibility for the action upon itself. Meanwhile, the Hunter Teams will be withdrawn—this is part of the voted decision."

"That, too?" said Ian.

"I'm sorry, sir. But you know," said Whallo, "they've been at a dead end for some hours now. The trail was lost in traffic, and the men might be anywhere in the central part of the city."

"Yes," said Ian. "Well, thank you for your message, Groupman."

"Sir!" said Whallo. He saluted again and went out.

As the door closed behind him, Ian's head turned back to face Pel and myself.

"You heard, gentlemen," he said. "Now, I've got work to do."

Pel and I left. In the corridor outside, Whallo was already gone and the young Force-leader was absent. Only Moro stood waiting for us. Pel turned on me furiously.

"Who asked you to show up here?" he demanded.

"Moro," I answered. "And a good thing, too. Pel, what's got into you? You act as if you had some personal axe to grind in seeing the Exotic mercenaries level Blauvain—"

He spun away from me.

"Excuse me!" he snapped. "I've got things to do. I've got to phone my headquarters."

Puzzled, I watched him take a couple of long strides away from me and out of the outer office. Suddenly, it was as if the winds of those massive forces I had felt for a moment just past in Ian's office had blown my head strangely clean, clear and empty, so that the slightest sound echoed with importance. All at once, I was hearing the echo of Pel saying those identical words as Kensie was preparing to leave the mercenary encampment for the nonexistent victory dinner, and a half-recognized but long-held suspicion in me flared into a raging certainty.

I took three long strides after him and caught him. I whirled him around and rammed him up against a wall.

"It was you!" I said. "You called from the encampment of the city just before we drove in. It was you who told the assassins we were on the way and to move into position to snipe at our car. You're Blue Front, Pel; and you set Kensie up to be murdered!"

My hands were on his throat and he could not have answered if he had wanted to. But he did not need to. Then I heard the click of bootheels on the floor of the polished stone corridor flagging outside the office and let go of him, slipping my hand under my uniform jacket to my beltgun.

"Say a word," I whispered to him, "or try anything . . . and I'll kill you before you can get the first syllable out. You're coming along with us!"

The Force-leader entered. He glanced at the three of us curiously.

"Something I can do for you gentlemen?" he asked.

"No," I said, "No, we're just leaving."

With one arm through Pel's and the hand of my other arm under my jacket on the butt of my beltgun, we went out as close as the old friends we had always been, Moro bringing up the rear. Out in the corridor, with the office door behind us, Moro caught up with me on the opposite side from Pel.

"What are we going to do?" Moro whispered. Pel had still said nothing, but his eyes were like the black shadows of meteor craters on the gray face of an airless moon.

"Take him downstairs and out to a locked room in the nearest police post," I said. "He's a walking stick of high explosive if any of the mercenaries find out what he did. Someone of his rank involved in Kensie's killing is all the excuse they need to run our street red in the gutters."

We got Pel to a private back room in Post Ninety-six, a local police center less than three minutes' drive from a building where Ian had his office.

"But how can you be sure, he—" Moro hesitated at putting it into words, once we were safe in a room. He stood staring at Pel, who sat huddled in a chair, still without speaking.

"I'm sure," I said. "The Exotic, Padma—" I cut myself off as much as Moro had done. "Never mind. The main thing is he's Blue Front, he's involved—and what do we do about it?"

Pel stirred and spoke for the first time since I had almost strangled him. He looked up at Moro and myself out of his gray-dead face.

"I did it for Ste. Marie!" he said hoarsely. "But I didn't know they were going to kill him! I didn't know that. They said it was just to be shooting around the car—for an incident—"

"You hear?" I jerked my head at Moro. "Do you want more proof than that?"

"What'll we do?" Moro was staring in fascinated horror at Pel.

"That was my question," I reminded him. He stood there looking hardly in better case than Pel. "But it doesn't look like you're going to be much help in answering it." I laughed, but not happily. "Padma said the choice was up to me."

"Who? What're you talking about? What choice?" asked Moro.

"Pel here"—I nodded at him—"knows where the assassins are hiding."

"No," said Pel.

"Well, you know enough so that we can find them," I said. "It makes no difference. And outside of this room, there're only two people on Ste. Marie we can trust with that information."

"You think I'd tell you anything?" Pel said. His face was still gray, but it had firmed up now. "Do you think even if I knew anything I'd tell you? Ste. Marie needs a strong government to survive and only the Blue Front can give it to her. I was ready to give my life for that, yesterday. I'm still willing. I won't tell you anything—and you can't make me. Not in six hours."

"What two people?" Moro asked me.

"Padma," I said, "and Ian."

"Ian!" said Pel. "You think he'll help you? He doesn't give a damn for Ste. Marie, either way. Did you believe that talk of his about his brother's military record? He's got no feelings. It's his own military record he's concerned with, and he doesn't care if the mercenaries tear Blauvain up by the roots, as long as it's done over his own objection. He's just as happy as any of the other mercenaries with that vote. He's just going to sit out his six hours and let things happen."

"And I suppose Padma doesn't care either?" Moro was beginning to sound a little ugly himself. "It was the Exotics sent us help against the Friendlies in the first place!"

"Who knows what Exotics want?" Pel retorted. "They pretend to go about doing nothing but helping other people, and never dirtying their hands with violence and so on, and somehow with all that they keep on getting richer and more powerful all the time. Sure, trust Padma, why don't you? Trust Padma and see what happens!"

Moro looked at me uncomfortably.

"What if he's right?" Moro said.

"What if he's right?" I snarled at him. "Moro, can't you see this is what Ste. Marie's trouble has always been? Here's the troublemaker we always have around—someone like Pel—whispering that the devil's in the chimney and you—like the rest of our people always do—starting to shake at the knees and wanting to sell him the house at any price! Stay here both of you, and don't try to leave the room."

I went out, locking the door behind me. They were in one of a number of rooms set up behind the duty officer's desk, and I went up to the night sergeant on duty. He was a man I'd known back when I had been in detective training on the Blauvain force, an old-line policeman named Jaker Reales.

"Jaker," I said, "I've got a couple of valuable items locked up in that back room. I hope to be back in an hour or so to collect them, but if I don't, make sure they don't get out and nobody gets in to them, or knows they're there. I don't care what kind of noises may seem to come out of there, it's all in the imagination of anyone who thinks he hears them, for twenty-four hours at least, if I don't come back."

"Got you, Tom," said Jaker. "Leave it up to me, sir."

"Thanks, Jaker," I said.

I went out and back to Expedition Headquarters. It had not occurred to me to wonder what Ian would do now that his Hunter Teams had been taken from him. I found Expedition Headquarters now quietly aswarm with officers—officers who clearly were most of them Dorsai. No enlisted men were to be seen.

I was braced to argue my way into seeing Ian, but the men on duty surprised me. I had to wait only four or five minutes outside the door of

Ian's private office before six senior commandants, Charley ap Morgan among them, filed out.

"Good," said Charley, nodding as he saw me, and then went on without any further explanation of what he meant. I had no time even to look after him. Ian was waiting.

I went in. Ian sat massively behind his desk, waiting for me, and waved me to a chair facing him as I came in. I sat down. He was only a few feet from me, but again I had the feeling of a vast distance separating us. Even here and now, under the soft lights of this nighttime office, he conveyed, more strongly than any Dorsai I had ever seen, a sense of difference. Generations of men bred to war had made him, and I could not warm to him as Pel and others had warmed to Kensie. Far from kindling any affection in me, as he sat there, a cold wind like that off some icy and barren mountaintop seemed to blow from him to me, chilling me. I could believe Pel, that Ian was all ice and no blood, and there was no reason for me to do anything for him—except that as a man whose brother had been killed, he deserved whatever help any other decent, law-abiding man could give him.

But I owed something to myself, too, and to the fact that we were not all villains, like Pel, on Ste. Marie.

"I've got something to tell you," I said. "It's about General Sinjin." He nodded, slowly.

"I've been waiting for you to come to me with that," he said.

I stared at him.

"You know about Pel?" I said.

"We knew someone from the Ste. Marie authorities had to be involved in what happened," he said. "Normally, a Dorsai officer is alert to any potentially dangerous situation. But there was the false dinner invitation, and then the matter of the assassins happening to be in just the right place at the right time, with just the right weapons. Also, our Hunter Teams found clear evidence the encounter was no accident. As I say, an officer like Field Commander Graeme is not ordinarily killed that easily."

It was odd to sit there and hear him speak Kensie's name that way. Title and name rang on my ears with the strangeness one feels when somebody speaks of himself in the third person.

"But Pel?" I said.

"We didn't know it was General Sinjin who was involved," Ian said. "You identified him yourself by coming to me about him just now."

"He's Blue Front," I said.

"Yes," said Ian, nodding.

"I've known him all my life," I said carefully. "I believe he's suffered some sort of nervous breakdown over the death of your brother. You know, he admired your brother very much. But he's still the man I grew up with, and that man can't be easily made to do something he doesn't want to do. Pel says he won't tell us anything that'll help us find the assassins, and he doesn't think we can make him tell us inside of the six hours left before your soldiers move in to search Blauvain. Knowing him, I'm afraid he's right."

I stopped talking. Ian sat where he was, behind the desk, looking at me, merely waiting.

"Don't you understand?" I said. "Pel can help us, but I don't know of any way to make him do it."

Still Ian said nothing.

"What do you want from me?" I almost shouted it at him, at last.

"Whatever," Ian said, "you have to give."

For a moment it seemed to me that there was something like a crack in the granite mountain that he seemed to be. For a moment I could have sworn that I saw into him. But if this was true, the crack closed up immediately, the minute I glimpsed it. He sat remote, icy, waiting, there behind his desk.

"I've got nothing," I said, "unless you know of some way to make Pel talk."

"I have no way consistent with my brother's reputation as a Dorsai officer," said Ian remotely.

"You're concerned with reputations?" I said. "I'm concerned with the people who'll die and be hurt in Blauvain if your mercenaries come in to hunt door-to-door for those assassins. Which is more important, the reputation of a dead man or the lives of living ones?"

"The people are rightly your concern, Commissioner," said Ian, still remotely, "the professional reputation of Kensie Graeme is rightly mine."

"What will happen to that reputation if those troops move into Blauvain in less than six hours from now?" I demanded.

"Something not good," Ian said. "That doesn't change my personal responsibilities. I can't do what I shouldn't do, and I must do what I ought to do."

I stood up.

"There's no answer to the situation then," I said. Suddenly, the utter tiredness I had felt before was on me again. I was tired of the fanatic Friendlies who had come out of another solar system to exercise a purely theoretical claim to our revenues and world surface as an excuse to assault Ste. Marie. I was tired of the Blue Front and people like Pel. I was tired of off-world people of all kinds, including Exotics and Dorsais. I was tired, tired. . . . It came to me then that I could walk out. I could refuse to make the decision that Padma had said I would make and the whole matter would be out of my hands. I told myself to do that, to get up and walk out, but my feet did not budge. In picking on me, events had chosen the right idiot as a pivot point. Like Ian, I cannot do what I should not do, and I must do what I ought to do.

"All right," I said. "Padma might be able to do something with him."

"The Exotics," said Ian, "force nobody." But he stood up.

"Maybe I can talk him into it," I said exhaustedly. "At least, I can try."

Once more, I would have had no idea where to find Padma in a hurry. But Ian located him in a research enclosure, a carrel in the stacks of the Blauvain library, which like many libraries on all the eleven inhabited worlds, had been Exotic-endowed. In the small space of the carrel, Ian and I faced him, the two of us standing, Padma seated in the serenity of his blue robe and unchanging facial expression. I told him what we needed with Pel, and he shook his head.

"Tom," he said, "you must already know that we who study the Exotic sciences never force anyone or anything. Not for moral reasons alone, but because using force would damage our ability to do the sensitive work we've dedicated our lives to doing. That's why we hire mercenaries to fight for us, and Cetan lawyers to handle our off-world business contracts. I am the last person on this world to make Pel talk."

"Don't you feel any responsibility to the innocent people of this city?" I said. "To the lives that will be lost if he doesn't?"

"Emotionally, yes," Padma said softly. "But there are practical limits to the responsibility of personal inaction. If I were to concern myself with all possible pain consequent upon the least, single action of mine, I would have to spend my life like a statue. I was not responsible for Kensie's death, and I am not responsible for finding his killers. Without such a responsibility, I can't violate the most basic prohibition of my life's rules."

"You knew Kensie," I said. "Don't you owe anything to him?" And don't you owe anything to the same Ste. Marie people you sent an armed expedition to help?"

"We make it a point to give, rather than take," Padma said, "just to avoid debts like that which would force us into doing what we shouldn't do. No, Tom. The Exotics and I have no obligation to your people, or even to Kensie."

"—And to the Dorsai?" asked Ian, behind me.

I had almost forgotten he was there, I had been concentrating so hard on Padma. Certainly, I had not expected Ian to speak. The sound of his deep voice was like a heavy bell tolling in the small room, and for the first time Padma's face changed.

"The Dorsai...," he echoed. "Yes, the time is coming when there will be neither Exotics nor Dorsai, in the end when the final development is achieved. But we Exotics have always counted on our work as a step on the way to that end, and the Dorsai helped us up our step. Possibly, if things had gone otherwise, the Dorsai might have never been, and we would still be where we are now. But things went as they have, and our thread has been tangled with the Dorsai thread from the time your many-times removed grandfather, Cletus Grahame, first freed all the younger worlds from the politics of Earth. . . ."

He stood up.

"I'll force no one," he said. "But I will offer Pel my help to find peace with himself, if he can, and if he finds such peace, then maybe he will want to tell you willingly what you want to know."

Padma, Ian, and I went back to the police station where I had left Pel and Moro locked up. We let Moro out and closed the door upon the three of us with Pel. He sat in a chair, looking at us, pale, pinch-faced, and composed.

"So you brought the Exotic, did you, Tom?" he said to me. "What's it going to be? Some kind of hypnosis?"

"No, Pel," said Padma softly, pacing across the room to him as Ian and I sat down to wait. "I would not deal in hypnosis, particularly without the consent of the one to be hypnotized."

"Well, you sure as hell haven't got my consent!" said Pel.

Padma had reached him now and was standing over him. Pel looked up into the calm face above the blue robe.

"But try it if you like," Pel said. "I don't hypnotize easily."

"No," said Padma. "I've said I would not hypnotize anyone, but in any case, neither you nor anyone else can be hypnotized without his or her innate consent. All things between individuals are done by consent. The prisoner consents to his captivity as the patient consents to his sur-gery—the difference is only in degree and pattern. The great, blind mass that is humanity in general is like an amoebic animal. It exists by internal laws that cohere its body and its actions. Those internal laws are based upon conscious and unconscious mutual consents of its atoms—our-selves—to work with each other and cooperate. Peace and satisfaction come to each of us in proportion to our success in such cooperation, in the forward-searching movement of the humanity-creature as a whole. Nonconsent and noncooperation work against the grain. Pain and self-hate result from friction when we fight against our natural desire to cooperate. . . ."

His voice went on. Gently but compellingly he said a great deal more, and I understood all at the time. But beyond what I have quoted so far—and those first few sentences stay printed clear in my memory—I do not recall another specific word. I do not know to this day what happened. Perhaps I half-dozed without realizing I was dozing. At any rate, time passed, and when I reached a point where the memory record took up again, he was leaving and Pel had altered.

"I can talk to you some more, can't I?" Pel said as the Outbond rose to leave. Pel's voice had become clear-toned and strangely young-sounding. "I don't mean now. I mean, there'll be other times?"

"I'm afraid not," Padma said. "I'll have to leave Ste. Marie shortly. My work takes me back to my own world and then on to one of the Friendly planets to meet someone and wind up what began here. But you don't need me to talk to. You created your own insights as we talked, and you can go on doing that by yourself. Good-bye, Pel."

"Good-bye," said Pel. He watched Padma leave. When he looked at me again his face, like his voice, was clear and younger than I had seen it in years. "Did you hear all that, Tom?"

"I think so . . . " I said, because already the memory was beginning to slip away from me. I could feel the import of what Padma had said to Pel, but without being able to give it exact shape, it was as if I had intercepted a message that had turned out to be not for me, and so my mental machinery had already begun to cancel it out. I got up and went over to Pel. "You'll help us find those assassins now?"

He was able to give us a list of five places that were possible hiding places for the three we hunted. He provided exact directions for finding each one.

"Now," I said to Ian, when Pel was through, "we need those Hunter Teams of yours that were pulled off."

"We have Hunters," said Ian. "Those officers who are Dorsai are still with us, and there are Hunters among them."

He stepped to the phone unit on the desk in the room and put a call in to Charley ap Morgan at Expeditionary Headquarters. When Charley answered, Ian gave him the five locations Pel had supplied us.

"Now," he said to me as he turned away from the phone, "we'll go back to my office."

"I want to come," said Pel. Ian looked at him for a long moment, then nodded, without changing expression.

"You can come," he said.

When we got back to the Expeditionary Headquarters building, the rooms and corridors there seemed even more aswarm with officers. As Ian had said, they were mostly Dorsai. But I saw some among them who might not have been. Apparently Ian commanded his own loyalty, or perhaps it was the Dorsai concept that commanded its own loyalty to whoever was commanding officer. We went to his office and, sitting there, waited while the reports began to come in.

The first three locations to be checked out by the officer Hunter Teams drew blanks. The fourth showed evidence of having been used within the last twenty-four hours, although it was empty now. The last location to be checked also drew blank.

The Hunter Teams concentrated on the fourth location and began to work outward from it, hoping to cross signs of a trail away from it. I checked the clock figures on my wrist unit. It was now nearing 1:00 A.M. local time, and the six-hour deadline of the enlisted mercenaries was due to expire in forty-seven minutes. In the office where I waited with Ian, Pel, Charley ap Morgan, and another senior Dorsai officer, the air was thick with the tension of waiting. Ian and the two other Dorsai sat still; even Pel sat still. I was the one who fidgeted and paced, as the time continued to run out.

The phone on Ian's desk flashed its visual signal light. Ian reached out to punch it on.

"Yes?" he said.

"Hunter Team Three," said a voice from the desk. "We have clear signs and are following now. Suggest you join us, sir."

"Thank you. Coming," said Ian.

We went, Ian, Charley, Pel, and myself, in an Expedition command car. It was an eerie ride through the patrolled deserted streets of my city. Ian's Hunter Team Three was ahead of us and led us to an apartment hotel on the upper north side of the city, in the oldest section.

The building had been built of poured cement faced with Castelmaine granite. Inside, the corridors were old-fashionedly narrow and close-feeling, with dark, thick carpeting and metal walls in imitation oak woodgrain. The soundproofing was good, however. We mounted to the seventh story and moved down the hall to suite number 415 without hearing any sound other than those we made ourselves.

"Here," finally said the leader of the Hunter Team, a lean, gnarled Dorsai senior commandant in his late fifties. He gestured to the door of 415. "All three of them."

"Ian," said Charley ap Morgan, glancing at his wrist unit. "The enlisted men start moving into the city in six minutes. You could go meet them to say we've found the assassins. The others and I—"

"No," said Ian. "We can't say we've found them until we see them and identify them positively." He stepped up to one side of the door and, reaching out an arm, touched the door annunciator stud.

There was no response. Above the door, the half-meter square annunciator screen stayed brown and blank.

Ian pressed the button again.

Again we waited, and there was no response.

Ian pressed the stud. Holding it down, so that his voice would go with the sound of its announcing chimes to the ears of those within, he spoke.

"This is Commander Ian Graeme," he said. "Blauvain is now under martial law, and you are under arrest in connection with the assassination of Field Commander Kensie Graeme. If necessary, we can cut our way in to you. However, I'm concerned that Field Commander Graeme's reputation be kept free of criticism in the matter of determining responsibility for his death. So I'm offering you the chance to come out and surrender."

He released the stud and stopped talking. There was a long pause. Then a voice spoke from the annunciator grille below the screen, although the screen itself remained blank.

"Go to hell, Graeme," said the voice. "We got your brother, and if you try to blast your way in here, we'll get you, too."

"My advice to you," said Ian—his voice was cold, distant, and impersonal, as if this was something he did every day—"is to surrender."

"You guarantee our safety if we do?"

"No," said Ian. "I only guarantee that I will see that Field Commander Graeme's reputation is not adversely affected by the way you're handled."

There was no immediate answer from the screen. Behind Ian, Charley looked again at his wrist unit.

"They're playing for time," he said. "But why? What good will that do them?"

"They're fanatics," said Pel softly. "Just as much fanatics as the Friendly soldiers were, only for the Blue Front instead of for some puritan form of religion. Those three in there don't expect to get out of this alive. They're only trying to set a higher price on their own deaths—get something more for their dying."

Charley ap Morgan's wrist unit chimed.

"Time's up," he said to Ian. "The enlisted men are moving into the suburbs of Blauvain now, to begin their search."

Ian reached out and pushed the annunciator stud again, holding it down as he spoke to the men inside.

"Are you coming out?"

"Why should we?" answered the voice that had spoken the first time. "Give us a reason."

"I'll come in and talk to you if you like," said Ian.

"No—" began Pel out loud. I gripped his arm, and he turned on me, whispering. "Tom, tell him not to go in! That's what they want."

"Stay here," I said.

I pushed forward until Charley ap Morgan put out an arm to stop me. I spoke across that arm to Ian.

"Ian," I said, in a voice safely low enough so that the door annunciator would not pick it up. "Pel says—"

"Maybe that's a good idea," said the voice from the annunciator.

"That's right, why don't you come on in, Graeme? Leave your weapons outside."

"Tom," said Ian, without looking either at me or Charley ap Morgan, "Stay back. Keep him back, Charley."

"Yes sir," said Charley. He looked into my face, eye to eye with me. "Stay out of this, Tom. Back up."

Ian stepped forward to stand square in front of the door, where a beam coming through it could go through him as well. He was taking off his sidearm as he went. He dropped it to the floor, in full sight of the screen, through the blankness of which those inside would be looking out.

"I'm unarmed," he said.

"Of that sidepiece, you are," said the annunciator. "Do you think we're going to take your word for the rest of you? Strip."

Without hesitation, Ian unsealed his uniform jacket and began to take off his clothes. In a moment or two, he stood naked in the hallway, but if the men in the suite had thought to gain some sort of moral advantage over him because of that, they were disappointed.

Stripped, he looked—like an athlete—larger and more impressive than he had clothed. He towered over us all in the hall, even over the other Dorsai there, and with his darkly tanned skin under the lights, he seemed like a massive figure carved in oak.

"I'm waiting," he said after a moment, calmly.

"All right," said the voice from the annunciator. "Come on in."

He moved forward. The door unlatched and slid aside before him. He passed through and it closed behind him. For a moment we were left with no sound or word from him or the suite, then, unexpectedly, the screen lit up. We found ourselves looking over and past Ian's bare shoulders at a room in which three men, each armed with a rifle and a pair of sidearms, sat facing him. They gave no sign of knowing that he had turned on the annunciator screen, the controls of which would be hidden behind him, now that he stood inside the door, facing the room.

The center one of the three seated men laughed. He was the big black-bearded man I had found vaguely familiar when I saw the solidigraphs of the three of them in Ian's office, and I recognized him now. He was a professional wrestler. He had been arraigned on assault charges four years ago, but lack of testimony against him had caused the charges to be dismissed. He was not as tall as Ian, but much heavier of body, and it was his voice we had been hearing. Now we heard it again as his lips moved on the screen.

"Well, well, Commander," he said. "Just what we needed—a visit from you. Now we can rack up a score of two Dorsai commanders before your soldiers carry what's left of us off to the morgue, and Ste. Marie can see that even you people can be handled by the Blue Front."

We could not see Ian's face, but he said nothing. Apparently his lack of reaction was irritating to the big assassin, who dropped his cheerful tone and leaned forward in his chair.

"Don't you understand, Graeme?" he said. "We've lived and died for the Blue Front, all three of us—for the one political party with the strength and guts to save the world. We're dead men no matter what we do. Did you think we don't know that? You think we don't know what would happen to us if we were idiots enough to surrender the way you said? Your men would tear us apart, and if there was anything left of us after that, the government's law would try us and then shoot us. We only let you in here so that we could lay you out like your twin brother, before we were laid out ourselves. Don't you follow me, man? You walked into our hands here like a fly into a trap, never realizing."

"I realized," said Ian.

The big man scowled at him and the muzzle of the heat rifle he held in one thick hand came up.

"What do you mean?" he demanded. "Whatever you think you've got up your sleeve isn't going to save you. Why would you come in here, knowing what we'd do?"

"The Dorsai are professional soldiers," said Ian's voice calmly. "We live and survive by our reputation. Without that reputation none of us could earn our living. And the reputation of the Dorsai in general is the sum of the reputations of its individual men and women. So Field Commander Kensie Graeme's professional reputation is a thing of value, to be guarded even after his death. I came in for that reason.

The big man's eyes narrowed. He was doing all the talking and his two companions seemed content to leave it that way.

"A reputation's worth dying for?" he said.

"I've been ready to die for mine for eighteen years," said Ian's voice quietly. "Today's no different than yesterday."

"And you came in here—" The big man's voice broke off on a snort. "I don't believe it. Watch him, you two!"

"Believe or not," said Ian. "I came in here, just as I told you, to see that the professional reputation of Field Commander Graeme was protected from events that might tarnish it. You'll notice—" His head moved slightly as if indicating something behind him and out of our sight. "I've turned on your annunciator screen, so that outside the door they can see what's going on in here."

The eyes of the three men jerked upwards to stare at the screen inside the suite, somewhere over Ian's head. There was a blur of motion that was Ian's tanned body flying through the air, a sound of something smashing, and the screen went blank again.

We outside were left blind once more, standing in the hallway, staring at the unresponsive screen and door. Pel, who had stepped up next to me, moved toward the door itself.

"Stay!" snapped Charley.

The single sharp tone was like a command given to some domestic beast. Pel flinched at the tone, but stopped—and in that moment the door before us disintegrated to the roar of an explosion in the room.

"Come on!" I yelled, and flung myself through the now open doorway.

It was like diving into a centrifuge filled with whirling bodies. I ducked to avoid the flying form of one of the men I had seen in the screen, but his leg slammed my head, and I went reeling, half-dazed and disoriented, into the very heart of the tumult. It was all a blur of action. I had a scrambled impression of explosions, of fire-beams lancing around me— and somehow in the midst of it all, the towering brown body of Ian moving with the certainty and deadliness of a panther. All those he touched went down, and all who went down, stayed down.

Then it was over. I steadied myself with one hand against a half-burned wall and realized that only Ian and myself were on our feet in that room. Not one of the other Dorsai had followed me in. On the floor, the three assassins lay still. One had his neck broken. Across the room a second man lay obviously dead, but with no obvious sign of the damage that had ended his life. The big man, the ex-wrestler, had the right side of his forehead crushed in, as if by a club.

Looking up from the three bodies, I saw I was now alone in the room. I turned back into the corridor and found there only Pel and Charley. Ian and the other Dorsai were already gone.

"Where's Ian?" I asked Charley. My voice came out thickly, like the voice of a slightly drunken man.

"Leave him alone," said Charley. "You don't need him now. Those are the assassins there, and the enlisted men have already been notified and pulled back from their search of Blauvain. What more is needed?"

I pulled myself together and remembered I was a policeman.

"I've got to know exactly what happened," I said. "I've got to know if it was self-defense, or . . ."

The words died on my tongue. To accuse a naked man of anything else in the death of three heavily armed individuals who had threatened his life, as I had just heard them do over the annunciator, was ridiculous.

"No," said Charley. "This was done during a period of martial law in Blauvain. Your office will receive a report from our command about it, but actually it's not even something within your authority."

Some of the tension that had been in him earlier seemed to leak out of him then. He half-smiled and became more like the friendly officer I had known before Kensie's death.

"But that martial law is about to be withdrawn," he said. "Maybe you'll want to get on the phone and start getting your own people out here to tidy up the details."

And he stood aside to let me go.

One day later, and the professional soldiers of the Exotic Expeditionary Force showed their affection for Kensie in a different fashion.

His body had been laid in state for a public review in the open, main floor lobby of the Blauvain City Government building. Beginning in the gray dawn and through the cloudless day—the sort of hard, bright day that seems impatient with those who will not bury their dead and get on to further things—the mercenaries filed past the casket holding Kensie, visible at full length in dress uniform under the transparent cover. Each one as he passed touched the casket lightly with his fingertips, or said a word to the dead man, or both. There were over ten thousand soldiers passing, one at a time. They were unarmed, in field uniforms, and their line seemed endless.

But that was not the end of it. The civilians of Blauvain had formed along either side of the street down which the line of troops wound on its way to the place where Kensie lay waiting for them. The civilians had formed in the face of strict police orders against doing any such thing, and my men could not drive them away. The situation could not have offered a better opportunity for the Blue Front to cause trouble. One heat grenade tossed into that line of slowly moving, unarmed soldiers, for example . . . But nothing happened.

By the time noon came and went without incident, I was ready to make a guess why not. It was because there was something in the mood of the civilian crowd itself that forbade terrorism, here and now. Any Blue Front activists trying such a thing would have been smothered by the very civilians around them in whose name they were doing it.

Something of awe and pity, and almost of envy, seemed to be stirring the souls of the Blauvain people, those same people of mine who had huddled in their houses twenty hours before, in undiluted fear of the very men now lined up before them and moving slowly to the City Government building. Once more, as I stood on a balcony above the lobby holding the casket, I felt those winds of vast movement I had sensed first for a moment in Ian's office, the winds of those forces of which Padma had spoken to me. The Blauvain people were different today and showed the difference. Kensie's death had changed them.

Then, something more happened. As the last of the soldiers passed, Blauvain civilians began to fall in behind them, extending the line. By midafternoon, the last soldier had gone by and the first figure in civilian clothes passed the casket, neither touching it nor speaking to it, but pausing to look with an unusual, almost shy curiosity upon the face of the body inside, in the name of which so much might have happened.

Already, behind that one man, the line of civilians was half again as long as the line of soldiers had been.

It was nearly midnight, long past the time when it had been planned to shut the gates of the lobby, when the last of the civilians had gone and the casket could be transferred to a room at Expeditionary Headquarters from which it would be shipped back to the Dorsai. This business of shipping a body home happened seldom, even in the case of mercenaries of the highest rank, but there had never been any doubt that it would happen in the case of Kensie. The enlisted men and officers of his command had contributed the extra funds necessary for the shipment. Ian, when his time came, would undoubtedly be buried in the earth of whatever world on which he fell. Only if he happened to be at home when the time came, would that earth be soil of the Dorsai. But Kensie had been—Kensie.

"Do you know what's been suggested to me?" asked Moro, as he, Pel, and I, along with several of the Expedition's senior officers—Charley ap Morgan among them—stood watching Kensie's casket being brought into the room at Expedition HQ. "There's a proposal to get the city government to put up a statue of him, here in Blauvain. A statue of Kensie."

Neither Pel nor I answered. We stood watching the placing of the casket. For all its massive appearance, four men handled it and the body within easily. The apparently thick metal of its sides was actually hollow to reduce shipping weight. The soldiers settled it, took off the transparent weather cover, and carried it out. The body of Kensie lay alone, uncovered, the profile of his face, seen from where we stood, quiet and still against the pink cloth of the casket's lining. The senior officers who were with us and who had not been in the line of soldiers filing through the lobby, now began to go into the room, one at a time to stand for a second at the casket before coming out again.

"It's what we never had on Ste. Marie," said Pel, after a long moment. He was a different man since Padma had talked to him. "A leader. Someone to love and follow. Now that our people have seen there is such a thing, they want something like it for themselves."

He looked up at Charley ap Morgan, who was just coming back out of the room.

"You Dorsai changed us," Pel said.

"Did we?" said Charley, stopping. "How do you feel about Ian now, Pel?"

"Ian?" Pel frowned. "We're talking about Kensie. Ian's just—what he always was."

"What you all never understood," said Charley, looking from one to the other of us.

"Ian's a good man," said Pel. "I don't argue with that. But there'll never be another Kensie."

"There'll never be another Ian," said Charley. "He and Kensie made up one person. That's what none of you ever understood. Now half of Ian is gone, into the grave."

Pel shook his head slowly.

"I'm sorry," he said. "I can't believe that. I can't believe Ian ever needed anyone—even Kensie. He's never risked anything, so how could he lose anything? After Kensie's death he did nothing but sit on his spine here insisting that he couldn't risk Kensie's reputation by doing any-thing—until events forced his hand. That's not the action of a man who's lost the better half of himself."

"I didn't say better half," said Charley, "I only said half—and just half is enough. Stop and try to feel for a moment what it would be like. Stop for a second and feel how it would be if you were amputated down the middle—if the life that was closest to you was wrenched away, shot down in the street by a handful of self-deluded, crackpot revolutionaries from a world you'd come to rescue. Suppose it was like that for you. How would you feel?"

Pel had gone a little pale as Charley talked. When he answered, his voice had a slight echo of the difference and youngness it had had after Padma had talked to him.

"I guess . . ." he said very slowly, and ran off into silence.

"Yes?" said Charley. "Now you're beginning to understand, to feel as Ian feels. Suppose you feel like this and just outside the city where the assassins of your brother are hiding there are six battalions of seasoned soldiers who can turn that same city—who can hardly be held back from turning that city—into another Rochmont, at one word from you. Tell me, is it easy, or is it hard, not to say that one word that will turn them loose?"

"It would be . . ." The words seemed dragged from Pel. "Hard."

"Yes," said Charley grimly, "as it was hard for Ian."

"Then why did he do it?" demanded Pel.

"He told you why," said Charley. "He did it to protect his brother's military reputation, so that not even after his death should Kensie Graeme's name be an excuse for anything but the highest and best of military conduct."

"But Kensie was dead. He couldn't hurt his own reputation!"

"His troops could," said Charley. "His troops wanted someone to pay for Kensie's death. They wanted to leave a monument to Kensie and their grief for him, as long-lasting a monument as Rochmont has been to Jacques Chrétien. There was only one way to satisfy them, and that was if Ian himself acted for them—as their agent—in dealing with the assassins. Because nobody could deny that Kensie's brother had the greatest right of all to represent all those who had lost with Kensie's death."

"You're talking about the fact that Ian killed the men, personally," said Moro. "But there was no way he could know he'd come face to face—"

He stopped, halted by the thin, faint smile on Charley's face.

"Ian was our Battle Op, our strategist," said Charley. "Just as Kensie was field commander, our tactician. Do you think that a strategist of Ian's ability couldn't lay a plan that would bring him face to face, alone, with the assassins once they were located?"

"What if they hadn't been located?" I asked. "What if I hadn't found out about Pel, and Pel hadn't told us what he knew?"

Charley shook his head.

"I don't know," he said. "Somehow Ian must have known this way would work—or he would have done it differently. For some reason he counted on help from you, Tom."

"Me!" I said. "What makes you say that?"

"He told me so." Charley looked at me strangely. "You know, many people thought that because they didn't understand Ian, that Ian didn't understand them. Actually, he understands other people unusually well. I think he saw something in you, Tom, he could rely on. And he was right, wasn't he?"

Once more, the winds I had felt—of the forces of which Padma had spoken, blew through me, chilling and enlightening me. Ian had felt those winds as well as I had—and understood them better. I could see the inevitability of it now. There had been only one pull on the many threads entangled in the fabric of events here, and that pull had been through me to Ian.

"When he went to that suite where the assassins were holed up," said Charley, "he intended to go in to them alone, and unarmed. And when he killed them with his bare hands, he did what every man in the expeditionary force wanted to do. So, when that was done, the anger of the troops was lightning-rodded. Through Ian, they all had their revenge, and then they were free. Free just to mourn for Kensie as they're doing today. So Blauvain escaped. And the Dorsai reputation has escaped stain, and the state of affairs between the inhabited worlds hasn't been upset by an incident here on Ste. Marie that could make enemies out of worlds, like the Exotic and the Dorsai, and Ste. Marie, who should all be friends."

He stopped talking. It had been a long speech for Charley, and none of us could think of anything to say. The last of the senior officers, all except Ian, had gone past us now, in and out of the room, and the casket was alone. Then Pel spoke.

"I'm sorry," he said, and he sounded sorry. "But even if what you say is all true, it only proves what I always said about Ian. Kensie had two men's feelings, but Ian hasn't any. He's ice and water with no blood in him. He couldn't bleed if he wanted to. Don't tell me any man torn apart emotionally by his twin brother's death could sit down and plan to handle a situation so cold-bloodedly and efficiently."

"People don't always bleed on the outside where you can see—" Charley broke off, turning his head.

We looked where he was looking, down the corridor behind us, and saw Ian coming, tall and alone. He strode up to us, nodded briefly at us, and went past into the room. We saw him walk to the side of the casket.

He did not speak to Kensie, or touch the casket gently as the soldiers passing through the lobby had done. Instead he closed his big hands, those hands that had killed three armed men, almost casually on the edge of it, and looked down into the face of his dead brother.

Twin face gazed to twin face, the living and the dead. Under the lights of the room, with the motionless towering figure of Ian, it was as if both were living, or both were dead—so little difference there was to be seen between them. Only, Kensie's eyes were closed and Ian's open; Kensie slept while Ian waked. And the oneness of the two of them was so solid and evident a thing, there in that room, that it stopped the breath in my chest.

For perhaps a minute or two Ian stood without moving. His face did not change. Then he lifted his gaze, let go of the casket and turned about. He came walking toward us, out of the room, his hands at his sides, the fingers curled into his palms.

"Gentlemen," he said, nodding to us as he passed, and went down the corridor until a turn in it took him out of sight.

Charley left us and went softly back into the room. He stood a moment there, then turned and called to us.

"Pel," he said, "come here."

Pel came; and the rest of us after him.

"I told you," Charley said to Pel, "some people don't bleed on the outside where you can see it."

He moved away from the casket and we looked at it. On its edge were the two areas where Ian had laid hold of it with his hands while he stood looking down at his dead brother. There was no mistaking the places, for at both of them, the hollow metal side had been bent in on itself and crushed with the strength of a grip that was hard to imagine. Below the crushed areas, the cloth lining of the casket was also crumpled and rent; and where each fingertip had pressed, the fabric was torn and marked with a dark stain of blood.

WHEN YOUR CONTRACT TAKES YOU TO THE DORSAI WORLD

by
SANDRA MIESEL

—excerpts transcribed from tape #183–34–8233, Basic Briefings for Off-Worlders, *57th ed. (Bakhalla, Kultis: Prajna Educational Services, 2345)*

To this day, the origin of the word "Dorsai" remains mysterious. Folk etymology suggests that the Dorsai are "the people who stand up," just as the dorsal fin of a swimming fish rises straight up from its body. Dorsal, in turn, is derived from the Latin *dorsum,* referring to any projection such as a summit, ridge, or mountain chain and from *dorsus,* a poetic term for a man's back.

But whatever the source of their name, planet and people proudly share it: the Dorsai world can rightly boast of breeding "men to match my mountains." Indeed, after more than two centuries together, one can scarcely imagine this starkly beautiful planet apart from its formidable people.

The Dorsai sun is Fomalhaut, brightest star in Piscis Austrinus, the constellation of the Southern Fish. It is one of those happy accidents of nature that the solar system of an A3 star should include a habitable world. Even this far from the primary, sunscreen and other radiation precautions are indispensable.

Approached from space, Dorsai seems all blue water and white clouds. Because the planet is in its most favorable interglacial phase, its oceans are at their maximum expanse. A mere 25 million square kilometers remain unsubmerged, and useless polar continents account for nearly half of this. The flooded areas, however, do afford excellent fishing.

Such land as projects above the waves is largely mountainous. Dorsai's young, sharp-toothed peaks include a few snow-capped giants that rise as high as six thousand meters. Since the major ranges trace a global Ring of Fire, seismic and volcanic activity is all too common. Moreover, coastal highlands condense moisture-laden sea air into chronic drizzle or heavy snowfall, which in turn feeds swift streams and icy lakes. Rivers are seldom navigable, but deeply indented shorelines provide many fine harbors. From spectacular crags to misty corries, the whole landscape shimmers with a special aliveness beneath Fomalhaut's clear white light.

Virtually all of Dorsai's 5 million natives live in one of three regions: Landfall, South Continent, and the Western Isles.

As the name suggests, Landfall was the site of Dorsai's first settlement. This subcontinental island 2 million square kilometers in area lies in the northern temperate zone. Blessed by a warm ocean current, Landfall's coastal plain is the best and broadest stretch of arable land on the planet. All of Dorsai's wheat and much of its sunflowers, sugar beets, and flax are grown here. By-products of these crops support extensive chicken-raising and provide winter feed for the herds of sheep, goats, and horses, which graze on the foothills of the Paladins.

Besides key agricultural enterprises, Landfall also supports Dorsai's most populous centers, including the capital, Omalu, an inland city of fifty thousand people. Here are the planet's government offices, its best hospital, and its spaceport, as well as fully equipped yards for assembling and repairing spacecraft and aircraft. The next largest community is Tar Beach, whose oilfield, petrochemical complex, and manufacturing facilities are small by the standards of any developed world. Finally, near Point Mikhail on the bleak northern coast stands the renowned Dorsai Military Academy, which operates as a self-sufficient town.

About 150 degrees east of Landfall, just below the Tropico del Sur, lies South Continent. With an area of some 5 million square kilometers, this is Dorsai's biggest, but also its driest and least populated land mass.

On its northernmost spot, Cape Doom, Gloryhole volcano glows like a natural lighthouse. Its western mountains, the Bloody Range, rise nearly straight out of the sea to make a cold desert of its lofty central plateau, the Empty Table. Here mineral wealth, including nitrates and sulfur, in addition to metallic ores, draws crews of seasonal miners, but no real towns exist in the area. As the continent curves south, the tableland steps down in a series of fissured cliffs called the Shikasta Country. Beyond these rocky wastes, the midsouth region of Gulistan offers grazing, but water is too scanty for farming. (In the last century, Mahub Van Ghent's attempt to control the deep wells at Suleiman's Drift led to a bloody clash still mourned by Dorsai.)

The northernmost section of the continent along the Drakanzee is a worthless dustbowl except during the brief wet season when the many-channeled Midnight River turns it to mire.

The east coast, however, from Iskanderbad southward to Osebeni, enjoys enough regular rainfall to be fertile. Its warmest districts yield crops including hardy grapes and soybeans that cannot grow anywhere else on the planet. Farther south, the variform pines of the vast Quathlamba forest provide wood pulp and a host of valuable organic chemicals, which are processed at the small port town of Witbaai.

Half a world away, the Western Isles, or "Sundowners," lie 120 degrees beyond Landfall in a great sweeping arc more than two thousand kilometers long. This archipelago—really a chain of half-submerged mountains—comprises more than a hundred sizable islands. Their combined area is perhaps one and a half million square kilometers, but only a fraction of this is arable.

Size and habitability vary dramatically. The southernmost and largest bodies, such as Caerlon, High Island, and Myogashima are green with glens, forests, and alpine pastures. The northernmost sprinkle of rocks called the Veil barely manages to grow lichen beneath the constant pall of mist that gives them their name. Cailleach is a wilderness of ashy rubble spewed by its mighty volcano, the Hag, but humor is life's sole dry feature among the hardy fishermen of the Pipsqueak Islands.

Shortage of cropland is the overriding factor in local economics. Fishing dominates the small islands, stock raising the large. Berries flourish in bogs; barley, rye, oats, buckwheat, and legumes occupy valleys; and potatoes fill hillside terraces. There is enough oil and natural gas for area needs, but neither these fields nor heavy-metal mines such as the nickel deposit on Caerlon offer much employment. So from colonial times on, service as mercenary soldiers has drawn surplus islanders off to the stars.

Although it was the second region to be settled, the Sundowners seems more the home of the Dorsai legend than anywhere else in this world. Here the harsh environment stretched spirits without breaking them. Those who can hold their own against sea and stone make fearsome opponents for other mortals.

All living things on Dorsai were introduced by humans. Marine ecology is the most elaborate. Myriad species thrive in these cold, nutrient-rich, shallow seas, including the planet's only wild mammals (seals, sea otters, and killer whales). The land supports an adequate assortment of birds, insects, and humbler organisms. Forests, chiefly of conifer and hardwoods, clothe the highlands wherever trees can grow.

Although they made prudent choices when stocking their world, the Dorsai also remembered that they were building a homeland, not a zoo habitat. They left room for Nature to be her unfettered self and sowed their woods with wildflowers. Because their lives are so disciplined, they savor spontaneity.

The same pragmatism and restraint that determine the way the Dorsai use their planet's resources are evident in all other aspects of their existence. They bring strategic and tactical thinking to bear on the struggle to stay alive.

Dorsai's planetary government, the United Cantons, does not so much govern as inform citizens. (Among developed societies, only the anarchistic arrangements among the Exotics are looser.) To this end, an excellent library is maintained at the capital, Omalu. Besides being a data bank, it is a central—and neutral—file for contracts. (Dorsai bargain as cannily among themselves as they do with off-world employers.) It aids the private sector by arming Dorsai military ventures with accurate facts and the public one by researching issues that affect the common good. Major policy decisions are taken by popular vote after electronic debate. Although consensus is informally shaped by the most respected community figures (the so-called "Grey Captains"), the duties of the elector, the official head of state, are mainly symbolic. There is no career bureaucrat class.

Not politics, but the telecommunications network and the weather service are the governmental functions likeliest to affect visitors' lives. Obviously, both are vital to a widely scattered population on a geologically active and meteorologically violent planet. Since off-worlders cannot expect to emulate the practiced vigilance of natives, they are strongly urged to wear weather-watchers at all times in order to receive broadcast warnings of hazards of sky, sea, or earth.

Dorsai are all too familiar with natural disasters: storm or wave, ashfall or tremor can threaten them and theirs at any moment. And with their agriculture so marginal, even minor variations in growing conditions can mean crop failure. Since each district has a subtly different microclimate, one valley's harvest may be fat while its nearest neighbor's is lean. Contingency planning for emergencies is a key duty of cantonal governments within a framework of planetwide consultation.

Self-defense measures are handled in similar fashion. So successful was their first trial by combat, the Dorsai have not been tested further since the ignominious rout of the Alliance-Coalition Expeditionary Force in 2185. Today's Dorsai are coolly aware that maintaining this legend of unconquerability is greatly to their advantage.

Most governmental business, however, is routine and undramatic. Services are supplied and problems are solved on the local level wherever possible, in accordance with the Dorsai preference for managing their affairs at the simplest stage of organization.

For instance, consider how the planet maintains an adequate level of health care. The cornerstone of the system is individual responsibility. Not only do Dorsai take care of their bodies, they learn paramedical procedures to assist others. (Accidents are the worst health hazard here.) The cantons support travelling medicians for routine maintenance and treatment. Critical cases are referred to regional hospitals, while the globally funded medical center at Omalu boasts an Exotic staff for advanced surgery and long-term rehabilitation.

This meshing of levels works because "neighborliness" is their guiding social principle. They have never forgotten the lesson the first Dorsai generation learned during the Outlaw Years: we must help one another or die. Survival demands solidarity. In practice, this means voluntary assessments, unstinting hospitality, and tactful charity. Community service is expected of all. Public opinion is a powerful incentive for co-operation—a reputation for selfishness can prove fatal.

Thus, patterns of everyday life on Dorsai broadly resemble those seen in pretechnological villages on Old Earth, but without the isolation and ignorance that blighted such places. Global communications make the difference. Most goods and services are sold via telemarketing. Atmosphere craft that require no special landing fields can reach the remotest areas. The electronic library network and Exotic-designed self-study programs carry learning to anyone seeking it, compensating for the lack of conventional higher education.

Even the culture's martial focus is made to serve social ends. When the fortunes of war bring people from various cantons together, lasting personal and professional bonds may form. The same individuals and families can choose repeated assignments together, because Dorsai military contracts are privately negotiated by freely assembled teams, unlike the coercive practices of the Friendlies and other groups.

To encourage unity among civilians, enrollment in children's training camps and adult home guard units deliberately mixes personnel from different areas. Beyond these policies, the strongest counterweight to excessive localism is simply the Dorsai awareness of themselves as *one* unique people. They understand the dynamics of their society well enough to make conscious adjustments when necessary.

Since the first difficult colonial days, the Dorsai have fought to maintain social balance between local and planetary government, between individualism and community. Being human, they do not always succeed. The temptation to impose one's will on another by force exists here just as it does in all cultures—Dorsai has known would-be warlords and bad neighbors. But no other society instills a sense of responsibility towards self and others as deeply or fiercely as this one does. Responsibility is the bedrock upon which Dorsai's acclaimed integrity and fortitude stand.

They learned in a harsh school that fidelity to principle is the ultimate pragmatism.

Because the constant need for cooperation imposes so much togetherness, Dorsai demand privacy and cultivate tact. They deal with each other in a brisk, objective, almost spartan style. They do not share their feelings easily. Visitors can expect courtesy, but no intimacy, from Dorsai associates.

Their self-assessments are invariably realistic—knowing exactly what to expect of each other in peace or war is essential for smooth functioning. For instance, the Rochmont Massacre in 2177 forced them to admit the deadliness of the infamous Dorsai "cold rage," the warrior fury their primitive ancestors glorified. Since Cletus Grahame's time, psychological training helps them keep this rage controlled unless deliberately released as hysterical strength for useful purposes.

Honest appraisal of their own abilities gives Dorsai such self-assurance, they sincerely respect the special gifts of other cultures. Indeed, their world would scarcely be habitable without goods and services perfected by the Ste. Marian agronomists, Exotic medicians and educators, Cassidan technologists, and so forth. Dorsai pay well for off-world expertise but insist on getting every bit of what they paid for. Furthermore, being committed to excellence themselves, they demand no less of their contract workers.

The source of these Dorsai traits must be sought in the family, the basic unit of their society. Observers from other cultures more conventionally free in personal relationships may find this aspect of Dorsai life especially alien. Here, the family is no mere temporary union, nor even a reproductive unit, but an entire network of relationships extending through time. Dorsai waste no tears on identity crises: they know where they came from, they know who they are, and they know what they wish their descendants to be. Kindred cleave to each other like clansmen.

Reputation follows lineage: praise or blame that falls on one family member falls on all. Ideally, young Dorsai strive to live up to their forebears' glory. But should they inherit shame instead, survivors may be driven to change their talented name or even flee the planet, as the ill-fated Van Ghents did.

Even religion, for those Dorsai who adhere to a particular faith, is of necessity home-centered. Most of the populace is too thinly scattered to maintain local churches, mosques, or temples. Instead, households conduct their own worship services either independently or with neighbors, supplemented by periodic visits from itinerant clerics.

Dorsai have almost Confucian reverence for ancestors. These days, traditional ethnic and religious rites honoring the departed, such as the Japanese *Bon* festival or the Christian All Souls' Day, mean more on

Dorsai than on Old Earth. Family history is faithfully recorded. Heirlooms are carefully preserved. Mementoes left by a family's founders have become virtual house talismans. The houses themselves take on a kind of life as generations pass. Even visitors respond to the romantic aura that clings to the oldest homesteads—for example, Fal Morgan in Foralie Canton. So vividly are the dead remembered in fact, relic, and legend, they almost seem to survive as unseen presences among the living who bear their blood.

Since the living regard themselves as stewards of their heritage, marriage is a matter of grave concern. (Rash impulses exist, but rarely affect behavior.) Dorsai prefer to marry young and often finance this step by short-term military service. Life's uncertainties drive Dorsai couples to want large families—large by the standards of Old Earth but not by those of the Friendly Worlds—and to want them quickly. Voluntary childlessness is unheard of here.

Although tours of duty on other planets multiply the opportunities for mixed marriages, few result. Dorsai is too harsh a world and too demanding a culture for most outsiders to successfully share. Visitors are cautioned not to entertain vain fantasies, no matter how attractive local people may appear.

Dorsai's original settlers established self-sufficient multigenerational households whose members held their property in common. This arrangement stressed mutual support for survival's sake: "Bare is a brotherless back." But over the past two centuries, Dorsai's population has increased a hundredfold. Economic development has brought diversification. Homesteads now operate like corporations instead of manors. Nuclear living is commoner than communal. Nevertheless, the old system continues in favor among commodity farmers, career military families, and South Continent miners. Immigrants still attach themselves to native families, often by legal adoption, in order to participate comfortably in Dorsai society.

Yet no matter where or how they live, today's Dorsai remain emotionally tied to some ancestral hearth and proudly display the emblems of their lineage. (For instance, the triple scallop shell device of Graeme is carved into a huge granite mantelpiece at Graemehouse in Foralie Canton.) Scattered relatives try to keep in touch and occasionally hold reunions. But Dorsai taste for cooperative living transcends simple nostalgia. Whether they reside in tiny villages or city complexes, nuclear families spontaneously link up with congenial neighbors to approximate the extended families of earlier times.

These domestic patterns affect child development. Formal education begins at home with one or more women in a family serving as teachers, supported by modern teaching aids. This continues through the primary years out in the countryside. Then those not destined for the Military Academy go on to district secondary schools. Youngsters from the most isolated areas board with other families while attending these institutions. Schooling stops at age eighteen except for local apprenticeship programs and limited vocational training in a few essential fields.

The psychological impact is even stronger. Children start absorbing Dorsai attitudes along with their mother's milk. The very structure of their homelife encourages a smooth transition from imitation to acceptance. Communal living instills discipline and consideration as well as diffusing bonds of affection and authority throughout the extended family. The presence of grandparents, aunts, uncles, cousins, or their equivalents modifies tensions between children and parents. With relationships running diagonally, vertically, and horizontally at the time, intensity of feeling may not always match closeness of blood: an aunt may seem more like a mother or a cousin like a brother. Moreover, since alternative role models are always at hand, children suffer less from the absence or death of a parent. They grow up firmly oriented towards group identity and group action, qualities that equip them to function well in any area of Dorsai life.

The "masculine" flavor of Dorsai society masks its matriarchal character. But the careful observer quickly discovers that women dominate everyday life in this Splinter Culture. First, demographics favor this situation. The planet has a surplus of females because job-related mortality rates are higher for males, and Dorsai refuse to tamper with the naturally occurring sex ratio. Secondly, work keeps many Dorsai men away from home for prolonged periods. (This holds for peaceful and martial occupations alike.) Women prefer to work locally, often processing the raw material men provide. (For instance, women pack, market, and devise new uses for the fish their menfolk catch.) Women are the chief administrators of households great and small. Aside from imported contract specialists, Dorsai's education, medicine, and information services are largely in the hands of women. More women than men are free to serve in government or civic posts. Thus practical considerations combine to make women the guardians of continuity. They shape the Dorsai ethos and instill it in new generations.

Note that Dorsai women started that shaping early, during their culture's formative years, when necessity forced them to fend for themselves. Foralie Canton's legendary chatelaine, the First Amanda Morgan, exemplifies the virtues of her sister pioneers two centuries ago. Originally from Old Earth, this formidable woman kept her birthname through three marriages and founded a dynasty that continues to produce distinguished soldiers. (At present, her namesake, the Second Amanda Morgan, is the planet's leading expert on military contracts.) In middle life, she successfully led homemakers against brigands during the Outlaw Years. In extreme age, she played a major role in local resistance to the Alliance-Coalition invasion, a campaign that could not have been won without women's valor.

Great households centered around such matriarchs remain the Dorsai ideal and are a perennial novelty to off-worlders. These establishments are, therefore, worth describing in some detail.

To begin with, these are rough-hewn versions of the traditional country estate (villa, manor, plantation, hacienda, station) built throughout Old Earth's pretechnological past. (Of course, on Dorsai, these are year-round homes of strictly practical construction and operate without servants.) Each homestead is separated from its fellows by huge tracts of land. Even if farming is not the family trade, space is needed for woodlots, pasturage, gardens, and landing sites for aircraft and spacecraft. With a whole planet at their disposal, the earliest settlers naturally chose the best real estate—well-watered, arable, and containing a defensible homesite. Scenic beauty was a not unappreciated bonus.

The design of any given homestead depends on climate and available materials. There are earth-sheltered structures green with turf and others set into cliff sides, but the majority are archaic-looking buildings of wood and stone. Adobe is occasionally found in South Continent's deserts, but the synthetic substances common elsewhere are entirely absent. Since they are built by self-taught local craftsmen, their architecture is more functional than elegant. Yet these houses inevitably suggest immense solidity. The finest ones fit their surroundings so well, they look as if they had simply grown out of the ground.

On closer inspection, a Dorsai homestead stands revealed as an entire complex of buildings. The main residence often shows signs of expansion over the generations—at the height of the system its walls may have had to shelter as many as thirty residents and entertain more. Although farms have the most outbuildings, any communal household will include shelters for vehicles and animals, storage sheds, a toolshop, and exercise facilities. Originally, power was generated on the spot, but now that equipment only operates during emergencies.

Animals will surely be at hand. Horses are kept for pleasure riding and are actually useful in rough country. (Long-term visitors may wish to learn horsemanship.) In the early years, when Dorsai was less mechanized, draft horses and shaggy ponies proved their worth. Mules produced from imported jackass semen are still prized in South Continent. Milk goats remain a standard feature, but these days, poultry raising has been relegated to commercial growers. Sheepdogs will be found if the family's herds of sheep and goats are large enough to warrant their use.

(These dogs are only bred on a few isolated islands and neutered or spayed before sale to preclude any possibility of feral packs forming.)

The household will also have extensive vegetable gardens and, if the climate permits, orchards of cold-tolerant fruit and nut trees. Small greenhouses are commonplace. Aside from their practical use for starting seedlings, access to live green plants boosts morale during Dorsai's long winters. Flowers, including tulips and the hardier strains of roses, brighten the brief growing season.

Despite their old-fashioned exteriors, these homesteads do enjoy the essential conveniences of civilized living. (Unlike extreme Friendlies, Dorsai see no virtue in hardship for its own sake.) Some visitors are startled by the contrast—a video screen in time-worn wooden panelling or sensor-cued lighting above a stone fireplace. Dorsai are willing to use automatic equipment that adds to the security or efficiency of their homes. They scorn as pointless luxuries, however, devices other cultures take for granted. Off-worlders must exercise caution in how they seat themselves: chairs will not float up to meet their bodies here. Nevertheless, handmade furnishings do provide adequate—if rustic—comfort, and the craftwork of generations has enriched initially stark interiors. The results inevitably charm nostalgia-minded observers, the sort who admire carved ceiling beams or shaggy wool rugs.

No two houses are alike, of course, but the general rule is to have large public areas and small private ones. Dining rooms in particular are huge, because sharing meals is an important sign of family unity. On the other hand, bedrooms, whether single or double occupancy, are mere cubicles, and children share a common nursery. Having a library, schoolroom, and infirmary right on the premises aids self-sufficiency. With so many mouths to feed, the kitchen may be a whole suite of rooms for processing and storing as well as preparing food.

From *sushi* to sauerkraut to scones, the major cuisines of Old Earth's cold regions are amply represented on Dorsai. Insofar as ubiquity makes a "national" dish, that honor goes to fish and chips, since seafood is the planet's cheapest protein and potatoes its major carbohydrate.

Constrained as they are by climate and terrain, Dorsai try to vary their limited bill of fare by genetics as well as cookery. No one district serves every dish, but visitors should be prepared for such novelties as purple lettuce, red broccoli, white carrots, yellow beets, and more kinds of potatoes than Old Peru or Ireland ever knew. There is an amazing assortment of leafy greens, legumes, squashes, onions, cole crops, mushrooms, and root vegetables. Some are unique; most are delicious. Tomatoes, hot peppers, ginger, and other cold-sensitive species can sometimes be coaxed to grow under glass in private homes. But only the commercial greenhouses geothermally heated by the Forge of Iblis in South Continent produce such foods in any quantity and always at a premium price that restricts their use to festive occasions.

Similarly, wheat is eaten less often than rye, oats, barley, millet, amaranth, or buckwheat. The ratio of labor to yield makes so-called wild rice the rarest starch crop and potatoes the commonest. (The latter will flourish even on those treeless isles where fisher-families must manufacture the very soil to plant them in.)

Orchards yield apples, cherries, plums, walnuts, hazelnuts, beechnuts, hickory nuts, pine nuts and other cold-tolerant species. Sunflower seeds are used like nuts, while nut oils and butters supplement sunflower oil and margarine. Every conceivable berry, from strawberries to cloudberries, is grown, plus juniper berries for flavoring and a relative of the bayberry for fragrant wax.

Since anything that *can* be fermented *is,* the Dorsai prepare a bewildering array of alcoholic beverages. Although their smoky-tasting whiskey is universally prized, other products are strictly local specialties that never leave the planet. Cantons—even individual families—seem to vie with one another in devising novel additions to neutral spirits, ales, and beers. Other drinks are prepared from fruits, beet-sugar, honey, and maple syrup. Attempts to make wine from *vinifera* grapes have never proven satisfactory, although hardy grapes are grown for eating. Provided due caution is shown with unfamiliar liquors, off-worlders should be able to find some concoction or other that suits them, but obviously parsnip wine, blueberry beer, or maple rum are acquired tastes. It cannot be stressed too strongly that Dorsai drink for conviviality, not oblivion. They view drunkenness as a lamentable loss of control.

Nonalcoholic beverages include cider and other fruit juices, herbal and variform *Thea* teas, a coffee substitute, and the milk of goats and sheep.

Most of Dorsai's milk, however, goes into cheese. Cultures and techniques developed on Ste. Marie yield many interesting varieties. Some are comparable to Old Earth's feta, fontina, gjetost, liptauer, chevre, and romano, but only certain cool caverns in the Paladin Mountains yield that incomparable blue-veined marvel known to gourmets among the stars as Fingal cheese. (Curiously enough, this delicacy did not win marketplace acceptance until Cetan consumer analysts were hired to merchandise it under its present brand name and packaging.)

Planetwide, mutton is the usual meat, with lamb and kid its preferred forms. The flesh of animals grazed on seaside pastures is especially flavorful. Chicken, turkey, and eggs are eaten oftener on Landfall than elsewhere because large commercial poultry growers can operate most efficiently here. There are no ducks or geese because of ecological considerations and difficulties adjusting breeding cycles. Although visitors are unlikely to be served seal or horsemeat, they should refrain from criticizing consumption by others.

Seafood—fish, crustaceans, mollusks—is the mainstay of the Dorsai table. Thanks to the variety of both catch and ethnic cusines, one can enjoy a different and delicious seafood dish every day of the long Dorsai year without repeating or exhausting the possibilities. The oceans also yield seaweed, which is eaten as a vegetable or processed for food additives and fertilizer. Krill and plankton are harvested for animal feed.

Every temperate zone herb is grown—and liberally used—on Dorsai. Saffron, patiently gathered from the autumn crocus, is reserved for special treats. Other flowers, including roses, nasturtiums, chive and squash blossoms, are pressed into service as flavorings or even eaten themselves. Mustard, Andean chili, and horseradish help satisfy the craving for hot tastes. Herb-flavored fruit vinegars add extra interest to pickled dishes. A few simple synthetics such as vanillin and citral are also available.

But tropical spices are sorely missed. The Dorsai contrive to import them in cunning ways to minimize cost. (But it is a point of honor to give the material away afterwards and not resell it.) For instance, electronic components may arrive nestled in bags of peppercorns instead of plastic foam. Although useful goods get higher priority, returning soldiers often devote a bit of their personal luggage allowance to spices. Wise visitors would do well to follow this example if such products are found on their homeworlds. Small packets of cinnamon, cloves, or the like make ideal hospitality gifts for Dorsai hosts. Thoughtful gestures do not go unnoticed here.

Good eating and good times go together on Dorsai. Those who have seen only uniformed Dorsai among the stars—and kept a respectful distance from them—must learn to relax with them when the occasions arise. And arise they will. Since Dorsai must endure long separations, they welcome any chance to be with their loved ones, if only for a simple gathering around the family hearth to toast raclette cheese and pop amaranth seeds. Indeed, their frugal lives would be intolerably grim without holidays. Some festivities (such as Freedom Day) are planetwide. Others are particular to a certain religion, locality, ethnic group, or family. Dorsai mark the seasons of the year and the stages of life: certain rituals accompany sowing and harvest, birth and death. Custom even decrees a special round of hospitality for the soldier home on leave.

On holidays Dorsai like to shed their practical everyday clothes for the kimono, kilt, or caftan of their ancestors. They feast as bountifully as they can and for that moment forget times when food was rationed by the mouthful. Besides eating, they enjoy singing and playing musical instruments. Folk dancing appeals to some, feats of strength to others. Displays of expert horsemanship are much admired.

Festivals aside, the prime season for recreation is winter, when most other activities come to a halt. Outdoors, snow sports attract all ages, while in foul weather, neighborhood and household gyms shelter lively ball games. Whatever their chosen pastime, Dorsai play with whole-hearted vigor—action is sweet.

Nor do they sit idle at home. Dorsai hands keep busy with needles, loom, or tools. (Their menfolk are formidable knitters.) The fruits of such labor do more than brighten their surroundings. The planet's domestic furniture, clothing, fabric, and fiber manufacturing began as cottage industries, as did production of luxury export goods. (The most precious of these, Veilpoint lace, started with a crippled woman's need for income.) Besides their intrinsic quality, the personal touch evident in Dorsai cashmere angora, fishskin leather, fragrance and flavor essences, liquor, cheese, and so forth is what commends them to the attention of elite classes on other worlds. Although the volume of this trade is small, its economic impact on participating families is considerable. Dorsai survival strategy depends on exploiting every possibility.

Of course, as everyone knows, what Dorsai sells to live is soldiers. The martial function defines this Splinter Culture. Every member acknowledges that "by spear my bread is kneaded." Not only do military contracts earn essential interstellar credits, military virtues—courage, loyalty, self-sacrifice, and discipline—shape the Dorsai ethic.

Yet surprisingly few take up arms for life. Their quality, not their quantity commands a premium price. No more than five percent of the population graduate from the Academy to become professional soldiers. They multiply their effectiveness in the armies of other planets by serving in training as well as command posts.

Temporary enlistment is far commoner. Many young people serve one tour of duty off-world to earn capital for their families and themselves. Their upbringing gives them significant advantages over recruits from other societies, for example Friendly draftees, who are too often treated as cannon fodder. A few Dorsai volunteers find military life so congenial, they stay on permanently as noncommissioned officers.

But whatever their career plans, all Dorsai receive elementary martial arts training from childhood according to the theories of Cletus Grahame. Home guard duty involves everyone. Even the disabled find ways to participate. This unique defense capability has kept Dorsai free from invasion for the past two hundred years.

In the half-century since Donal Graeme gave our worlds temporary unity, there has been less fighting among the stars and therefore less demand for soldiers. As their earning power shrinks, some Dorsai share the complaint of medieval *condottiere* Sir John Hawkwood: "I live by war and peace would be my undoing." What does the future hold for Dorsai? Surely these valiant and ingenious people will find a fitting role so that their noble qualities will remain part of our race forever—the backbone of the organism called Man.